AL

MW01233882

The Odyssey of Walker Garrett

The writing is excellent and the story moves along at a fast clip, which keeps you turning pages to see what will happen next.

Kristy Shelton, author of *The Blinders Trilogy*

As a combat veteran myself, I really value an author who somehow seems to understand the mind of the soldier; the courage required, the doubt about the mission and especially the hidden fear.

Bill Zarrett, Amazon review

The characters, the events, and the exotic places all come alive and you feel that you are there watching the story unfold.

Ruth Bennett, Amazon review

I was hooked from the beginning chapters. The way the author wove Walker's story with known historical characters brings history to life. His vivid descriptions of places are brilliant.

Bill Burton, Facebook post

I came to truly care about the characters in the story, and their journey mattered to me more with each page. Great history, and a great human journey in one amazing odyssey.

David Fincher, Amazon review

WALKER GARRETT, SECRET SERVICE

MICHAEL GLENN

PAGETURNERBOOKS, LLC

CONTENTS

FOREWORD

Walker Garrett, Secret Service is a sequel to *The Odyssey of Walker Garrett.* The reader will better understand and enjoy the present volume if you have first read the earlier one. It tells how young Walker left his rural home in North Alabama to join his mentor and idol, General Joseph Wheeler, for the campaign in Cuba in 1898, during the Spanish-American War. While there, he encountered Captain John Pershing and the black soldiers of the Tenth Cavalry ("Buffalo Soldiers"), Theodore Roosevelt and his Rough Riders, and befriended José, a Cuban rebel. At the conclusion of that campaign, Walker's unit was sent to the Philippines to take part in the war there, as the U.S. sought to "civilize and Christianize the Filipinos."

When the Boxer Rebellion broke out in China in 1900, Walker was part of the contingent sent there to participate in the multinational force which rescued the besieged international communities in Tientsin and Peking. While protecting some missionaries from the "Boxers," he unexpectedly found himself separated from his unit, crossing the Gobi Desert to Mongolia, and going from there to Russia. The group crossed Russia on the newly-completed Great Siberian Railway, and continued onward across Europe and the Atlantic Ocean.

He shared all of these travels with a black soldier, L. G. Dixon, of the Tenth Cavalry Regiment, with whom he shared a personal connection, both being from the same area of North Alabama. In fact, in the closing pages of *The Odyssey*, Walker is shocked to learn that they are half-brothers. Upon their arrival back in the U.S., they were immediately court-martialed and acquitted of the charge of having deserted in China, and then awarded medals for their courageous service.

After an absence of two and a half years, Walker returned home a changed man as a result of his globe-circling adventures and experiences. While he was gone, both of his parents had died. He had nurtured a romantic interest in Abigail Dancy, who had written letters and sent him small crocheted items as tokens of her interest, but he eventually concluded, sadly, that she was not seriously interested in him. He and Dixon, lacking a plan for their lives, accepted employment in the Secret Service, having met its director, John Wilkie, on the liner while crossing the Atlantic. After a brief training program, they were assigned to protect the president, William McKinley, who had just been reelected in 1900.

President McKinley began his second term in 1901 with an extended tour of the western states by rail, hoping to use his victory to heal persistent sectional divisions. The Secret Service had only recently begun to provide presidential protection, and sent four agents along as bodyguards. That is where the present volume begins.

❧

Please note that this is a work of historical fiction. Fictional characters and events are products of the author's imagination, and any resemblance to any actual persons, living or dead, is entirely coincidental.

When real historical people appear as characters, and real historical events are described, accuracy is the objective, though occasional liberties may be taken which do not affect the general historicity of the text. An appendix of historical notes is provided at the end of the book, in which fact is separated from fiction. Notes are provided for each chapter, and the reader is encouraged to consult them as each chapter is read.

1

"JUST LIKE OLD TIMES"

It was the finest train anyone in Decatur, Alabama, had ever seen. And it should have been—it was carrying the President of the United States on a tour of the country, and no cost had been spared in making this train a spectacular sight. The nine-piece brass band on the platform of the train station struck up a spirited rendition of "Dixie" as the impressive locomotive slowed only slightly while rumbling through the small town. Pennons and banners decorated the buildings nearest the track, and crowds of farmers, shopkeepers, and schoolchildren cheered and waved little flags. President William McKinley stood on a deck at the rear of the last car, waving in return. It was over in a matter of seconds, as the regal eight-car train disappeared into the distance. "Dixie" trailed off into silence barely halfway through the first verse, and after a moment, the people gradually began to quietly disperse to their homes and businesses. After all, it was not yet noon, and there was still work to be done.

"Did you see them?" Walker Garrett stepped back from the window of the staff car near the front of the train and made a futile effort to straighten his wind-blown, sandy-brown hair.

"Yup," nodded L. G. Dixon, with a grin. "They was at the far end of the platform. Daisy was wearin' a blue dress and Mama had a red scarf 'round her head and a yellow apron. They waved at us." He paused, and then added, "Dancy?"

Walker shrugged. Abigail Dancy had corresponded with Walker over the past three years while he traveled the world, courtesy of the U.S. Army. However, he doubted that she—a wealthy man's daughter—really cared for him, a farmer's son. Even now that he was a Secret Service agent traveling with the president, he sensed that her interest in him was only casual.

"Don't matter, no ways. We got more important things to do."

As if on cue, the door at the end of the car opened with a rush of wind, and a voice called out, "Dixon! Garrett! Foster wants to see us—now!"

George Foster was in charge of the small squad of Secret Service agents. A husky, graying six-footer with a lined and weathered face, he had been with the president since the first inauguration in '97, having previously been the doorkeeper of the state legislature in McKinley's home state of Ohio. The security of the president had been his sole responsibility until recently, when a handful of men had been brought on to assist him. Their training had been minimal—the procedures for actually keeping the president safe were still evolving, and each situation presented a new set of challenges to be solved.

Four men stood around a small table in the dining car, on which lay a map of Memphis. There were circles and lines drawn on the map with a charcoal pencil, and several X's and arrows. Foster motioned for them to sit.

"We'll be in Memphis this afternoon," he began, "and that's when we really start doing our job. These two days of riding the rails have been the easy part, but now comes the work. There's only the four of us, so it's important that we be vigilant and execute our plan." He fixed a penetrating glare on each man, pausing for a moment before continuing.

"We arrive at the Calhoun Street Station," he said, tapping his finger on the map, "where an artillery salute will be fired, and a company of Confederate veterans will serve as an honor guard. There will be large crowds to hear the president speak at Court Square, a reception at the Nineteenth Century Club, and a banquet at the Peabody Hotel. Those locations are all marked, with each man's position indicated." He rotated the map around to face them and gestured toward it. "Look this over, and let me know if you have any questions."

The three spent a long minute studying the map, and then the third man—a stout, mustached New Yorker with bushy red eyebrows —cleared his throat. "Chief, I understand our assigned locations all right, but—" he hesitated—" but what are we actually supposed to *do*?"

Foster coughed involuntarily, and stared. "Stover, you hold your position and watch the crowd. Be on the lookout for anyone suspicious or dangerous-looking. If anyone advances toward the president, head them off. The Memphis police will be primarily responsible for securing the area, but we'll be the closest to the president. Don't let anyone get past you. Is that clear?"

Stover's face reddened. "All our training was for the Executive Mansion," he said defensively, "not for traveling across the country with him speaking to large crowds in the open air. If somebody wants to get him—"

"Nobody's going to get him!" interrupted Foster, angrily. "No Lincoln or Garfield on *my* watch! *Is that clear?*"

There was an uncomfortable silence, and then each man nodded that he understood.

"Just one thing, Mr. Foster," said Walker, tentatively pointing to the map. "It looks like you've got Dixon and me pretty far from the speaker's platform in Court Square. How can we stay between the president and the crowd?"

"I want you two to mingle with the crowd. That's why I told you to bring some old clothes—to fit in with the crowd and not be noticed. Keep your eyes and ears open in case you pick up something. If you hear anybody saying anything threatening, stick close to them. Don't forget that the president was once a Union major in the Civil War, and we're in Memphis. Some old rebels never got over losing the war. I don't trust them."

Walker opened his mouth to object, but Dixon kicked his foot under the table, and he closed it without speaking. Walker's father had fought for the Confederate Army during the war, as had his mentor and idol, General Joseph Wheeler. The idea that Confederate veterans could not be trusted around the president made his jaw muscles tighten and his nostrils flare.

"Yes sir, Mr. Foster," said Dixon, nodding. "We'll be all eyes and ears. You can count on us, sir."

"I'm especially counting on you, Dixon. Low-class troublemakers would never suspect that a colored man is a federal agent, and they might be less careful what they say around you." Then he added, somewhat reflectively, "You know, I wasn't sure it was a good idea to bring a Negro with us, but I'm beginning to understand Mr. Wilkie's thinking, and now I agree with him. You'll be very useful, Dixon." He gave Dixon an approving nod, apparently not noticing his astonished expression, and tapped the side of his head. "Eyes and ears!" And then he looked at all of them and repeated emphatically, "Eyes and ears!"

Walker kicked Dixon's foot under the table as he said, enthusiastically, "Yes sir, Mr. Foster! Eyes and ears!" Walker and Dixon saluted out of habit, drawing a glare from Foster. They all rose from the table and left the dining car—Foster going back to the president's private car, and the three agents forward to the staff car.

When the door had shut noisily behind them, Walker turned to Dixon and made a show of smoothing and adjusting the lapels on his suit coat. "Did you hear that, Dixon? You're going to be very useful. Your mama would be so proud of you!"

Dixon knocked Walker's hands away and scowled. "I notice he didn't say *you* would be useful, Garrett! Who's going to be proud of *you*?" He bit his lip when he saw Walker's grin instantly change to a grimace. Walker's parents had both died the previous year, and he was still grieving their loss.

"Nobody, I reckon. Maybe General Wheeler."

"Are you talking about the Congressman, Joseph Wheeler? The Confederate general?" asked Stover. "Why would he be proud of *you*?"

"My pa served with him in the Civil War," Walker explained, "and I grew up on his plantation near here. In fact," he said as he pointed out the window, "that's it yonder, through the trees—Pond Spring!"

Stover grunted in surprise as he peered toward the white house in the distance. "So, he knows you from when you were growing up around here?"

"He was also my commanding officer in Cuba, and for a while in the Philippines."

Stover grunted again and stared at Walker. "You fought in both of those places?"

"And in China, during the Boxer Rebellion," chimed in Dixon. "Both of us did."

The look of disbelief on Stover's face was almost comical. "Sure you did," he sneered sarcastically. "And I'm the King of England!" Glaring angrily, he pushed past them and exited the car, slamming the door shut behind him.

"I don't think he's going to be very useful," grinned Walker, and they both burst into laughter.

"It's Courtland!" Walker suddenly exclaimed, and leaped to the window and put his head out. He barely had time to wave at the dozen people standing on the unpainted platform of the dusty old depot before the train steamed past at full speed. There was a blur of familiar faces, and hands raised in reply, and a speckled hound lying on the platform lifted his head briefly, as if wondering what all the fuss was about. In seconds, pine trees were all that could be seen from the train window.

Walker stepped back and stood for a moment, staring blankly into space. He raised a hand to brush at his tousled hair, but instead just rubbed his eyes. In his mind he saw again the figures of his mother and father waving as the little country train took him away—a vision frozen in time. His color paled, and for several seconds, he forgot to breathe.

Dixon looked at him quizzically. "Courtland?" he asked.

Walker cleared his throat. "That's where I said good-bye to Mama and Papa, three years ago. It was the last time I saw them. I was headed in the other direction—to Decatur, and on to Tampa. That's when it all started for me." His voice trailed off and he heaved a deep sigh, thinking of his parents' graves under the oak tree at Pond Spring. The two took facing seats by the open window and silently watched the trees and fields rush past. The rest of the day passed quietly.

By late afternoon the train was approaching Memphis, and it was time to prepare for their assignments. They changed from their new three-piece suits into scuffed boots, faded dungarees, floppy hats, and two very shaggy and ragged camel's hair coats. Each carried a .38 revolver in a shoulder holster, concealed by the coat.

"We look like a couple of scruffy tramps," Walker said, with a shake of his head.

"Just like old times," Dixon agreed, with a note of satisfaction in his voice.

Within minutes, the locomotive hissed to a stop under the platform roof at the Calhoun Street Station. While the presidential party was being greeted by local dignitaries in the spacious interior, Walker and Dixon slipped out on the opposite side of the train and made their way around to the front of the station to mingle with the crowd of onlookers. The brick and stone façade of the Victorian-style building, with its round, pointed turrets at each of the front corners, gave it a very solid and imposing look. A company of white-bearded Confederate veterans in their gray uniforms, shouldering ancient rifled muskets, lined the path from the entrance to the carriages waiting at the street. An artillery squad fired a twenty-one-gun salute as the party emerged through the arched doorway into the sunlight. McKinley waved cheerily as he and his wife climbed into the ornate carriages which would take them and the rest of the party into the city center. Walker noted that only a few hands waved in response, and the crowd seemed less than enthusiastic. The mood that he sensed from those around him made him uneasy. Catching Dixon's eye across the way, he tapped the side of his head meaningfully—*eyes and ears*! Dixon replied with an almost imperceptible nod.

It was only a mile up Main Street to Court Square, where the president was to give a speech. A dozen mounted policemen escorted the carriages. Walker and Dixon walked briskly on opposite sides of the street, which was lined by curious spectators gazing impassively at the passing cortege. *This feels more like a funeral procession*, Walker thought. *This is not a good start to the president's tour.*

Court Square was already filled with a waiting crowd. McKinley sat on the speaker's platform with his cabinet members, the mayor, the president of a bank, and the pastor of a large local church, who led a lengthy prayer. Most of the audience stood throughout the event, while Mrs. McKinley and the cabinet members' wives sat on the front row of seats. A group of school children sang some patriotic songs, and a band played "The Star-Spangled Banner," followed by "Dixie."

Meanwhile, Walker and Dixon strolled casually around the perimeter, studying faces and overhearing bits of conversation. There wasn't much conversation to overhear, actually. The audience was eerily quiet, and Walker began to feel a sense of dread that he could not shake.

"This place is giving me the heebie-jeebies," Dixon murmured as they passed each other.

"Me, too," Walker replied, and they paused, surveying the scene.

On impulse, he suddenly asked, "If you were trying to assassinate the president here today, how would you do it?"

Dixon gave him a startled look, and then furrowed his brow. "I'd shoot him with a rifle from a tall building, far enough away that I could make my escape before anybody could get to me."

Walker stared at him, taken aback. "You just now thought of all that, right here on the spot?"

"Well, what would *you* do? You got a better plan?"

"No. I reckon that's exactly what I would do, too. Are there any tall buildings around here that would serve the purpose?"

They turned away from the crowd and looked in all directions.

Both pointed simultaneously to a three-story building two blocks away to the west, along the Mississippi River front.

"That's the only one," said Dixon. "Trees block the view from these others, and this one over here is too close. That one is perfect. It's maybe three hundred yards at the most, but it's a clear line of fire, and a good man with a rifle could make the shot, easy."

Walker squinted as he studied the roof of the distant building, and suddenly he felt a shiver run up his spine. "Do you see what I see?" he gasped. He had spied the figure of a man, apparently crouching behind the parapet of the flat-roofed building, and what appeared to be the barrel of a rifle flashed in the sun for a split second. Without another word, the two began running down the street toward the waterfront.

As they left the square, the band was just finishing its performance. Mayor "JJ" Williams stepped to the podium and began his introduction of the president. Taking full advantage of the opportunity to share a platform with the President of the United States, the mayor waxed eloquent, delivering an impassioned speech of his own in a loud voice which carried down the street, reaching the ears of Walker and Dixon as they ran.

"I hope he keeps it up," panted Dixon. "We need all the time we can get!"

They tried the front doors of the building, but found that, due to the presidential visit, businesses were closed and the doors were locked. Running around to the side alley, they found the external fire escape, but the ladder section had been pulled up and was ten feet off the ground.

"Boost me!" cried Walker, putting one hand against the rough brick wall and raising his foot high. Dixon made a stirrup with his hands, and taking Walker's foot, raised him up. Walker grabbed the rungs of the ladder and, climbing to the first deck, released the catch and let the ladder drop down to Dixon, who rapidly followed him up to the top. The fire escape did not ascend all the way to the roof, but only to the third-floor windows. Walker crouched, and Dixon stepped up on his thigh, and then stood on his shoulders, bracing with his hands against the wall. Walker stood up straight, and Dixon was able to grab the top edge of the parapet and scramble up onto the roof. There, he found a rope ladder that the rifleman had used, with a large hook attached. He hooked it onto the parapet and dropped the rope over to Walker, who then joined him on the roof.

Turning, they saw a man kneeling at the far corner of the roof, his long rifle barrel resting on the edge of the low wall, but not yet taking aim. Beside him was another man, also kneeling, with a short, repeating rifle in his hands. Both men were focused on the gathering in the square, and did not see the two men walking quickly toward them.

"Lay those rifles down and step away!" ordered Dixon firmly. The clicking sounds of the two .38 revolvers being cocked gave added emphasis to his words. The man with the lever-action repeater instantly sprang to his feet and whirled around, shock written on his face. Apparently giving no consideration to following Dixon's order, he worked the lever handle down and back up, and started to raise the rifle. Walker leaped forward and struck the man in the head with his revolver, leaving a bloody gash on the side of his face. The man staggered backward and, tripping over his own feet, plunged over the side of the building with a surprised yelp. Walker, keeping his gun pointed at the other man, took a quick look over the edge to see the prone figure lying on the street below, with a spreading circle of blood around his head.

"Lay the rifle down and—" began Dixon again, but the rifleman wasn't listening. Clearly much older than the other, with a straggly white beard and wearing a threadbare gray Confederate field jacket, he let go of the rifle to put both hands on the parapet and gaped down at the body below.

"Marlon! No!" It was a heart-wrenching cry. "That's my son! You killed my son! You damned bastard! You killed my son!" In a frenzy he lunged at Walker, reaching for him with bony, claw-like hands, his face distorted by grief and rage. He grabbed at the revolver and they both fell, wrestling and struggling. The report of the gunshot was muffled, and the struggling ceased.

Walker rolled away from the body and sat up, looking at his smoking gun, speechless.

"You alright?" asked Dixon, holstering his weapon.

"Yeah, I reckon so. That happened fast."

"Let's get out of here. We don't want any trouble with the police." They hurried back across the roof and climbed down the rope to the fire escape, and then down to the ground. Exiting the alley to the street, they took a longer route back to the Square to avoid attracting attention. By the time they arrived, the mayor was finishing his long-winded, flowery speech, and finally getting around to introducing the president.

McKinley stepped to the podium, greeted by a smattering of applause, and spoke for about an hour to the mostly quiet audience. Tennessee and all the other former Confederate states had voted for his opponent, Democrat William Jennings Bryan, in the previous year's election, and there was little love shown for the Republican. During the speech, Walker and Dixon devoted almost as much attention to the nearby rooftops as they did to the crowd.

At the conclusion of the speech, the presidential party reentered the carriages to ride to the Nineteenth Century Club for a reception. The carriages were again accompanied by mounted policemen, and Walker and Dixon went on foot. It was less than a mile to the stylish, white, three-story mansion belonging to the elite women's club. Even though women could not vote, these wealthy women—whose husbands were economic and political leaders of the city—were also a political force, promoting social and urban reforms. While the McKinleys and others mingled with the members inside, Foster and Stover stood guard outside the front door, and Walker and Dixon watched from across the street.

"What're you fellas doing here?" Two policemen were walking toward them. "You lookin' to cause trouble?"

"No, not a'tall," replied Dixon. "We—"

"I seen both of 'em at the Square," interrupted the other policeman. "Walking 'round, watchin' ever'body. They're up to no good, if you ask me."

The two officers stood menacingly in front of them, slapping their nightsticks into their hands in a threatening manner. The taller of the two took a step closer, lip curled in disdain.

"Stalkin' the president, are you? Followin' him 'round town?"

"I reckon they're plannin' to cause some trouble. That's what I think."

"I think we oughta work 'em over. Find out what they're up to."

"We're just doing our job," said Walker quickly. They both raised their hands shoulder high, palms out, as a show of non-resistance. "We're helping protect the president."

"*You?*" exclaimed the tall policeman, contemptuously. Both laughed harshly. "I've seen better men than you going through the trash looking for food. We got a cell with your names on it, and that's where you're going. Now—get moving, and come along with us!" With that, he jabbed his nightstick into Walker's chest, pushing him back a step. The other policeman did the same to Dixon. Suddenly, there were other policemen surrounding them, all brandishing night-sticks—at least four more, Walker thought. The situation looked serious.

"Stop!" called out a voice. "Leave those men alone!" It was Stover, running across the street, huffing and puffing. Foster still stood by the door, arms folded across his chest, watching.

"Says who?" demanded the tall policeman.

Stover pulled his suitcoat open to reveal his Secret Service badge pinned to the inside. The handle of his revolver peeked out, also. "Secret Service," he said. "These are two of our agents. They are part of the presidential security detail. Leave them alone."

"You tellin' me that a n----r is a Secret Service agent?" sneered the shorter policeman. "I don't believe it. Can't be!"

"It's true," asserted Stover. "They were in the army, too. Fought in Cuba, the Philippines, and China. With General Wheeler."

"*Wheeler?* You mean "Fightin' Joe" Wheeler? The Confederate cavalry hero?" The question was asked in tones of awe and disbelief.

"The one and only," responded Walker, dryly.

Dixon cleared his throat meaningfully and pulled open his

ragged coat to expose the Secret Service badge. Walker did the same. The wide-eyed policemen gawked and unleashed a string of profanities as they turned and walked away, shaking their heads. Stover returned to the front steps of the mansion, and resumed his post beside Foster.

"Looks like I was wrong about Stover," said Walker. "He's pretty useful, after all."

"Does this mean he's the King of England now?" grinned Dixon. They laughed.

After a moment of silence, Walker asked, in a lowered voice, "What do you think we should tell Foster about what happened back at the Square?"

"Absolutely nothin'," replied Dixon, firmly. "There's two dead men back there, and we don't want nothin' to do with it. It ain't nothin' but trouble, and nobody needs to know nothin' about it."

"But shouldn't Foster know? It's his job to know these things."

"Maybe so, but Foster is by-the-book, and he'll report it to the police. Do you think Memphis is going to just let us outsiders waltz in here and kill two of their finest citizens, and then just waltz out of town, just like that? I don't think so. They don't appear to be too fond of the federal government around here as it is—how much clappin' and cheerin' did you hear from that crowd? They'll hang us high. If you want to tell Foster, just leave me out of it. I wasn't there and don't know nothin' about it."

"I guess you're right," Walker conceded, reluctantly.

"I *am* right," Dixon retorted. "Didn't you hear the band play 'Dixie' right after 'The Star-Spangled Banner'? And that shooter was wearing a Confederate coat and using a Civil War musket. That minie ball would have torn McKinley in two. And did you notice how those policemen acted when Stover mentioned General Wheeler? Like he was a *god*.

"Garrett," he continued earnestly, "these people ain't got a federal bone in their bodies. The sooner we can get out of this town, the safer I'll feel. Don't go stirring the pot. It won't do any good, and could get us killed."

"Alright," agreed Walker, with some exasperation. "Not a word about it."

After the reception, the group returned to the train to change into evening wear for a sumptuous banquet at the famous Peabody Hotel. Walker and Dixon, back in their three-piece suits again, stood on steps at the rear of the president's carriage, as if they were coachmen. Dining on lobster and duck, the guests listened to several speeches and toasts. The elaborate affair lasted until almost midnight, and finally, at one-thirty in the morning, the train steamed out of Memphis, heading south toward New Orleans, more than four hundred miles away.

The men climbed into their bunks, exhausted. No one felt like talking, and the click-clacking of the rails was the only sound. *That was a close call today,* Walker thought to himself. *Four agents are not nearly enough for this job.* The words 'eyes and ears' kept bouncing around in his head, and he groaned audibly. As he drifted off to sleep, the rhythmic rocking of the car gave him the strange sensation that he was riding a camel again in the Gobi Desert. And then the blackness mercifully descended, and he knew nothing until morning.

2

"LOST CAUSE"

"I bet you southern boys've never seen anything like *that* before, have you?" Stover smirked, gesturing with his thumb over his shoulder at the towering St. Louis Cathedral. A landmark of New Orleans, the massive, triple-spired, white cathedral fronted on Jackson Square with its equine statue of General Andrew Jackson, little more than a stone's throw from the Mississippi River.

"That is quite nice," agreed Dixon, nodding. "Don't you think so, Garrett?"

"Definitely," Walker concurred. "Reminds me of one that we saw in Paris. I wonder if it's as beautiful inside as the one in Irkutsk?"

"Dammit!" Stover snapped, before Dixon could reply. "Stop it! Do you take me for a fool? Foster told me that you two really were in Cuba, the Philippines, and China, but now you're going too far! Next, you'll be saying that the St. Charles Hotel isn't as nice as where you stayed in some place like London or Rome!"

"No," said Walker, shaking his head. "The one where we stayed in London was pretty plain. But the St. Charles is just as nice as the ones in Berlin and Moscow. Wouldn't you agree, Dixon?"

Dixon opened his mouth to speak, but Stover held up his hand to stop him. Red in the face, and with a trembling voice, he snarled, "If you expect me to believe that you fellows went all the way around the world, you've got another think coming. This may be a joke to you, but I don't appreciate having my leg pulled like this. It's disrespectful! We may need to have a little talk with Mr. Foster. You won't be laughing, *then!*" He whirled about and, with clenched fists, stormed off to the carriages, which awaited the return of the president and Mrs. McKinley, who were being given a tour inside the cathedral.

Walker and Dixon watched with raised eyebrows as Stover departed. After several seconds of silence, Dixon said quietly, "Personally, I think the hotels in Europe were all much better than the St. Charles, because I got to stay in the nice rooms, not in some dinky closet next to the back door."

"Well, I'm sleeping in the dinky closet too, you know," replied Walker, uncomfortably. "That's just the way it is down here in the South."

"Yeah, but for you, it's a *choice*. I appreciate it, but it ain't the same. I wouldn't even get *that* room if I wasn't a Secret Service agent with the president, and you know it."

The conversation was cut short when the presidential party emerged from the cathedral and boarded the carriages en route to the steamboat landing. The next item on the itinerary was a paddlewheel steamboat tour of the riverfront. A jazz band was already playing on the upper deck of the majestic *St. Louis* when they arrived at the wharf. Dancers whirled gaily in colorful costumes, and the mood was festive. Before Walker and Dixon could board, however, Foster waved them over to the side and handed them a small object wrapped in cloth.

"This is one of Mrs. McKinley's shoes," he said. "The heel broke in the cathedral, and she can barely walk in it. I want you two to take it to a shoe shop and get it fixed before the boat gets back to the dock. I told the president you'd take care of it. You've got about two hours, so get moving." Without waiting for a response, he turned and hurried to the boat, making it just as the boarding ramp was pulled away.

Disappointed, Walker turned to Dixon. "I was really looking forward to a boat ride."

"Apparently fixing Mrs. McKinley's shoe is more important than providing security on the boat," Dixon grumbled. "Let's shake a leg— we ain't got much time."

They obtained directions to a shoe repair shop from an elderly woman selling flowers from a cart in the Square. It wasn't far away— two long blocks north to Bourbon Street, and three blocks east. They hurried up Pirate's Alley, a narrow passage between the cathedral and the Cabildo, the seat of the state Supreme Court, where the president had delivered a speech earlier that day. All told, it was maybe half a mile from the wharf, and in ten minutes they were standing in front of Plessy's Shoe Shop.

A bell tinkled above the door as they entered. Dixon placed the shoe on the counter, and a man wearing a leather apron and rolled-up sleeves emerged through a curtain from a back room.

"Which one of you was here first?" he asked. Walker showed no reaction, but he was surprised that the man would apparently serve a colored customer before a white man. *That wouldn't be taken well in most places in the South*, he thought.

"We're together," replied Dixon. The man's eyebrows rose slightly, but he said nothing.

"We need to get this shoe fixed real quick," he continued, pointing at the shoe sitting wrapped in cloth on the counter. "It belongs to Mrs. McKinley, the president's wife. They're on the *St. Louis* right now, but they'll be back in a couple of hours and it has to be ready for her."

"Sure it does," chuckled the man. "I get president's shoes in here all the time, and governors, and kings, queens, and popes. Everybody wants it done real quick, too."

"No, it's true," Dixon objected. "We're Secret Service bodyguards, traveling with the president's party." They pulled their coats open to show their badges.

"Well, why didn't you say so? Let me take a look at the shoe." He unwrapped the cloth, and picked up the shoe. "The heel came loose, here," he pointed. "All it needs is a few small nails and a little glue under the pad. Shouldn't take more than a few minutes. Wait right here." He turned to head back through the curtain, shoe in hand, when Dixon spoke again.

"I'd like to speak to Mr. Plessy, if you don't mind."

"I'm Plessy. I said it would be done in a few minutes—is there a problem?"

"No—it's just that—well, you're a *white* man. I thought you might be the famous Plessy from the court case a few years ago."

Plessy laughed shortly. "That's me, alright. I may *look* white, but I'm one-eighth black, and that's enough to make me a Negro in Louisiana. And if you're a Negro, you can't ride in the same railroad car as the white folks, even if you're whiter than some of *them*. Strange world, ain't it?" With that, he disappeared behind the curtain.

Walker's mind flashed back to a scene he had witnessed on a train three years ago in Birmingham. A well-dressed black man had been evicted from the whites-only car, and at the time he had thought it appropriate. It seemed like a lifetime ago.

"I've heard of him," Walker said slowly. He removed his fedora and scratched his head. "Surely he can't really be *that* Plessy! I thought Plessy was a black man, but this fellow is a white man—or at least, he sure looks white. I'm getting confused," he said, shaking his head.

"Being a colored man ain't really about your *color*," said Dixon, tersely. "It's about who your mama is. Once you been written down on the 'colored list,' your descendants will be on that list 'til Jesus comes back—no matter what *color* they are."

"So," mused Walker, "because somebody decided that Plessy—who is one-eighth black and seven-eighths white—was a colored man, he has to ride in the colored passenger car. What difference does it really make, though? Didn't the Supreme Court say the cars had to be alike? Equal?"

"Garrett, have you ever *been* in the colored car? Do you really think they are the same? Is our dinky closet at the hotel *equal* to the rooms Foster and Stover have, or just *separate*?"

Walker opened his mouth to reply, but then realized that he had nothing to say, so he closed it. With a frown, he put his hat back on and turned to watch passersby on the street.

Plessy returned with the shoe after a few minutes, and pronounced the shoe to be "good as new." He rapped the heel on the counter as if to prove it. "No charge," he smiled. "Tell the president and his missus that it's a token of my appreciation for his service in the war. Us *black* folks owe him and the rest of the Union Army a debt of gratitude!" He laughed out loud, amused at referring to himself as being black. "We *black* folks may be a lost cause today, but someday that will change!" And he retired through the curtain for the final time.

Back out on the rough cobblestones of Bourbon Street, they dodged carriages and horse excrement in the street. The shoe repair had been done so quickly that they had no need to hurry. Standing on a street corner, waiting for a freight wagon pulled by six mules to pass, Walker turned to Dixon.

"He said black people today are a 'lost cause.' What did he mean by that?"

"It's obvious, ain't it? He means that colored folk are being beat down and pushed aside, and nobody seems to care," Dixon replied grimly. "And it don't look like there's any hope for things to get better any time soon, but he thinks that, eventually, it will. I hope he's right."

"That reminds me of the Civil War," Walker said. "The South was fightin' for a 'Lost Cause' and couldn't win, but wouldn't quit. There's something noble about that."

"Bah!" Dixon snorted derisively. "'Lost Cause'? Garrett, they *lost* 'cause they was fightin' for the *wrong* cause. Not quittin' wasn't noble —it was *stupid*. And ever since, they been pretending they didn't *really* lose." He glared at Walker and poked him in the chest with his finger. "Us colored folks won't win *our* cause 'til Southern white folks admit they lost *theirs*."

Walker knocked Dixon's hand away. Through clenched teeth he snapped, "It wasn't stupid!" and abruptly stepped out into the street without looking.

Dixon shouted "Garrett!" and violently jerked him back to the curb just as a two-horse carriage hurtled past with clattering hooves, narrowly missing him. "Watch where you're going! You could have gotten killed!"

Shaken and pale, Walker straightened his hat and took a deep breath. "Thanks," he said quietly, and then added, "We can't talk about the Civil War no more."

"Alright, brother," said Dixon, with a penetrating gaze. "Not another word."

"Beware!" The cackling cry of an old crone came suddenly from behind them. They spun about to see a hunched figure draped in a black robe, with a hood pulled over her head, extending past her gaunt and wrinkled face. She stood in the doorway of a tiny alcove beneath a sign which read, "Claire Voyant: The Seer of New Orleans." Walker blinked and reflexively took a step backward.

"Beware!" she croaked again, pointing a crooked, bony finger at both of them.

"Beware of what?" asked Dixon, rather brusquely.

"Beware the left-handed assassin!" She lifted her face toward them, and Walker thought he could feel her cataract-glazed eyes staring into his very brain. Her upper lip curled, exposing two yellow teeth. "The man you protect is Eglon, the fat king," she cackled. "Beware Ehud, the left-handed assassin! He will do his duty!" She snapped her fingers, somehow releasing a small cloud of white smoke, and then shuffled quickly back into the dark interior.

They looked at each other blankly. "How did she know we are protecting someone? Someone who could be assassinated—a political leader?" wondered Walker aloud.

"Crazy gypsy!" spat Dixon. "It don't mean nothin'! Let's get back to the wharf."

Before they had walked a block, a sultry feminine voice called out, "Hey there, handsome!"

Walker stopped and turned to look. Dixon took another couple of steps and then turned to glare impatiently at Walker, hands on hips.

"Up here, handsome!" The voice was coming from a second-floor balcony overlooking the sidewalk. Walker looked up to see a striking young woman with long dark hair, red lips, and a very low-cut neckline, revealing deep cleavage. She sensuously tossed her hair out of her face and leaned over the railing. "My, but you're a handsome fellow!" she cooed. "Come up here and let's get to know each other! I'll make it worth your while!"

Walker's jaw dropped and he stood frozen in his tracks. For the second time, Dixon grabbed him roughly by the arm and began dragging him away. Walker stumbled and almost fell, but Dixon did not relent.

"But she—she—but I—" Walker groped helplessly for words and tried to stay on his feet as he looked over his shoulder.

"I know," Dixon hissed. "You ain't never seen nothin' like that before. Listen to me—you didn't see *that* neither. Get it outa your head. We got a shoe to deliver to Mrs. McKinley. Here—you carry the shoe. Keep moving!" And he kept a firm grip on Walker's arm, hustling him along, as the woman's calling voice faded away behind them.

"Lord a-mercy!" Walker breathed, as they turned down Pirate's Alley toward the riverfront. "You can let go of my arm, now."

Dixon released his arm and gave Walker a disgusted look. "Garrett," he said, shaking his head, "you're a lost cause, farm boy. A lost cause."

"Well, at least I'm a *handsome* lost cause," Walker replied, with a smirk. Dixon groaned and smacked him hard on the back with the flat of his hand, and they then laughed and joked all the way to Jackson's Square.

At the wharf, they watched the regal *St. Louis* churning its way around the bend in the big river, heading back to its berth. A sizeable crowd was there to see the president—in fact, to Walker it seemed that the crowd which had seen the president off on his tour two hours ago had never left, and had even grown larger. A short distance away, at another berth, was a steamboat with the name *Natchez* proudly emblazoned on its sidewheel façade.

Pointing to it, Walker asked a uniformed steamboat attendant at the boarding gate, "Say, is that the famous *Natchez* that lost the race to the *Robert E. Lee* a few years ago?"

The attendant drew himself up with squared shoulders and jutted his chin forward in a belligerent posture. With a scowl, he snapped, "No *sir*! The *Natchez* ain't never lost no race to *nobody*! She's the fastest steamboat on the river, and anybody that says otherwise is lyin'!"

"But that's not right," Walker objected. "Everybody knows that the *Robert E. Lee* got to St. Louis ahead of the *Natchez* and won the race. The *Lee* broke the old record the *Natchez* set by more than thirty minutes!"

"That may be true," growled the attendant, "but that don't mean the *Natchez* got beat. The truth is they deliberately let the *Robert E. Lee* finish first."

"Why on earth would they do that?" Walker exclaimed. "People all the way from New Orleans to St. Louis watched those two boats race up the river, and a mountain of money was bet on both sides. Deliberately losing would have caused a huge scandal! The captain would've been shot!"

"Or lynched," added Dixon, shaking his head. "What makes you think the *Natchez* threw the race?"

"It's common knowledge on the river," sneered the attendant, with a curled upper lip. "They was about to win, when they realized that forever after, the name of the great General Lee would be 'sociated with defeat. It was a hard pill to swaller, but they knew they had to do it. They steered the *Natchez* into a cove under cover of darkness, and waited 'til the *Lee* plowed past. Then, after a while, they got back out on the river and follered 'em on to the finish line." He folded his arms and concluded philosophically, "Ain't no shame in finishin' second, when it's for a good purpose."

"Sort of like a 'lost cause'?" suggested Dixon, giving Walker a knowing look.

"'Zactly!" agreed the man, with an emphatic nod. "That's 'zactly what it is. You do what has to be done—that's all you *can* do." At this moment, the *St. Louis* was almost to the dock, and the attendant walked away, busy with his duties.

Dixon turned to Walker, shaking his head. "Garrett, you see what I was tellin' you? These people think their Confederate war heroes are *gods*. They wouldn't let a dadgum steamboat named *Lee* lose a race, even when there was thousands of dollars ridin' on it. It just ain't *natural*."

"I admit it's hard to understand," Walker said, reluctantly.

"There ain't no understanding it a'tall! Why, I could make loads of money horse-racing down here. Just give me any ol' nag. I'll name it 'Robert E. Lee,' and none of 'em would dare win the race! I could rob 'em blind! You know it's true!"

"I think you're taking it a bit far, there."

"Oh? What if I named it 'General Wheeler?' Would you let me win the race, or would you pass me, knowin' that the next day's newspapers would all run the story about General Wheeler losin' the big race?"

"I would—" Walker began confidently, and then hesitated. "I would—well, I think I would—"

"Like I said—you're a lost cause, Garrett," said Dixon, disgustedly. "Just a lost cause."

Dixon took the shoe from Walker's hand and delivered it to Foster at the boarding ramp as the boat came to a stop. Walker stood for a long moment, deep in thought, and then slowly followed.

The presidential party disembarked, entered the carriages, and amid much cheering and waving, headed off to the train station. The railroad cars had already been ferried across the river on barges, and were awaiting the arrival of the group. By late afternoon, the reassembled train departed for Texas, leaving behind the bands and cheering crowds, and for a few hours at least, the passengers enjoyed peace and quiet.

Walker sat alone in the dining car after everyone else had retired early. The staff removed the dishes and white tablecloths, talking to each other and laughing. He started a letter to Abigail Dancy, but struggled to find words and began scribbling random notes and drawing designs. The electric lights in the car were dimmed, and the setting sun cast long shadows across the landscape outside. Soon, it was night, and Walker could see nothing but his own reflection in the window glass. Distracted by his doodling and writing, he did not notice the sound of the door at the end of the car opening behind him, and he was badly startled by the deep, resonant voice which suddenly spoke, right at his elbow.

"Is this seat taken, young man?"

The pencil literally flipped from his fingers into the air as the blood rushed to his face and he instantly drew his feet under him in order to stand up.

"Don't get up! I'll join you, if you don't mind." President William McKinley put his hand firmly on Walker's shoulder, pushing him back down onto his seat. "I hope I'm not interrupting anything?"

"Sir! No sir! I was just—I was—" Walker felt that he couldn't breathe, and his eyes were like saucers. He swallowed hard and tried to control his shaking hands.

McKinley lowered himself into the opposite chair, scooting it back to make room for his ample stomach. He wore slippers, and a loose dressing gown over an open-collared white shirt, and dark trousers, apparently having been in the process of changing clothes when he decided to return to the dining car. Seeing the president in such casual attire was completely confusing to Walker's mind."

"Andrew!" called the president, waving to one of the staff. "Bring us two mugs of hot cocoa, and some of those delicious pecan cookies, if there are any left!"

"Yes sir, Mr. President," came the reply. "It'll be just a few minutes, sir."

"As you may have guessed, I'm William McKinley," smiled the president, extending his hand to shake Walker's. "And with whom do I have the pleasure of sharing this bedtime snack?"

Coughing nervously and clearing his throat, Walker said hoarsely, "Garrett, sir. I'm Walker Garrett, one of your Secret Service bodyguards."

"Ah, yes! Garrett!" McKinley nodded as if remembering something. "George—that's George Foster—has told me about you. You and—the other agent, the colored one—"

"Dixon, sir."

"Yes, Dixon, that's right—George told me about you two. You had quite an experience in the army, didn't you?" Without waiting for a reply, he continued, "I can tell from your accent that you're from the South. Where do you call home, Garrett?"

"Courtland, Alabama, sir. We passed through it on the way to Memphis. I actually lived on General Joseph Wheeler's plantation near there. My father served—"

"Wheeler!" exclaimed McKinley, interrupting. "Remarkable man! We need more like him. He chose the wrong side in *that* war, but he has righted his course since then, and he's a true patriot today. Glad to have him with us in Washington!"

"Yes sir, Mr. President! The General is a hero to the South, and we would follow him anywhere. We Southerners are patriotic, and we love our country as much as anybody!"

"Yes, I see that, everywhere I go in the South," agreed the president. "But I also see signs of continuing discontent and resentment. That's why I've talked about sectionalism in every speech I've made on this trip. In fact, that's why we starting mixing soldiers from all parts of the country in each company in the army—so they would get to know men from all over, and build bonds of friendship."

"Yes sir, I noticed that while I was in the army! I think it worked very well."

"Excellent!" McKinley beamed. Just then, the hot cocoa and cookies arrived, and the conversation halted while they indulged in the refreshments. After disposing of a couple of cookies and half of the mug of cocoa, the president, with a serious expression, fixed his gaze on Walker.

"Garrett," he said, looking troubled. "I want to ask you about something. This will be confidential, just between you and me. Agreed?"

"Yes sir, Mr. President," Walker replied earnestly, surprised at the sudden seriousness of tone.

"When I was sitting on the speakers' platform in Court Square, in Memphis, I saw something down the street that disturbed me. I am sure that I saw a man fall from the roof of a building, and then I saw men struggling on the roof." He paused, studying Walker's face, which had gone pale.

"We received a telegram yesterday from the mayor, saying that they found the body of a dead man on the roof, next to a rifle, and wearing a Confederate army jacket. The man who fell down to the street was also dead, and also had a rifle. Two men were seen running away—one of them a white man, and the other colored. The mayor agreed to keep this from the press, but felt that we should know about it. Can you shed any light on this for me?" His expression was not angry, but his eyes were focused intently on Walker's as he waited for a response.

Walker sat silent and motionless for several seconds, not breathing. He stared at McKinley, feeling suddenly cold inside. Finally, he shook himself back to life and, taking a deep breath, spoke slowly and hesitantly, his voice almost a whisper. He couldn't lie to the president.

"Yes sir, I can. That was me and Dixon, sir. We didn't intend to kill anybody, but they attacked us when we told them to put down their rifles. It just sort of happened, y'know?" The words began to come more easily, and Walker told the story in detail, leaving out nothing. When he finished, he sighed and shrugged. "And that's all there is to tell," he concluded.

"You did well," McKinley nodded. "You probably saved my life! However, this has to be kept secret. It wouldn't do for this to get out to the public. Do you understand?"

"Oh, absolutely, Mr. President!" Walker exclaimed, relieved. "We won't tell a soul"

"Good! Not another word about it, then." Taking another slurp of cocoa, the president asked, "Are you a Bible student, Garrett?"

The question surprised Walker. He had heard that McKinley was a very religious man, and felt a bit uneasy at having to admit that he was not. "No sir. I always went to church with my folks, and I believe in the Bible, but I don't really study it, sir."

McKinley pointed to the paper on which Walker had been scribbling. "You've written 'Eglon' and 'Ehud' here. You know that story, don't you?"

"No sir. Someone mentioned those names recently, but I don't know what they mean."

"It's a fairly obscure story from the Old Testament. Eglon was the king of Moab, and they were oppressing the Israelites. God sent Ehud to deliver them. Ehud, who was left-handed, concealed a double-edged sword under his robe, and asked for a private audience with the king. He drove the sword into Eglon's belly—he was very fat—and the fat covered the hilt of the sword. Ehud then escaped out a window. It's an amazing story—one of my favorites in the Bible."

"I see," Walker mused. "That's very interesting, sir. I'll have to do more Bible reading!"

"Yes, indeed," agreed the president, rising from the table. "We all should do more Bible reading! It's been a pleasure, Agent Garrett!" He extended his hand again.

"Yes sir, Mr. President. Thank you, sir!"

As McKinley turned to leave, a thought suddenly occurred to Walker. "Mr. President! You might like to know, sir, that Mrs. McKinley's shoe was fixed today by a cobbler named Homer Plessy. He said there was no charge—and to tell you that he appreciated what you and the Union Army did for black people like him. Except that he's not actually black. Did you know that he is seven-eighths white? He's as white as I am, sir, but has to sit in the colored car on trains. Very strange, it seems to me."

"Homer Plessy! Yes, I know that name. I wish I could have met him. Ida will be pleased to know that he's the one who repaired her shoe. Thank you, Garrett!" Without further ado, the president ambled off to his own private car.

Walker finished his cocoa with a large gulp, grabbed two more cookies, and taking his sheet of paper and pencil, left in the opposite direction. Back in his bunk, the realization began to sink in that he had actually had a conversation with the President of the United States—and even shared cookies and cocoa! He longed to write a letter to his parents to share this incredible experience, and felt their loss more deeply than ever. *I'll write a letter to Abigail tomorrow*, he thought. *Or maybe I'll write the General.* He was so excited that it was impossible to fall asleep until after midnight.

3

"REMEMBER THE ALAMO"

F lags, parades, bands, and multitudes of school children marching on streets covered with flowers, lined with cheering and waving crowds—that was Houston, and later that same day, Austin. Audiences numbering in the thousands heard McKinley's speeches, and in Austin, the state capitol, he addressed the legislature. The state governor welcomed the president in Houston and traveled with him to Austin. Mayors and other dignitaries filled the platforms, along with the president's cabinet members. Texans seemed to be trying to outdo the other Southern states in showing the president true Southern hospitality.

The scene was repeated in San Antonio, with the addition of an honor guard of Union and Confederate veterans, wearing their blue and gray uniforms, respectively. Even the buildings along the parade route were festooned with banners and flags—the city was a riot of patriotic colors. Upon reaching Alamo Plaza, the men took their seats on the grandstand, and the introductions and speeches began. The Alamo itself provided a backdrop for the occasion.

Typically, while the president gave his speeches, Mrs. McKinley attended receptions with the ladies. This time, however, she insisted on visiting the Alamo, privately. The historic battle site was within a stone's throw of the grandstand, and since women were not supposed to be seated on the platform with the men, she decided to take advantage of the opportunity to do some sight-seeing. Walker was assigned to escort her. Wearing a wide-brimmed sun hat and using a silk parasol as a walking stick, the First Lady took Walker's arm as they strolled slowly across the plaza toward the adobe mission with its distinctive arched façade. The large crowd was gathered in front of the grandstand for the speech, and almost no one was at the Alamo itself. Once inside the building, it was relatively quiet. The thick walls not only kept out the noise of the crowd, but also the heat of the Texas sun, making the interior pleasantly cool and shady.

"Thank you, Mr. Garrett," she said, releasing his arm. "I'm sure you would prefer to be back there with the others, rather than walking around with me."

"No ma'am, not at all!" Walker responded with a warm smile. "It's an honor, and I'm excited to get to see where so many American heroes died fighting for our country!"

A contemptuous snort came from the shadows across the room. Walker turned to see a heavily-mustached man wearing a serape drop a smoking cigarette to the floor and crush it under his boot, as he exhaled twin plumes of smoke from his nostrils. When he stepped forward and spoke, Walker could see that he was a Mexican, with a strong Hispanic accent.

"Eet was not 'your country' they were fighting for," he said, disdainfully. "They fought for *Texas*, and for independence from Mexico, which they had no right to do. And they were not heroes— they were foolish rebels who should have retreated and saved themselves. They wasted their lives for no good reason! I speet on their memory!" And he spat on the floor, glaring defiantly at them.

Seeing that Walker was about to make an angry response, Mrs. McKinley held up her hand and said, "Mr. Garrett, let's not argue with this man. Please take me into the next room. I would like to see the rest of the place."

Holding his tongue with great difficulty, Walker said only, "Yes ma'am," and turning his back on the man, walked with her out of the room. However, the man apparently interpreted this as a sign of timidity, and followed them.

"I think he is intoxicated," whispered the First Lady. "Try not to provoke him. We don't want trouble." Walker nodded, but doubted that this would turn out well.

"I speet on ze United States," the belligerent man continued, spitting on the floor again.

Mrs. McKinley pressed on Walker's arm to keep him moving forward. "Let's go into the courtyard," she murmured. Before they could reach the outer door, however, the man spoke again.

"I speet on President McKinley," he declared, making a harsh, juicy noise deep in his throat, preparing to spit again.

At that, the First Lady spun about and, pointing an accusing finger, snapped angrily, "How dare you speak disrespectfully of the President of the United States! I happen to know that he is a very fine and decent man, not like you at all! You should mind your manners, sir!"

Now it was Walker tugging at *her* elbow and urging caution. "Ma'am, let's go out into the—"

"Ha!" the inebriated bully shouted derisively. "'A fine and decent man?' Why should I show respect to *him* when he does not show respect for *my* country? He should geeve back to us ze land your country stole from us! Geeve back California, Arizona, New Mexico, and Texas! Geeve back all ze gold you took from our land! And ze silver! And—"

Before he could continue his tirade, a trio of uniformed policemen suddenly burst into the room. Two of them grabbed the man by his arms, and amid much shouting and struggling, dragged him out. The third man, apparently their commanding officer, bowed to Mrs. McKinley, tipping his hat and apologizing profusely for the disturbance as he backed hastily from the room.

When all was quiet again, Mrs. McKinley looked at Walker and said, "Not a word about this to William! It would upset him greatly to know that I had been treated so rudely!"

"Yes ma'am," nodded Walker. "Not a word, ma'am." When they

reached the courtyard, he spoke again. "Why did he say that the U.S. stole that land? We won it fair and square in a war that Mexico started, didn't we?"

"Well, not necessarily," she replied, a little hesitantly. "Some people think President Polk was responsible for starting the war. He claimed that 'American blood was shed on American soil,' but not everyone believed him. Abraham Lincoln, as a congressman, challenged him to prove it, but the war was already starting. At the end of the war, we took almost half of Mexico's territory as compensation for the expense the war cost us. Mexicans have never accepted this, and still claim that they were robbed."

Walker digested this slowly, and after a long moment asked, "What do you think about it, Mrs. McKinley? Do you think it was fair?"

She paused to choose her words carefully before answering. "Whether the outcome was fair or not depends on how you think the war started," she said quietly. "If Polk was right, and if Mexican soldiers shed American blood on American soil, then it was fair. If Lincoln was right, then it wasn't. Either way, the Mexican War set in motion a series of events which indirectly led to our Civil War a few years later. More than a half million American men died on those battlefields. You have to wonder if getting all that land from Mexico was worth it."

Walker cleared his throat and gave his head a quick shake. This was a lot to absorb. He made a mental note to discuss this with General Wheeler when he got back to Washington.

"It's always interesting to see how one thing leads to another," she continued, talking as much to herself as to Walker. "The Texas Revolution made the Mexican War possible, and the Mexican War helped make the Civil War possible. Just think, Mr. Garrett—" she gestured broadly with her hand toward the buildings of the Alamo—"It all started right here!"

Walker grunted softly and looked around, seeing with new eyes. He felt as if the weight of history was suddenly pressing down upon him. "I've always heard it said, 'Remember the Alamo!'"

Walker grimaced. "After today, I'll never remember it the same way again."

They continued to explore the site for a while, and then rejoined the rest of the party in the plaza. Everyone climbed back into the carriages for another short parade, during which they were led by a colorful marching band back to the train station. Within minutes, the steam whistle blasted a shrill scream and the tall wheels of the presidential locomotive began to turn. They were soon racing through the flatlands of west Texas, with nothing in sight for miles but scrub brush and an occasional weather-beaten tree.

"Ain't exactly Alabama, is it?" commented Dixon, as they watched the passing landscape through the window.

"Not by a long shot," agreed Walker.

"New York, either," added Stover. The two Alabamians looked at him in surprise. "What?" demanded Stover, indignantly. "Did you think the whole state of New York was skyscrapers and asphalt?"

"Yeah, kinda," admitted Walker. "And tenement slums and big crowds of immigrants. But then, we only passed through New York City, from the dock to the railroad station."

"New York *State* is a lot more than just New York *City*," scoffed Stover. "You'll see. This tour ends in Buffalo, at the Pan American Exposition. You'll get to see a lot of really pretty country." Then he added, making a face, "For two fellows who traveled all the way around the world, you sure don't know much about your own country!"

"Tell me this, Stover," said Dixon, with a raised eyebrow. "Before you came on this trip, did you think the South was all cottonfields, shacks, and mules?"

Stover was visibly taken aback by the question. He blinked, and opened his mouth and closed it without speaking, twice. Finally, his face reddening, he sheepishly admitted, "Yes, that's exactly what I thought. I admit the South is not what I expected—except for the humidity. I'm kind of glad to be out here in the Southwest where the air is drier, even if it's not much to look at."

"You ain't *seen* humidity 'til you've been in the jungle in the Philippines," asserted Dixon. "You can go swimming without even gettin' in the river."

"The jungle!" exclaimed Stover, with an involuntary shiver. "I hear they've got snakes big enough to swallow a man whole!"

"Don't I know it!" Walker almost yelled. "A giant python attacked me in the dark, and would've got me if I hadn't cut his head off with a machete!"

Stover stared, wide-eyed for several seconds, and then, glaring, snapped, "You're pulling my leg again, Garrett! Stop it!"

"He ain't messin' with you, Stover," said Dixon. "It's a fact. Show 'im, Garrett."

Walker stood and pulled off his jacket, unbuttoned his shirt, and slipped his left arm out of the sleeve. Pointing to a double row of puncture wounds encircling his upper arm, he said, "That's where it grabbed my arm. It wrapped 'round my body and was squeezing the breath out of me. If I hadn't had that machete, I wouldn't be here talkin' to you now."

Stover became pale and looked like he was going to be sick. Fixing his pained eyes on Walker's, he asked, "How do you sleep at night?"

"I just try not to think about it," Walker said, quietly. "There's a lot of things I try not to think about." Buttoning his shirt, he paused and added, "Too many."

After a moment of silence, Dixon spoke up. "I saw you went into the Alamo with Mrs. McKinley. Anything interesting in there?"

"Yes! It was very interesting to see where all those heroes fought to the death. Travis, Crockett, Bowie—it all came to life. Seemed real, not like reading about it in a book!"

"Now, those men were *real* heroes," declared Stover, making a fist. "Faced with overwhelming odds, they fought for what they believed in, knowing they probably wouldn't survive. That takes real courage —and character!"

A thought flashed through Walker's mind, and he voiced it slowly, even as he grappled with its meaning. "Facing overwhelming odds. . . not much chance of winning. . . but fighting for what you believe in. . . ." He paused reflectively. "Would you call that a 'lost cause?'"

"Well, sure!" replied Stover, emphatically. "I'd say that's the very *definition* of a lost cause. Why? Does that mean something special?"

Dixon was frowning, but Walker ignored him. "There was a Mexican man inside the Alamo, and he called the Alamo defenders 'foolish rebels,' and said they 'wasted their lives for no good reason.' Do you think he was right?"

"Just because he doesn't agree with their reason doesn't mean they didn't *have* a good reason," argued Stover. "They were fighting for something they believed in—something that was important to *them*—and that made it a cause worth fighting for—and worth dying for. I respect that."

"Does that apply to the Confederate soldiers in the Civil War, too?" persisted Walker. "They fought for a cause they believed in, against overwhelming odds. Just because somebody else doesn't agree with their reason doesn't mean they didn't have one that they thought was worth fighting—and dying—for."

"The men at the Alamo fought for *freedom*," interjected Dixon, irritably. "Confederates fought for *slavery*. That's the opposite thing, and no matter what they believed about it, it was wrong. Calling it a 'lost cause' don't make it any better."

"General Wheeler didn't own any slaves," argued Walker. "Neither did my pa. Hardly any of the men in gray owned slaves."

"Don't matter," averred Dixon. "If they'd a'won the war, slavery would still be going on today, and you know it. Whether it was *their* cause or not, it was *the* cause. So it ain't no difference."

Walker glared at Dixon as he considered this argument. Finally, after a long moment, he growled, "Alright—I see your point. It wasn't the cause that *every* man was fightin' for, but it was a cause for *some*— for the ones that owned slaves, anyway."

"And they were the ones that ran the government," nodded Stover. "They decided to have a war for their own selfish reasons. The common man carried the load—that's the way it always is. The rich man always comes out on top."

"I guess so," Walker consented, reluctantly. "I reckon the soldier and the politician saw things different ways. General Wheeler once told me that politicians see things the way they want them to be, but soldiers have to see them the way they are. Since he is both a soldier and a politician, I guess he knows what he's talking about."

"As I see it," Stover said, folding his arms authoritatively, "the most important thing is to stand up and fight for what you believe in, and never quit. It's not always the end result that matters the most—sometimes it's the fighting for it, even against the odds, that counts just as much."

"*Especially* against the odds," corrected Walker. "Remember the Alamo!"

4

CINCO DE MAYO

"Cinco de Mayo?" Dixon scratched his head. "What's that?" He held in his hand a flyer, printed on yellow paper, announcing festivities to be staged in the city of Juarez that day.

"I'm pretty sure it means 'fifth of May,'" replied Walker, also scratching his head. "But I don't know what makes today so special to the Mexicans."

"Well, here's our one chance to find out!" Dixon adjusted his bowler hat and began walking toward the International Bridge, which connected El Paso, Texas, to the Mexican city of Juarez, on the other side of the Rio Grande. Walker shrugged, and hurried to catch up.

The presidential train had arrived in El Paso at nine in the morning on May 5. Due to it being Sunday, McKinley had requested that there be no parades, ceremonies, or other official celebrations that day. He and the First Lady, along with some others in his party, attended a church service in the morning, and then enjoyed a quiet afternoon and evening at their hotel. Foster gave his three agents the afternoon off, and while he and Stover relaxed at the hotel, Walker and Dixon headed out to see the town. El Paso was suffocatingly quiet, seemingly deserted. In contrast, the sounds of laughter and peppy Mexican music floated across the river, stirring the curiosity of the two. It was only a short walk across the bridge, and they quickly found themselves caught up in the colorful and exuberant celebration which filled the streets of the small town of Juarez.

It seemed there was a band playing on every other corner, with men, women, and children of all ages dancing in the streets. Street vendors sold food from carts, and since Walker and Dixon had not eaten since breakfast, they went from one to the next, sampling everything. Fortunately, the vendors readily accepted their dollars, and repeated the names of the dishes—burritos, enchiladas, fajitas, and others. They were thoroughly enjoying themselves until they ate their first jalapeño peppers.

"What's the matter, Garrett?" asked Dixon, his mouth full. "You look like you just swallered a load of gunpowder and lit a—" His chuckle was cut short, however, as he bit into a particularly hot pepper in his burrito. Suddenly, he too was wheezing and wiping tears from his eyes. Seeing their distress, the vendor laughed and handed each an amber-colored bottle to drink. It didn't help—the liquid burned in their throats, producing coughing and choking. However, the stinging sensation created by the peppers was worse, and they quickly emptied the bottles in an attempt to quench the fire.

"My head is sweating," gasped Walker, as they staggered away. He fanned himself with his fedora and loosened his shirt collar.

"Good Lord!" exclaimed Dixon, looking at the label on the bottle. "Do you realize we just drank a whole damn bottle of tequila? We better find some place to sit down quick, before we *fall* down. We're about to be really drunk."

It was their good fortune that, as they stumbled along the sidewalk, they were suddenly overwhelmed by nausea. They hurried into a narrow alley, just in time. Stepping back out onto the street a couple of minutes later, a pale Walker wiped his mouth with a handkerchief and belched loudly. "I think I feel better," he groaned, and then added, "maybe."

"I hope nobody strikes a match in that alley anytime soon," said

Dixon hoarsely, as he spat on the ground. "The whole town'd go up in smoke."

"My head hurts," winced Walker. "Let's go to that park over there and sit down."

They sat on the ground in the Plaza de Armas, a large, green square, criss-crossed with walking paths. An imposing twin-towered church loomed over the plaza. Without talking, they watched the strolling pedestrians and playing children, listened to the lively music, and rubbed their aching temples. Walker noticed a man sitting on a nearby bench who appeared to be inserting bullets into a small, round device. After watching this for a moment, curiosity got the better of him, and he got up and walked over for a better look. The man's face was shielded by a broad-brimmed sombrero, and he wore a tan leather jacket and dusty boots with spurs.

Walker had acquired a small Spanish vocabulary while in Cuba and the Philippines, but almost two years had passed since then, and he struggled to find the right words to get the man's attention. The man, suddenly noticing that he was being watched, looked up at Walker with a frown, his dark eyes smoldering.

"Qué deseas?" he snarled. *What do you want?*

Walker, flustered, raised his hands apologetically and, after a false start, managed to ask, "Perdón—que es?" *Pardon—what is it?*

The man glared for a long moment, and Walker thought he was not going to answer. Before he could retreat to his sitting place, however, the man suddenly relaxed and motioned Walker to come closer. Dixon stepped over to join them.

They both uttered exclamations of amazement upon realizing that the small device was a firearm—a palm pistol. It fit snugly into one's palm, with a short barrel protruding between the fingers. A squeeze of the hand discharged a .32 caliber bullet. The flat, circular body of the weapon held eight rounds of ammunition. The man reluctantly allowed them to heft it in their hands and get the feel of it, but then immediately reclaimed it, and slipped it into his jacket pocket. Walker and Dixon were so animated in their admiration that he finally grinned, teeth flashing in contrast with his dark brown skin. After nodding and politely touching the brim of his hat, he abruptly hurried away across the plaza as if he suddenly had somewhere to go.

"What a devilish piece of work that is!" exclaimed Walker, watching the man leave.

"The gun, or the man?" scowled Dixon. "That gun ain't got but one purpose, and that's to murder somebody up close. Just point and shoot. Pure murder."

"That's true," Walker admitted. "But I'd sure like to have one! I wonder if one of these stores around here sells them."

With nothing better to do, they crossed the plaza, looking for stores that might sell firearms. As they approached the cathedral, three muted gunshots rang out, with an eerie echo.

"Did those shots come from inside the church?" asked Walker in astonishment.

"Sure sounded like it," Dixon nodded. "Who shoots a gun inside a church?"

In answer to his question, a man wearing a wide sombrero and a tan leather jacket ran out a side door of the cathedral and leaped into the saddle of a waiting horse. The horse reared dramatically, and then galloped down the street and disappeared around a corner.

"Dixon!" exclaimed Walker incredulously. "That was the man—the man in the plaza with the palm—"

"I know it, Garrett," interrupted Dixon. "I saw it, too. He murdered somebody in there. What did I tell you? Let's go see."

They ran into the church, stopping briefly inside the door to let their eyes adjust to the dim interior light. A small group of people was clustered near the main altar, and there were sounds of weeping as they knelt beside a body lying on the floor. A priest spoke quickly and quietly, repeatedly making the sign of the cross. Halfway down the aisle, the two watched silently, hats in hand, and after a moment, walked back outside. Squinting in the bright sunlight, Walker decided that obtaining a palm pistol did not seem so important anymore.

"I don't feel so good," he said, putting a hand on his stomach. "I don't think I got rid of all that tequila. How about we head back to the hotel?"

"Suits me."

They strolled casually through the crowds, musicians, and vendors back to the bridge to El Paso. At the hotel, they went to their small, windowless room next to the kitchen and stretched out on the bed.

"Did you get a good look at the body?" asked Walker. "I couldn't see much."

"It was a man in a suit," yawned Dixon, half asleep already. "Not a priest."

"The people around the body looked well-dressed," reflected Walker. "They definitely weren't poor people. Upper class, I'd say. Not like the man with the palm pistol."

"Maybe that's why he did it," mumbled Dixon, as he turned onto his side toward the peeling wall. "Lot of that goin' around, seems." A light snore indicated that the conversation was finished for now.

The next morning, the cabinet wives and Mrs. McKinley were taken in a carriage across the bridge to Juarez for a sumptuous breakfast, hosted by a prominent local banker and several local dignitaries. Walker and Dixon, having already visited the city, were assigned to accompany them. The various speakers at the breakfast all spoke English, and from their remarks Walker learned that Mrs. McKinley was the first First Lady to visit a foreign country while in office. He joined in the applause, and noted that the Mexican hosts seemed very pleased that their city was honored with this distinction. It was also said that, while the ladies of the presidential party had come to Juarez, several thousand of the city's residents had crossed over to El Paso to hear President McKinley's speech. *I guess that's why this place is so quiet today,* thought Walker, glancing out the second-floor window at the nearly empty street below.

Suddenly, however, he did a double-take, and stared intently at a passing figure in the street. A man wearing a wide-brimmed sombrero and a tan leather jacket rode past on a trotting horse, going north. He watched until the man was lost to view, and then caught

Dixon's eye across the room. Frowning, he tapped the side of his head: *eyes and ears!* Dixon nodded and took several soft steps toward the door.

The breakfast concluded without incident, however, and as everyone was shaking hands and engaging in small talk, prior to departing, Walker approached a well-dressed Mexican businessman.

"Buenos días!" he ventured. "Do you speak English?"

"Yes—somewhat!" he smiled, shaking hands warmly. "Thank you for coming to Juarez!"

"My friend and I were here yesterday, also," Walker nodded. "The Cinco de Mayo celebration was very nice! Until we ate some hot peppers, that is!"

"Oh! I am so sorry to hear that!" he laughed. "I hope that you are alright today?"

"Yes, we're just fine now, but we are watching out for anything that looks like a hot pepper!" They both laughed, and agreed that the breakfast had been very good.

"By the way," Walker said, more seriously, "when we were here yesterday, a man was shot to death in the cathedral. Do you know who he was, and why he was killed?"

The businessman blinked and froze for a few seconds before responding. "He—ah, he was a leading citizen in Juarez—a wealthy —ah—" He cleared his throat and frowned in concentration. "A very bad thing—I am sorry you saw that. We have troublemakers—*insurgentes*—bandits—" He appeared to be about to say more, but then abruptly, with a tightly civil smile, he simply said, "Adiós, señor!" and walked briskly away.

Dixon strolled casually over to Walker. "What did you say to that fella to upset him like that?" he whispered.

"Just asked who the man was that got shot in the cathedral yesterday, that's all. He said it was a wealthy, leading citizen, and that they have rebels and bandits around here. He seemed kind of unhappy that we saw that."

"Well, I should reckon so! It makes their town look pretty bad to have rich folk getting shot in church, especially in front of visitors."

Walker suppressed a smile and gave Dixon a severe look, as they followed the ladies out to the carriages. They mounted the horses they had been loaned by the El Paso police, and trailed the carriages to the bridge and across onto American soil. There was a large gathering on the far side of the bridge, where President McKinley and the rest of his party had arrived at the conclusion of their tour of the city. Dignitaries representing El Paso and Juarez were all shaking hands with the president and his cabinet, and there was much bowing and hat-tipping. The president's visit to El Paso was ending and farewells were being extended all around.

From his vantage point in the saddle, Walker had a good view of the crowd, numbering at least in the hundreds. He walked the horse slowly around the periphery, studying the people, watching for anything unusual. A slight disturbance caught his eye—a man was roughly pushing his way through the crowd toward the front. He was wearing a broad sombrero, and Walker could see a tan leather jacket. His heart leaped into his throat, and he decided in a split second that he had no chance of intercepting the man on foot. Kicking his heels into the horse's flanks, he rode into the crowd, holding his coat lapel open to expose his Secret Service badge.

"Step aside!" he ordered, as he received angry looks and objections. "Make way!" Catching up to the sombrero, he reined the horse to turn in front of him. They were only twenty yards from the president. The man was startled to find his path blocked by a horse, and looked up at Walker with a furious expression, which turned to shock as he recognized his face—and saw that he was staring into the barrel of a .38 revolver. He took a step back, looking left and right, and Walker could see that he was calculating his chances. The sombrero was suddenly knocked from his head, falling over his face. Grabbing it with his right hand, he turned to find a second horse crowding against him from behind—with Dixon astride. When he heard the distinctive clicking of two revolvers being cocked next to his head, he shrugged and raised both hands in surrender.

Dixon reached out and took the palm pistol from the man's left hand. He instantly dropped to the ground and scurried underneath

Dixon's horse, causing it to jump in alarm, snorting loudly. The man bolted through the crowd while Dixon worked to control his horse, and Walker prodded his to go around Dixon in pursuit. The sombrero was nowhere in sight, however, and it seemed that the man had simply disappeared into thin air. They corralled a man wearing an identical sombrero, and another wearing a tan leather jacket, but neither was the man they sought. They realized that he was being assisted by fellow Mexicans in escaping from the "gringos."

"Forget it," growled Dixon. "He's gone, but we've got his gun, and whatever he did in Juarez yesterday is none of our business."

Following a short parade back to the train station, the presidential party left El Paso at noon sharp, rolling toward the Arizona Territory. Walker heaved a deep sigh of relief that they had managed to avoid disaster yet again. The train would not stop again until it arrived in Phoenix, early tomorrow morning. Meanwhile, there would be time to relax and get some sleep.

After lunch, he settled into his usual seat by the window in the staff car, with some paper and pencils. He would try again to write a letter to Abigail Dancy. Before he could begin, however, Dixon slid into the opposite seat.

"Well, Garrett, we've been lucky so far. Maybe we oughta take up playin' cards."

"Not me! I don't like depending on luck. It never holds out."

"We better hope it does, at least 'til we get the president back to D.C. We got another month of this to go. I don't know if I can take it that long."

"By then we'll both have a permanent nervous twitch," agreed Walker, shaking his head. "This is almost as bad as dealing with those Chinese Boxers, never knowing when they're gonna come at you."

"Well, at least we can relax while we're on this train," shrugged Dixon. "This is the best part of this trip—even if the countryside ain't much to look at around here."

They watched the desert for a moment before Dixon spoke again. "Here—" he pushed a metal object across the table toward Walker. "You said you wanted one of these."

"The palm pistol?" Walker picked it up eagerly, turning it over and examining it. "Shouldn't we show this to Foster and tell him what happened?"

"Garrett, we've been through this already. Foster don't need to know everything. He's got enough to worry about as it is. Besides, it would just make more trouble for everybody."

"I guess you're right. Are you sure you don't want it? You're the one that got it away from him, so you've got first claim to it."

"No, you're the one that saw him first and headed him off. That was nice work, Garrett. Keep it—you deserve it."

"Thanks! I will!" Walker put the weapon back down on the table and looked Dixon in the eye. "Do you realize what happened today, Dixon?"

"What do you mean?"

"Remember that gypsy fortune teller in New Orleans? She said we would protect the king from the left-handed assassin."

"That crazy old hag didn't know what she was talkin' about," scoffed Dixon. "What's that got to do with what happened today, anyway?"

"When you took the palm pistol from that fellow, do you remember which hand he was holding it in?" He paused, with eyebrows raised as he waited for Dixon's answer.

"I think it was—" Dixon knit his brows, thinking hard. "It was his —his left hand, wasn't it?"

"That's right! He was holding the pistol in his left hand. In fact, I remember now that when we were on the plaza in Juarez on Sunday, he put it in his left coat pocket. He was left-handed, Dixon!" Walker beamed triumphantly. "You realize what that means, don't you?"

"It don't mean nothin', Garrett! Nothin'! That old hag didn't predict this. You don't really believe in that gibberish, do you?"

"It ain't gibberish if it works," argued Walker. "You heard what she said, and you saw what happened. How do you explain that?"

"I don't have to explain it," growled Dixon. "I don't believe in it, and that's that."

Just then, the compartment door opened and Stover joined them, squeezing into the seat beside Walker, who quickly slipped the palm pistol into his pocket. "How are you Southern boys liking this lovely scenery?" he grinned.

"As long as we keep moving, I ain't complaining," responded Dixon.

"I'm glad it's early May, and not August," said Walker. "It's going to be hot as hell out here in the summer time, and I mean that literally."

"Say, what were you two doing in the crowd today on your horses?" asked Stover. "It looked like you were riding over people. Good thing Foster didn't see that."

Walker and Dixon exchanged a warning look. "We saw some ruffians trying to start a fight, and thought we should break it up," explained Walker smoothly.

"Didn't want anything to disrupt the president's visit, you know," added Dixon, glancing casually out the window.

"Where did you two learn to ride like that?" Stover persisted. "I don't suppose you picked that up in Cuba, or the Philippines!" He laughed a high-pitched, nasal laugh, which did not seem to go with his stocky build.

"The U.S. cavalry taught me to ride," said Dixon seriously, "but the best riders I ever saw were the Comanches. We 'Buffalo Soldiers' learned a lot from them."

"You fought Indians on the plains?" Stover's face went blank. Dixon nodded.

"General Wheeler taught me to ride," chimed in Walker. "But the best riders I've seen were the Mongols. They were practically *one* with their horses. I try to ride like they did."

Stover sat silent for a moment, and then his eyes narrowed and he glared at each of them. "Comanches? Mongols? Will you two ever stop? I can't get a straight answer out of either of you about anything!" Smacking his palm angrily on the table top, he stood red-faced, gritting his teeth, and stormed out of the car.

"I'm trying to feel sorry for him," sighed Dixon, "but I can't quite do it."

"Me neither," agreed Walker. "He's alright, mostly, but he needs to loosen up some."

"If he don't," mused Dixon, "by the time we get back to D.C., he'll be the one with a permanent nervous twitch."

This struck them as very funny, and as they laughed loudly, Walker could feel his tension beginning to release. He hadn't realized until then just how much pressure he was under. Then, after gazing out the window at the barren landscape passing by, Walker slid a sheet of paper toward Dixon. "Time to write a letter home."

Dixon sighed. "Ain't got nothin' better to do, I guess. Don't know what to say, though. Ain't nothin' happened." He grinned at that, beginning to laugh again.

"We can tell them about Cinco de Mayo, hot peppers, and tequila," suggested Walker, helpfully.

"Might not want to mention the tequila," chuckled Dixon, "or what happened in the alley after that!" And they bellowed laughter until tears ran down their cheeks. Finally, emotionally drained, they settled down to writing. The two worked on their letters until dinnertime, and then, after making the meal last as long as possible, turned in early.

5

SILVER BUGS, GOLD BUGS, AND RED BUGS

At eight o'clock the next morning, the train hissed to a stop at the station in Congress, Arizona Territory. McKinley and his entourage had come to visit one of the country's most productive gold mines. In fact, there were more than thirty active gold mines in Congress, some with shafts extending several thousand feet underground. The cheering crowd of grimy miners which met them at the station was almost drowned out by a brass band and a host of shrieking steam whistles. It was bedlam.

"They sure do seem to like the president," commented Walker to Stover, as they stood on the platform awaiting McKinley's exit from the car. He had to almost shout into Stover's ear to be heard, even though they stood shoulder to shoulder.

"They ought to," yelled Stover, not taking his eyes off the crowd, "after what he's done for them and the gold mining business!"

Before Walker could ask what he meant, the president appeared and, smiling and waving to the excited gathering, descended to the platform and began shaking hands with the group of local politicians and mining executives. A tour of the largest mine was planned, and the group set off on foot, the mine being only a short distance away. The president was surrounded by his Cabinet members and their wives, along with the local group and a good many reporters and photographers, so that only Foster was able to be close by. The other three Secret Service agents trailed along the periphery of the crowd.

The mouth of the mine shaft was a twenty-foot-wide hole in the ground, braced with timbers and strung with electric lights. Most of the party headed deep into the mine, descending in sturdy cages, lowered by thick ropes. As they disappeared into the depths, Walker murmured aloud to himself, "Now I know what it means to go to hell in a handbasket!" A reporter standing nearby overheard him, and began scribbling on a notepad, nodding to himself.

Nervously backing away from the shaft, Dixon shook his head adamantly. "If the good Lord had a-wanted me to go down a hole like that, he woulda put a million dollars down there with my name on it. 'Til then, I ain't going."

The president and Mrs. McKinley, accompanied by most of the press and some of the dignitaries, went into one of the downward-sloping tunnels, walking alongside the narrow railroad tracks on which the ore carts traveled. Foster was beside the president, as usual, and the other three agents continued to follow behind the group. It was the first time for each to be in a mine, and they were uneasy at the reality of being underground. The muffled voices and laughter of those at the front of the group seemed to float from far away, and despite the electric lights strung along the sides, the flickering shadows created a spooky atmosphere.

Sensing the tension building for Walker and Dixon, Stover played a prank on them. He was walking in the middle between them, with one at each side. Stover suddenly hissed, "Watch out!" and grabbed each by their arm. Walker and Dixon went airborne, with arms and legs flailing wildly, uttering half-strangled cries of alarm. Crouching, with wide eyes searching desperately for the cause of the warning, both were reaching into their coats for their revolvers. And then they saw Stover doubled over, laughing—or rather, wheezing—through his nose. Hands on his knees, he fought to silence his mirth. A couple of those at the rear of the group heard the disturbance and turned to see what was going on, but otherwise no one noticed.

"Stover," Dixon growled fiercely, "you coulda give us a heart attack."

Stover, still choking on his laughter, only held out his hand about knee-high, palm down, indicating how high they had jumped. He flapped his arms like a bird in flight, and wheezed even more violently.

"That's nothing," said Walker nonchalantly. "We jumped a lot higher when that lion charged us in Africa."

Catching on immediately, Dixon nodded agreement. "That's right —we jumped all the way to the top of a palm tree, and threw coconuts down at him. I remember now!"

Stover stopped wheezing and put his hands on his hips, glaring at them. "Africa? Lions? Coconuts?" He shook his head. "I don't believe a word either of you says anymore. Not a word!" He turned and stomped angrily back toward the tunnel entrance, and Walker and Dixon could hear him muttering "Comanches! Mongols! Boxers! Lions! Bah!"

"Quick thinkin' there, Garrett."

"Serves him right," Walker scowled. "I think I peed on myself." They began giggling silently, and Dixon held out his hand, waist-high, indicating how high Walker had jumped, and flapped his arms. Walker held out his hand head-high, pretending to measure Dixon's leap, and they both struggled to keep from laughing out loud.

When the tour was finished, the president's group emerged from the tunnel back into the brilliant sunlight. The rest of the party ascended from the depths of the mine, and everyone walked back to the station, chattering about their amazing experience. After much hand-shaking and posing for photographs, they boarded the train. As the brass band played and the steam whistles blasted, the tall wheels began turning. President McKinley stood on the back platform of his car and waved to the cheering miners until they were lost to view.

It had been only a three-hour visit, but it felt more like a full day to Walker. He heaved a deep sigh as he settled into his usual seat by the window in the staff car. Setting his hat aside, he loosened his collar, rested his chin in his hand, and closed his eyes.

"Don't go to sleep," warned Dixon, taking the opposite seat. "You'll miss lunch."

Walker grunted, and reluctantly sat up straighter. "I could never be a miner," he groaned. "Being underground like that just wears me out. I'm beat."

"We didn't even go into the deep part," nodded Dixon. "They woulda had to bring me out on a stretcher. I don't see how they do it all day, every day."

Just then, Stover came into the car. When he saw the two of them sitting by the window, he stopped short. His eyes narrowed and his jaw tightened, and he turned to leave. Walker held up his hand to stop him.

"We were just kidding about the African lion, Stover. You got us good in the tunnel, and I was just getting you back, that's all. Are we even?"

Stover hesitated, with his hand on the door handle. He frowned, but then smirked a bit sheepishly. "I did get you fellows, didn't I?"

"You made Garrett pee on hisself," Dixon agreed. "He nearly jumped all the way down to the president."

"Well, you left a dent in the top of that tunnel," Walker retaliated, indignantly. "I was afraid it was gonna cave in on us."

All three laughed heartily, and Stover took a seat with them, loosening his collar and fanning himself with his hat. "Going to be a hot one today," he said. They agreed, and then they were quiet as they all gazed out the window at the desert.

"Say, Stover," said Walker suddenly, "what did you mean when you said the miners ought to love the president because of all that he's done for them? What has President McKinley done for miners?"

"Not just *any* miners," said Stover. "Gold miners in particular. Don't you remember all the fuss in '96 about 'Free Silver' and the gold standard? People were going crazy—everybody was either a 'gold bug' or a 'silver bug,' wearing lapel pins to show which side they were on. Bryan was for silver, and McKinley was for gold. When McKinley won, gold won. That's why these miners love McKinley."

Walker made a face. "I remember hearing about it, but I wasn't old enough to vote in '96, so I didn't pay that much attention. It had something to do with the money, didn't it?"

"It had *everything* to do with the money!" Stover declared. "Bryan and the Democrats wanted the government to coin silver and put more money into circulation to help fight the depression we were in. McKinley and the Republicans wanted to use only gold to back the money. That makes gold more valuable, which is good for gold miners. See?"

"Yes, but I don't understand. What's wrong with using silver to put more money into circulation? Wouldn't that make it easier for folks to have money and make a living?"

"Not necessarily. If everybody's got more money to spend, the prices of everything will just go up, and then you're no better off than before. And if your income doesn't keep pace with the rising prices, you might very well be *worse* off."

"Then why did all the Democrats vote for it?" argued Walker. "They must have thought they'd be better off. They couldn't all be wrong, could they?"

"What about all the Republicans?" countered Stover. "Were they all wrong? They just saw things from different points of view. I don't think either one was necessarily right or wrong."

"Sounds like the Democrats were optimists, and the Republicans were pessimists," opined Dixon.

"I don't think so," disagreed Stover. "Look at it like this—is a dollar more valuable when there's a lot of them, or when there's only a few of them?"

"When there's only a few of 'em," chorused Walker and Dixon.

"And if you're a big banker or financier, like J. P Morgan or John D. Rockefeller, and you've got a vault full of gold-backed dollars, do you want the government shoveling out a bunch of silver dollars into the economy?"

Walker and Dixon only grunted and stared, thinking hard.

"The people that have the money want it to be worth as much as possible, so they can charge higher interest rates on it. Having fewer dollars in circulation suits them just fine. Those who don't have money—and have to borrow it—want more dollars in circulation because it means lower interest rates." Stover glared triumphantly. "*Now* do you see?

"That's why the 'Free Silver' movement was supported by the farmers in the South and Midwest," he continued. "Farmers are always borrowing money, and paying it back after the harvest. Northern businessmen wanted the gold standard, and they got it. Northern factory workers didn't support the silverites because factory workers don't borrow money—not from banks, anyway."

"That makes a lot of sense," admitted Walker, slowly. "But does that mean that President McKinley is pro-business and anti-farmer?"

"No, he doesn't have to be anti-farmer to be pro-business," disagreed Stover. "After all, farmers are businessmen, too. And that's why he's traveling across the South and West—to show them that they matter to him, even if they didn't vote for him. But think about this—who do you think is paying for this train? It isn't the farmers! It's those railroad executives that are eating in that fancy dining car with the president right now.

"When you're the president, you need to know which side of the bread the butter is on," Stover said, as he rose from his chair. "McKinley knows exactly what he's doing. He's the smartest president we've had since Lincoln." Tugging his watch from its pocket, he announced, "Speaking of bread and butter, it's time for us to go eat, too! Let's get to the dining car and see what they've left us."

Pausing at the door, Dixon turned to Walker. "So, Garrett—are you a 'silver bug' or a 'gold bug?'"

"Silver looks like a lost cause," he said ruefully. "I reckon Pa is rolling over in his grave, but I have to go with the 'gold bugs.'"

"Same here," nodded Dixon. "Let's eat."

That afternoon, McKinley attended a ceremony at the Phoenix Indian School. His entourage sat in a grandstand as seven hundred Native American children marched before them in military ranks, wearing uniforms, while a band played patriotic music. At the conclusion of the performance, all seven hundred turned their eyes toward the president, and proclaimed with one voice: "I give my head and my hand and my heart to my country; one country; one language and one flag." The grandstand erupted in applause, and the children knelt in place as the superintendent stepped to the podium to deliver his remarks.

Standing with Dixon at the side of the grandstand, Walker listened with one ear while he closely watched the children. Their expressionless faces, devoid of any childlike joy or interest disturbed him. The superintendent spoke of the progress being made in achieving the mission of the school to assimilate the native children into white culture, and to "civilize and Christianize" them. These phrases reminded Walker of those used to justify the war in the Philippines, and the policy of "benevolent assimilation." *The methods we're using to assimilate the Filipinos aren't always so benevolent,* he thought. *I hope these children are being treated better than that.*

When the superintendent finished speaking, Walker turned to walk away, and bumped into a lanky, bespectacled man standing close behind him. Both apologized and were about to go their separate ways when Walker noticed a red ribbon on the man's lapel, indicating that he was on the staff of the school.

"Excuse me," he said quickly, opening his coat to flash the Secret Service badge. "I'm with the president's group. Are you with the Indian school?"

"Yes," he replied. "I'm one of the teachers here. Can I help you?"

"I was just wondering—are the children always like that?"

"Do you mean neatly-dressed, orderly and well-disciplined? Yes, they are! We stress those things here. It's a part of 'civilizing and Christianizing' them. Assimilation is what we do."

"Actually, I was referring to how sad they all look," replied Walker. "Don't they like being here at the school?"

"*Like it?*" the teacher laughed as if the thought was genuinely funny. "Since when do students at *any* school *like* it? School is *work*. It prepares you for what comes later. If they were happy, it would mean that we weren't running the school properly."

Walker blinked twice. Dumbfounded, he could not think of anything to say.

"I thought Indians always had long hair," said Dixon.

"Not here!" scoffed the teacher, contemptuously. "First thing we do when they get here is cut their hair and take their Indian clothes away. Teach them to pray. Eat civilized food. Wear shoes. If they speak anything other than English, we wash their mouths out with soap. 'Kill the Indian and save the man.' That's the idea!"

"But why do their parents send them here, if they are going to have their native culture taken away from them?" asked Walker, innocently.

The teacher stared at him incredulously. "'Send them here'? Are you joking? The government takes the children away from their parents and *brings* them here. They don't have a *choice*. It may seem cruel, but it's for their own good. Dozens of Indian schools all across the country are doing the same thing. It's been this way for decades, and it's necessary!"

Walker opened his mouth, but Dixon cut him off, putting his hand on Walker's shoulder. "Thank you, sir, for explaining to us how the school works. We'll be moving along now." Pushing Walker ahead of him, he steered him away from the grandstand, toward the waiting carriages. "We've got work to do, Garrett. Stay focused."

An hour later, the presidential party was safely back on the train and rolling westward out of Phoenix. Sitting at his customary window, Walker watched the sun set in brilliant colors over the distant mountains. He felt dazed at the enormity of what he had witnessed and heard that day. He could not erase from his mind the images of the bronze-skinned children with their dull, dead eyes. It was time to go to the dining car for dinner, but he had no appetite.

The door opened noisily, and Dixon stepped into the car. "I was wondering where you were," he said in a tone of surprise. "Ain't you coming to eat?"

"Not hungry," was all Walker could say, and turned his face back toward the window.

Dixon sat down, and studied him in silence for a long moment.

"Listening to that superintendent and the school teacher, I felt like I was back in the Philippines," Walker said, finally. "Benevolent assimilation. Civilize and Christianize. Teaching their children English." He shook his head sadly. "I halfway expected him to say they used the water cure on them."

"I understand," nodded Dixon. "And we used military force to put down an insurrection both here and there. That's what I was doing on the plains for fo' years before we went to Cuba. 'Might makes right,' they say, but it ain't true. I'm no saint, but I know this: *Right makes might*. No matter how mighty the wrong is, *right* wins in the end. Fightin' for what's right ain't no lost cause, Garrett—it's a sure thing."

Walker sighed. "Dixon, you oughta be a preacher."

Dixon sniffed derisively. "Actually, I was thinkin' 'bout running for president."

Walker laughed out loud before he could stop himself. "I'd like to see that!" he exclaimed. "Dadgummit, lieutenant! You've got *my* vote!"

"I'll count on it. Just a few million more to go with it, and we'll be poppin' champaign corks."

"I b'lieve I've found my appetite," Walker said suddenly, standing up. "Lead the way!"

When they reached the door, Walker spoke once again. "I take back what I said earlier today about being a 'gold bug.'" Dixon gave him a curious look. "I'm going to be a 'red bug,'" he continued. "Red for *right*. That's what I'm going to stand for—not money."

He gave a nod toward the window. The red sun was sinking beyond the purple mountains, its rays decorating the high clouds with brilliant colors. The scene was breath-taking.

Dixon smiled. "Two 'red bugs', then, Garrett. That's us."

6

GRIM ENDS

W alker rubbed his eyes and blinked rapidly. "Is California completely covered in flowers?" he asked incredulously. "I thought we saw a lot of flowers in Redlands this morning, but this is unbelievable!"

"I feel like I just walked into a flower shop," echoed Dixon, looking right and left at the massive banks of flowers of all colors lining the street. "A really *big* flower shop!"

The arrival of the president in Los Angeles coincided with the city's annual *Los Fiesta de las Flores* festival, a celebration of the history and culture of Southern California. The main event was a magnificent floral parade, complete with Spanish and Indian dancers, Mexican vaqueros, American military units, bands, floats, and a hundred-foot-long Chinese dragon. McKinley was the guest of honor, and he and his entourage were seated in the grandstand, waving as the parade passed.

Watching the colorful, undulating dragon snake past them, Walker leaned over to Dixon and said, "If the Boxers had had a few of those, they might've won!"

"They almost won anyway," Dixon countered. "What they needed was bullets."

"I don't even want to think about that," shivered Walker. "That would have been—" and he left the sentence unfinished, unable to come up with a word awful enough to express his horror at the prospect. After several seconds, he added, "I didn't know there was so many different kinds of people in California. Reminds me of that song we used to sing in Sunday School—'Red and yellow, black and white, They are precious in His sight."

"Maybe 'Jesus loves the little children of the world,'" Dixon frowned, completing the verse, "but nobody else does. Too many children sufferin' and dyin' all around the world, if you ask me." Walker could only nod in agreement, wincing at the memories of what they had seen in several war-torn countries, not to mention the Indian school in Phoenix.

The parade lasted almost two hours, after which the McKinleys were taken to the home of an old friend for dinner and to spend the night, while the rest of the group had accommodations in a hotel. Walker and Dixon accompanied the president, while Foster and Stover went to the hotel to get some sleep. They would relieve Walker and Dixon after midnight and guard the president until morning.

The carriages went down a stately avenue, paved with macadam, and lined with trees and impressive mansions. The horses became very skittish at the approach of a loud motorcar, whizzing along at more than ten miles per hour. Walker had seen a few of these contraptions from a distance or parked silently beside buildings, but this was his first close look at one in operation, and he studied it carefully as it passed. The driver, his face hidden behind a sporty cap, goggles, and a scarf, waved a gloved hand, apparently unaware of who occupied the carriage.

Their destination was a lovely, Spanish-style, two-story structure with a tiled roof and several chimneys, surrounded by beautiful flowering shrubs and palmettos. "The Bivouac," it was called, the home of Harrison Gray Otis, publisher of the *Los Angeles Times* newspaper. The carriage stopped under a portal at the side door for the passengers to disembark before proceeding onward to the carriage house. Otis and his wife came out to greet their guests, and he and the president embraced, shook hands, and shared jovial good humor, obviously pleased to be reunited. Otis was at least as stout as McKinley, and in his suit and tie, with his white mustache and goatee, he conveyed a sense of authority and importance.

While they were exchanging greetings, Walker extended his hand to assist Mrs. McKinley in stepping down from the carriage. She smiled, "Thank you, Agent Garrett! That is so nice of you."

Walker noticed that her right index finger was wrapped in a white bandage, and she seemed paler than usual. "Are you alright, ma'am?" he inquired politely.

"Oh, it's nothing," she shrugged, with a wan smile. "Just a little cut. Too much shaking hands! That's what I get for wearing these rings!" She joined her husband and the Otises, and as they entered the house, Walker heard her ask to lie down for a while before dinner. *She does not look well at all,* he thought. *I hope she's not getting sick.*

He and Dixon walked around the house twice, making a plan for their nighttime guard duty. The mansion was located on a street corner, so it was exposed on two sides. There were a good many trees, besides bushes, a small, ornamental fish pond, and a gazebo in the elaborate grounds. A large park was barely a hundred yards away, its trees offering protective cover to anyone desiring to approach the house unseen. They decided to post themselves at the two rear corners of the house, from which they would be able to cover three sides. The main street front was the least likely side to be the target of any attack, so they would check it periodically. Satisfied with their plan, they relaxed in the gazebo, watching the sunset paint the sky red and purple.

"What did you think of that automobile?" asked Walker. "Wasn't that something!"

"Nah! Give me a good horse any day," sneered Dixon. "Them things are loud, and they stink up the air with that smoke they put out. Besides, they always breaking down, and then you got to fix 'em." Shaking his head, he repeated emphatically, "Nah! I'll stick with a horse. You can have your motor car."

"It looks like a lot of fun to me," Walker grinned. "I'll probably never be able to afford one, but they do look like fun."

Just then, a kitchen worker brought their supper on a tray to the gazebo. She was a pretty, young black woman, dressed in a white blouse, black skirt with a white apron, and a red scarf wrapped around her head. Dixon stared for several seconds before clearing his throat and speaking in a forced casual tone, "Good evening, miss! We sho' do thank you for this wonderful supper. Mighty nice of you!"

"There's more where that came from," she smiled shyly. "Can I get y'all anything else?"

"What's this green stuff?" asked Walker, peering closely at the plate of food.

"It's called 'guacamole,'" she answered. "It's a Mexican dish made from avocadoes."

"What's an avocado?" he asked again.

"You'll have to excuse my partner," interjected Dixon, doffing his hat. "He's from Alabama, and he don't get out much. Grits and chitlins are all he knows about."

"Oh my!" she exclaimed, and laughed a very pleasant laugh. "And where might you be from, sir? I believe I hear a southern accent!"

"That's a long story," Dixon replied, rising from the bench. "I'm from Alabama too, but I've been all over the world—Cuba, the Philippines, China, Europe—lots of places."

"The Philippines! The General was in the Philippines!" she said in surprise. "He was a hero in the war."

"What general is that?" asked Walker immediately, his brow furrowed. The only person he thought of as 'the General' was Joseph Wheeler.

"Why, Mr. Otis, of course! He runs the newspaper now, but he was a general in the war, and likes to be called that."

"Are you sayin' that the Mr. Otis that lives in this house is the same Otis as the general who was in the Philippines?" Dixon was amazed, as was Walker. They stared at each other.

"I thought everybody knew that!" she laughed again. "I heard them talkin', and he and the president's both from Ohio, and fought in the Civil War, too. They goes way back together."

"Well, if that don't beat all!" Dixon marveled. "That is very interesting! By the way," he added, with his most charming smile, "if I want anything else, who do I ask for?"

"Just come to the kitchen door and ask for Jenny—that's me," she smiled, her eyes twinkling. "And who might be askin'?"

"Secret Service agent L. G. Dixon, miss," he bowed. "At your service!"

Jenny laughed delightfully again. "Well, Mr. Dixon, y'all enjoy your supper!" She turned to go, but Walker spoke up with one more question.

"There ain't no jalapeno peppers in this, is there? I don't care to be lit up just now."

She giggled and assured them that there were no jalapenos, and they watched as she crossed the garden and disappeared back into the house.

When she had gone, Dixon blew out a noisy big breath through pursed lips and fanned himself with his hat. "Good Lord!" he gasped. "I think I just saw a angel!" Looking upward, with raised hands, he exclaimed, "Take me home, sweet Jesus!" and then added, as an afterthought, "But not just yet—I got other things on my mind right now."

Walker snorted, his mouth full of black beans and rice. "So, I don't get out much, you say? Grits and chitlins are all I know about?"

"Shake it off, Garrett. This ain't about you." They proceeded to devour the food without further conversation.

Walker belched and pointed to his clean plate. "I don't know what some of that was, but it was pretty good!"

"It was *fantastic*," corrected Dixon. "Best ever."

"Are you talkin' about the food, or about Jenny?" Walker grinned.

"Both," Dixon said, dreamily. "I may just stay here in Los Angeles."

"I'm sure 'the General' would be happy to give you a job in his kitchen," said Walker. "Do you remember when we saw him in Manila?"

"Yeah. I didn't recognize him without those batwing sideburns. And I think he's gained some weight."

"I've thought many times about what he said that day," Walker mused, stroking his chin. "General Wheeler was there, along with Captain Pershing and Governor Taft. Otis said that Filipino insurgents had fired on American troops. Aguinaldo claimed it was an accident, and wanted to negotiate, but Otis said that 'the fighting, having begun, must go on to the grim end.'" Walker shook his head. "I remember it word for word, just like it was yesterday."

"You think that if he'd just talked with Aguinaldo that maybe the war wouldn't have started?" Dixon asked.

"I don't know," Walker sighed. "What I do know is that when you won't talk to people, bad things happen. And 'the grim end' ain't got here *yet*, even after we caught Aguinaldo. They're still fightin' in the jungles over there, and ain't no tellin' how many people have died because of it. Seems to me, if you could avoid a war by talking and negotiating a deal, that'd be the smart thing to do."

"You'd think so," Dixon agreed. "Doesn't sound like 'benevolent assimilation,' does it?"

"I reckon the Filipinos don't want to be 'civilized and Christianized,'" said Walker sarcastically, referring to President McKinley's stated goals for the war. "I think the president is a good man with good intentions, but he does not understand the situation there." They stood in silence for a moment, each deep in thought.

"Time to get to work," said Dixon abruptly. "Let's do a walkaround, and then take up our posts." Within a few minutes, they had completed their inspection and each was in his respective station at the rear corners of the house. Invisible among the trees in the darkness, Walker had an unobstructed view of two sides of the house and the street. He couldn't see Dixon in the shadows about fifty yards away. The moon was almost full, but passing clouds intermittently blocked its light. The only sound was that of the myriad nocturnal insects; their songs reminded Walker of the many nights he had spent in tropical jungles in Cuba and the Philippines, and his mind began to wander down vivid memory trails, reliving old times.

Shortly before midnight, the sharp sound of a twig snapping jolted Walker back into the present. Someone was moving stealthily through the trees a few yards behind him. He felt a tingling sensation as the hairs on the back of his neck rose, and all his senses were on full alert. Silently drawing his revolver from its shoulder holster, he slowly turned, barely breathing as he listened and watched for any hint of movement. The moonlight, filtered through a wispy cloud, created a dappled effect in the darkness, and he caught a glimpse of a shadowy figure out of the corner of his eye.

Crouching, he tip-toed quickly along a stone-paved walkway to intercept the intruder's path. He heard two more twigs snap, and a muttered curse. Stepping out from behind a tree, he confronted the man, cocking the hammer on the revolver with two distinctive clicks. "Stop right where you are!" he challenged. "What are you doing here?"

Startled, the man's knees buckled and he almost fell down as he uttered a frightened half-cry from deep in his throat. He carried a burlap sack by its neck, holding it carefully, as if its contents were fragile. He steadied himself, looking frantically right and left, his eyes wide and face pale, even in the dark.

"What are you doing here?" demanded Walker again, more loudly. "And what's in that sack?"

Suddenly, in Walker's left ear came the clicking sound of a pistol being cocked, right next to his head. "Drop yer gun, and don't make no sudden moves, or I'll blow yer brains out!" a rough voice ordered.

"Yes sir," said Walker, as he released the hammer and let the gun drop to the ground with a soft thud. He held both hands up. "Before you shoot me, you should know that I'm a Secret Service agent of the federal government. You'll never get away with it."

"Sure, you are," jeered the voice. "And why would the federal government be watchin' the Otis house? Do you take us for idiots? Yer just some security guard he hired to watch the place."

"My badge is inside my jacket," insisted Walker, pointing. "Look—I'll show you!"

"No you don't!" growled the man, and quickly extended his arm, the gun barrel only inches from Walker's temple. "One false move and yer gone! I won't warn you again."

For the third time, there was the distinctive sound of a hammer being cocked, this time behind the threatening gunman. "Put the gun down easy," came Dixon's calm, low voice. "Nobody needs to get killed here tonight."

Taking advantage of the distraction, Walker instantly swung his arm and knocked the man's pistol away. Pivoting in one smooth motion, he drove his right fist into the man's jaw, knocking him sprawling. Dixon seized the man's weapon, while Walker quickly retrieved his own. The man with the burlap sack made another frightened sound in his throat and appeared about to flee the scene.

"Don't try it!" Walker snapped, pointing the gun at him. "Put down the bag, and get on the ground." The man hesitated, and then obeyed, trembling violently. The two agents had them sit on the ground in the open where the light was better. "What's in the sack?" Walker demanded.

The two men flinched in fear as Walker dropped it on the ground in front of them. and the one who had been carrying the sack raised his arms as if to shield himself. Holstering his gun, Walker opened the bag and reached in. "Be careful!" begged the gun-wielding man. "You don't know what yer doin'!" Walker felt the object tentatively, frowning. Lifting it out carefully, he was shocked to see that he held a bundle of four sticks of dynamite, wrapped in a length of fuse.

"Good Lord!" exclaimed Dixon. "*Dynamite*? You were planning to blow up the president of the United States with *dynamite*?"

"What are you talking about?" the man gasped. "We're here to blow up *Otis*. We don't know nothin' about the president. He ain't here, anyway!"

"Yes, he *is* here," scowled Walker. "He and Otis are friends, and the McKinleys are spending the night here. That's why we Secret Service agents are guarding the house—we provide security for the president." He pulled his jacket open to show his badge, glinting in the moonlight. Dixon did the same.

"Oh, hell!" the man breathed, his face showing despair. "We didn't know! We never would've come here tonight if we'd knowed the president was here. We ain't no assassins. You got to believe us! Honest!" The other man nodded vigorously, making whimpering noises.

"So why are you trying to kill Otis?" asked Dixon. "What's he ever done to you?"

"He runs the *Times*, and we work there—or used to, 'til he fired us. We been trying to unionize for two years, but he keeps shutting us down, locking us out—he's a tyrant. Long hours, low pay—treats us all like dirt. We've had enough of it, and came here to get even." He clenched his fists and shook his head in anger. "I hate that man! But honest to God, we didn't know the president was here! We don't mean no harm to the president!"

Walker and Dixon stepped away a few steps to talk quietly. "Do you believe him, that they didn't know the president was here?" asked Dixon.

"Yeah, I do. I think he's tellin' the truth." They studied the two men for a moment in silence, and then Walker whispered, "What do you think we ought to do with 'em? We can't take 'em to the police and leave the house unguarded. Reckon we ought to just hold 'em here 'til Foster comes in a couple of hours?"

"Good question," Dixon murmured, scratching his head. "On the other hand, we're not here to protect Otis, and they ain't a threat to the president—at least not anymore."

"What are you saying?" Walker hissed in astonishment. "Are you thinking that we should just let them *go*?"

"We've got their gun and the dynamite," mused Dixon. "They're scared half to death. The president is safe. If Otis treats his workers bad enough that they want to blow him up, that's *his* problem—not ours. We've done our job."

"Are you serious?" Walker was aghast. "These men brought dynamite to blow up—"

"Who's got the dynamite *now*?" interrupted Dixon. "And the gun?

They didn't know the president was here, and we've eliminated the threat. If you ask me, we took care of business, and the job is done. Finished."

Walker stared at Dixon for a long moment, and then at the two slumped, dejected men sitting on the ground. "I don't know . . ." he hesitated.

"'The fighting, having begun, must continue to the grim end,'" said Dixon quietly, but with a hard tone of voice. "He started this war with his workers, so let him continue to the 'grim end' on his own. We don't work for him."

When Walker still hesitated, Dixon continued. "Garrett, remember those surrenders we was escorting to the stockade in Manila? Remember what you said we should do with them? Pershing saw us release them, and he let us off."

"*Let us off*? He sent us to *China*, in case you forgot about that."

Dixon burst out laughing, and Walker had to smile ruefully, in spite of himself. Taking a deep breath, he made his decision. Giving Dixon a nod, he turned to the two men.

"My partner and I are going inside the house to use Mr. Otis's telephone and call the police," he said firmly. "You two sit right here and don't move 'til we get back, you hear?"

The men's blank expressions were almost comical, but then they nodded rapidly. "Yes sir, Mr. Secret Service man. We'll be right here when you get back!"

Walker put the dynamite back into the sack, and Dixon shoved the pistol into his belt. "We won't be gone but just a minute," Dixon said gruffly. "Behave yourselves."

They walked toward the house without looking back until they reached the kitchen door. Turning around, they saw no sign of the two men. "I hope this doesn't come back to bite us," worried Walker.

"Maybe we'll get sent back to China again," speculated Dixon.

"Anything but that!" groaned Walker. "If I ever see another Boxer, I'll light this dynamite and throw it at him!"

"Speaking of dynamite, what do you think we ought to do with it?"

"There's a lake in the park just down the street," Walker suggested. "It wouldn't take a minute to run down there and heave it in."

"Sounds good to me. Take this pistol and throw it in, too." When Walker glared at him, Dixon added, "It was your idea, y'know."

At the lake shore, Walker hurled the sack as far as he could throw it into the water, and watched it disappear from view. He followed it with the pistol, and then returned to the Otis mansion at a quick trot. Standing once again in the shadows of the trees behind the house, he and Dixon silently watched a cloud slowly pass in front of the moon. Dixon cleared his throat and said, "By the way, how did you know Otis has a telephone?"

"I have no idea if he has a telephone or not. Just said that to give us an excuse to walk away."

"Quick thinking there, Garrett."

"I reckon you don't want to tell Foster about this?"

"Tell him about *what*?" Dixon replied, meaningfully. "No point in adding to his worries."

Walker rubbed his eyes and sighed. "We are definitely shipping out to China. No doubt about it."

"That's a pretty grim end. Reckon Jenny would go with me?"

"I have a feeling Jenny's not keen on grim ends. Abigail Dancy, either."

"Looks like it's you and me, then," grinned Dixon. "That's a pretty grim end, itself!"

"Can't argue with that," Walker smiled. "Could be a lot worse, though—we could be working for Otis!"

"Nope," frowned Dixon. "I'd be diving into that lake, fishin' that dynamite back out of there."

Walker laughed as Dixon headed back to his post, but immediately began to wrestle with much more serious thoughts. *What if that man hadn't stepped on the twig? What if Dixon hadn't arrived in time to save me? I could be dead. There could be a huge, smoking hole in the side of The Bivouac right now, and the president could be dead. Talk about grim ends! This could have gone wrong in so many ways!* Walker shivered, despite the warm night air. *Did we do the right thing in releasing those two? What if they come back in a few days and are successful? Innocent people—like Jenny—could be hurt.*

Walker decided that he had to at least warn Otis. Whether or not he heeded the warning would be his own responsibility. Before the presidential train left Los Angeles two days later, he penciled a cryptic note and dropped it off at a post office.

OTIS—YOU HAVE ENEMIES AND YOUR HOUSE IS NOT SAFE. BE ON GUARD OR YOU WILL COME TO A GRIM END.

I've done what I can, he thought. *I hope that, this time, he will talk to them.*

7

TROUBLE IN PARADISE

I t was early afternoon when the train pulled out from the Santa Barbara station. The president had spent three hours in the picturesque small town, touring in a beautiful, rose-covered carriage, and speaking to a crowd of people that numbered almost twice the town's population. The air was full of excitement and energy.

"California sure seems to love the president!" marveled Walker.

"Well, it's the first state we've been to that voted for McKinley in the election," observed Stover. "All the other states so far went for Bryan and the Democrats. That might have something to do with it."

"Maybe," conceded Walker, "but he got a pretty warm reception in the Democrat states, too—except for Memphis. Southerners have been very hospitable, I think."

"Yes, the Southern Democrats *like* the president," agreed Stover, "but the Republicans *love* him! That's why he's made this trip through the South, just like when he visited Georgia and Alabama a couple of years ago. He's trying to pull the country together."

"What are you talking about? McKinley visited Georgia and Alabama? When was that?" Walker was in disbelief. "I never heard anything about that!"

"Let's see," Stover thought, tugging at his mustache. "It was right before Christmas, and the war in Cuba had just ended, so it must have been December of '98. He went to several cities in Georgia, including Savannah and Atlanta, and then went to Tuskegee and visited the school run by Booker T. Washington. He went to Montgomery, the capital city, too. I remember reading all about it in the newspaper."

"December of '98?" repeated Dixon. "We were on our way across the Pacific then. No wonder we didn't hear about it. You say he went to Tuskegee?"

"That's right. He started in Savannah and retraced Sherman's path across Georgia to Atlanta, in reverse. Then he went to Tuskegee. In Montgomery, he stood on the steps of the capitol building and gave a speech on the very same spot where Jefferson Davis took his oath of office at the start of the war. He won over the old Confederates—a great success, everybody said."

"Well, if that don't beat all!" exclaimed Dixon. "The president of the United States went to Tuskegee, Alabama, and visited Booker T. Washington! That's just—just—" he groped for words, and finally made a helpless gesture and said, "I just can't hardly believe it!"

"Booker Washington has visited the president in the Executive Mansion, too, y'know," added Stover. "More than once. They talk about politics, race problems, things like that."

"Then why doesn't he get more votes in the South," asked Walker. "He didn't win a single Southern state last year."

"You two don't keep up with politics much, do you?" said Stover. It was more of a statement than a question.

"We were out of the country for a good while," defended Walker. "Besides, I'm just now old enough to vote. Never really thought much about it, before."

"Well, the short and sweet of it is that Democrats—and farming states in general—are against tariffs, annexation of foreign territories, and the gold standard, and Republicans are for all of it," Stover explained. "And those are the three biggest issues in American politics today. When you think about it, it's really something that Southerners have welcomed McKinley the way they have. Showing respect to a black man isn't likely to win you many votes in the South. It wouldn't be surprising if they were all as chilly as Memphis was."

"Yeah," Walker grunted, giving Dixon a meaningful look. "Memphis was definitely *not* a warm reception."

"It came close to being *real* warm," Dixon replied, returning the look.

Stover, thinking that they were referring to the confrontation with the Memphis police at the women's club, waved a hand dismissively, and said, with a grin, "Oh, don't worry about that little mix-up, fellows! Everybody needs a little help now and then. I was glad to bail you out."

Walker blinked and looked at Dixon again, unsure how to respond. Dixon, without missing a beat, smiled and clapped Stover on the shoulder. "And we sure did appreciate it, Stover. The last thing we needed right then was to get hauled down to the police station like a couple of tramps. Good thing you were there!"

"That's right!" agreed Walker, nodding emphatically. "That was a big help!"

"Don't mention it," Stover waved his hand again. "You know, before we got to Memphis, I was thinking that protecting the president was going to be too much for just the four of us, but things have been real quiet. No threats or danger—not even one person has tried to get too close to the president. The only thing you two have had to do was get Mrs. McKinley's shoe fixed! I'm not sure that we are even needed at all!" He sighed and folded his arms, as he turned to look out the window at the passing scenery.

Walker's nostrils flared and he sent Dixon a piercing glare with narrowed eyes. Dixon raised both eyebrows and gave an almost imperceptible shake of his head. Walker drew a deep breath and let it out noisily, as he also folded his arms and stared out the window.

Noticing this, Stover sympathized, "I guess we're all a little bored. But it's better this way than if we were having to fight off assassins and crazies, like that idiot Guiteau. No, I'll take boredom any day over that."

A minute passed with no sound other than the rhythmic clacking of the rails. The scenery was spectacular—the Pacific Ocean reaching to the western horizon, and mountains practically looming over the town to the east. Palm trees with their graceful, slender trunks were almost close enough to touch, and not a single cloud disturbed the perfect blue sky.

Stover sighed again and cracked his knuckles loudly. "Have you ever seen such a beautiful place as this!" he exclaimed. "This is paradise on earth!"

Dixon saw the look in Walker's eyes and gave him another quick shake of his head, but Walker ignored him. "Oh, I don't know. The prettiest scenery I've seen was in Hawaii. The white sandy beaches, palm trees, the surf rolling in, the mountains—it was a lot like this, but even more beautiful, I'd have to say, especially under the tropical moon. That was amazing, wouldn't you agree, Dixon?"

Dixon could feel Stover tensing, but then gave in to temptation. "Personally, I prefer forests and mountains, like we passed through in Russia, just across the border from Mongolia. When we came down that mountain to Lake Baikal—that was the most beautiful sight I've ever seen. That water was so crystal clear, and deep blue. Nothing can beat that!"

"Damn it!" Stover exploded, pounding his fist on the table. "It's always *something* with you two!" Standing abruptly, he snapped, "I need some fresh air," and barreled through the door into the next car, leaving them alone.

"We'll regret this, one of these days," predicted Dixon.

"Not me," Walker shrugged. "I'm just a bored shoe-fixer. Lucky I haven't had to do anything to save the president from a crazy assassin, or anything like that."

"It's not his fault that he doesn't know about those, you know," said Dixon, with a frown. "We're just gonna have to swallow our pride. Nobody knows what we've done, and we don't want them to."

"True," Walker scowled. "But *I* know, and it ain't easy listening to somebody say we haven't done nothing."

"Let it go, Garrett. Just let it go. It ain't worth gettin' sideways about it. Won't do you no good to get upset. Just let it go."

Walker sighed. "Alright. I'll let it go," he said, still with a note of irritation in his voice. "And we'll need to figure out a way to make things right with Stover. We don't want there to be hard feelings."

The train soon turned inland and tracked northward through a broad valley. There were fields and orchards as far as the eye could see, with misty, gray mountains in the distance. The president's party arrived in Monterey late that evening, having returned to the coast after traveling almost four hundred miles in one day. As the night-time shadows deepened, Walker found himself standing alone on the veranda of the luxurious Hotel del Monte, gazing out at Monterey Bay as it shimmered under a half-moon. He shivered in the cool sea breeze, and shoved his hands into his pockets for warmth. Suddenly, Stover was standing beside him, sharing the view. After a minute of silence, Walker spoke.

"We were on our way to the Philippines, and we stopped over in Hawaii to provide security for the annexation ceremony. We were there for only a few days, but it was really beautiful." He gestured toward the bay, and added, "This reminds me a lot of Hawaii."

"Well," Stover seemed to relax a bit. "Hawaii must be a beautiful place, then."

"I decided that all places have their own kind of beauty," Walker said, quietly. "Even the Gobi Desert, with no trees, and not much water or grass—even that place had its own kind of beauty. You just had to learn to see it."

Stover grunted, but said nothing. Another long minute passed.

"I also learned to see beauty in all kinds of people," Walker went on, talking more to himself than to Stover. "When I left home, I thought white people were all that really mattered. But I made friends in Cuba and the Philippines, and I saw that the people in Hawaii and China cared about the same things we care about. And of course, there were the black troops—especially Dixon. We're like brothers." Walker couldn't suppress a smile at that. "It changed me," he said, simply.

More silence, as Stover gave Walker a curious look. Unsure of how to respond to Walker's confession, he finally grumbled, "I guess this trip across the U.S. must be pretty boring to you two."

"Not at all!" Walker exclaimed. "It's been great to see so much of our own country! I'm loving every minute of it. It's amazing how many different kinds of people live here, and we're all Americans! There's no other place like it!"

"You should come to New York!" chuckled Stover, loosening up. "There's people from all over the world, all in one city: Chinese, Arabs, Africans, Jews, Italians, Irish—you name it, we got it."

"That sounds amazing!" grinned Walker. "I can't wait to go there. Maybe the president will visit New York and we'll get to go along."

"We'll probably pass through New York City on the way back to Washington from Buffalo," Stover said.

"Buffalo—isn't that where Niagara Falls is?"

"Yep—I've been there. It's like nothing else you've ever seen. Magnificent!"

"Ooh!" Walker breathed. "I am really excited now. This trip—this *country*—is just amazing!" He rubbed his hands together in anticipation. "So much to see. . . ." his voice trailed off.

Stover studied him for a moment. "Yes," he said, finally. "There is."

Walker heaved a sigh of satisfaction. "You want first watch, or second?" he asked.

Stover produced a coin from his pocket. "Heads, you take first; tails, I do." Flipping the coin into the air, he let it fall to the marble floor where it bounced twice and came to a rest with a ringing sound. "Heads," he announced, holding up the coin. "See you at midnight, Garrett."

"Say, isn't that a *silver* coin?" asked Walker, with a mischievous grin. "Better not let President McKinley see that!"

Stover snorted in disdain, waved his hand dismissively, and headed off to bed.

The next morning was a busy one for the president. There was a grand reception, hosted by the city mayor, at which McKinley made a speech to a large crowd. Another speech soon followed, given to an assembly of Union Army veterans in nearby Pacific Grove. Next on the agenda was a tour of the coastline, following a scenic seventeen-mile route. However, the president returned to the hotel instead, leaving the rest of his entourage to take the tour without him. Mrs. McKinley's finger had become infected, and she had developed a fever, in addition to dysentery. Fortunately, her personal physician, Dr. Marion Rixey, had accompanied them on the trip, and he lanced and drained her swollen and inflamed finger. The president anxiously stayed by her side the rest of the day. On the following day, he canceled his scheduled appearances and left abruptly for San Francisco, where better medical care was available. The mood on the train was apprehensive, and conversation was limited.

The McKinleys were guests of the wealthy industrialist, Henry T. Scott, a leading citizen of San Francisco. His Victorian mansion, with its ivy-covered walls, corner turrets, arches, and balconies, stood across the street from Lafayette Park, a lovely green space surrounded by fine homes. The First Lady rested there while being treated by the best doctors in the city. Unfortunately, her condition worsened dramatically, and her husband canceled all of his engagements to be with her. It was feared that her life was in danger, as her fever reached a hundred and four degrees, and she was unconscious most of the time. The entire nation's attention was focused on her health, and reporters gathered in the park daily, awaiting updates.

Mayor Phelan insisted on providing police protection for the Scott home, so the Secret Service agents were not needed around the clock. Foster remained with the president, as always, and Stover lounged in the house, reading books borrowed from the Scott's library. With time on their hands, Walker and Dixon explored the city on horses rented from a local stable.

Following directions suggested by one of the policemen, they meandered through the adjacent neighborhood, gawking at the palatial mansions with elaborate architecture and exotic landscaping, being passed by expensive motor cars and carriages drawn by teams of fine, matched horses. Continuing eastward through the wealthy Nob Hill district, they were astonished at the steepness of the hills, and had to rein their mounts to the side to avoid the streetcars, crowded with passengers.

"Is everybody in San Francisco rich?" Walker asked aloud, to no one in particular.

"Maybe that gold rush had something to do with it," speculated Dixon. "Is that one over there a house, or a hotel?"

"I don't see a sign in front of it, so it must be a house," replied Walker, skeptically.

"You can tell this is the rich folk's part of town," observed Dixon. "It's the highest land around, and you can look down on ever'body else."

"You can even see San Francisco Bay out yonder," marveled Walker, pointing. "Let's go take a look."

After descending a long hill, they found themselves in China-town. The contrast was remarkable. There were no mansions to be seen, or decorative landscaping, flowers, or motor cars. The streets were busy, crowded with Chinese men dressed in dark tunics, many carrying large baskets on poles across their shoulders. All commercial signs were in the Chinese language, with diverse wares displayed in stalls and racks outside the shops. Some featured textiles, and others ceramic goods, fruits and vegetables, raw meat, or fish. Freight wagons and carts lined the curbs, with almost no draft animals—Walker guessed that they relied on manpower to haul them. Walker and Dixon were the only non-Asian men in sight, and also the only ones on horseback, and wearing western-style suits and hats.

"You feel a little conspicuous?" asked Walker, uneasily.

"I just hope there ain't no Boxers here," replied Dixon. "We're outnumbered pretty bad."

"We could always pray up a thunderstorm if things get rough," Walker grinned, referring to an incident that had occurred in Mongolia as they fled from the Boxers.

"That'll be your job," Dixon said, with a shake of his head. "I'll believe it when I see it."

"I saw it, and I still don't believe it," agreed Walker. "That was a sure 'nuff miracle."

Their conversation was suddenly interrupted by a loud ruckus from inside a shop. They heard men's voices shouting and a female screaming, and then the door burst open and several individuals spilled out onto the sidewalk and into the street. An austere, dark-haired white woman in a long black dress held a half-naked Chinese girl firmly by the arm as she backed away from a group of angry, threatening Chinese men. The woman was jabbing her finger at the men while raising her voice in a commanding tone, and the men were shaking their fists and shouting. The men began encircling the two females, drawing closer, their faces contorted by rage. Walker could not understand anything being said, but he could understand the danger the woman and child were facing.

Dixon whistled a sharp, shrill blast, which produced an instant shocked silence as everyone in the melee stopped shouting and stared up at him. "Ting!" barked Walker, in his most authoritative voice. *Halt!* He hoped he had remembered the correct word. Both pulled back their coats to reveal their badges and the handles of the revolvers in the shoulder holsters.

"Clear out!" snapped Dixon, with a wave of his hand. The men hesitated only for a few seconds, and then withdrew, scowling, and retreated back into the dark interior of the shop. Just that quickly, the crisis was past, and activity on the street returned to normal.

"Thank you so much!" exclaimed the woman, with a look of great relief. "I was beginning to be afraid we weren't going to get away this time!"

Walker dismounted and tipped his hat. "Agent Walker Garrett, of the United States Secret Service, ma'am," he began. "What on earth is going on, here?"

"I'm rescuing this girl from prostitution," she said, with a defiant expression. "Hundreds of girls like her are sold into slavery and forced to be prostitutes. Chinese *tongs*—gangs—run these opium dens, with brothels in the basement. The girls are so abused, they usually don't live more than five years. Someone has to do something about it, and if the city government won't do it, I will!"

"Ain't that kind of dangerous, ma'am?" asked Dixon.

"I don't care," she said through clenched teeth. "I'll do whatever it takes to free these girls!"

"Can we escort you to a safe place?" asked Walker.

"It's just a couple of blocks from here to the Mission House," she said, "but if you don't mind, that would be very nice."

Dixon remained in the saddle, while Walker walked alongside the two. "What's your name, ma'am?" he asked.

"Donaldina Cameron," she replied. "I run the Occidental Board's Presbyterian Mission House. We give these girls a safe place to live, teach them work skills, and teach them about Jesus. We give them a chance to have a decent life.

"By the way," she added, "where did you learn Chinese?"

"I don't actually speak Chinese, ma'am," he said, modestly. "I just picked up a few words while I was in China with the army last year, dealing with the Boxer Rebellion."

"Oh my! I'm sure *that* was exciting!"

"That would be one way to describe it, I s'pose," interjected Dixon.

"I don't mean to be rude," Walker said, apologetically, "but why do the gangs use such young girls for—for *that*—instead of grown women?"

"Girls are not valued highly in China," explained Cameron, frowning. "Their families sometimes sell them, or Chinese gangs kidnap them and ship them over here. It's called the 'Yellow Slave Trade.' It's just easier to get young girls. They are brought here as children and made to do domestic work until they reach puberty, and then they are forced into prostitution. It's the devil's work, and I will go to hell and back before I let it go on."

Walker was trying to think of something to say in reply, when she continued. "Turn around and look. Tell me what you see."

"A street full of Chinese people," offered Dixon.

"Look closer. What do you notice about them?"

"They're all wearing the same kind of clothes," said Walker. "Dark jackets and baggy pants."

"Look closer," she insisted. "What else do they all have in common?"

They studied the scene for several seconds, and finally Dixon said in a tone of amazement, "They're all *men.*"

"That's right," she nodded. "Ninety percent of the Chinese here are men, and it's against the law for them to marry a non-Chinese woman. That doesn't justify enslaving girls for sex, but you can see how unfair the situation is for everyone. In Chinese, a prostitute is called 'a hundred men's wife.' In other words, they're everybody's wife."

"That's awful," breathed Walker, in shock.

"I can't save them all," Cameron sighed, "but I'll do what I can, as long as I can. God help me!"

Only another block away, they stopped in front of a sturdy, four-story brick building. The sign over the front door identified it as the Mission House. Cameron and the girl climbed the steps and turned to face them.

"Will you be safe here?" asked Walker.

"More or less," she replied, with a shrug. "We get threats all the time. We've found dynamite sticks on these front steps, and wedged into our windows. No explosions yet, though."

"You're risking your life, you know!" exclaimed Walker, and immediately felt stupid for stating the obvious.

"God will provide," she smiled. "I'm not afraid." She opened the door, and then turned back once again. "Thank you both so much. God has used you today in a wonderful way! Bless you!" And then the two disappeared inside, and the door closed behind them.

Walker swung back into the saddle, and they stayed there in front of the Mission House for a minute without talking. "You know," reflected Dixon, "she's a lot like Harriet Tubman—risking her life to help get people out of slavery. That is a brave woman."

"Who's Harriet Tubman?" asked Walker, with a blank expression.

Dixon gave him a disgusted look. "Garrett, I keep forgettin' you went to the white boy's school. You don't know *nothin'.*" Prodding his horse, he began the ascent back up the hill from Chinatown. Walker followed, frowning.

Upon returning to the Scott house, they learned that Mrs. McKinley's condition had continued to deteriorate. Three solemn doctors, carrying black satchels, exited the front door as they were arriving. Inside, all was very quiet, and the atmosphere was heavy.

"Trouble in paradise," Stover muttered to them under his breath. "Things don't look good."

Paradise? Walker reflected on what he had just seen in Chinatown. *It's only paradise for some,* he thought, *not for all. For some here, trouble is all they know.* Sighing heavily, he asked softly, "How much trouble can you have in paradise, before it isn't paradise anymore?"

Stover blinked, and then furrowed his brow in thought. No one had an answer.

8

UNLEASHED

"I had forgotten how big these things are!" breathed Walker in awe.

"Never been this close to one before," nodded Dixon. "Not a'tall like those troop transports we were on."

They stood on a pier, almost within arm's reach of the *USS Ohio*, the navy's newest battleship. It had been under construction for two years in the Union Iron Works shipyard, and was now ready to be launched. Named for President McKinley's home state, the launching was one of the main events scheduled for the western tour. Fortunately, Mrs. McKinley was finally improving enough that the president could leave her bedside, and he was to give a speech for the ceremony the next day. Walker and Dixon had been dispatched to visit the shipyard and report on the security preparations.

Workers scurried about the ship like ants on a giant anthill, painting, welding, and hammering. The massive hull rested in a cradle of concrete and wood beams, held in place by thick blocks, with its stern pointing downward toward the end of the slip and open water.

"It's like she's just sitting here, waiting to be unleashed," admired Walker.

"That's a good way to put it," came a voice from behind them. Startled, they turned to find themselves facing a sturdy, middle-aged man wearing a naval uniform. "Captain Everett Thomas, at your service," he announced, without smiling. "I understand you fellows are presidential bodyguards, looking over the security arrangements?"

"Yes sir," they chorused, saluting. "Secret Service agents Garrett and Dixon," offered Walker. "We were just admiring your beautiful ship, captain."

"We never been so close to a battleship before," added Dixon. "Very impressive!"

"It's a floating city," nodded Thomas. "It has telephones, electric lights, plumbing, water purification—all behind eleven inches of Krupp steel. The big rifles fire 870-pound high-velocity shells, and the secondary batteries fire hundred-pound shells, and there's an assortment of smaller guns. There are two torpedo tubes. This will be one of the most formidable warships in the world when it gets in the water. 'Unleashed' is a good way to put it."

Walker whistled softly. "How do you *get* it in the water? Does it just slide down that big ramp?"

"*Just slide down the ramp*?" The captain spat on the ground. "Launching a battleship is one of the most complex tasks of all! A hundred different things could go wrong and end in disaster. The launch is a high-precision work of art, requiring dozens of skilled workmen, each doing their jobs at exactly the right time. After two years of hard work and three million dollars spent, there's no room for error. And the fact that there will be thousands of spectators watching—including the President of the United States—only adds to the pressure!"

Walker and Dixon responded to this with stunned silence, staring wide-eyed at the huge steel ship. "But, of course, we've done this before, so we know what we're doing," the captain quickly added, noticing their expressions of concern. "Nothing will go wrong, I assure you!"

They both nodded, a bit uncertainly. "Where do you reckon would be the safest place to stand?" asked Dixon, innocently.

The captain glared at him furiously, and for a brief second Walker thought he was about to explode. Instead, he spun on his heel and stalked away, motioning curtly over his shoulder for them to follow. They gave each other a frown, shrugged, and then hurried to catch up. He led them on a quick tour of the yard. Thomas pointed out the wharf where the president would arrive on a transport tug, the platform where he would stand to deliver his speech, and the grandstand from which the spectators would watch.

"The entire Pacific Squadron will be in the Bay," he concluded tersely, "and city police—mounted and on foot—will be all over the yard, so the president will be completely safe and secure. No reason for any concern for his welfare. *And*—" he paused to glare at Dixon again—"the ship will *not* fall over on him. I *guarantee* it." Before Dixon could respond, the captain was marching away. The tour was clearly finished.

"I think you rubbed him the wrong way," Walker observed.

"Seemed like a fair question to me," Dixon growled. "A mite touchy, I'd say."

They mounted their horses and headed for the front gate, letting the animals walk while they took one more admiring look at the massive ship. Just before they reached the exit, an ear-splitting steam whistle released a long blast. The horses panicked, rearing and twisting about, and tossing their heads in a frenzy of fear. It was all Walker and Dixon could do to stay in their saddles. No sooner had they brought the animals back under control than a flood of workmen came pouring out of the ship, down the gangplanks, and heading for the gate. Shouting, laughing, and carousing, some walking and some running, they just kept coming out of every opening. There seemed to be no end to the flow.

"Must be dinner time!" yelled Dixon.

"Let's get out of here before they run over us!" Walker yelled back. They left the shipyard at a brisk canter, glad to get away. Slowing to a trot after a short distance, they continued along the waterfront. It seemed that everyone was getting off work for lunch at the same time, though, and the streets were becoming crowded with pedestrians. Walker noticed that they were getting some hostile looks from the rough-clad shipyard workers, so they decided to detour through a nearby commercial district.

"I'm getting' kinda hungry, myself," said Dixon. "Let's see if we can find a place to get a bite to eat."

They dismounted in front of a small restaurant, and tethered the horses to a post. The sign over the door said "Soon Lee Diner." They seated themselves on a bench along the wall, placing their hats beside them. A Catholic priest and a man wearing a rumpled suit were eating at a nearby table, but otherwise the place was empty. A short, pig-tailed Chinese man wearing a stained white apron came out from the kitchen and approached them, wiping his hands on a towel.

"Tooah polka lice bowz, tooah cuppa teah, on dollah," he said matter-of-factly, and waited for their response.

After a second's hesitation, Walker nodded and said, "Yes, thank you."

As the man disappeared back into the kitchen, Dixon stared at Walker. "What was that? Something about lice? Are you crazy?"

"I actually understood him," Walker said, in a tone of surprise. "Two bowls of pork and rice, and two cups of tea, for a dollar. Sounds reasonable."

"Huh!" grunted Dixon, studying Walker curiously. "Not bad for a Alabama boy."

"You're a Alabama boy, too, y'know."

"Let's just let that be our little secret, if you don't mind."

Walker was thinking of a retort when their food arrived: Two good-sized wooden bowls full of steaming white rice, with diced fried pork, onions, and boiled eggs, and two cups of hot tea, with a small pot for refills. They inhaled the aroma with closed eyes, and then dug in with gusto. "I didn't realize how hungry I was," Walker said, with a grain of rice stuck to his lip.

Dixon didn't bother replying until he finally dropped the spoon into the empty bowl. "Good stuff," was his verdict, punctuated with a belch.

Just then, the door opened and a dozen workingmen barged into the diner, talking loudly and scuffing their boots on the rough wooden floor. When they saw Walker and Dixon, they stopped short and fell silent, staring coldly at them. The hostility was palpable, and the atmosphere instantly became tense.

"Something wrong, fellas?" asked Walker, spreading his hands.

"I seen you at the shipyard," accused one of them. "Snoopin' around."

"Spies!" rasped another. "Tryin' to find somethin' to use 'gainst us, ain't you?"

"What are you talking about?" objected Dixon, in amazement. "We ain't spies, any more than you are."

"Then what the hell was you doin' at the shipyard? Lookin' to buy a battleship, or somethin'?" A burly, tattooed worker seemed to be the leader of the group. He approached the table in a threatening manner, fists on hips.

Walker and Dixon pulled back their coats to show their silver badges, also exposing the pistol butts. The workmen's reaction was completely different than that of the Chinese gangs. Instead of retreating, they surged forward angrily, with clenched fists. Walker quickly pulled his revolver and slammed it down on the table with a hard, heavy sound.

"I'll thank you to keep your distance, fellas," he warned. Dixon held his gun in his lap, but the cocking of the hammer could be heard by all. The workers took a step back.

"Police!" spat the burly leader. "I knowed you was police!" The other men raised their voices, cursing and threatening with pointing fingers and clenched fists.

Soon Lee, emerging from the kitchen, saw what was happening and began waving his arms and shouting a mixture of Chinese and fractured English. He produced a large kitchen knife and sliced the air back and forth with it. The situation appeared to be descending into chaos.

"Stop this, right now!" The priest stepped over to the table, holding both hands out in a gesture of restraint. "This is not the time nor the place for violence! All of you, just step back, now." The workers complied, stepping back again, clearly respectful of the cleric. Soon Lee retired to the kitchen door, where he continued to mutter in Chinese and jab the air with the knife.

"Father Yorke! You know they oughtn't be in here! They's our enemies!"

The priest turned to Walker and Dixon. "Who are you, and why are you here?" he demanded. His tone was firm, neither friendly nor hostile.

"We're not police," Walker replied, in a similar tone.

"We're Secret Service," added Dixon, showing his badge again. "See for yourself."

The priest bent close and studied the badge. "Secret Service," he confirmed. "And what is the Secret Service?"

"I tole you they was spies," hissed one of the workers, nodding vigorously.

"Secret Service agents are not spies," Walker snapped, becoming irritated. "We provide protection for the President of the United States. He's coming to the shipyard tomorrow for the launching of the *Ohio*, and we're doing an advance security inspection."

"Liars!" snarled the burly man. "Ain't no way a n----r is a federal agent!"

"Stop it!" ordered Father Yorke. "His badge says he's Secret Service, and I believe him. They're here on behalf of the president, and we will respect that. Do you agree?"

The men sullenly nodded. The leader spoke again, and demanded, "But how come you two are in *here*? You tryin' to start trouble?"

"We're not the ones trying to start trouble," Walker growled. "We were minding our own business 'til you all came in."

"Besides," added Dixon, "a colored man can't get a meal just anywhere, you know. We figured a Chinaman would care less what color a customer is."

"Satisfied now?" asked Father Yorke. "You men take a seat and get your food. No more trouble."

The crisis now past, Walker and Dixon holstered their weapons. "Thank you, Father Yorke," said Walker. "You were a big help."

The priest shrugged. "No need for violence—yet."

Walker and Dixon looked at each other. "What do you mean by 'yet,' Father?" queried Dixon.

"There's a storm brewing on the waterfront," Yorke replied, with a shake of his head. "I fear that violence may be inevitable. I wish that it could be avoided, but I'm beginning to think that there are worse things than violence. Not so many years ago, slaveowners whipped their slaves into submission. The corporations and police are treating the wage-earning laborers of San Francisco the same way. The fuse is burning short, and I fear an explosion is imminent."

"Is the president in any danger?" asked Walker anxiously.

"Not at all," interjected the man in the rumpled suit. He beckoned them to come over to the table he shared with Father Yorke. "Foruseth," he said, extending his hand. "Andrew Foruseth. I'm one of the union leaders. There'll be violence only if the bosses and police want it—and they'll want it, if experience teaches us anything. They'll stop at nothing to crush a strike."

"Do you have any chance at winning, if it comes to that?" asked Walker, skeptically.

Furuseth sighed. "Less than fifty-fifty," he admitted. "But does that mean that we should just lie down and submit to their abuse? Do the bosses have all the rights, and the workers have none? The employers combine against the strikers and blacklist them—makes it impossible for a man to get a job anywhere. Do the workers not also have the right to combine? Animals form packs, herds, and flocks for their protection. Are workers less than animals?" He paused as if waiting for their response. When none was forthcoming, he continued.

"Who will stand up for the workingman, if we don't stand up for ourselves? Blood and bone is all we've got, and that's what we'll use when push comes to shove. The power of the working class will be unleashed."

"They'll put you behind bars," warned Dixon. "Lock you up and throw away the key."

Furuseth shrugged. "They can't put me in a smaller room than I've always lived in. They can't give me plainer food than I've always eaten. And they can't make me lonelier than I've always been."

That simple declaration left Walker and Dixon with no words. They sat quietly for a long moment, absorbing its impact. Father Yorke broke the silence, speaking quietly. "We don't anticipate any major developments for a few weeks yet, so the president's visit will go smoothly. He'll have a warm reception tomorrow, don't worry about that." Then, fixing them with a direct gaze, he added, "Keep all this to yourselves, if you please. We don't want to stir up anything prematurely. Agreed?"

"Absolutely!" said Walker, and Dixon nodded agreement. They shook hands again, and the two stood to leave. Walker drew two silver dollar coins from his pocket and put them on the table. "That's for us and you. Good luck—you've got a hard road ahead."

Soon Lee's hand appeared from nowhere and took the coins. Dixon pulled two bills from his pocket and nudged Walker. "Tell him I want to pay for the workers' meals—six dollars."

Walker quickly searched his limited Chinese vocabulary. "Foo sheir," he ventured. Soon Lee's blank expression showed that he did not understand. Dixon pointed to the long table where the dozen workers were eating, and extended the bills. Soon Lee's eyes widened, and he pointed to Dixon and then to the workers. Dixon nodded. Soon Lee bowed, and they did the same.

As they were reining their horses about to leave, the diner door opened and the burly worker stepped out onto the sidewalk. He raised a hand, pointing to Dixon, and said, "Thank you—you're a good man." Dixon touched the brim of his hat, and they trotted away.

"That was mighty nice of you, in there," Walker commented.

"I thought so," Dixon replied drily.

Walker shook his head and laughed. "You realize that you over-paid, don't you?"

"Soon Lee deserves it. Chinamen have a hard time here. Besides, what am I gonna spend that money for, anyway? Let's get back and make our report."

The next day was one that Walker would not soon forget. The president was driven to a wharf in a closed carriage, escorted by a company of mounted police. Boarding a transport tug, he joined his cabinet and other dignitaries for a two-mile voyage to the shipyard. The four Secret Service agents were all aboard as they steamed down the bay, surrounded by the warships of the Pacific Squadron, bedecked with colorful signal flags from bow to stern. The battle-ships and cruisers fired salutes with their biggest guns, and the roar was deafening. There were dozens of other boats on the water, all decorated with American flags and banners. Every pier and wharf were packed with spectators, waving flags and cheering at the top of their lungs as the president's boat passed. The rooftops of waterfront buildings, and even a nearby hillside were covered with people.

A special moment came when the tug passed close to a troop transport crowded with soldiers just returned from the war in the Philippines. The men went crazy with enthusiasm, shouting and waving. A band on board the ship began playing the "Star-Spangled Banner," and McKinley stood at the railing and waved his handker-chief until he was some distance away.

Finally arriving at the shipyard, the president was greeted by the more than four thousand workers who had built the *Ohio*. Their patriotic enthusiasm was second to none, as their cheers reverberated across the bay and echoed off the buildings. The presidential entourage stepped onto the pier, and proceeded to walk up a long white sheet of muslin between cheering and clapping workers packed on either side. Foster and Stover walked just ahead of the president, and Walker and Dixon followed immediately behind him. Walker found that the noise was so great that it interfered with his ability to think clearly and stay focused, and he was relieved when McKinley mounted the platform.

Walker did not listen to the speeches, which were frequently interrupted with roars of applause, but closely watched the multitude of spectators instead. Mrs. McKinley had been scheduled to break a bottle of champagne against the ship's hull for the christening, but due to her illness a sixteen-year-old girl from Ohio—the daughter of a friend of the president—did the honors. The bottle was suspended from a red, white, and blue ribbon, and the girl spoke the words, "I christen thee 'Ohio,'" and released it to another roar of applause. The bottle shattered against the steel prow; the final keel block fell away, and the steel behemoth began to slide down the slip toward the water, gaining speed as it went. A band began playing, but Walker couldn't tell what the music was, due to the deafening roar of the crowd.

Walker suddenly noticed that Dixon was not standing beside him at the platform stairs. Looking quickly about, he spied him several yards away, poised to sprint in case the ship wobbled. He couldn't help but laugh.

The launch had been timed to coincide with high tide, at just after noon, and when the stern of the ship plowed into the bay, it made a huge splash. The ship's progress then slowed, and it settled smoothly and quietly into the water. The *Ohio* had been unleashed.

McKinley's exit was immediate and quick. He hurried to a waiting closed carriage, and with the mounted police escort, raced from the shipyard to return to the Scott home, back to Ida's bedside. Stover sat in front with the driver, Foster inside with the president, and Walker and Dixon perched on the rear, standing on footmen's posts. Gripping the handholds with white knuckles, and with their coattails flapping, they enjoyed the ride immensely. It was an exhilarating conclusion to an exciting and memorable morning.

As the First Lady's condition continued to slowly improve, the president decided to keep a few more of his scheduled appearances. It was a very busy day, beginning with a visit to the Presidio army base to welcome troops returning from the Philippines, and to dedicate the newly-built military hospital there. As it turned out, the returning troops were the same ones who had cheered so lustily for the president from their transport ship in San Francisco Bay at the launching of the *Ohio*.

More than two thousand blue-clad soldiers, wearing brown slouch hats, stood at attention on the Presidio parade ground. Booming cannons announced McKinley's arrival, and a band played "Hail to the Chief" as he walked to the reviewing platform. As he climbed the steps, a bugle sounded, and the men gave a great shout and cheer. The commander-in-chief saluted the assembly, and the men finally quieted down, at least temporarily. The president's brief speech was interrupted by cheers several times as he praised the men for their service, and for bringing honor to the flag. "You have done your duty," he said.

Walker's mind strayed back to the Philippines, as he remembered the scenes of death and destruction he had witnessed there. *Not much honor, that I could see,* he mused. *'Benevolent Assimilation'? Not much benevolence, and not much assimilation, either. These men are lucky to be done with it.*

After the speech, the president visited the hospital, speaking to each wounded soldier and extending his sympathy, shaking hands and giving salutes. As he and others went bed by bed down a long, airy ward, Walker, Dixon, and Stover stood by the entry. Surveying the large room, filled with bandaged men, many with missing arms or legs, Walker recalled the various bullet wounds he had suffered. Leaning toward Dixon, he murmured, "There, but for the grace of God...."

"Yeah," Dixon whispered, nodding. "I know."

"He's a good man," Stover said softly, with a nod toward the president.

"He has a good heart," Walker agreed.

"He means well," Dixon conceded, and then quickly added, "You can tell the men really appreciate it."

"Yes, they do!" came a deep voice from behind them. "And so do I! Major Schuyler, of the Forty-Sixth. These are my men." The three agents introduced themselves and shook hands. The major motioned for them to step outside the room, and then continued, "You heard what the president said out there—'they've done their duty'—it's your turn now, gentlemen. Join the army and do your share. It's every man's duty to serve his country."

"You're talking to a couple of veterans right now," Stover replied with a grin, before either of them could speak. "Garrett and Dixon fought in Cuba, the Philippines, and then in China. They've done their duty, and then some!"

"Excellent!" nodded Schuyler, and then suddenly stopped and stared at the two. "Did you say Garrett and Dixon? You're not the ones who swam the Pampanga River at flood stage with ropes to make a ferry for the army to cross, are you?"

"That would be us," Dixon admitted, almost sheepishly. "Stupidest fools in the whole United States Army."

"We got a medal and a cigar for doing that," remembered Walker, with a grin.

"And two bullets," added Dixon. "Don't forget that little detail."

"Well, I must say!" exclaimed Schuyler, tugging at his bushy mustache. "I stand in the presence of heroes! How is it that you are already back in the States, and in the Secret Service?"

"Well, sir," said Walker hesitantly, "we sorta got separated from our unit in China, and things got complicated after that."

"I see," replied Schuyler, even though he obviously didn't. Extending his hand for a final shake, he said abruptly, "It's a pleasure, men." He then marched briskly down the aisle and joined the group. Their voices could be heard across the ward as he greeted the president and the others, exchanging pleasantries.

Walker sensed Stover's eyes boring into him. Glancing sideways at him, he asked, "Something wrong?"

Stover squinted and frowned. "You two swam a river at flood stage, under enemy fire, dragging ropes?"

After a few seconds of silence, Dixon shrugged and said, "It was a really good cigar."

Walker's shoulders shook with silent laughter. "Took me three days to smoke it!" he gasped.

"That's 'cause you didn't have any matches," Dixon snorted,

elbowing Walker in the ribs. Walker leaned forward, hands on knees, barely able to stand up, he was laughing so hard.

Stover stared at them, shaking his head in disbelief, and then couldn't suppress a one-sided grin. The grin almost turned into a chuckle, but he quickly cleared his throat and regained his composure. Stepping back into the ward, he growled over his shoulder, "You two are impossible!"

The rest of the day was an exhausting whirlwind of receptions, speeches, and ceremonies. The president met with Civil War veterans, Mexican War veterans, unions, and political clubs. One reception was at the fabulous Palace Hotel, which left Walker amazed at its size and grandeur. The day ended with McKinley wielding a shovel at the groundbreaking ceremony for a monument commemorating Admiral Dewey's famous naval victory over the Spanish at the beginning of the Spanish-American War in 1898. Listening to the president speak to so many different groups in rapid succession, Walker was astonished at his eloquence. National pride and unity were his consistent themes, and he touched the hearts of each audience. *He always seems to know exactly what to say,* Walker thought. *No wonder he's been elected twice. You can't help but admire and like him. He's a good president, even if the South didn't vote for him.*

The next day, the doctors pronounced Mrs. McKinley fit to travel. The rest of the tour had already been canceled, and after almost two weeks in San Francisco, it was time to return to Washington. The most direct route across the continent was chosen—that of the original transcontinental railroad, finished with a golden spike over thirty years earlier. After crossing the bay by ferry, they boarded the presidential train in Oakland. The steam whistle sounded, and with a slight jerk, the train began to move, slowly gaining speed.

Walker had a sense of being home again, as he stowed his things in the familiar bunk car. From his accustomed window seat, he could see the skyline of San Francisco across the water. It had not been a particularly pleasant stay, he reflected, considering the First Lady's nearly fatal illness, but he would not soon forget Father Yorke and Andrew Foruseth, and especially not Donaldina Cameron. *There are some remarkable people here,* he thought. *If they can only find a few more like them, it will be a great city.* The track angled northeastward, turning toward the Sierra Nevada mountains, and the bay was lost to his view. Walker settled back in the seat, rested his head against the window frame, and closed his eyes. Until then, he hadn't realized how tired he was.

9

"A CLOSE THING INDEED"

The return trip to Washington took five days. The train did not stop, except to take on coal and water. The dramatic mountain scenery kept Walker and Dixon at the windows for the first day, but the endless prairie that followed reminded them of the ocean-like expanse of the Siberian steppes. To pass the time, the agents played cards, wrote letters, slept, or simply talked. Dixon wrote to his mother, to his sister, and to Jenny. Walker had only Abigail Dancy, to whom he wrote a lengthy description of the trip, omitting the violent incidents. This was still not enough to fill the time, and out of sheer boredom Walker conceived an idea that gave him a sense of excitement.

"Dixon," he announced with a grin, "I'm going to write a book!"

"You? Write a book? You don't even *read* books—how you gonna *write* one?"

"I do too read books," Walker retorted—"just not lately. I read lots of books on the ships and trains over the past two years. General Wheeler's books, and books that Reverend Roberts loaned me."

"What're you gonna write about?" Dixon was still skeptical. "You got to have something to say if you're gonna write a book."

"I'm gonna write about my adventures in the army," Walker

beamed. "I'll start from the time I left Courtland, and tell about all that happened in Cuba, the Philippines, China—and all the other places. It should make for some interesting reading, I think."

"Nobody will believe it," Dixon scoffed. "Just like Stover, they'll think it's a bunch of made-up stories."

"Don't matter," Walker shrugged. "It will still be a good book. A lot happened, and I want to write it down before I forget it."

"What will you call it? 'Alabama Cracker Goes Round the World?'"

"I was thinking more like, 'The Adventures of Walker Garrett,' maybe."

At that point, Stover entered the car with a mug of coffee, swallowing the last of a donut. Hearing the last words by Walker, he wanted to know what they were talking about, and Walker explained his idea.

"I like it," he nodded. "You've got some real stem-winders to tell— charging up San Juan Hill, swimming that river in the Philippines, fighting the Boxers—I'd like to read it, myself!"

"I think he should call it 'Alabama Cracker Sees the World,'" chuckled Dixon.

"Very funny," frowned Walker. "I was thinking 'The Adventures of Walker Garrett.' Or, how about 'Around the World in a Thousand Days,' like that book by Jules Verne."

"I've got it!" exclaimed Stover. "There was a famous Greek myth about a man who traveled a long way to get home. It was called 'The Odyssey.' You could name your book 'The Odyssey of Walker Garrett!'"

"Hmmm," mused Walker for a few seconds. "No, that sounds a little too uppity for me. I'll have to do some more thinking on this. But for now, I'm gonna get started writing. Good thing I've got Dixon here to help me remember everything."

"I don't work for free," Dixon warned.

Walker laughed as he drew his meager supply of writing paper from his bag. "I'm gonna need a lot more paper," he said. "And a bunch of pencils."

By the time the locomotive finally hissed to a stop at Washington's Baltimore & Potomac Railroad Station, Walker had run out of paper for writing. It didn't matter, because the next several days were extremely busy. Getting the McKinleys resettled in the Executive Mansion and reestablishing security routines required the full concentration of all of the Secret Service agents, including those who had not participated in the trip. Since the president had been away for thirty-two days, there was an even greater than usual number of people who wanted to see him, and many who wanted to express their concern for Mrs. McKinley. The size of the crowds taxed the agents' ability to keep order. At the end of each day, Walker and Dixon were exhausted, and they dragged themselves back to the room they rented at the home of a black minister.

Reverend Moses Wright and his wife, Hannah, welcomed both of them with warm hospitality. They ate at the table with the family— which included four children—shared conversation in the parlor, and Hannah even washed their clothes. Moses not only preached for the local African Methodist Episcopal congregation, but he and Hannah ran a small school for black children at the church building during the week. They were cheerful, generous people, and Walker quickly came to feel at home there.

They had been back in Washington for a few days, and things were settling into a routine. After church one Sunday in early June, the pastor asked Walker and Dixon to step outside the house with him while Hannah finished preparing the noon meal. He led them to the front porch, where a grandfatherly black man waited, fanning himself with his hat. He had a short white beard, and his suit was plain, but neat, with a crisp white shirt and a black bow tie. His black shoes were highly polished, shining in the sun.

"This is my good friend, Brother Henry Brown," began Wright. "After the church service this morning he said he had something to tell me. When I heard it, I knew he should tell you, too. I think it's important."

Henry cleared his throat a bit nervously and, fidgeting with his hat, proceeded to tell his story. "I drives a cab heah. I doan listen to what folks talks about, but sometimes I hears things." He hesitated for a couple of seconds, then continued. "Yestiddy, I picked up two fellas at the train station. One of 'em had just come in on the train, and t'other one was meetin' him. Whilst we was goin' along, they was talkin', an' I understood what they was sayin'."

"What do you mean, you 'understood' them?" asked Dixon.

"They was talkin' in Spanish," Henry explained. "My mama was Mexican, an' we lived on the Texas border 'til after the War, 'fore I come to D.C. to find work. I ain't heard nobody talkin' Spanish in a long time, so I listened. I knowed I shouldn't, but I couldn't help myself."

"That's alright, Brother Brown," nodded the reverend. "You didn't do anything wrong."

"Well," continued Henry, "the one in the fancy gray suit with the diamond stickpin was tellin' t'other one—t'other one was wearin' a red vest, and it looked right tacky, if'n you ask me. No gen'lman would wear somethin' like that, 'specially not with green pants an' brown boots. An' it's too warm now for a leather coat. I knowed he weren't from 'round here."

"What were they talking about?" prodded Walker.

"The gen'lman give him some money—I don't know how much—an' told him that the *target* would be driving his wife 'round the city on Sunday afternoon, an' there wouldn't be no guards with him. He say t'would be easy to get close enough to do the job. He also say he was giving him a train ticket to New York, so he could be on the next ship out."

Walker and Dixon looked at each other in alarm. It was well-known that President McKinley drove the First Lady about the city in a carriage on Sunday afternoons. Could he be the 'target?'"

"Where did these men get out of the cab?" asked Dixon, frowning.

"The gen'lman got out at the corner of Pennsylvania Avenue and 24th Street. He tole me to take t'other one to the Surratt Boarding House. I wondered to myself 'Why that one?' 'cause it was a fur piece to go. An' then he say to t'other one, in Spanish—" here, Henry hesitated again, giving the reverend a nervous look.

"Go ahead, Brother Brown," encouraged the pastor. "It's important."

Clearing his throat again, Henry said, "He say—in Spanish—that this was the right place for him to stay, 'cause it was *symbolic*. He say he would understand why when he got there."

"Thank you, Brother Brown," smiled Wright, shaking his hand. Walker and Dixon also thanked him and shook hands. As Brown left, Wright turned to them with a somber expression. "Well, what do you think?" Walker and Dixon gave each other another look of concern.

"Wasn't the Surratt House where John Wilkes Booth's gang stayed while they planned Lincoln's assassination?" asked Walker. "I thought she was hanged with the others."

"She was," nodded Wright, "but the new owners kept the name—it's famous and apparently attracts business."

"What's at Pennsylvania and 24th?" asked Dixon. "Aren't there some foreign embassies in that area?"

"That could be the Spanish embassy," said Wright, "but I'm not certain. It would make sense, since they were speaking Spanish."

Just then, a church bell sounded, indicating one o'clock.

"I'm afraid we're not going to be able to stay for dinner today, Reverend," said Dixon.

"We don't have any time to waste!" added Walker, and they began running down the street. It was almost two miles to the Executive Mansion. "I wish we had our horses here," panted Walker.

"Maybe we can catch a cab," suggested Dixon. It was highly unlikely that any cabs would be out on a Sunday afternoon, but suddenly they heard the clopping of hooves approaching from behind them. Turning, they were astonished to see Brother Brown in his cab.

"Hop in, fellas!" he waved. "I'll get you there in a jiffy!" When they had piled into the rear seat, he snapped the reins and called to the horse, "Giddap there, Napoleon! We got to move smart, now!" Napoleon trotted briskly, as if he knew the stakes were high.

When they reached the Executive Mansion and jumped to the ground, Dixon flipped a gold coin to Henry. "That's for Napoleon!

Give him some extra oats from us!" They dashed madly for the front entrance, where two Secret Service agents stood guard.

"Thank you, sah!" responded Henry enthusiastically. He tipped his hat, and Napoleon snorted and tossed his head.

They were dismayed to find that the presidential couple had already departed for their afternoon drive. Mrs. McKinley had just recently recovered enough strength to be able to sit up in bed, but the doctors apparently felt that some fresh air would be good for her, and so they had approved the outing. Within minutes, four agents on horseback were galloping in pursuit, hoping that the president was taking his usual route. Sure enough, they spied his carriage about a half-mile from the Mansion, not far from the Washington Monument. The canopy was up, to protect the First Lady from the heat of the sun. They were in no hurry, letting the horse walk as they waved to pedestrians along the street.

Not wanting to disturb the McKinleys' outing unnecessarily, they reined in their horses a short distance behind the carriage, but close enough to respond quickly to any threat. "You two stay with the carriage, and watch for a man in a red vest," directed Dixon. "Me and Garrett will scout up ahead." They cantered past the carriage, turning their faces away so that the president would hopefully not recognize them. Reaching the Mall, they stopped and looked carefully in all directions for a suspicious figure, without success.

Walker rode forward into the trees. Now that he was out of the bright sunshine and into the shade, he could see much better. Catching a movement out of the corner of his eye, he glanced and saw the man in the red vest less than fifty yards away, partially hidden behind a tree trunk. To Walker's surprise, the man was on horseback. His attention was focused on the president's approaching carriage, and he did not notice Walker.

Advancing further into concealment, Walker drew his revolver and motioned to Dixon to go toward the man's position. Dixon, still in the sun, could not tell what Walker wanted him to do, and shading his eyes with one hand, made a questioning gesture. Walker pointed again, jabbing the air with his finger. Dixon, unable to see what

Walker could see, leisurely walked his horse in the man's direction. Walker, using the trees for cover, paralleled Dixon's movement.

He was less than fifty feet away when the red vest man apparently decided it was time to make his move toward the president. The man had one hand ominously inside his leather coat as he came trotting from the shade of the trees. Walker and Dixon converged on him simultaneously, guns in hand.

"Halt!" barked Walker. The man's shocked expression was almost comical, as his mouth fell wide open. However, instead of obeying the command to stop, he kicked his mount into a full run, attempting to dash between them toward the carriage. He did not know that he was challenging two well-trained riders with combat experience. Also, his rented gelding was no match for the steeds ridden by the agents, and they quickly jammed him between them, forcing him to a halt. When he reached into his coat again, Dixon put his gun barrel to the man's temple, and his resistance ended abruptly.

Walker reached across and relieved him of the weapon—a Mauser 7.63 mm "broom handle" pistol—the same model that Spanish soldiers had carried in the recent war. Walker had taken one from a dead soldier in Cuba, and had used it until he ran out of ammunition for it. Dixon took hold of the reins and led the horse as they escorted their prisoner to a police station. Along the way, he attempted to break free by lunging at Walker, trying to unhorse him. This was a mistake, as he received a sharp elbow in the face, giving him a bloody nose.

The police seemed unsure whether or not to detain the man, since he had not actually committed a crime. No one at the station spoke Spanish, and the man remained stoically silent during questioning, so it was not clear if he knew English. However, due to his attempted flight and brandishing a weapon in the vicinity of the president, they agreed to hold him until more evidence was produced.

As they left the station, Walker suddenly had an idea. Turning to Dixon, he said, "Henry said this man is staying at the Surratt Boarding House. If we search his room, we might find some proof of what he was doing here." Dixon agreed, and so they went straight to the small establishment. It was a simple, box-like, four-story structure, with guest rooms on the upper three floors, and a dining area on the ground floor. The proprietor answered the door, and upon seeing their silver five-point-star badges, let them in and showed them to the man's upstairs room.

"His name is Juan W. Puesto," he said. "At least, that's what he signed on the guest book, downstairs."

"Juan Puesto!" echoed Walker. "'Juan' is the Spanish name for *John*, and 'puesto' means a *stall*, like in a barn or stable. It could mean a *booth*, also. You've got a 'John W. Booth' staying at the Surratt Boarding House—*again*."

"Well, I'll be damned!" gaped the proprietor. "If that ain't a coincidence!" Chuckling to himself, he went back downstairs, leaving them to search the room.

"Yeah," muttered Dixon, with a shake of his head. "That ain't no coincidence. I call that 'evidence.'"

"Yup," agreed Walker. "We may have to borrow that guest book."

The search took only a minute. There wasn't much to examine, and lying on the table in plain view was a small book, which turned out to be a personal diary, with dates and places for each day's entry. The would-be assassin had apparently kept a journal of his thoughts and actions. It was written in Spanish, but they felt sure it would provide the proof of his diabolical plan. After briefly debating what to do with it, they decided to take it to the police station, since it would be the city's responsibility to prosecute the case.

"We got one more stop to make," Dixon said, as they left the police station. "The Spanish embassy. We need to find out who that fellow with the diamond stickpin is."

"Shouldn't we let somebody from the State Department handle that?" argued Walker. "That's over our heads, isn't it?"

"Yes," agreed Dixon, "but we can't wait 'til tomorrow. The president is s'posed to be dead already, and whoever that man from the embassy is, he's probably makin' tracks for somewhere else right now. We got no time to waste."

They hurried to Pennsylvania and 24th Street, finding that it was indeed the Spanish embassy. It was surrounded by a ten-foot brick wall, with a wrought-iron gate at the entrance. Walker dismounted and approached the gate. Just inside was a small booth, manned by a uniformed soldier. "Hablas inglés?" Walker asked. *Do you speak English?* The soldier shook his head. Stepping backwards into the guard booth, he lifted a telephone receiver to his ear, and spoke rapidly into the mouthpiece. He then motioned for them to wait. In about a minute, a door opened and a man came out of the embassy and walked toward them. His suit was not expensive, and he did not have a diamond stickpin.

"May I help you?" he asked politely.

"I hope so," Walker replied, trying not to sound too concerned. "We'd like to speak to a man who works here at the embassy, but we don't know his name. Maybe you can help us figure out who he is."

"Who are you, and why do you need to speak to this man?" asked the embassy officer.

Thinking quickly, Walker opened his coat to show his badge. "We're law officers, and we have reason to believe that this man may be in danger. We'd like to talk to him, and make sure he's alright."

The Spanish official studied them silently, stroking his chin. Sensing that he needed to press further, Walker continued. "A witness told us that this man dresses expensively, and wears a diamond stickpin in his lapel. The witness heard threats being made. We wouldn't want any harm to come to a foreign guest in our city, so we'd like to see him. It will only take a moment."

The official frowned, making a dismissive gesture. "I can assure you that the man of whom you speak will come to no harm in this city. He is completely safe—you have no reason to worry. Thank you for your concern."

"We really need to see him for ourselves, sir," Walker objected. However, the official was already walking back to the embassy, ignoring Walker's protests.

Back in the saddle, he turned to Dixon with a scowl. "How can he be so sure that man is not in any danger? You'd think he'd be at least a *little* concerned about it."

"Think about what he said," Dixon countered. "He said he would 'come to no harm in this city.' What if he isn't *in this city* anymore? Henry said he gave Mr. Red Vest a train ticket to New York. Maybe he's heading to New York himself, to sail back to Spain."

"Let's get to the station, then," Walker nodded. They hastened as fast as they could safely push the horses in the summer heat. Hurrying into the lobby, they approached the ticket window. "When does the next train for New York leave?" he asked.

"It's leaving right now. Track Number Two," the ticket clerk replied, pointing toward the train shed exit. They ran out to the platforms. There was no train on the first track, so they had a clear view of the cars on track Number Two. Before they could head for the stairs to the tunnel beneath the tracks, the train began to move, hissing and huffing. They stood helplessly watching as the cars rolled past, just a few yards away.

As one of the first-class cars passed, a man inside the compartment stood, facing the window, and reached out with his arms to pull the curtains. There was a quick flash of light from his suit lapel before the curtains closed.

"Did you see that?" asked Dixon, excitedly. "That was him! The man with the diamond stickpin!"

"I saw it," nodded Walker. "He's got away, but maybe we can telegraph New York and have him picked up there." As they were about to mount their horses, Walker scratched his head and asked, "Why do you s'pose the Spanish would want to kill President McKinley, anyway? He never did anything to them."

Dixon stared at Walker, hands on hips. "Maybe they didn't appreciate him sinking their navy and taking Cuba, Puerto Rico, Guam, and the Philippines away from them."

Walker's face reddened. "Oh, yeah. I forgot about that."

Dixon shook his head. "I swear, Garrett—you need to stay out of the sun."

It was a silent ride back to the Executive Mansion from the train station. They returned their sweaty horses to the stable and made sure that they were well-cared for. By the time they walked back to

Reverend Wright's house, the family was sitting down for supper. "Y'all wash up now, y'hear!" greeted Hannah with her usual warm smile. "I reckon y'all must be 'bout starved."

"Yes ma'am!" they chorused, and headed for the wash basin on the back porch. After a delicious meal of cornbread, peas, fried okra, and slices of fresh tomato, the men withdrew to the shade of a tree in the front yard, while the children helped their mother clean up the kitchen and wash the dishes.

"So, what happened?" asked Wright, as he struck a match to light his pipe.

Walker and Dixon exchanged a look. "Thanks to you and Brother Henry, the president is alive tonight," Dixon replied. The reverend blinked, and he coughed a puff of smoke.

"You're exaggerating, aren't you, Brother Dixon?"

"No sir, not even a little bit. The man in the red vest was waiting to shoot the president at the Mall, and we got there just in time. The police have him now."

"We searched his room at the Surratt Boarding House," added Walker. "We found his diary, which will probably prove what he was up to."

"But the man with the diamond stickpin got away," concluded Dixon. "Took the train to New York. We'll let the authorities there know, so they can arrest him before his ship sails."

"Well, if he's a diplomat, he has immunity and can't be arrested," Wright said, drawing on the pipe. "But you've done a marvelous job today, gentlemen! You saved the President of the United States from an untimely end. You should get medals for this!"

"If anybody deserves a medal, it's Henry," averred Walker. "He's the one that made this possible."

"We'll make sure the right people know about that, too," Dixon promised. "If it wasn't for his eye for detail, we wouldn't have known what to look for."

"Like the old hymn says," Wright smiled, "'God moves in a mysterious way, His wonders to perform.' It was a close thing, gentlemen, a close thing indeed. We must thank the good Lord for His providence." The reverend promptly bowed his head and began to pray aloud. Walker and Dixon bowed their heads respectfully, and added their 'Amen' at the conclusion.

"Thank you, Reverend," Walker said. "I'm going to head to the room, now. I want to write a few more pages in my book while the daylight lasts. I'll see y'all in the morning." At a small table in their shared room, he wrote until it was too dark to see the print, and then crawled into bed, mentally exhausted.

10

REVOLUTIONARY WHEELS

"Any news from Decatur?" asked Walker.

Dixon, sitting on his bed, looked up from the letter he was reading. "Mama says Daisy's doin' real good in school. This'll probably be her last year, though, since colored girls can't go past the eighth grade. She's still making a little money with her crocheting." He held up a small, crocheted green square with a white flower in the middle. "It's a magnolia blossom. She sent one for you, too." And he tossed a green and white square onto Walker's bed. "Says she's glad we got a good place to stay, where we can eat good. Wants to know when we're comin' to visit."

"Tell her 'thank you'—that's really nice!" Walker admired the needlework. "I'll keep it with the others." He was quiet for a moment, studying the letter in his hand, and then looked up to see Dixon eyeing him expectantly, waiting for his own report. He shrugged. "Abigail says she'll be spending the summer with relatives in Charleston again, like she always does. Come fall, she'll be with other relatives in Richmond. Just the usual."

"Richmond ain't that far," nodded Dixon. "Maybe you could drop down there for a visit."

"Don't think so," Walker shook his head. "Mr. Dancy wants her to get married to one of her cousins—a second cousin, I think—in Charleston. He's about twelve years older than her, and he hasn't proposed yet, but she thinks he will, this summer. He's a rich man, she says, so I figure she'll say 'yes.'"

"That's just what 'Dancin' Dancy needs," Dixon sneered—"a rich man that can afford to hire help to do all the work in the house. She wasn't your kind, anyway, Garrett."

"I reckon so," Walker sighed. "Can't say that I'm surprised." He refolded the pastel yellow stationery and put it back into the matching yellow envelope. "We'll be busy, anyway. Two months in Canton, and then straight to Buffalo. I won't have time to think about her much."

Dixon cleared his throat. "I been meanin' to talk to you about that, Garrett. I don't think I'm going to Canton. They don't need all of us there, so I'll be stayin' here. Foster approved it this morning."

"Not going to Canton?" Walker was aghast. "Who am I supposed to talk to, and do things with? You can't leave me with just Stover!"

"Stover's not so bad, and it won't be for long. I may even join you before summer's out, if things here go smoothly."

"What things?"

"I want to bring Mama and Daisy here," Dixon said earnestly. "There's colored schools here where Daisy can get more education, and Mama can find work easy, cookin' for big shots. I even thought you and me could rent a house, and we could all live together."

"Oh!" was all that Walker could say at first, as his mind grappled with this unexpected turn. Taking a deep breath, he continued, "I see. Yes—I understand—that's a good idea. Really good—I like it. Alright, that's what we'll do!"

Pleased at Walker's response, Dixon grinned. "I need to get them up here as soon as possible so Daisy can get squared away and start school in the fall. Moses and Hannah can help find us a place to live, and help Mama find somewhere to work. There ain't no future for them in Decatur."

"I said your Mama would be proud of you, didn't I! I was right, too. I'll get by without you in Canton, I guess, since it's for a good cause. You better show up in Buffalo, though!"

"Count on it! I'll be there, for sure. Right now, you need to start packing for Ohio, and I got to send Mama a telegram and some travelin' money, and start lookin' for a house we can afford. Lots to do!"

The next few days were a whirlwind of activity. Walker and Stover were sent to Canton a day ahead of the presidential party, shepherding a small mountain of trunks, boxes, and bags. Canton was more than three hundred miles northwest of the capital city, through the Appalachian Mountains, with a stop in Pittsburgh. Despite leaving on the first train of the morning, it was almost dark when they finally arrived. They hired a wagon at the train station, and hauled the baggage to the cavernous Saxton-McKinley house—a three-story, red-brick mansion in the French Second Empire style, complete with Mansard roof and wrap-around porch. Ida's sister, Mary Barber, and her husband and five grown children lived on the lower floors of the house, while the McKinleys made their home in an apartment on the third floor. The pulley lift was large enough for only one person at a time, so Stover and Walker had to carry the heavy trunks and baggage up the three-story spiral staircase together. By the time they finished, it was nine o'clock, and they were exhausted and sweating profusely in the muggy heat.

"Lord a-mercy," Walker groaned, as they stood fanning themselves on the front porch. "I b'lieve I'm gettin' the shakes."

Stover blew a spray of sweat from his mustache, and wiped his forehead with a handkerchief. "You and me both," he agreed.

"Where do you reckon we're s'posed to sleep tonight?" Walker asked.

As if on cue, the front door opened and Mary Barber joined them on the porch. "Thank you, gentlemen! You've certainly worked hard tonight, and I know you're tired. One of my daughters is bringing you each a glass of cold lemonade in just a moment to refresh you."

"Thank you kindly, ma'am," responded Walker, gratefully. "That's mighty nice of you!"

"A room has been reserved for you at the Farmer's Hotel," she continued. "It's just a across the street, and they will provide you with whatever you need to make you comfortable."

"A bath and a clean bed will make *me* comfortable," Stover grunted, squeezing more sweat from his mustache with a forefinger and blowing it toward the bushes at the edge of the porch. Barber gave him a horrified look, which he did not see, and stepped away from him. Walker suppressed a smile and made a mental note to never grow a mustache.

Just then, the door opened and two young women came out, each carrying a tall glass of lemonade, complete with slices of lemon and chunks of ice. Walker blinked as he looked at the girl handing him the glass. She was clearly in her teens, with brown hair and eyes that could be seen twinkling, even in the dark. "Hello!" she said, flashing a smile. "I'm Kate. What's your name?"

"Katherine!" objected Mrs. Barber. "Mind your manners!"

"And I'm Ida," said the other young woman, curtsying as she handed a glass to Stover. Mrs. Barber stamped her foot and put her hands on her hips, frowning. The girls giggled.

Walker grinned. "Walker Garrett," he said. Raising the glass as if making a toast, he added, "Thank you very much for the lemonade. This is delicious!"

"You're welcome!" Kate beamed. "I made it myself!"

"Good night, then, gentlemen!" interjected Mrs. Barber forcefully, herding her daughters toward the door with outstretched arms. "Just leave the glasses by the door and we'll get them later."

Walker and Stover could hear the girls' laughter as the door closed. They looked at each other with raised eyebrows. "Canton just got a lot more interesting!" Walker observed.

Blowing another spray of lemonade and sweat, Stover shrugged. "Just remember—they're the president's nieces. Don't bite off more than you can chew, or you'll be on the next train back to D.C.—or Alabama."

"True," agreed Walker, setting his empty glass down beside the door. "I'm ready for that bath and bed." They shouldered their duffel bags and headed across the street. Farmer's Hotel was not fancy, but was comfortable and quiet. Within an hour, they had washed off the sweat and were turning down the sheets on the beds.

"Long day," yawned Walker as he stretched out, plumping the pillow under his head.

"No snoring allowed," Stover growled. He laid down, and within seconds began snoring. Walker groaned, turned on his side, and put the pillow over his head. He hardly moved a muscle all night.

Foster arrived with the McKinleys the next evening, along with the president's usual traveling staff: a stenographer, a typist, a telegraph operator, and of course, his personal secretary, John Cortelyou. They set up their office at the "Campaign House," which was a half-mile away from the Sexton-McKinley House, and also lodged there. Foster, Walker, and Stover lodged in the hotel, due to it being so much closer to the president.

Foster assigned them to sentry duty at the front door. No problems were expected, but the presence of two Secret Service agents at the front door would make any would-be trouble-makers have second thoughts. McKinley objected that it was excessive and unnecessary, but Foster and Cortelyou insisted, and so he relented.

After one week, Walker and Stover were allowed to split the duty, with one standing the post and the other having leisure time. It was during this free time that Walker explored the city and developed a relationship with the Barber family. Nineteen-year-old William and twenty-year-old Ida were the closest to Walker in age, but it was seventeen-year-old Kate who showed the most interest. Two older brothers worked at a bank, and were seldom present during the day, but they allowed Walker to borrow their bicycles to go riding with the younger siblings.

Instead of the traditional long dresses or skirts which reached the ankles, Kate and other bicycle-riding young women wore a variety of more practical styles. Walker had never seen girls wearing bloomers —baggy calf-length pants, with stockings. Initially astonished at this, Walker decided that he liked it. He was less enthusiastic about men's cycling fashions. He felt foolish wearing knickerbockers and leggings, an open-necked shirt, and cloth cap, but since all the other young men on bicycles were similarly dressed, he decided to conform. He couldn't help thinking that he was glad Dixon was not there to laugh at him.

One pleasant July morning, he found Kate and William waiting for him on their bicycles. Kate stood astraddle of hers, with one foot on the ground and the other on a pedal. "Walker—get a bike! William and I are taking you to Meyers Lake!" She seemed quite excited, and William was grinning.

"What's Meyers Lake?" he asked, a bit suspiciously.

"It's an amusement park a few miles outside of town. It's the best place on earth! You're going to love it!"

"What's an amusement park?"

"Walker! Don't be silly! Everybody knows what an amusement park is! They have a roller coaster, and a roller skating rink, and lots of things to do for fun! Hurry up!"

"What's a roll—never mind. I'm coming!"

A few miles of brisk pedaling brought them to a lovely lake in a natural setting—mostly natural, that is. Green forest lined the shores around most of the lake, but the rest was festooned with various attractions, including restaurants, food and drink vendors, halls for billiards, dancing, skating, and bowling, besides the roller coaster and a narrow-gauge train station. The lake was dotted with boats, and a roped-off area near a bath house was for swimming. There were bandstands and gazebos, and people strolling about, eating ice cream.

"Come on, Walker!" cried Kate, laughing, as she grabbed his arm. "We have to ride the roller coaster!"

When Walker saw the string of little carts sitting on the narrow track, he was surprised. He had expected something unusual—something exciting. This looked like it was going to be very dull and boring. He reluctantly wedged himself into the cart beside Kate, who couldn't stop talking about how much fun it was going to be. William sat in the cart behind them. Walker forced a smile and told himself to try to enjoy it. The carts moved slowly out of the station and crept around a curve in the track. Kate stamped her feet in a frenzy of anticipation, and Walker almost laughed out loud, thinking she was putting on an act.

Suddenly the cart dropped like a rock and accelerated like a bullet out of a gun. Walker involuntarily shouted in alarm, and Kate squealed in delight. The cart darted right and left, slamming them from side to side, bouncing up and down like a bucking horse. Walker's eyes and mouth were open wide and his knuckles were white as he gripped the safety bar in front of him. The cart slowed as it climbed a steeper hill, giving Walker a chance to catch his breath—until it reached the top and then dove insanely down the other side, twisting in a sharp banking turn. Walker screamed in mortal fear, certain that he was about to die. There were a couple more bone-jarring turns, and then, without warning, it abruptly slowed to a stop back in the station. It was time to get out. The ride had lasted about two minutes.

Walker sat frozen, still gripping the restraining bar. "Step right this way, sir!" said the attendant, raising the bar and gesturing them to exit. Walker drew a deep breath—his first in at least a minute—and practically crawled onto the platform, his knees wobbly. Kate was literally dancing around him, laughing hysterically.

"Walker! Did you like it? You scream like a girl! That was so much fun! Let's do it again!" She grabbed his arm again and dragged him toward the line of waiting riders. William, also laughing, took Walker's other arm, as they all staggered together to the back of the line.

"Let's come back later for this," Walker gasped. "I'd like to paddle a boat, or something. Anything that won't try to kill me."

"Skating!" she whooped. "That's what we should do next! Come on, Walker—I'll teach you to roller skate!" Walker felt a sense of dread as he let her lead him to the roller skating rink. Within a few minutes, he was sitting on a bench beside the polished wooden floor of the rink, looking skeptically at a pair of boots with wheels under them.

"This doesn't look like a good idea," he said, doubtfully.

"Hurry up, Walker!" Kate urged, as she laced up her roller skates. "You'll get the hang of it in no time!" She launched out onto the floor, twirled about twice, and whisked away around the rink, hair flying out behind her.

"That looks pretty easy," Walker said to William.

William gave him a pitying look. "I'll help you," he said sympathetically, and extended a hand.

Walker waved him off. "If she can do it, I can do it," he said firmly, and pushed out onto the floor. His legs went in two different directions, and he twisted in mid-air and landed face down. He looked up to see William's shoulders shaking with silent laughter as he extended his hand again. This time, Walker grasped it and climbed carefully back to his feet, only to sit hard on the floor as his feet shot out from under him. With William's help, he made it to the railing and hung on to it like a drowning man to a life jacket. Kate rocketed past, and then spun about. With pink cheeks and shining eyes, she held out her hands to Walker.

"Take my hands, Walker! I'll help you get started!"

Surrendering his grip on the railing one hand at a time, he took her hands. She skated backwards slowly, towing him as he crouched unsteadily, concentrating intensely. Without warning, he lost his balance, and as he fell backward she was pulled forward, landing squarely on top of him. Almost nose to nose, she exclaimed, "Walker Garrett! You did that on purpose, didn't you!"

"What? No! I didn't—I wouldn't—I—" he blushed furiously as they scrambled to their feet. "I don't think roller skating is for me. Maybe I should just—"

"We are not quitting! Absolutely not! I'm going to teach you to roller skate if it's the last thing I do!" With Kate on one side and William on the other, Walker painfully made several rounds of the rink, until he was finally moving on his own. Gradually he gained confidence, and speed, enjoying the wind in his hair. *I'm getting pretty good at this,* he thought. As he completed another trip around the floor, he saw Kate and William on the bench, removing their skates.

"Come on, Walker," she called. "Let's go get something to eat!"

"How do I stop?" he called back, approaching rapidly. He aimed for the gap in the railing, and almost made it. He slammed into the rail and doubled over it, landing on his back in front of the bench.

"Not like that," she replied, looking down at him with an arched eyebrow. "I'll teach you that next time."

Later in the day, they went to the bath house and rented swim suits. Walker donned the knee-length shorts and tank-top, thinking it was strange to swim wearing clothes, and in the presence of females, no less. Nevertheless, the cool water was a welcome relief from the afternoon heat. He and William swam out to the middle of the lake and back. Women's swimwear was too voluminous for swimming, so the ladies had to be content with wading near the shore. Kate, standing in waist-deep water, scowled as they returned.

"I think it's stupid for women to have to wear these bloomers in the water," she fumed. "Why do you men get to swim, and I have to just wade like a little child?"

"Same reason why men get to vote, and women don't," William grinned. That was clearly not the best thing to say. Kate's chin jutted forward and her eyes flashed like lightning. She took a deep breath and was about to give William a high-volume tongue-lashing, but he laughed and held up his hands. "It was a joke, Kate! You know I don't agree with it, any more than you do. Women will get the vote some-day, and you'll get to swim, too. All in good time!"

"Hmph!" she scoffed. "If it wasn't for bicycles, we girls would still be stuck inside the house, wearing corsets and doing needlework." She turned to Walker. "What do you think about it, Walker? Do you think women should vote?"

"There was a time when I would have laughed at the idea," Walker said. "But while I was with the army in the Philippines and in China, I saw women who were incredibly brave and selfless, risking their lives to help others. They were as brave as any man, and they changed my thinking. I now know that a woman can do anything a man can do—including riding bicycles and roller skating—and even voting!"

Mollified, Kate smiled. "Thank you, Walker. I knew you were smart."

William studied Walker for a few seconds and then asked, "You were in the Philippines and *China*? How's that?"

Walker explained briefly that he had fought in Cuba, and had then been sent to the Philippines, and then to China during the Boxer Rebellion. "I got to see a lot of the world," he shrugged, "but I don't recommend doing it that way."

"Is that how you got that scar?" she asked, pointing to his cheek. "And that notch in your ear? And that one on your shoulder? And this one on your arm?"

"And a few more that you can't see," he said, uncomfortably. He suddenly felt that his scars made him ugly, and he looked away, his hands moving unconsciously to cover them.

Seeing this, she touched his arm. "You must be very brave, Walker," she said. "Our oldest brother, James, was in the navy during the war, and died in Hong Kong last year. I admire anyone who fought for our country."

"Me too," added William. "I hope you don't mind if I ask—what about those two rows of scars on your left arm? It looks almost like something really big bit you."

"Maybe I'll tell you that story sometime," Walker said softly. "For now, let's just say that there are some really big snakes in the jungle over there." Their eyes widened, and Kate put a hand on her stomach as if she felt nauseated. "Let's head back to town, if you don't mind," he suggested. "This has been an amazing day, and I'm plumb tuckered out."

Arriving back at the Saxton-McKinley House, Walker went around to the front porch, where Stover was standing his post at the front door. Painfully climbing the steps, he asked, "Anything exciting happen today?"

"Not hardly," replied Stover. "You look like you've had it pretty rough, though."

"I feel like I've been wrasslin' a wild pig, and lost." He twisted and stretched, as his back cracked audibly. "You ever been roller skating?"

"Do I look like a fool?" scoffed Stover. "You'll never get me up on those demon wheels. No sir, I'm perfectly happy here on the porch."

Just then came the sound of a series of loud bangs and pops, and a steam-powered automobile dashed around the corner and hissed to a jerking stop in front of the house. Walker stared in disbelief as he recognized the passenger.

"Is that—?" he pointed.

"Yup," nodded Stover impassively. "The president went for a ride."

McKinley exited the car in much the same unsteady manner as Walker had done earlier at the roller coaster. The driver sped off, his machine banging and popping as he went, leaving a trail of smoke behind. The president walked slowly toward the house, his hands out to each side, palms down, as if balancing himself. When he reached the porch, Walker asked, "Sir, do you need a hand up the steps?"

"Thank you, Walker, but I believe I can manage." Taking deep breaths and exhaling noisily, he reached the top successfully, and turned to gaze back toward the street. "Mr. Stanley is overoptimistic, I think, when he says those things will someday replace horses." With a shake of his head, he disappeared inside the house.

Walker kept his eyes fixed on the street, careful not to look at Stover for fear that he would burst into laughter. *I guess that's how I looked to Kate and William today,* he thought. *We all need time to get used to new things.* It occurred to him suddenly that all of these new things used wheels. *Kate said bicycles changed life for girls. Automobiles will change it for everyone. Wheels are changing the world,* he mused. *Horses don't have a chance.*

After pondering these profound thoughts for a moment, he turned to Stover. "Wheels," he said reflectively, and paused.

Stover eyed him skeptically. "What about them?"

"They're pretty revolutionary, don't you think?"

Stover snorted involuntarily. "Garrett, that's the dumbest thing I've heard you say yet. You need to stay away from that roller skating rink. You must've banged your head."

"Well, it makes a lot of sense to me," Walker shrugged. "I'm going to get cleaned up for supper. See you in a little while." He descended the steps and crossed the street to the Farmer's Hotel, being sure to look both ways in case a bicycle or automobile might be coming.

11

GOOD-BYE AND HELLO

Walker stood on the front porch of the Saxton-McKinley House, idly watching traffic on Market Avenue, his thumbs hooked behind his belt buckle. To pass the time, he had already counted twenty bicycles, two automobiles, nine horse-riders, and a dozen horse-drawn wagons and carriages. *Not bad,* he thought, *considering that it's not even mid-morning yet. If this keeps up, it'll be a new record.*

The door opened behind him, and Kate stepped to the threshold. "Walker, would you mind helping me for just a minute, please?" He was delighted, of course, and immediately forgot about counting traffic and followed her into the house. There was a rolling cart at the foot of the spiral staircase, bearing two covered trays.

"This is Martha's day off, and the lift is out of order," she explained. "Mama said for me to take Aunt Ida's breakfast up to her, and I can't carry both trays up the stairs, especially not in this long skirt."

"Say no more," replied Walker, gallantly. "I'll be glad to help." He thought it seemed a bit late for breakfast, but decided that it wasn't any of his business. They each took a tray and ascended the stairs to the third floor. Mrs. McKinley sat in an armchair by a window, with a lap rug over her knees. Walker had not seen her since they arrived in Canton, almost two months ago, and he thought she was looking well. Kate positioned a small table in front of her, and put the dishes on it, removing the silver domes to release clouds of steam from the hot food.

"Why, if it isn't Agent Walker Garrett!" the First Lady smiled. "I haven't had a chance to talk with you since San Antonio. Do sit down! How are you doing?"

"I'm doing very well, thank you, ma'am. Kate and William have been keeping me busy whenever I'm not standing post. You look like you've made a complete recovery!"

"Yes, I think that awful infection is finally behind me. I nearly died, you know! It's so embarrassing to have caused everyone so much trouble, and I'm looking forward to being more active now." She lifted some scrambled eggs with her fork. "I hope you'll pardon my rudeness if I eat while we talk."

Kate did most of the talking, chattering brightly about the fun they'd had while riding the bicycles about town and countryside. She regaled her aunt with accounts of Walker's misadventures at Meyers Lake, and shared bits of local gossip. "Aunt Ida—did you know that Walker is writing a book about his travels around the world?" She reached over and patted his arm, beaming. "He's been across both the Pacific and Atlantic Oceans, across China and Russia and Europe —I want to travel too! I want to take a tour of Europe like you did before you got married. Wasn't that just the most wonderful thing to do!"

Pushing her empty plate back and touching her lips with a napkin, Mrs. McKinley nodded. "Yes, my dear! It was an amazing experience, and I so hope that you and your sisters can do something like it, also. Be sure to do it before you marry, though! After that, you won't have the freedom to do as you please."

Walker decided that it was a good time for him to get back downstairs, but as he began to rise to his feet, he noticed a large basket on the other side of McKinley's chair. It was full of crocheted slippers. He did a double-take and almost sat back down. Noticing this, the

First Lady smiled. "See what I do with my time, Walker? I crochet slippers and donate them to charities, like orphanages and hospitals."

"I see—" Walker said hesitantly. "So, you make slippers for the orphans and sick people?"

"Not exactly," she laughed. "Some people will pay a lot of money for a pair of slippers crocheted by the First Lady. The charity can auction the slippers and use the money to support its cause. I've crocheted almost three thousand pairs since I became First Lady. It may not be much, but I do what I can."

"Three thousand pairs!" Walker exclaimed in astonishment. "That is amazing! *You* are amazing, ma'am—I had no idea! That's just —just—" he groped for words.

"That's enough, Walker," she interrupted, putting her hand out to motion for quiet. "Thank you, though." Then, continuing in a serious vein, she gave him a direct look. "Before you go, Walker, I want to thank you for helping protect my husband. I worry about him every day. It gives me great comfort to know that brave men such as you are watching out for him. Please be on your guard!"

"Don't you worry, Mrs. McKinley. We'll take good care of your husband."

She frowned. "Don't make promises you can't keep. I know you will do your best, but look at what has been happening across Europe. Kings, czars, emperors, empresses—so many have been assassinated by anarchists. Russia, Italy, France, Spain, Germany— they are everywhere! And so many immigrants from those countries are pouring into America—can we really believe that none of these murderers have come here? We've had two presidents assassinated in less than forty years, and I desperately fear that my William may be next! I did not want him to be reelected, but he felt that he had to do it for the country." She wrung her hands anxiously. "Just be watchful! Don't let them hurt him!" And she dabbed at her eyes with the napkin.

"Yes ma'am," he said quietly, feeling very uncomfortable. "I promise that we will do our very best to keep him safe." She squeezed his hand, and he returned downstairs alone, leaving Kate with her aunt. Back on the porch, he heaved a troubled sigh. *If she only knew how close her husband has already come, so many times! A Confederate minie ball in Memphis. A palm pistol in El Paso. Dynamite in Los Angeles. A mounted gunman in Washington. But for the grace of God, he would already be dead and buried. I just hope our luck holds out.*

A few days later, the McKinley entourage gathered on the platform of the train station, preparing to leave. The original plan had been for the McKinleys to finish their western tour by stopping in Buffalo, New York on the way back, for the Pan-American Exposition. Mrs. McKinley's illness had prevented that, causing them to cut the tour short and return directly to Washington. Now that she was much improved, they had decided to go from Canton to Buffalo and attend the Exposition.

The McKinleys bade farewell to family and friends at their house. Walker and Stover spent the morning transporting baggage and loading it onto the four-car train, and he did not have a chance to say good-bye to William or Kate. With everyone finally on the train, it was time to pull out of the station. Tight-lipped and glum, Walker stood on the step, holding the handle of the collapsible door, and took one last sweeping look around the platform. Just as the train whistle sounded a final warning, he caught a glimpse of a figure sprinting madly from the stairwell. It was Kate—rosy-cheeked, with hair flying. Judging from her outfit, she had ridden her bicycle to the station. The train jerked and began to move, but she was faster, and caught up to Walker.

"Walker!" she shouted breathlessly. "Take this!" She pulled a small, crumpled violet-colored envelope from her belt and held it out as she ran alongside the train. He took it and, holding onto the door handle, leaned as far out as he could and kissed her on the top of her head.

"I'll miss you!" he called, as she slowed to a walk. She put her fingers to her lips and blew him a kiss, and then stood waving. Walker thought he saw her wipe a tear from her cheek. The train left the station behind, but Walker stayed in the gangway between cars for several minutes. Putting Kate's envelope in his pocket to read later, he blew his nose and washed his face in the lavatory, feeling deeply saddened at the parting. When he felt ready, he entered the car and slid into the seat beside Stover, who gave him a curious look.

"You alright, Garrett?"

Walker sighed. "Yeah. I'm alright." He didn't sound convincing. Stover watched him for a few seconds, and then, with a barely perceptible smile, said, "You're going to love Niagara Falls. You've never seen anything like it!"

Grateful for the diversion, Walker replied, "Tell me about it."

"It's like thunder, except that it never stops," Stover began, using both hands to paint a picture in the air. He went on for quite a while. Walker nodded frequently, but his heart ached and his mind was back at the Canton train station.

Most of the train's route ran along the shore of Lake Erie, and the water was in sight most of the time. Walker was duly impressed with the size of the lake, and Stover was not irritated when he compared it to Lake Baikal, in Russia. "On a clear day, you can sometimes see all the way across to Canada," Stover noted, "at least at the eastern end, which is narrower."

Late that afternoon, the train slowed as it approached the station in Buffalo. "Well, it's back to work," said Stover. "I didn't know I was going to be a part-time baggage handler, as well as a presidential bodyguard."

"I know what you mean," Walker nodded. "Not very flattering, is it?"

They moved into the gangway, waiting for the train to stop. Stover turned to Walker and said gravely, "You got attached to the president's little niece, didn't you?"

"Yeah, I did. She's something special."

"I'm sure she is. But it won't work. You know that, right?"

"What do you mean?" Walker's face reddened.

"It's just a fact. Her kind is not for the likes of you and me. She's from a rich family, and her uncle is the President of the United States. I'm sure she likes you, too, but don't make the mistake of trying to hold onto something you can't keep. Remember it, but let it go."

Walker's eyes narrowed and his nostrils flared. Stover held up both hands defensively. "Don't get angry with me, Garrett. I'm just giving you good advice. You're young, and I don't want to see you get messed up."

"Thanks," said Walker gruffly. "I'll think about it."

Stover nodded and slapped him on the back. "Let's hit the ground running," he said, and pulled the door open as the train hissed to a stop.

To Walker's surprise, the party was not staying at a hotel in Buffalo, but at a private residence. An old friend of McKinley's, John Milburn, was the president of the Pan-American Exposition, and had offered the use of his large home. To Walker's further surprise, Dixon was already at the house when they arrived. Walker gripped the handle of a heavy suitcase in one hand, and bent his knees to reach for the handle of another with the other hand, when a familiar voice spoke right behind him.

"Don't try to show off, Garrett! One is enough!"

Setting the suitcase down, he turned to see Dixon grinning at him. "Leave something for the rest of us to do, cracker!"

"When did you get here, stranger?"

"Just a couple of hours ago. We got a little room at the back of the house, as usual."

"Fine with me! Good to see you!" Walker smiled for the first time that day. He hadn't realized how much he had missed Dixon over the past two months. Suddenly, he was already starting to feel like his old self again.

After supper, Foster gave the agents their duty assignments. Mainly, they would stand guard at the doors, on a rotating basis, whenever the president was in the house. Local police would patrol the streets around the neighborhood. In addition to detachments of soldiers and police, all of the agents would accompany the president to his scheduled events at the Exposition the following day, and to Niagara Falls on Friday. Security would be tight. For the night's assignments, Walker drew the first shift, and when Stover relieved him just before midnight, he tiptoed quietly into the room he shared with Dixon. Dixon was sleeping soundly, so he did not turn on the light, and went to bed without having read Kate's note.

When he awoke the next morning, Dixon was still at his post, having relieved Stover in the early hours. Taking advantage of a few minutes of privacy, he opened the pastel violet envelope and extracted the folded paper. Leaning toward the window to catch the early morning light, he bent over the note and devoured its message eagerly.

> *My dear Walker,*
>
> *Having you here has made this the best summer of my life. I wish you did not have to go, but I know you must. It makes me happy to know that Uncle William is being protected by you! I hope you can come back sometime. Stay safe!*
>
> *With warmest affection,*
> *Kate*

Walker smiled, and then he grinned. *Who says it can't work? We'll see about that!* Hearing footsteps approaching the door, he quickly folded the note and tucked the envelope into his duffel bag, just as the door opened.

"Let's grab some breakfast," Dixon said. "We got a big day ahead of us!"

"Right behind you!" Walker grinned. "I'm ready for it!"

12

THE UNTHINKABLE

The events of Thursday, September 5, reminded Walker of the western rail tour. Rows of colorfully-uniformed soldiers, mounted police escorts, brass bands playing patriotic music, thousands of flags waving—and, of course, massive crowds of cheering citizens—it was an emotional celebration of such intensity that it seemed at times to be on the verge of losing control. The escorts had to force the crowd aside to allow McKinley's carriage to pass. Walker concluded that the only threat to the president was not from a would-be assassin, but from the possibility that the crowd itself would, in its enthusiasm, sweep over him and cause him injury. *If anyone tried to harm the president, this crowd would tear him to pieces,* he thought. *Mrs. McKinley can relax—her husband is safe here!*

The president, accompanied by the First Lady, Milburn, Cortelyou, and other officials proceeded to visit the exhibits in the various buildings. At noon they enjoyed a sumptuous luncheon with dignitaries, after which the crowd waiting outside cheered itself hoarse as they caught sight of the party exiting the building. A military band performed a concert as McKinley inspected some large artillery pieces. By late afternoon, the exhausted couple returned to the

Milburn House to rest and have dinner. The activities of the day were as nothing, however, compared to what took place that evening.

They returned to the park as twilight was descending to experience the daily highlight of the Exposition—a spectacle known simply as the "Illumination." Tens of thousands of visitors jammed the Midway, expectantly watching the Electric Tower which rose in the center of the park. John Philip Sousa's band played patriotic music as the crowd gathered and the presidential party was escorted to its place. Finally, when the sun was completely gone, the lights in the park were all suddenly turned off and the thousands of spectators became perfectly silent in the darkness, holding their breath in anticipation. It began with a faint, pink glow, like the approach of dawn, and grew in intensity until, within seconds, blinding light burst forth from the Tower in a blaze of glory, as the multitude collectively gasped in awe. The Tower itself was a riot of color, with hundreds of thousands of colored lights outlining its every facet.

The crowd buzzed with quiet fascination for several minutes, absorbing the scene to scattered applause. And then as a special treat due to the president's visit, the lights were dimmed and fireworks began exploding overhead. The massive rockets boomed like artillery shells, creating artistic pictures in vivid colors. With each thunderous eruption, the crowd roared with excitement, faces turned upward, illuminated by the spectrum of brilliant light. It seemed to Walker that it would never end, but at last, the ground-shaking grand finale faded into darkness, and all was quiet. Without delay, the president's carriage drove quickly from the park, and headed back once again to the Milburn House. Walker was glad to have his perch on the rear step of the carriage, and to not have to contend with the crowd.

His nerves tingling and ears ringing, Walker doubted that he would be able to go to sleep any time soon. Fortunately, he had the first shift again, and spent the next few hours alone at the front of the house, thankful for the quiet and semi-darkness. He gazed up at the stars, noting that they were not nearly as numerous as when viewed away from the city. He smiled as he remembered how, on his foreign travels, he had often drawn comfort and inspiration from the stunning heavenly display. Even now, he still felt a sense of smallness and humbling insignificance in the presence of such incomprehensible vastness. *I know you're still out there, even if I can't see all of you,* he thought. *No matter what changes down here, some things will never change, and I'm going to hold onto those things.* The reality of the unseen was an intriguing concept to Walker, and he became so absorbed in these reflections that he was actually disappointed when Stover came to relieve him, and it was time to go to bed.

The next morning, the president and a group of about a hundred guests boarded a special train to visit Niagara Falls. The train consisted entirely of parlor cars—equivalent to first-class accommodations, far superior to the common coach. Each passenger had an individual, roomy, plush seat in an attractively decorated car, and refreshments were served continuously. Walker, Dixon, and Stover settled into seats at the end of the last car. Slurping a swallow of lemonade from a frosted glass, Walker closed his eyes and purred in satisfaction.

"I like traveling with the president!" he exclaimed. "This is nice!"

"Beats the colored car all to pieces," nodded Dixon. At this, Stover snorted his lemonade and proceeded to suffer a violent coughing fit which lasted a whole minute, leaving him red-faced and teary-eyed. When he finally regained his composure, Dixon gave him a raised eyebrow and said, "If you don't believe me, just try it."

"Try what?" asked Stover hoarsely, as he raised his glass to his lips again.

"The colored car," replied Dixon. Stover snorted his lemonade again, and had another coughing fit, until lemonade came out his nose. Other passengers were turning to look at him, so he got up and went out into the gangway, where he could still be heard coughing and wheezing.

"What was it like, spending two months with him in Canton?" asked Dixon.

"Not bad at all," shrugged Walker. "He snores, but other than that, it was alright. I like him." Sipping lemonade, he added, "Canton was nice, too. I got to be good friends with a nephew and a niece of the

McKinleys. We rode bicycles a lot." Dixon nodded and did not appear inclined to say anything, so Walker continued, "Are Beulah and Daisy coming to Washington?"

"Already there. Found a house for all of us, a couple of streets over from Reverend Wright's house. Mama's already got a position as cook for a good family, and Miss Hannah's helping Daisy get ready for school to start."

"Well! You *have* been busy, haven't you! I can't wait to see them, and eat some of your mama's cooking!"

Just then, Stover reentered the car and sat down. Giving Dixon a warning look, he picked up his lemonade glass and, pausing halfway to his mouth to make sure Dixon wasn't going to say something, he took a quick drink.

"See? That wasn't so hard, was it?" asked Dixon mischievously.

Apparently Stover hadn't actually swallowed yet, and he immediately began heaving, hyperventilating through flared nostrils, and finally, putting the glass back to his mouth, he spat the lemonade back into it. He set the glass down loudly, pushed it away, and raised his hands in surrender. "I give up," he said, shaking his head. "I can't drink anything with you around."

The three laughed together, and Walker said, "Stover knows all about Niagara Falls. Tell Dixon what you told me. It sounds really exciting."

"It's like thunder, except it never stops," Stover began, repeating most of what he had told Walker two days before. His monologue lasted until the train reached its destination.

Carriages were waiting for them, and the entire party enjoyed a drive to Prospect Park and Goat Island. They had a good view of the American Falls, the Bridal Veil Falls, and of course, the famous Horseshoe Falls. Rainbows shimmered in the dense mist, and the noise was just like Stover had described—thunderous. Walker was awestruck, and had to keep reminding himself that he was not there to see the sights, but to guard the president. The agents were careful to stay close enough to the presidential couple to provide protection, but not close enough to interfere with their socializing. After a luncheon at a hotel, the party visited an electrical power generating station, and then boarded the train back to Buffalo.

McKinley had one more item on his schedule for the day—a hand-shaking reception at the Temple of Music. Cortelyou had tried twice to cancel this event, for security reasons, but the president insisted on keeping it—meeting the public was one of his favorite things about being the president. Mrs. McKinley went to the Milburn House to rest while he returned to the park for the reception. Afterward, he was to join her for a dinner at the home of a supporter.

Despite the late afternoon heat, a very large crowd waited patiently outside the doors of the Temple of Music. Soldiers and policemen kept everyone out while the finishing touches were applied inside. Potted plants lined the path from the entrance to the exit. The president took his place in front of a large, draped American flag, flanked by Cortelyou and Milburn. Other dignitaries formed a line, with police and soldiers also close by. The Secret Service agents positioned themselves as close as they could get, chafing at the crowd around the president. The magnificent pipe organ began playing a composition by Johann Sebastian Bach. Walker thought that a more cheerful piece of music would have been better.

When everything was set, a signal was given, and the doors were opened. The eager admirers came, single-file, flowing between the potted plants, sweeping toward the president. Walker glanced at McKinley and saw him smiling warmly as he extended his hand to the first person in line. *He really does enjoy this,* Walker thought. *He really does care about the people. And they really do care about him.*

McKinley had a practiced method for shaking hands. Reaching out with his right hand, he would take the greeter's extended hand and, cupping their elbow with his left, pull them forward as he smiled and thanked them for coming, and simultaneously reached for the next person's hand. With his politician's efficiency, he could shake fifty hands a minute.

Walker watched a little girl present her doll to the president to shake his hand. His eyes twinkling with pleasure, McKinley shook hands with the doll, and then took his signature red carnation from his lapel and presented it to the child, and patted her head as he turned to the next in line. *I've never seen so much love showered on anyone as this,* Walker marveled. *And he loves them back. No wonder the crowds go wild whenever they see him.*

Standing only a few feet away, Walker kept a close eye on the people in the line, watchful for any indication of danger. As a swarthy, foreign-looking man reached the president, Walker took a step forward, ready to pounce, but the man moved on without incident, and he relaxed. The next person in line was a boyish-looking young man. He had a handkerchief draped over his right hand, which appeared to be injured, as he held it awkwardly against his stomach. He reached out to the president with his left hand. Normally, people who approached the president were required to have their hands visible and empty, but due to the heat, many carried handkerchiefs, and the rule was not being enforced. McKinley accommodatingly reached out with his left hand to grasp the other man's hand. That's when it happened.

From under the handkerchief came the explosion of a gunshot, followed quickly by a second. The handkerchief caught fire from the muzzle blast, and the gunman raised the weapon to fire a third shot, but was prevented by being knocked to the floor by the next man in line—a powerful, six-foot six-inch tall black man. Walker immediately secured the firearm. The scene was wild, and soldiers gave the young man a severe beating, leaving a small puddle of his blood on the floor.

The organ music stopped and screams of fear and confusion erupted from the crowd, both inside and outside the building. Those inside tried to flee, while those outside tried to push in to see what had happened. It was chaos for several minutes, but guards at the doors prevented anyone from entering, and the soldiers and policemen ushered those already inside to the exits as quickly as possible—in some cases, at bayonet point.

McKinley staggered backward, stunned, his hand going to his large stomach, where a growing red circle appeared. He was assisted to a nearby chair, as pandemonium ensued.

"I done my duty," rasped the gunman, roughly held between two soldiers, as he spat blood on the floor. He was quickly hustled out a side door and taken to the nearest police precinct.

The president was promptly taken in an electric-powered ambulance to the infirmary to be treated for his wounds. As the ambulance made its hurried departure, escorted by mounted police, the crowd outside gave an audible, collective groan and stood in shock, not knowing where to go or what to do. Eventually they straggled away and the music hall, which only moments earlier had been busy with life and energy, was then empty and silent.

13

THE FACE OF A KILLER

Walker stationed himself at the entrance to the infirmary. A small, curious crowd began to gather, but he made it clear that no one was allowed to enter. Hearing a quiet step behind him, he glanced over his shoulder.

"Well, if that don't just beat all!" Dixon joined him in the doorway. "And just as I was startin' to think that this was an easy day, too."

"You ain't kidding," agreed Walker. "What kind of man shoots the president in public in broad daylight with guards all around? He's got to be crazy as a loon."

"He didn't look crazy, though," demurred Dixon. "Did you hear what he said? 'I done my duty.' I'd like to know what he meant by that."

"Maybe we'll find out, if they don't beat him to death at the jail."

"They just might, if the president dies in here. This ain't a real hospital, and it ain't a real operating room, and the real doctor is out of town. They got a doctor that normally takes care of pregnant women working on him. It don't look good, if you ask me."

"Looks like we may be here for a while, then," Walker sighed, removing his fedora to brush an unruly lock of hair out of his eyes. "Might as well get comfortable."

. . .

Despite concerns raised for his safety, McKinley had insisted on personally greeting the public. "No one would want to hurt me!" he had laughed. And yet, now he lay on the operating table as the doctor probed his stomach in search of the bullets that had struck him.

The surgery was completed as the sun was setting. Ironically, despite the Exposition featuring the many uses of electricity, there was no electricity in the makeshift operating room, and lighting was improvised by holding up a bed pan by the window to reflect the fading sunlight onto the patient.

The ambulance carried him to the Milburn House, where he was attended by nurses and his wife. Soldiers and police surrounded the house, giving it the appearance of a military camp. Telegraph machines were installed in the living room, and tents were set up around the house for the multitude of reporters who gathered. Large oxygen tanks were carried into the president's bedroom on the second floor to assist with his labored breathing, and electric fans circulated the air to keep him comfortable. The Milburn family relocated to a downtown hotel so that the entire house could be used for the president's needs. A steady stream of visiting dignitaries passed through over the next few days, as the president's condition permitted.

Walker and Dixon stood at the front door of the ivy-covered stone and brick mansion, surveying the busy scene. The door opened behind them and Foster stepped out. His rigid expression indicated the immense strain he felt, and his tight voice failed to conceal the pain he carried. "There's not much that you two can do here," he said. "Stover's with me. Go get yourselves something to eat. I'll see you tomorrow morning, and we'll figure out where to go from here."

"How is the president, sir?" asked Walker.

"And how are *you* doing, sir?" added Dixon. "You don't look so good."

"The president is resting. They couldn't find one of the bullets, but the doctor thinks it won't be a problem. It's a wait-and-see situation right now, so don't talk to any reporters." Foster ignored Dixon's question.

"Yes sir," nodded Walker. "Mum's the word."

"By the way," added Foster, "you won't be able to sleep here tonight. This place is filling up with political, medical, and military people. No room at the inn, I'm afraid—not even in the stable. You'll have to find a place for yourselves. Get a receipt."

"Will do. And you take care of yourself too, sir."

Foster's only response was to turn and go back inside the house. As the door shut, Walker's and Dixon's eyes met, and they both immediately shook their heads.

"He looks like he's on the edge," said Dixon. "I've never seen him so tight."

"I guess it's understandable. He probably feels responsible. I sure hope the president recovers, or Foster might just—I don't know what, but it won't be pretty."

They decided against going back into the Exposition grounds to find a meal. Strolling through the nearby business district, they found a small diner with a somewhat dingy façade and a working-class menu. After downing a bowl of beef stew and dark bread, they sat quietly at a corner table and relaxed.

Suddenly, something occurred to Walker. "Say, do you remember what that gypsy fortune teller in New Orleans said? 'Beware Ehud, the left-handed assassin! He will do his duty!' How could she have known this would happen?"

"Garrett! Don't go crazy on me. That old hag didn't know nuthin' about nuthin'. It's just a bunch of gibberish. That's all!"

"How can you say that? She said we were protecting the 'fat king', and President McKinley is pretty heavy. And that fella reached out to shake hands with his *left hand*! And he said 'I done my duty.' You heard him! That's too much for coincidence!"

"So you think she predicted the future? Nobody can do that."

"Then how do you account for her saying those things? Don't it seem really strange to you?"

"Yes, I admit it's strange. I can't account for it. I just don't believe in it, that's all. And even if it's true that she predicted this, there ain't nuthin' we can do about it now. It's done happened."

"True," Walker frowned. "It happened. Maybe we should have been paying more attention, I don't know. I just think we failed at our job. I'm feeling really bad about this."

"We all feel bad about it. But second-guessing ourselves ain't goin' to help anything. Nobody in the crowd noticed him having a gun. That sneaky rat got past the guards at the door, and all the soldiers and police between the president and the door. By the time he reached McKinley, we didn't have a chance to stop him. It was too late."

"Maybe," Walker muttered. "I just know I can't go back to Canton. I let them down. I sure hope he pulls through."

The restaurant was only about half full. The other patrons were locals, dressed in rough working clothes, some with muddy boots and sooty faces. Stew and beer seemed to be the universal fare, as no one actually looked at a menu, but merely sat on benches at long tables and waited to be served. They did not pay any attention to Walker and Dixon, although there were a couple of curious glances at Dixon. Black men in suits were apparently not a common sight there.

"Say," grunted one, with his mouth full of beef stew, "didja hear what 'appened over to the Exposition today?"

"No—did somebody get fried on all that 'lectricity they got runnin' all over the place?"

"Worse than that—some fool shot the president!"

"You mean President *McKinley*? Are you pullin' my leg?"

"Nope—it's a fact. I heered it was a anarchist, like what shot them European kings and queens. I never thought it'd 'appen here."

"Well, y'know we did have some anarchists threw a bomb at the police in Chicago a few years back. I reckon they're everywhere!"

"Don't s'prise me none. The rich folks got so much and us workers got so little, it ain't no wonder that somebody tries to do somethin' 'bout it. Morgan, Rockefeller, Vanderbilt—them folks got more money than the rest of the country put together. Shoulda shot one of *them*, 'steada the president."

"Maybe somebody will. If a fella can get close enough to the president to shoot *him*, then ain't *nobody* safe no more."

At this point, Walker and Dixon made their exit. It was now dark, and the evening air was much cooler than in the afternoon. There was little traffic, and gas lights were only on the street corners, casting long shadows. After walking about for over an hour without finding any available lodging, they began to think that they were going to have to sleep in a field or sneak into someone's hay loft. Turning a corner, they found themselves standing in front of a police precinct headquarters.

"Reckon they got any spare beds in there?" Dixon laughed.

"Well, it wouldn't be the first time we spent a night in jail," grinned Walker. They had found themselves in a cell in Moscow, Russia, during their journey around the world. It was probably the low-point of their adventures, and Walker had been sure he was destined for a Siberian labor camp.

"You got any better ideas?" Dixon sounded serious.

Walker shrugged. "Can't hurt to ask, I guess."

Stepping inside, they went to the front desk and were greeted brusquely by a burly, red-haired sergeant. "What d'you want?"

"We're Secret Service agents," Walker said, and they showed their Secret Service badges for his inspection. He blinked and looked at them critically for a few seconds, and then repeated, "What do you want?"

"As you know," Walker continued, "the president was shot today. He is recovering at the Milburn House, which is where we were staying, but now we need somewhere to spend the night. Do you have any spare beds we could use?"

"What the hell do you think this is, a *hotel*?" the sergeant roared in disbelief. Over his shoulder, he yelled, "Hey Cap'n! Get a load of this! Two Secret Service agents want to sleep here t'night!"

A tall, bony-faced police captain emerged from an office and came to the counter. Other policemen appeared from nowhere, gathering around them, and Walker and Dixon suddenly felt that they were being stared at like a circus side-show. The captain gave them a long frowning look, and then smiled broadly—a bit maliciously, Walker thought.

"Why, yes, we *do* have spare beds," he said in a tone that made Walker uneasy. "It's a cell with four bunks in it and only one prisoner, so you'll have your choice of beds.

"Sergeant," he continued in a voice dripping with sarcasm, "show our guests to Cell Number Five. Since it's the Secret Service's responsibility to protect the president, I think this is the perfect place for them to spend the night." The group of policemen burst into laughter, clapping one another on the back as they hooted with glee.

"Follow me," sneered the red-haired sergeant, and, taking a ring of large keys, he led them down a corridor lined with iron-barred cell doors on each side. Walker could see shadowy figures in the cells as they passed. Halfway down the corridor the sergeant stopped and unlocked a cell door. Gesturing magnanimously, he waved them to enter.

"Dinner will be served shortly," he said, and laughed as he clanged the door shut behind them. The laughter of the other officers could still be heard until the squeaky door at the end of the corridor was slammed shut, and then it was remarkably quiet. Three naked light bulbs spaced down the corridor provided limited light.

Walker and Dixon sat down on an empty lower bunk. The other lower bunk was occupied by an ordinary-looking young man, who lay with his face to the wall. After a long moment of silence, Walker spoke softly. "Hey mister, are you awake?"

There was no response.

"We're Secret Service. Our job is to protect the president," offered Dixon.

This produced an immediate reaction, as the man rolled over and twisted into a sitting position so quickly that he seemed to be almost in a panic. He brought his knees up in front of him, feet on the bunk, and held his hands up palms outward, defensively.

"I been beat enough. I done my duty—that's all I done. Don't beat me no more." He wasn't whining or begging, but spoke simply, as if merely stating facts. Even in the dim light, the bruises on his face were plainly visible, and his upper lip looked swollen.

Walker and Dixon stared at each other. "So that's what the captain meant," Walker muttered out the side of his mouth. "The 'perfect place' for us to spend the night."

Dixon exhaled with a whistling sound. "No, we're not going to beat you. We would like to talk to you, though."

"I got nothing to say to you. I done my duty. That's all. Leave me alone."

"What do you mean, 'you done your duty?'" asked Walker. "How was it your duty to shoot the president?"

"The government only serves the rich. It oppresses the poor. Capitalism exploits the working man. Everything is for the rich man." The words came spilling out rapidly, as if repeating a well-rehearsed story. The man leaned forward, fists clenched, as he ranted. "McKinley never done nothing for the working man, so I killed him. He got what he deserved! He was the enemy of the good people—the good working people. I am not sorry for what I done, though I am sorry for Mrs. McKinley. I would have shot more, but somebody hit me in the face, and then everybody jumped on me."

"Are you an anarchist?" asked Walker.

"I am an anarchist. I don't believe in voting; it is against my principles. I don't believe in marriage; I believe in free love. I don't believe in one man having so much service, and another man should have none. We anarchists believe in the 'propaganda of the deed.' Actions speak louder than words, and an act of violence does more to expose the injustice of society than making a speech or writing a book. When people understand why I shot the president, they will see the truth!"

"Some folks might say you're crazy," observed Dixon skeptically.

"I am not insane. I fully understood what I was doing. I planned it all very careful. I realized that I was sacrificing my life, and I am willing to take the consequences. I made up my mind several months ago that all rulers must be exterminated, and I determined to do something for the cause I love. You may not understand it or agree with it, but I'm not crazy."

"No, I dcn't think you are," Dixon replied thoughtfully. "I *don't* understand or agree with you, but you're clearly not crazy. Honestly, I kinda wish you *were*."

Just then the door at the end of the corridor opened with a long, ear-piercing screech, and a voice called out, "Supper time, losers!" A cart with a squeaky wheel was pushed slowly down the shadowy corridor, and metal bowls of food were passed through slots in the bottom of the cell doors.

Walker picked up one of the bowls that were slid into their cell. "Well, Dixon, looks like this is our lucky day—cold beef stew and stale crackers!"

"Just push my bowl back out."

"Let me have it," said the anarchist quickly. "I'm starving."

"You can have all three, if you want 'em," replied Walker, pushing the bowls toward him on the floor. "By the way, what's your name?"

"Czolgosz. Leon Czolgosz," he answered, as he began hungrily spooning stew into his mouth. "It's Polish," he added.

"I thought all anarchist assassins were Italian," said Walker.

"Not anymore," smirked Czolgosz, with his mouth full.

"McKinley may not die, you know," Walker probed. "Apparently, only one of your bullets actually went into him. They patched him up at the infirmary."

"He'll die. It may take a few days, but he'll die. Nobody survives a bullet to the belly like that—especially not a fat man."

"So, what will your defense be, if you're not crazy?" asked Dixon.

"I'll plead guilty. They'll hang me. Case closed. Everybody's got to die sometime."

Walker and Dixon were speechless at the man's utter disregard for his own fate. They watched silently as he finished off two and a half bowls of stew and noisily slid them back into the corridor. He belched, stretched, and laid back on the bunk.

"I'm tired of talking," he yawned. "Want to sleep now." Turning his face back to the wall, he was soon snoring lightly.

"Me too," said Dixon. "I call the bottom bunk."

"Sleep tight," frowned Walker, and with a meaningful glance toward the sleeping Czolgosz added, "but not too tight."

"We're not important enough for him to want to kill," murmured Dixon. "No worries there. Besides—" and he tugged at his coat lapel, briefly exposing the handle of the revolver in its shoulder holster.

Walker nodded. "I hope you're right."

Walker climbed up into the top bunk and tried to find a comfortable position among the lumps of the thin mattress. With no bedsheet and no pillow, it did not promise to be a restful night. He placed his hat over his eyes to block out the dim light from the corridor and tried to turn off his brain. It took a while, but he finally found sleep.

14

A LIFE IN THE BALANCE

The president's condition slowly improved over the next few days, and the doctors were cautiously optimistic that the worst was past. The Milburn House was a veritable beehive of activity as cabinet members and key senators and congressmen arrived to pay their respects and give the presidential couple their best wishes. Even Vice-President Theodore Roosevelt arrived the day after the shooting and quickly left again, as the president's life seemed safe. The nation heaved a collective sigh of relief, and the stream of visiting government officials gradually abated.

Walker and Dixon found more comfortable lodging in the city, and spent most of their time strolling through the Exposition. With the Milburn House surrounded by police and soldiers, there was little else for them to do. They found the exhibits interesting, but not as impressive or varied as those they had seen in Paris the preceding year.

"I'd like to see that cyclorama of Missionary Ridge," commented Walker.

"What the heck is a cyclorama? And what's a Missionary Ridge?"

"I read about it. A cyclorama is a huge painting done in a circle, and you stand in the middle to look at it. This one is sixty feet high and over three hundred feet around. It shows the Civil War battle of Missionary Ridge, which was at Chattanooga."

"Who won?"

Walker, about to reply, shut his mouth abruptly and glared at Dixon.

"That means the Northern boys won, I reckon," smirked Dixon. "Count me in."

Walker scowled. "It might still be interesting to see it. I never saw a painting that big before. If there was just an Eiffel Tower here, this would be a close second place to the Paris Exposition."

"Are you forgetting that you nearly peed your pants up there on that thing?" scoffed Dixon.

"I seem to recall that I wasn't the only one," grinned Walker. "We couldn't get down from there fast enough!"

"And then there was that exhibit about the American Negro. All those colleges, books, and inventions by colored folk—that was very impressive to me."

"That fellow DuBois was impressive!" enthused Walker. "A professor from Harvard! We heard him speak three languages—why, he's probably the smartest man I ever met, next to Roosevelt."

"Roosevelt!" scoffed Dixon. "If he was half as smart as he thinks he is, he'd be the smartest man in the history of the world!"

"Well, look at all the things he's done! He's done more than any other two men, and he's just forty-two and the vice president. General Wheeler predicted he'd become president and change the world. There ain't nobody like Teddy Roosevelt!"

"If he actually done all the things he claims to have done, I'd probably be more impressed. But I was there at San Juan Hill, and I know what really happened. And so do you."

"Well—" was all Walker could think of to say, so he said it again as he searched for a suitable reply. It was true that Roosevelt had claimed the victory was won by himself and his "Rough Riders," despite the key role played by the Tenth Cavalry Regiment of black soldiers. He had almost thought of something to say when Dixon, looking at a tourist map of the Exposition grounds, made a thoughtful "humm?" sound.

"Found something worth going to see?"

"Maybe. Hadn't noticed this before—it's called 'The Old Plantation.' Wonder what that is."

"I heard of that. I picked up a newspaper last evening and saw something. Let me see."

Walker pulled a thin, folded newspaper from his back pants pocket. Fumbling through its pages for a minute, he announced triumphantly, "Here it is!" and began to read aloud.

"Genuine southern darkies, two hundred of them, ranging in years from wee, toddling pickaninnies to negroes, grey and bent with age, can be seen each day at the Exposition at their different occupations and pastimes. Lovers of negro melodies will have a feast. Many of the darkies will be selected because of their special talents as singers and banjo players and they will dance and sing to the seductive tinkling of instruments exactly as the Negroes of the South used to do in the long, long ago."

Dixon stopped and stared at Walker. "Well, if that don't just beat all! What do they think slavery was *like*? Singin', dancin', and playin' a banjo all day? Do they think all that cotton picked itself? What do they think all them slaves was runnin' away *from*? Banjo music?"

"Well, now," said Walker hesitantly, "it does say 'genuine southern darkies,' and says that they are 'selected from the best class of southern darkies.'"

Dixon snatched the newspaper from Walker's hands, wadded it up, and hurled it at a nearby trash can. "Garrett, you will never be nuthin' but a white boy."

"I guess you don't want to go see 'The Old Plantation,' then?"

Dixon knocked Walker's hat off his head with a flick of his hand. Walker spun about and deftly caught it in the air, smoothly returning it to its place. "I'll assume that means 'no,'" he frowned.

"Well, at least you got *one* thing right," Dixon scowled. And then, abruptly he added, "I'm hungry. Let's get something to eat."

"There's a place over there—the Boston Inn."

They seated themselves at a table in a corner and began to examine the menu.

"What might I get for you gen'lmen?" asked a deep voice with a pleasant southern accent.

Looking up they were shocked to recognize the intimidating figure of "Big Ben" James Parker—the tall, muscular black man who had knocked Czolgosz to the floor, preventing him from firing a third shot. Parker had been hailed as a hero ever since the shooting and repeatedly interviewed by reporters. Souvenir hunters had even bought buttons and snips of clothing from him.

"You're Parker, aren't you?" asked Walker. "We're Secret Service agents. I remember you from the Temple of Music. You saved the president's life!"

"Let me shake your hand!" exclaimed Dixon, rising and extending his hand.

Parker seemed genuinely embarrassed. "I tried to do my duty. That's all any man can do," he said humbly. "I'm glad I was able to be of service to the country."

"Where are you from? You don't sound like you're from around here," observed Walker.

"I'm from Georgia—Atlanta, Savannah—I've been around a bit. Worked in Chicago, here and there. Came to Buffalo a few days ago for a job."

"Well, it's a good thing you did! Otherwise, we'd be having a funeral by now!" Dixon said, looking up at the tall black man. "You ever think about working for the Secret Service?"

"No, but I was a constable in Savannah serving warrants, so I'm no stranger to law enforcement. Y'all reckon they'd hire me?"

"Talk to George Foster—he's our boss," nodded Dixon. "Looks to me like you'd be a good candidate!"

"Thank you kindly, brother. I'll keep it in mind. Now, what can I fetch y'all to eat?"

They ordered two bowls of baked beans and sausage, with corn-bread muffins. After Parker had disappeared back into the kitchen, they sat for a moment in silence, contemplating the coincidence of meeting the man they'd heard so much about.

"Did you hear what he said?" asked Dixon. "'I tried to do my duty. That's all any man can do.' Does that remind you of anyone?"

"You mean Czolgosz? 'I done my duty.' That's what *he* said."

Dixon rubbed his eyes. "How can two people have such different ideas about their duty? One man says it's his duty to *kill* the president, and the other man says it's his duty to *save* him. How can that be?"

"I don't know," Walker mused, shaking his head. "Duty is what you're honor-bound to do because it's right. It would be wrong not to do it. How can a man think it would be wrong not to kill someone? That doesn't make sense."

"Depends on what you believe in, I reckon. Czolgosz says he's a anarchist. Don't believe in marriage or voting. Believes the working people are oppressed. Maybe he believes he was honor-bound to do something for the workers."

"Well then, he definitely failed," Walker frowned. "Not only didn't he kill the president, but lots of anarchists have been arrested since the shooting. From what I've read in the papers, they don't agree with what he did, either. Even the working people are calling for his execution. I don't know where he got the idea that it was his duty to shoot the president, but it was the wrong idea."

"Yes suh, it *was* the wrong idea," said the deep voice in that slow, Georgia drawl. So intent had Walker and Dixon been in their discussion that they had not noticed the return of Parker. He placed steaming bowls of beans and sausage in front of them, and a cloth-lined basket of cornbread muffins.

"But those crowds of people 'round the jail hollering for his neck in a noose, they got the wrong idea, too," he continued. "We seen too many lynchings across the South, and other parts of the country. More than a hunnerd a year, every year. It ain't nobody's duty to kill nobody else without a fair trial. It's wrong. We got to start respectin' the law and doing our duty to treat people right, even when we don't agree with them. Otherwise, we're worse than Czolgosz."

"Amen, brother," breathed Dixon softly. Walker just blinked and stared. Parker, suddenly awkward and fearing he'd said too much, turned to attend to other diners, and did not return to their table.

They ate in silence, each deep in thought. Afterward, they strolled casually down the Midway, passing literally hundreds of pieces of sculpture, and many fountains, gardens, and exhibits. Reaching the entrance, they saw the swelling tide of visitors pouring into the grounds to enjoy the nighttime electric light show.

"Why don't we drop by the Milburn House and see how the president is doing?" suggested Walker.

"Whatever suits you," shrugged Dixon. "I'd just as soon drop by the jail and see how Czolgosz is doing, but I don't really want to wrangle with those coppers again. They might want us to spend the night."

Hopping onto a streetcar, they rode back into town, got off and walked four blocks to the Milburn House. As they approached the house, they both noticed that something was different. The crowd of reporters was milling about in the front yard, pressing up against the steps. Armed guards formed a barrier, keeping them away from the house. There was a buzz of excitement in the air.

Circling around to the back door, they showed their credentials to the guard and were admitted. They found Foster standing in the kitchen, arms folded across his chest, head bowed, and a grim expression on his face. He looked up as they entered the room. Before they could speak, he shook his head.

"Can't talk now, boys. The president has taken a turn for the worse. It's not looking good. The doctors are up there with him now. There's nothing you can do here, but come back tomorrow and I'll give you an update."

Foster turned and walked slowly through a door into the dining room, seeming a bit lost. Through the open door, they briefly caught a glimpse of men in business suits sitting around the dining table, looking tense and concerned. Stover, expressionless, stood at the far end of the room by a window, hands clasped behind his back, military style. They could hear telegraph keys tapping away in the living room. The door closed, and the kitchen became oppressively silent.

"Well, I sure wasn't expecting *that*," said Walker, stunned. "I thought he was supposed to be getting *better*, not *worse*."

"Looks like Czolgosz was right," frowned Dixon. "Nobody survives a belly shot for long. Especially when the bullet goes right through the stomach."

"Don't count him out yet," bristled Walker. "This may be just a temporary downturn. He'll bounce back in a day or two."

"Whatever you say," replied Dixon impassively. Placing his hat on his head, he added, "Let's get out of here. I need some air."

15

THE CHANGING OF THE GUARD

The president did not bounce back, however. Instead, his condition deteriorated rapidly. The executive cabinet hurried back to Buffalo, and an urgent telegram was sent to Vice President Roosevelt, vacationing in the Adirondacks, urging him to come immediately. Anxious crowds gathered around the Milburn House and in the city, and a growling mob began forming at the jail where Czolgosz was confined. By that evening the reports being given to the waiting press had changed from 'He is holding his own' to 'He is still alive.' A somber mood settled on the entire city.

The end came shortly after midnight. The president lost consciousness around nine o'clock, and shortly after two o'clock a.m., Saturday, September 14, he died. After days of being told that the president was expected to recover, the nation was in shock at his sudden collapse. The telegraph keys rattled furiously, and by mid-morning the newsboys were waving "hot off the press" newspapers and shouting the headline, "President is Dead."

Foster gathered his small team in the garden behind the Milburn House. At the end of a shaded, brick-laid walking path, he sat tiredly on a bench beside a bird bath and a statue of the Virgin Mary, his shoulders slumping, eyes fixed on the ground. Colorful petunias filled the glade, and birds sang in the branches overhead. A cool morning breeze brought the fragrant scent of honeysuckle blossoms. Walker thought it somehow incongruous for such loveliness to coexist with the grief and shock they all felt. He noticed that Foster's hands were trembling, and he looked like he hadn't slept in a while. Finally, with a heavy sigh, Foster spoke.

"We failed. But it wasn't your fault, men. I let you down. I'm sorry." He sighed again, and paused, rubbing his eyes. "We're going to be blamed and criticized by some, but try not to let it bother you. Mr. Wilkie sends his support and encouragement. He wants us all to continue to work and protect the new president. He promises to ask for more funding to hire more agents, and to get more authority to do our jobs effectively. We never should have had to deal with all those police and soldiers in there, but with only four of us. . . ." His voice trailed off, and he sighed again. Then, he straightened up and shook his head as if clearing his thoughts.

"Stover, I want you on the next train back to Washington. Take charge of the Executive Mansion and lock it down tight. No visitors—*nobody*—is allowed inside."

"Yes sir, Chief."

"Vice President Roosevelt is on his way here, and should arrive this afternoon. Garrett and Dixon—I want you to meet him at the train station. Take one of Milburn's carriages, and I'll arrange for a squad of mounted police as an escort. Guard him with your lives. Take him to the Wilcox house, and when he is ready for the swearing-in ceremony, bring him here. Any questions?"

There were no questions. Foster stood and took a step toward the house, but then stopped and turned. "I'm proud of the work you've all done," he said quietly. "Keep it up." And then he walked slowly to the house and entered through the kitchen door. The three agents looked at each other with questions in their eyes, but no one spoke. Then, single-file, they too headed up the path toward the house.

That afternoon, Walker and Dixon stood on the crowded train platform, being jostled by the hurried passengers, most of whom were coming to visit the Exposition. Despite the number of people moving about, there was very little noise. The news of the president's death seemed to have left everyone with no words.

"Think he'll remember us?" asked Dixon, fanning himself with his bowler hat.

"Of course he will!" scoffed Walker. "He wrote that letter for our court-martial hearing, you know. It hasn't been *that* long."

"Yeah, well, he might *say* he remembers us, but I don't believe he really *will*. If he says anything that shows that he really does remember us, I'll buy you a steak and gravy supper at the Boston Inn."

"Alright—and if he doesn't, I'll buy *you* one." They shook hands on the wager, and resumed watching the passing throngs.

Shortly after one o'clock the special express train bearing the vice president came steaming into the station, its powerful driving wheels locking and skidding to a screeching stop for the final few feet. The accordion door of the leading passenger car banged open and the sturdy, energetic form of the young vice president landed on the platform and, without pausing, strode vigorously toward the station exit.

"Colonel Roo—I mean, Mr. Vice President!" called Walker, waving his hat as he ran to catch up. "We're here to take you to the Wilcox House, sir! Mr. Wilcox is waiting in the carriage. Come right this way!"

The three climbed into the carriage, with Roosevelt in the rear seat with Ansley Wilcox, a friend of his who lived in Buffalo. Dixon guided the team into traffic, and they moved at a quick trot down the broad avenue, escorted by a dozen mounted policemen.

"Everyone will be glad to see you, Mr. Vice President," Walker said over his shoulder. "It's a very sad day, sir."

Roosevelt gave no reply or indication that he had heard at all. Dixon raised an eyebrow and a barely perceptible smile tugged at the corner of his mouth. Walker frowned, and they completed the short trip in silence.

When the carriage came to a stop, Roosevelt was the first one to hit the ground. He was about to charge up the path to the house when he stopped short and turned abruptly. "Haven't I seen you somewhere before?" He squinted through his pince-nez spectacles.

"Yes sir," nodded Walker. "We were both at San Juan Hill, with the Tenth Cavalry Regiment. I was an aide to General Wheeler."

"Yes, yes, yes—you went into the block house through a hole in the roof. Isn't that right? Incredible bravery!"

"Thank you, sir. You wrote a letter for us to the army, last year. It helped get us acquitted of the charge of desertion, and that led to us working for the Secret Service. Thank you very much, sir."

Roosevelt's head bobbed up and down with a quick, jerky motion. "Ah, yes! I remember now—the two of you got separated from your unit in China and wound up crossing the Gobi Desert into Russia and traveling all the way around the world to get back home. Splendid! What a bully adventure! I envy you!"

He shook their hands vigorously, with a toothy grin. Walker winced at the crushing power of the man's grip, and thought he could see energy radiating from him like ripples on a lake. *There's no one else like this man,* he thought.

The front door of the house closed behind Roosevelt, and Walker rubbed his hand gingerly. He noticed that Dixon was doing the same. "That man is a human tornado," he said in an awed tone.

"Yeah, but Washington D.C. ain't the same as San Juan Hill. He's going to have to learn to take it slow, and not go chargin' around all the time."

"I don't know," replied Walker slowly. "I expect that the folks in Washington are going to have to learn how to do some charging around if they're going to keep up with this president. I don't think he knows how to slow down."

"Huh," Dixon grunted. "You may be right." After a short pause he added, "I reckon you'll be wanting that steak and gravy for supper tonight?"

"Yup!" grinned Walker. "And I hope my hand recovers enough by then to eat it!"

When Roosevelt emerged an hour later in borrowed formal wear, including a silk top hat, they delivered him to the Milburn House to pay his respects to Mrs. McKinley. She was too distraught to receive visitors, however, and the autopsy was still being conducted on the president's body, so they returned him to the Wilcox home. The mounted troopers rode alongside all the way, much to Roosevelt's displeasure. The six cabinet members followed in separate carriages and they all assembled in the library, where the vice president positioned himself in front of a stained-glass window which cast a soft light over the room.

The library was crowded with the cabinet, local dignitaries, journalists, and a federal judge who was to administer the oath of office. Walker and Dixon stood protectively at the door, while Foster paced outside it, unable to bring himself to enter the room. The library clock struck three-thirty. The judge directed Roosevelt to raise his right hand, and within a minute he was officially sworn in as the President of the United States.

The room emptied. Roosevelt remained behind to meet privately with his cabinet. Foster motioned for Walker and Dixon to step aside for a word.

"We'll be here until Monday, and then go to Washington. That's where the funeral will be. Until then, the police and soldiers will be around the president—around Roosevelt—so get some rest." He paused, and then added with a meaningful look, "You'll need it."

The return to Washington was a somber, heartbreaking journey. The train bearing the slain president's casket was draped in black, and the crowds that stood silently alongside the track no longer cheered gaily and waved flags, but instead wore black and wept openly. No bands played patriotic music. Men removed their hats and bowed their heads. The scene was morbidly depressing, and yet Walker could not take his eyes away from the window as the train rumbled through town after town. He felt bonded to the people by grief, and immersed in their sadness. Studying the sea of mournful faces, he wondered, *What are they thinking? How are they really feeling, deep inside? What will they talk about tonight around the supper table?*

He still felt guilty for having allowed the tragic deed to take place, and constantly replayed the events in his mind, vainly trying to imagine how he might have prevented it. Eventually, he closed his eyes and instinctively began to pray. He prayed for Ida McKinley, for her family in Canton, for Kate and William, for the multitudes lining the tracks, and for President Roosevelt. It occurred to him that Czolgosz might need someone to pray for him, too, but couldn't bring himself to do it. However, the thought wouldn't go away, and finally he surrendered to it, and offered up a prayer for the assassin's soul. Strangely, as soon as the prayer was said, he immediately felt much better, as if a burden had been lifted from his heart.

Upon arriving in Washington that evening, Dixon led Walker to their new home—a narrow, shotgun-style, wood-frame house with blue window shutters. As soon as they stepped through the front door, Beulah and Daisy rushed to greet them with hugs and tears. Daisy clung to Dixon, resting her head against his chest, with his arm around her shoulders, while Beulah put her arms around both Dixon and Walker and repeatedly murmured, "So sorry! So sorry!"

After a long moment, she said, "I know y'all must be hungry! I fixed somethin' special for supper, to help y'all feel better."

"I thought I smelled something really good," responded Walker, inhaling deeply. "Is that fried chicken livers I'm smelling?"

"It is, indeed!" beamed Beulah.

"And okra and cornbread!" added Daisy, grinning through her tears.

"I'm half starved," moaned Dixon, sniffing the air. "I could eat a whole chicken right now, by myself."

"It'll just take a few minutes to heat it up, so y'all put your things away and get washed up," Beulah said over her shoulder as she bustled off to the kitchen. "Daisy, get that peach cobbler out of the pie safe and put it on the table, and whip some cream."

"Peach cobbler!" exclaimed Walker, wide-eyed. "I done died and gone to heaven!"

"You and me, both," echoed Dixon. "Come on, Garrett. I'll show you where our room is."

Sitting at the kitchen table with its red and white checkered cloth, Walker was able to relax for the first time in days. He listened to Beulah and Daisy tell about their move from Alabama to Washington, about Beulah's new employer, and Daisy's new school. It was dark outside, and the house did not have electricity, so a candle provided light. Fatigue was catching up with Walker, and the flickering shadows had a hypnotic effect. After his head bobbed up and down for the third time, Beulah reached across the table and squeezed his hand.

"Mr. Walker, you need to go to bed, 'fore you go to sleep right here at the table!"

"We both do," agreed Dixon, scooting his chair back from the table. "We'll see y'all in the morning."

Moments later, Walker pulled his boots off as he sat on his bed. He looked across the room at Dixon, who was hanging his shoulder holster and pistol on the bed post. "Dixon," he said, "You done good." Nodding, he repeated, "You done good."

Dixon understood his meaning, and also nodded. "Yup," he grinned. "I did."

16

"BOOKER T"

The next month was a whirlwind of activity for the new president and the Secret Service. The memorial for McKinley in the capitol was followed by the new First Family's moving into the Executive Mansion—which Roosevelt directed should now be referred to as the 'White House'—and the establishing of new routines for everyone. The Roosevelts were the first presidential family with small children since Lincoln, and this profoundly affected the atmosphere in the White House and expanded the role of the security forces. Roosevelt himself was much more active than his predecessors, and this required the Secret Service agents to also be constantly on the move. By mid-October, things had just begun to settle down a bit when the president stirred up a controversy that threatened to overwhelm his administration, and even posed a threat to his personal safety.

It began innocently enough, with Roosevelt extending an invitation to black leader Booker T. Washington to dine with him. Washington was the most prominent black figure in America, having established a college in Tuskegee, Alabama. "Booker T," as he was commonly known, was already in the city visiting a friend, and

Roosevelt decided to take advantage of the opportunity to discuss topics concerning Southern politics and race relations. Both men knew that it would be a matter of significance for a black man to eat at the president's table, but felt that it would be worth the risk. Neither anticipated the fury of the Southern white reaction that followed.

When he emerged from the White House at about ten o'clock that evening, Booker T climbed into a carriage to be driven to the train station to catch the last train to New York.

"Evening, sir," said Dixon, touching the brim of his hat.

"It is indeed a good evening," responded Washington in a powerfully resonant voice, as he settled into the rear seat. "At least, I hope that it is."

"What do you mean, sir?" asked Walker, as Dixon snapped the reins and the carriage began to move forward.

"Not everyone will approve of a colored man dining with the president and members of his family. I just hope that this doesn't turn into a problem for either of us, that's all."

"It probably will, at least in the South," said Dixon skeptically. "Agent Garrett and me, we're both from Alabama, and we understand what it's like down there. If the southern press gets wind of it, they'll stir up a big ruckus for sure."

"You're probably right," Washington replied. "It was a chance worth taking, though. In our society, status is closely tied to where and with whom you are allowed to eat. This was an important opportunity for my race, and I couldn't refuse it out of fear for my personal welfare."

"You're a brave man, Mr. Washington," Walker observed. "I hope you'll be careful, sir. You don't have security guards like the president does. You might want to think about that."

"Hopefully that won't be necessary, Agent Garrett, but thank you for the thought."

They were soon at the train station. Booker T exited the carriage, carrying only the small satchel he had taken to the White House.

"Don't you have any more baggage than that, sir?" asked Dixon.

"It's being sent ahead for me," smiled Washington. "But let me give you this." He unfastened the buckle of the strap and opened the satchel. From it he produced a small volume, which he handed to Dixon.

"I hope you'll enjoy reading that, Agent Dixon. It's my autobiography—*Up From Slavery*. It's just been published, and I want as many of our people to read it as possible. I believe that it will encourage them. When you finish with it, pass it on."

With that, the well-dressed, handsome man disappeared into the station. They stood watching until he could no longer be seen, and then turned the carriage back down Pennsylvania Avenue.

The feared southern reaction was not long in coming. The next day, newspapers across the South, from Memphis to the Carolinas to Virginia, were boiling in rage at the president for sharing a table in the White House with a black man. Racial epithets and threats of violence abounded. Roosevelt was accused of promoting race-mixing, and a U.S. senator from South Carolina snarled that it would require killing a thousand blacks to put the race back in its place, clearly implying that lynchings were needed. The hatred and fury unleashed upon both Roosevelt and Washington were breath-taking.

Five days after the dinner, both men attended the bicentennial celebration of Yale University, in New Haven, Connecticut. Roosevelt was to deliver a speech on the third day of the festivities, while Booker T would be a member of the audience. There was no plan for the two to interact at the event, but the simple fact that both were present served to escalate the tensions and heat generated by the much-debated dinner.

The Secret Service was on high alert, with all ten of the agents assigned to guard the president traveling with him on the special overnight train. After breakfast in the dining car, Foster addressed the group, describing the day's planned itinerary, and giving out assignments to the agents. To avoid the crowds, the president's train was not actually going to stop at the station, but at a crossing near the Yale campus, where carriages would be waiting. In conclusion, he glared around at the group.

"This is not going to be another Buffalo," he asserted grimly. "There'll be no hand-shaking—no close contact. We are going to be at the president's elbow everywhere he goes. We're going to be in front, behind, to the right, and to the left. Anybody that wants to get to the president will have to go through us! Keep your eyes peeled! If you think you see a threat, don't hesitate—react immediately!" He waved his hand to dismiss them.

"Something tells me the Secret Service needs more than ten agents," Dixon muttered to Walker as they filed out. "It's one thing to protect him in the White House, but out in the open, twenty-four hours a day? Gotta sleep *some*time."

"Dixon! Garrett!" barked Foster. "Front and center!"

The two stepped aside to let the other agents exit the car, and then hesitantly walked back to Foster.

"Sir," began Dixon, "I didn't mean—"

"I have a special assignment for you two," rasped Foster, cutting him off with an irritated wave of his hand. "The president and Director Wilkie are concerned that Mr. Washington may be vulnerable to violence. The president fears that his having had dinner with Washington could expose him to danger, and he wants us to make sure it doesn't happen. We may be in the North, and the northern press has supported the president's dining with Washington, but don't forget that President McKinley was shot in Buffalo—also in the North. Geography is no protection. They want us to make sure Mr. Washington comes to no harm while the president is in town.

"And that's where you two come in," he continued, folding his arms across his chest. "While the other agents are looking out for the president, you'll be shadowing Washington. Stick close to him everywhere he goes. Make sure nobody lays a hand on him."

"Yes sir," they replied in unison, saluting out of habit. Foster frowned.

"So, we're protecting Mr. Washington, not the president?" Walker sounded confused.

"I can assure you it wasn't *my* idea," scowled Foster. "We're short-handed as it is, and detaching two agents to guard somebody that isn't even our responsibility just makes it that much harder to do our job. But nobody asked me, and nobody asked you, either."

"Why us, sir?" asked Dixon curiously. "And not any of the other agents?"

"You have both already met him, and you're both from Alabama, so you have a double connection with him. Also, Dixon, you're the only colored agent we have, and that may make it easier for you to follow close in some of the places he might go. Last, I know you two have been through a lot together, so you should make a good team. Any concerns?" Foster's tone of voice and steely glare made the question more of a challenge than a query.

"No sir," nodded Dixon quickly. "We'll make sure Mr. Washington stays safe. You can count on us, sir." Both saluted again.

"For the last time, cut out the saluting!" he snapped irritably. "This isn't the army!" Just then, the train braked noticeably, and they heard the sound of its steam whistle. "We're stopping. One of the carriages will take you to the station to meet Washington, and bring you back to the campus. Now get going—his train is due in half an hour."

The large crowd that had gathered at the station for the arrival of the president was disappointed when his train steamed through without stopping. When Walker and Dixon arrived a short while later, the platform was almost deserted. They watched the last stragglers slowly leaving, with only a few scattered individuals left in sight. A distant whistle was faintly heard, and they saw a plume of smoke from the approaching locomotive.

"If I see anybody with a handkerchief wrapped around his hand," Walker muttered to Dixon, "I'm gonna knock him down and ask questions later."

"Not if I get to him first," Dixon replied, with a meaningful look.

As the passengers began disembarking from the train, they spotted Washington emerging from a car a short distance away. They went to meet him, and when only a few feet separated them, a stranger suddenly stepped in front of Washington. He wore work-man's clothes and boots, and a faded corduroy jacket, with uncombed hair and a light beard stubble. He hailed Washington loudly in a tone that sounded superficially friendly, but Walker thought that it sounded more mocking than congenial, and he suspected that the man was intoxicated.

"Why, you're Booker T. Washington, ain't you? I recognize you from pictures in the newspaper. You're one of the biggest men in the whole damn country! Yes sir, ain't nobody bigger'n Booker T. Washington!" Washington tried to sidestep the man, but he pressed in closer and continued speaking loudly.

"I never met nobody as 'portant as you are, Booker T! I thought I was goin' to meet Mr. Roosevelt, but he didn't even stop here. Just rolled right on through. That's just as well, I reckon. I used to think he was a big man too, and I was all for him, but after he let you eat dinner with him, well, that finished him as far as I'm concerned. I'm done with Roosevelt! But you, Booker T—"

Walker put his hand firmly on the man's shoulder. "That's enough! Mr. Washington has appointments to keep. Step aside, and let him pass."

"Says who?" demanded the man, belligerently.

Walker pulled back his coat to show the silver badge and the handle of the revolver. "Let him pass," he repeated, locking eyes with the man. The odor of beer was strong.

The man held up both hands defensively. "I wasn't doing nothin' but talking. Ain't no crime to talk to a feller, is it? A man ought to be able to talk to somebody if'n he wants to."

The man continued to talk loudly as he trailed them out to the street. He appeared to resent being ignored, and his speech became louder and more abusive. As they drove away in the carriage, he shouted a curse, and Walker, sitting beside the driver, glanced back to see him making an obscene gesture.

"Welcome to New Haven, Mr. Washington," said Dixon drily.

Washington laughed in his rich, deep voice. "I've experienced much worse, Agent Dixon! But thank you both for intervening—it's a bit early in the day to have to smell beer-breath!"

They delivered their charge to Dwight Hall, where the guests of honor were gathered in preparation for their ceremonial march to the Hyperion Theatre. Thousands of students and visitors crowded the walkway, slowing the procession of robed academics and honorees. Not only were Secret Service agents walking alongside the president, but several mounted police accompanied them, as well. No one was going to be allowed to get near him. Walker and Dixon stayed within an arm's length of Washington.

Roosevelt was seated on the stage with dozens of other noted guests, while Washington sat in the audience. The three-thousand seat auditorium was packed to the rafters, and the energy of the crowd was electric. A Supreme Court justice gave a speech, remarking that "Yale men can recognize a true Washington, whether his name be George or Booker." This reference to Booker T produced a burst of cheering and applause. The university president then read a list of those receiving honorary degrees, and each was applauded vigorously, none more so than Samuel Clemens. Walker had read several books by "Mark Twain," and was thrilled to get to see his favorite author, even if only from a distance.

Finally, after a pause, President Hadley said, "One name yet remains—" and the crowd roared so loudly and for so long that he had to wait for silence before continuing. "To Theodore Roosevelt—" he began, but had to wait again for silence, as the room erupted with more cheering. Eventually he managed to get through his introduction of the president and present him with an honorary doctorate degree. "President Roosevelt is a Harvard man," he declared, "but his perseverance for truth and right will make him glad to be an adopted son of Yale." Predictably, an avalanche of cheering and applause again swept down upon the assembly, as Roosevelt came forward to receive his award and make a brief speech.

Within minutes, the program was concluded, and as many of the audience as could reach the stage sought to shake hands with the president and the others. The Secret Service agents rushed from the wings and struggled to keep the situation under control. Roosevelt chafed at the security measures, and managed to shake a few hands before the agents established a perimeter around him.

It seemed to Walker that the emotional response to Roosevelt's presence equaled anything he had seen during his time with McKinley. *Has McKinley been forgotten so quickly?* he wondered. *It's as if he was never here.* The thought saddened him, but he put it out of his mind, forcing himself to concentrate on Washington, watching carefully as he was bumped and jostled by the crowd.

The rest of the day was busy with a luncheon for college presidents, and a reception, both on the campus. Walker and Dixon kept a respectful distance as Washington socialized with cabinet officials, U.S. senators and congressmen, Supreme Court justices, corporate tycoons, army generals, admirals, and other college presidents. Musical ensembles played quietly in the background, to the tinkling of silver and crystalware. *I can't tell if this place is a cathedral or a castle,* Walker thought, as his eyes traced the massive fireplace, high beams, and stained-glass windows.

Leaning over to Dixon, he whispered, "I had no idea Mr. Washington was so—"

"Me neither," Dixon breathed, equally impressed. "He's come a long way from where he started. You should read his book. He was a slave 'til he was eight or nine years old."

Walker blinked. "That *is* a long way to come."

Late in the afternoon, Washington motioned to them. "Gentlemen, it's time for me to get back to the station. My train will be leaving in less than an hour, and I don't want to be late." While Dixon went to summon the carriage driver, Walker fidgeted nervously. "Agent Garrett, is there something on your mind?"

"Well, yes sir. Something is bothering me. Something I observed today. I don't know what to make of it, sir."

"Care to share it?"

Walker sighed deeply. "We traveled all across the United States with President McKinley, and everywhere we went, people clapped, cheered, and waved flags like it was the Second Coming. It was amazing. Now, it's been barely a month since Buffalo, and people are cheering the same way for Roosevelt. I don't mean any disrespect to President Roosevelt, but it just seems to me that people have already forgotten about McKinley. Do you see what I mean? Have I got it all wrong, sir?"

"No, Agent Garrett—I understand, and you don't have it wrong, but there is something here that you may be missing. President McKinley was a good man, and the nation was devastated when he passed. His death left a big hole in the hearts of the people, and they are looking for something to fill that hole."

He paused and put his hand on Walker's shoulder. "Mr. Roosevelt is a good man, too, and I believe that he is the right person to fill that hole. I know that a lot of people think he's a bull in a china shop, but he is willing to listen and learn, and that is a very important quality for a leader to have." He patted Walker's shoulder and smiled sympathetically. "The country needs Mr. Roosevelt right now because we've lost McKinley. The enthusiasm you are seeing for Roosevelt is a sign of how much everyone is missing McKinley."

"I didn't think about it like that," admitted Walker. "That makes sense. Thank you, Mr. Washington!"

The carriage arrived and Washington got in and sat beside Dixon, while Walker climbed up to sit beside the driver. With a light slap of the reins, the horse began trotting at a casual pace. The Union Station was about a mile from Yale, which would take them no more than ten or twelve minutes. The driver, being local, knew a shortcut, and turned off the main street to go through an industrial area, between dark, gloomy warehouses. There was litter in the street, and empty crates stacked along the curb.

"Why are we going through here?" demanded Walker. "Shouldn't we stay on the main avenue?"

"This will save us a couple of minutes," said the driver. "Less traffic, too."

"We don't need to save a couple of minutes," retorted Walker. "This doesn't look like a good place to be. Turn around and go back."

"Nothing to worry about!" argued the driver. "We'll be there in no time."

Before Walker could reply, two men suddenly appeared from behind a pile of crates. One of them grabbed the horse's bridle and dragged him to a halt, while the other cocked a pistol and pointed it at Walker. "Well, if it ain't Booker T hisself! Get out of the carriage, Booker—we gonna finish our conversation!"

"You're the man that was at the train station this morning!" exclaimed Walker, standing up.

"That's right, and you're gonna be sorry you acted so high and mighty! I know you got a gun under that coat, so just keep your hands away from it, or I'll put daylight through you for sure!"

"I'll just put 'em in my coat pockets," said Walker, pushing his hands into the pockets on each side of the suit coat. "See? Out of sight."

"Smart fella," he sneered, and turned his gun toward Washington and Dixon. "Both you n----rs get out! We gonna have us a little fun!" The man holding the bridle laughed a rough, evil laugh.

Two gunshots rang out in quick succession, and the gunman staggered back and fell to the ground, a red blotch spreading on his chest. The horse, startled, tossed his head with a frightened snort and pawed the pavement. The man holding the bridle, seeing his partner fall, turned and ran down an alley. As soon as he let go of the bridle, the driver immediately slapped the reins harshly and the horse leaped forward, causing Walker to sit down hard, his hat landing in the carriage.

"Garrett—you're on fire!" called Dixon.

Walker looked down and saw the smoldering black circle growing on his coat pocket, and a small wisp of smoke rising. Quickly pulling a red handkerchief from his pants pocket, he patted it out, leaving a blackened goose-egg around a finger-sized hole. "Looks like I'm gonna need a new suit," he said ruefully.

"Next time, pull that pistol out of your pocket before you shoot it," advised Dixon, handing him his hat.

Walker turned to the driver, giving him a hard look. "Mum's the word." It was an order.

"Mum's the word," he agreed eagerly. "I didn't see nothing."

At the station, Washington expressed curiosity about the weapon Walker had used, so he showed him the diminutive palm pistol. Washington marveled at the its effectiveness, and Walker offered it to him. "No, no," he declined, almost in alarm. "It wouldn't do for me to go about armed, and especially not to shoot a white man. Even if I *am* Booker T. Washington, it would be a huge mistake. Thank you for the offer, but you keep it, Agent Garrett."

They walked Washington to his train and saw him safely aboard. They did not leave the platform until the train pulled out and he was on his way. Returning to the waiting carriage, they sat together for the ride back to the university campus.

"Reckon we ought to tell Foster?" asked Walker.

"Garrett, how many times are we going to have to go over this? He don't need anything more to worry about. Just let it alone. Nobody needs to know."

"It would just make trouble for everybody, right?"

"You're catching on. Let's just keep our heads down and git out of town. Mum's the word!"

For the rest of the evening, Walker carefully kept his hand down by his side, covering the conspicuous blemish on his coat. No one seemed to notice. At the conclusion of a dinner given in honor of the president, the party finally boarded the train near midnight. Walker, unable to sleep, gazed out the window at the scenery gliding past, reflecting back on the day's events. He decided that Booker T's explanation of why the crowds cheered so enthusiastically for Roosevelt was probably correct, though he still felt uncomfortable about it. It also concerned him that Washington would not carry a weapon for self-defense because, as a black man, he risked more by being armed than by not being armed. *That man needs a bodyguard,* he thought. *If he won't protect himself, somebody ought to do it for him. Maybe I'll talk to Foster about it.*

The view from the train changed constantly. He had slept through all of this on the trip northward, so these sights were all new to him. The route closely followed the coastline, and he was able to see the ocean at times. Small towns came one after the other, with few breaks, and it seemed to him that New York City went on forever. Somewhere south of New York, he dozed off. When he awoke, the sun had risen, and the train was passing through Baltimore. In another hour, they were in the capitol, and it was a new day.

17

HOME

W alker sat on his bed, carefully reading from some sheets of pastel yellow stationery. A matching yellow envelope lay on the bed beside him. So absorbed was he that he did not notice Dixon's entering the room.

"Letter from 'Dancin' Dancy?'"

"Yeah." After a short pause, Walker shrugged and began folding the papers. "Says she's sorry about McKinley getting shot, even if he was a Republican. Her pa is pretty steamed about Beulah coming up to D.C. He can't find a good cook to replace her."

Dixon interrupted with a laugh. "Hard times at the Dancy house!" he chuckled. "He may have to actually pay somebody what they're worth, if he wants good help."

"That rich cousin in Charleston proposed to her on Labor Day," Walker continued. "She says she told him she'd have to think about it, and hasn't given him an answer yet. She's been in Richmond, visiting her other relatives since right after the assassination. He's coming up to see her next week, and wants an answer."

"Here's your big chance, Garrett! Trot down to Richmond ahead of 'im and throw your hat in the ring. Maybe she'll see the light and make you a happy man." Dixon started laughing again.

"Very funny," Walker scowled. "She'd throw my hat right back at me—after she got through laughing." Putting the letter back into the envelope, he added, "Nope—I'd just as soon keep my hat on my head, thank you."

Dixon shrugged. "You don't know, 'til you know. Anyway, you still sweet on that girl in Ohio—McKinley's niece?"

"I reckon that's over with and done. I wrote her a letter saying how sorry I was that we let her uncle get shot. That was six weeks ago, and she hasn't written back. I don't blame her. I'd probably feel the same way."

"Speaking of blaming somebody, it's a shame about Foster. He did what he could with what they gave him. It just wasn't enough, and it ain't his fault."

Walker nodded. "The big brass have to have somebody to put the blame on, and he was the scapegoat. Now he gets to sit at a desk and do paperwork. It's Congress that ought to get the blame for not giving the Service the resources and authority to do the job right. Maybe that'll change now."

"Don't bet on it," Dixon scoffed. "By the way, they're electrocuting Czolgosz today in New York. Auburn prison. They're gonna fry him with seventeen hunnerd volts. Wonder how he feels about doing his duty *now*?"

"I'm kind of surprised that he has lived long enough to be executed," Walker said. "I would have bet that a mob would've dragged him out of his cell and lynched him before he ever got out of Buffalo."

"If he'd been black, that would have happened, for sure," Dixon frowned. "No colored man that did what he did would have ever seen the inside of a courtroom."

Walker stood abruptly. "Just remembered I've got to run over to the tailor and pick up my suit before he closes shop. He said he could just replace the pocket and nobody will ever notice. I hope he's right —it would save me a lot of money. See you at supper!"

The tailor's promise was good—the new tweed material perfectly matched the rest of the coat, and it looked as good as ever. Feeling generous, Walker picked out a colorful necktie to go with the suit.

On the way back, enjoying the autumn chill in the air, he took a different route and passed the AME church where Reverend Wright preached. On the spur of the moment, he decided to stop for a visit. He entered the front double-doors and walked into the semi-dark sanctuary, down the center aisle toward the carved oak pulpit. Pink light from the setting sun filtered through the high windows and bathed the silent room with an ethereal glow. A crucifix of dark, stained wood hung on the wall, bearing the twisted figure of the crucified Jesus. Mesmerized, he sat down on the front pew and fixed his eyes on the cross and its holy burden. He had seen many such icons in churches in America and Russia, but those were usually made of shining silver or gold, sometimes decorated with jewels. The stark simplicity of the dark wood made the figure seem alive and organic, the woodgrain highlighting its tortured contours. Walker studied it for several minutes, and then closed his eyes and bowed his head.

A slight sound startled him, and he turned quickly to see Reverend Wright taking a seat beside him. "Brother Walker! I didn't mean to interrupt you. This is a pleasant surprise! How are you doing?" smiled the pastor. "What brings you here?"

"Reverend Wright! It's good to see you, sir! I was just passing by and thought I'd see if you were here. Haven't seen you and Hannah in a while."

"Well, I am so glad you did! It has been a while, indeed. How have things been going for you and Dixon?"

"Pretty crazy ever since the assassination, really," Walker admitted, in a sad tone of voice. "We feel bad that it happened, but there's been no time to mourn. Too much to do, especially with President Roosevelt being such a whirlwind all the time. He never stops, and that means we never stop, either."

"I see," sympathized Wright, nodding sagely. "You have unresolved grief, and perhaps also a bit of guilt—feeling responsible for the tragedy?"

"A little, yes—well, actually a lot, to tell the truth."

"I wasn't there, of course," Wright reflected, "but I've read the newspaper accounts of what happened, and more importantly, I know you and Dixon. I've seen your dedication to your work—it's a *mission* to both of you, not just a job to do. If anyone could have prevented this terrible thing, you would have been the ones to do it. Unfortunately, sometimes there's just no explanation for what happens. We just have to accept it, learn from it, and move forward."

"I've heard people say that it must have been God's will for McKinley to die. He even said so on his deathbed. Do you believe that, Reverend? Was it God's will for Czolgosz to kill the president?"

"That's not a simple question, Walker, nor an easy one. Many theologians argue that everything that happens in this world is God's will. If you hit your thumb with a hammer, or stump your toe, or spill coffee on your pants—it's all part of God's plan. Maybe they are right, but I do not think so. God gave us all the power of choice, and we can choose to do good or to do wrong. When we choose to do wrong, there are consequences, and sometimes we suffer the consequences of other people's bad choices. Czolgosz chose to do wrong, and President McKinley—actually, the entire nation—suffered the consequences. God is able to take these bad things and turn them into something good, though. It may be that Roosevelt is God's way of turning Czolgosz's bad choice into something good. Time will tell."

"That makes a lot of sense—a whole lot of sense. Thank you, Reverend. I feel better already!"

"I'm glad for that! Was there anything else on your mind?"

"No sir, I think that's all for now," and he started to rise, but his eye again caught sight of the crucifix. "That crucifix—I was looking at it a few minutes ago. Something about it strikes me as odd."

"Oh? What's that, Brother Walker?"

"See how dark the wood is? It makes Jesus look almost black. Shouldn't you put some white paint on him to make him look right?"

Reverend Wright threw his head back and laughed so loudly that it echoed in the spacious room. Taken aback, Walker blinked. *Did I say something funny?*

"Pardon me for laughing!" Wright chuckled. Wiping a tear from his eyes as he regained his composure, he gave Walker an amused look. "Why do you think Jesus should be painted white?"

"Well," Walker said defensively, "I've seen lots of paintings of Jesus in museums and books and in the Bible, and he's always a white man. He *was* white, wasn't he?"

"Who painted those pictures, Walker?"

"I don't know, but I've heard of Rembrandt, Leonardo da Vinci, Michelangelo—people like that."

"Yes, that's true, and many others also. They were European artists—white men. They painted Jesus to look like themselves. But Jesus wasn't a European, you know. He lived in Palestine. Do you know what the people who live there look like, Walker?"

"No, I guess not. Don't Arabs live in that part of the world?"

"Yes, they do! What do Arabs look like?"

Walker fidgeted uneasily. "Kind of dark, I think. Black hair. Beards."

Reverend Wright smiled and nodded. "Very good! The Jews who lived in that part of the world looked like that, too. Jesus would have looked like them."

"But Jesus was the Son of God, not a Jew!"

Wright put a hand gently on Walker's shoulder and spoke softly. "Yes, he was the Son of God, but he was also the son of *Mary,* and he was *Jewish.* He was much more than merely Jewish, of course—he referred to himself as 'the Son of Man.' He was part of all mankind—white, black, Chinese, Mexican, Indian—we are *all* his brothers and sisters, and we can all see ourselves in him. That's why he can be the Savior of the whole world!"

Walker looked back up at the crucifix, and gazed at it for a long moment. "I never thought about it like that before. I guess he's more than I realized."

"He's more than any of us realize!" Wright smiled benevolently. "He was God in the flesh, and he still lives today. That's why we worship him and pray to him."

Walker sighed and gave his head a quick, vigorous shake. "That's about all I think I can handle for now, Reverend," he said, standing up and extending his hand. "I better run along or I'll be late for supper."

"Come again, any time!"

Walker hurried down the street, carrying his bundle under his arm, with dry leaves crunching underfoot. The last red glow of the sun was disappearing behind the treetops, and the temperature was dropping rapidly. The first stars of the evening began to twinkle. *I miss getting to talk to General Wheeler,* he thought, *but it sure is good to be able to talk to Reverend Wright. He's a smart man. Maybe as smart as the General.*

He was still reflecting on Wright's words when he got to the house. He stood in the yard for a moment, absorbing the scene in front of him, his breath fogging in the chill night air. Through the kitchen window he saw Daisy take a skillet of cornbread out of the oven and put it on the table. A steaming pot of vegetable soup was on the stove. He heard Dixon's voice and Daisy's reply as if from a great distance, but could not make out the words. A chair scraped harshly on the floor as it was pulled out from the table, and dishes and utensils clinked and rattled faintly. *This is just like home,* he thought. Then he realized, *This is home. This is my family now. I belong here.* A sense of calm settled over him—a feeling of peace like he had not known in a very long time, and he smiled as he walked slowly into the house.

18

GUARDING ROOSEVELT

"What'sa matter, Garrett?" Dixon grinned. "Didn't you enjoy your hike with the president?"

"Good Lord!" breathed Walker, eyes closed, as he leaned forward, hands on knees. "That man is an animal." He stood up painfully and rubbed his lower back. "Twenty miles in the rain and mud. I never walked so fast in my life—practically running. Then we swam a river —in February, mind you. It was so freezing cold, I thought I was gonna die. Then we got to the other side and climbed a cliff. One slip and you'd break your neck. And all the way, he's tellin' me to hurry up." He shook his head in disbelief. "Why am I the lucky one that gets to go on these hikes?"

"Because you're young, and you can keep up," Stover said, sipping a cup of coffee. "I'd never make it back. They'd just have to bury me somewhere out there in the Virginia countryside."

"I'll stick to riding with him," nodded Dixon. "Even that's dangerous. He gallops at full speed on that stallion of his—"Bleistein"—and shoots at stumps with his pistol, jumping fences and walls. He don't slow down for streams, gravel, or mud. I got so splattered last time, you couldn't tell I was a colored man."

The door of the Secret Service office opened and "Big Bill" Craig stuck his head in. "Let's go, men!" he barked, in his distinctly Scottish accent. "Time for your training session!" Craig had taken Foster's place as the chief agent of the presidential detail. At six feet four inches and two-hundred sixty pounds, he was an imposing giant of a man, and strong as an ox. He had been in charge of physical conditioning for the British Army for years, and also taught boxing, fencing, and hand-to-hand combat techniques. He gathered the three agents in a large storage room that had been converted into a makeshift gym, at Craig's request. A naked light bulb hung from the ceiling, and some thin mattresses covered the floor. A large, cylindrical canvas bag hung from a hook at the far end of the room.

Standing about three feet in front of Stover, Craig ordered him, "Hit me in the jaw as hard as you can." Stover didn't move, and Craig repeated the order. Stover stepped forward and poked a fist feebly at Craig, stopping short of his chin, unable to bring himself to actually hit him. Craig quickly slapped Stover's face smartly with his right hand, and then with his left. With anger in his eyes, Stover unleashed a full-force right punch at the larger man's face—it never landed. Craig grabbed his arm and, with a lightning quick move, flipped Stover head over heels. A cloud of dust erupted from the old mattress when he slammed down on it, and Craig twisted his arm, forcing him over onto his stomach. Stover sneezed violently twice in the dust cloud, and let out a pained cry, pounding the mattress with his free hand. Walker and Dixon stared with wide eyes.

"That was judo," Craig said tersely. "You're going to learn how to neutralize attackers and take control of any situation quickly."

"Can't we just shoot 'em?" asked Walker innocently.

"Not if they're not armed, or if there is a crowd of people around," Craig answered. "And you may not have time to draw your weapon. You need more options than just shooting a gun. This training will give you those options." Walker nodded.

Positioning himself in front of Walker, Craig shot out a left hand and whacked the side of his head, and then did it twice more. When Walker put up his right hand defensively, Craig slapped him with the other hand. Left followed right followed left, and then Walker, like

Stover, threw an angry punch, and like Stover, landed on his back in a cloud of dust. Craig unceremoniously stepped to Dixon and began slapping him. Within seconds, Dixon joined them on the mattress.

"Now, you're going to learn to do that," Craig growled. "On your feet!" For the next hour he put them through a workout that left them sweating and panting. While Craig worked with one, the others pounded on the punching bag. The air in the room became hot and stale. Finally, he announced the end of the session. "You've made a good start, men! We'll continue three times a week, and you can come in here to work with the punching bag whenever you want. And do those exercises I showed you, every day. See you next time!" And he was gone.

Stover collapsed against the wall, his wet hair plastered to his forehead. "That man is trying to kill us," he wheezed, blowing a spray of sweat from his bushy mustache. "How can I protect the president if my arms and hands are broken and I can't stand up straight?"

"Look at it this way," grunted Dixon, rubbing his back. "If we survive this training, we'll be really good at protecting the president."

"And if we don't," Walker added, "I won't have to go on any more of those demon hikes."

"Every cloud has a silver lining, I reckon," Dixon chuckled. "Let's get out of here, before he comes back."

This became their routine over the next few months, as winter turned to spring. Thanks to Craig's workouts, the agents were in the best physical condition of their lives, and they were becoming increasingly proficient in the hand-to-hand fighting techniques he taught them. Walker actually learned to enjoy the murderous hikes with Roosevelt, and was able to keep up without any goading from the president.

Roosevelt even joined them in the tiny gym occasionally, and demonstrated his own mastery of judo and jiu-jitsu, besides boxing. Nothing angered him more than for the agents to give less than their best effort to beat him in combat. Once, when Walker landed a solid right to Roosevelt's head, the president countered with a right of his own, and knocked Walker out cold for several seconds. When he revived, with ears ringing he listened to Roosevelt shouting at him not to let his guard down. "Keep your gloves up!" he snapped. "Never give your opponent an opening!"

In April, the president and Mrs. Roosevelt traveled to Charleston to attend the South Carolina Interstate and West Indian Exposition. Walker was interested in seeing the city where Abigail had spent so much time. There was no time for sight-seeing, however, and after a presidential speech and a brief tour of the exhibits, they quickly left. The most interesting part of the visit, in Walker's opinion, was the excursion to Fort Sumter. He felt the stirrings of his old Southern pride as he contemplated the birthplace of the Civil War, but his pride was tempered by the knowledge of what lay in wait for the South in that war. The Secret Service agents were on edge during the visit, due to the outburst of rage against the president over the White House dinner with Booker T. Washington. Nowhere was that anger more vituperative than in South Carolina, and as a result they were all tense, anticipating trouble that did not materialize.

Finally, with the arrival of July, Congress ended its annual session, and it was time for the president to begin his summer vacation. This meant taking the family to his Sagamore Hill estate, near Oyster Bay, on the north shore of Long Island, New York. The twenty-two-room Queen Anne house sat on a hill at the end of a mile-long winding drive through the woods from tiny Cove Neck, which was a couple of miles from the hamlet of Oyster Bay.

However, just because he was on vacation and Congress was scattered across the country did not mean that the president was not working. Half of every day was spent with Cortelyou, reading and writing letters and telegrams, digesting the news, and planning policy decisions. Official business was always completed by noon, and Roosevelt spent the rest of the day romping and playing with his children, riding and hiking.

Walker was astonished at how playful the president was when with his children. He led them on walks, played lawn games, and wrestled—always losing. What amazed him even more was that "Big Bill" Craig joined in the fun. Watching the powerful warrior who mercilessly drilled the agents in hand-to-hand combat getting down on all fours and pretending to be a wild animal for them to hunt left Walker speechless. Craig was especially close to four-year-old Quentin Roosevelt, who would sit in his lap as they read comics together.

There were frequent visitors, many of them important and powerful. Among them were the German Kaiser's brother, various wealthy businessmen, cabinet members and Supreme Court justices, athletes and soldiers, and *lots* of relatives. There was a large family gathering for the Fourth of July, with several representatives from the Hyde Park branch of the Roosevelts attending, including twenty-year-old Franklin, a lanky college student who idolized his older cousin Teddy. The president's favorite niece, Eleanor, also visited, but did not seem to get on well with her cousin, Alice. Eleanor was rather plain and shy, while Alice was an international celebrity, widely regarded as an American "princess." Walker was shocked to see Alice smoking cigarettes and sipping alcohol. *The president needs to control his daughter better than that,* he thought. *She's going to cause a scandal!*

He mentioned this to Dixon while the two stood guard duty together. "Not your problem, Garrett!" he shrugged. "If the president wants to let her run wild, that's between him and her. You keep your mouth shut about it, and don't say nuthin' to nobody."

"Of course, I won't say nothing. It just seems like—I don't know, just not right."

"Maybe you oughta throw your hat in *that* ring, now that 'Dancin' Dancy' passed you by. Seems to me they're two birds of a feather. You'd be right at home."

"Very funny," scowled Walker. "She doesn't even know who I am. Maybe I forgot to tell you, but Abigail turned down that cousin's proposal. She said she just couldn't marry somebody that much older than her, 'specially since she wasn't in love with him."

"Well, them's two good reasons not to marry somebody, I reckon. Clears the road for you, though. Like I said before, trot down to Richmond and get on your knee. All that crocheting wasn't for nuthin', you know." Dixon laughed and slapped his knee in merriment.

"She's not in Richmond. She usually spends summers with the relatives in Charleston, but since she backed out of marrying one of 'em, she decided to stay in Decatur this summer. Says she's doing the cooking—they still ain't found anybody to replace Beulah, and it's been a year now. Since her mother passed on a while back, it's all on her now."

"You're *kidding!*" Dixon cackled. "'Dancin' Dancy' in the *kitchen?* I'd have to see it to believe it. That just ain't *natural!* What's the world *comin'* to?"

Walker sighed and shook his head. "Did you ever hear back from Jenny?"

"Jenny? Who's Jenny?" Dixon made a wry face. "There's a mighty fine young lady at Reverend Wright's church, though. Sings like a angel, and looks like one, too. I ain't managed to meet her yet, but I'm workin' on it." He held up both hands, with fingers crossed.

"Ask him to introduce you to her."

"Garrett! That's the best idea you ever had! That's exactly what I'll do, soon as we get back home!"

Before returning home, however, they had one more job ahead of them—Roosevelt was launching a barnstorming tour of New England and it was "all hands on deck" for the Secret Service agents. The midterm elections were approaching, and the president was to campaign for his fellow Republicans. The tour was only twelve days long, lasting from late August to early September, but there were dozens of towns, dinners, receptions, speeches, and parades, and doubtless thousands of hands to shake. Providing adequate security would be no small task.

They steamed out of Oyster Bay aboard the presidential yacht, the USS *Sylph*, a 123-foot graceful, steel-hulled beauty. Less than four hours later, they dropped anchor in New Haven, Connecticut, where Roosevelt had received an honorary degree from Yale University a few months before. Walker and Dixon exchanged an uneasy glance, and Walker unconsciously dropped his right hand to the pocket of his suit, where he felt the outline of the palm pistol. A short parade, in which the president was escorted by Connecticut National Guard troops to the accompaniment of cheering crowds, was quickly followed by a short speech by Roosevelt in Meriden, twenty miles north by rail. Another twenty miles inland brought them to the state capital, Hartford, where he attended a formal dinner and gave another speech before spending the night with a prominent Republican.

In Hartford, Roosevelt rode from the train station to the capitol in an electric automobile, escorted by bicycle-riding policemen and mounted troops. The Secret Service agents followed closely in carriages. Throughout the day, Walker could not stop thinking about the attempts on McKinley's life, and constantly studied the nearby rooftops and watched the crowds along the street, trying to anticipate threatening movements. By the end of the day, he was drained and tense, and slept poorly.

They made their way back to the coast, where Roosevelt boarded a private yacht to Newport, Rhode Island, where he stayed with a former Rough Rider comrade, and the next day traveled by train to Boston, with numerous whistlestops along the way. Walker lost count of the small towns where the president gave short speeches from the train platform. Over the next two days, he gave eleven speeches in three states. Constant movement, cheering crowds, brass bands, parades—it all became a blur to Walker as they passed through New Hampshire, Maine, and Vermont. He found that he couldn't even remember which state he was in. The president gave six speeches in six different towns on Labor Day. Walker wondered how Roosevelt found the energy to keep up such a pace, until after one stop he observed the president board the train and throw up in the toilet of his Pullman car. *I guess he's human, after all,* he thought, and he quickly and silently walked away.

The following day was particularly grueling, as the president visited eight towns in Massachusetts. He gave speeches, inspected factories, attended luncheons, and shook hands. The agents hovered close by, carefully examining each person who approached.

Wednesday, September 3, was the final day of the tour, and thus was welcomed with a sense of relief by Walker and the other agents.

The day's itinerary started bright and early as the governor arrived to join Roosevelt for a parade into the town of Pittsfield. Walker was by now so used to cheering crowds, waving flags, steam whistles, and bands that he hardly noticed them. Roosevelt gave a speech at nine o'clock and then climbed into a carriage to go to another scheduled event a few miles away. Roosevelt sat in the right rear seat, with Governor Crane to his left. Cortelyou sat facing them, and Craig was on the front left, beside the driver. The Secret Service agents piled into other carriages to follow.

As they proceeded down South Street in downtown Pittsfield, disaster struck. An electric trolley came from behind the caravan of carriages, the driver somehow unaware that trolley service had been suspended for the duration of the president's visit. The trolley passed the carriages bearing the Secret Service agents and the president's staff, and just as it approached the lead carriage, its driver made a left turn across the tracks, not expecting there to be any trolley traffic.

The trolley driver clanged his bell frantically and the occupants of the carriage turned to look. Craig stood up and cried out, "Look out! Hold fast!" But it was too late. The trolley crashed into the carriage, splintering it to pieces. Roosevelt was thrown out like a rag doll, suffering facial bruises and injuring his left leg. The governor was miraculously unhurt, and Cortelyou only smashed his nose on the carriage door. One of the four horses was killed. Craig, however, fell onto the tracks and was run over, his skull and upper torso crushed beneath the steel wheels of the trolley.

Craig's loss was devastating to the president and to all of the agents. Walker was stunned at the suddenness of the accident. He had seen a lot of bloodshed while in the army, but the bloody mess on the tracks was horrifying, and made him feel sick to his stomach. At the remaining stops on the day's itinerary, Roosevelt, limping and sporting a black eye, split lip and bruised cheek, spoke only a few words and asked the crowds not to cheer, out of respect for the memory of "Big Bill." Upon reaching Bridgeport, he asked to be excused from making a speech at all, and boarded the *Sylph* to return to Oyster Bay.

It was very late in the afternoon when the silent entourage reached Sagamore Hill. No one had much appetite for eating dinner, and the lights were turned out early. Walker took his guard post on the drive, thankful for the quiet darkness. As he gazed up at the starry sky, he remembered the conversation with Reverend Wright. *It wasn't God's will for Craig to die,* he thought. *God didn't make that happen —it was a consequence of someone's bad decision. Somehow, though, God will make something good out of it. I don't know how, but I believe it.* These thoughts gave Walker a measure of comfort, even as the sadness remained.

19

SURPRISES

Only three days after the return to Oyster Bay, Roosevelt made another quick trip into the South, this time to Chattanooga, but without the First Lady. His face still bruised from the accident, he made brief speeches from the train at innumerable stops along the way. Walker thought surely this would be the last trip for a while, and he was more than a little surprised—and not particularly pleased—to learn that barely a week later the president was setting off on another campaign tour. This time, he was heading through the Midwest and Upper Plains states. Cincinnati, Detroit, and Indianapolis were the first cities to be visited, and the itinerary included Minnesota, Wisconsin, and Iowa, and other states along the way.

It was to be an eighteen-day barnstorming tour, covering far more territory and with more campaign stops than the New England tour. With the exhaustion of the previous trip still fresh in his memory, Walker regarded the prospect of an even longer outing with trepidation. He could tell that the other agents felt the same way, though no one complained. By the time they returned, they would have been away from their homes and families for nearly seven weeks. Smiles and laughter were rare.

Things went very differently than planned, however. Following an outdoor reception at Sagamore Hill to celebrate his first year in office —an event at which the president shook the hands of more than nine thousand well-wishers in three hours—they departed. It rained steadily as the presidential train crossed Pennsylvania into Ohio. From Cincinnati it was a day-long train to Detroit for another speech and a parade. Roosevelt was on his feet for hours at a time, and something was clearly wrong. Pale in the face, he lacked his usual energy on stage, grimaced frequently, and sweated profusely.

When leaving the venue the next evening in Logansport, Indiana, he hesitated before a sloping path to the waiting carriages. Walker quickly stepped to the president's side with a raised umbrella and offered his arm. Roosevelt was about to decline, but Walker insisted, saying, "Mr. President, this isn't San Juan Hill. Let's do this together, sir." Without a word, Roosevelt gripped his arm and leaned heavily on Walker as they descended slowly and carefully to the street. "This is serious," Walker whispered to the attending navy medic. "He needs help."

The medic apparently agreed, for when they arrived in Indianapolis the next day, four surgeons awaited them. They examined Roosevelt's injured left leg, and promptly sent him to the nearest hospital. The mounted Secret Service agents galloped ahead of the carriage, making sure there was no traffic at intersections. The surgeons opened a large swelling on the president's shin, drained and cleaned it. By the time they were finished, it was five o'clock. After allowing Roosevelt a couple of hours to recover from the sedation, he was carried on a stretcher to the train, which departed immediately for Washington. The tour had lasted less than a week.

"I can't help but feel like we've been through this before," Walker said to Dixon as they sat on the train, looking out at the incessant rain.

"You mean like when Mrs. McKinley got sick and we had to cut the trip short?"

"Yeah. She nearly died, you know. I sure hope the president is going to be alright."

"He probably will," Dixon shrugged. "He's a tough one. It'll take more than a bum leg to put him down."

"Well, it was a little scratch on her *finger* that nearly did it for Mrs. McKinley," Walker reminded him. "Little things can turn into big things. I just hope they caught it in time."

"You got a point, there," admitted Dixon. "The docs will have to keep a close eye on him."

"I hope that will be enough," Walker mused. "They thought President McKinley was going to be fine, until all of a sudden, he wasn't. And *then*, all of a sudden, he was *dead*."

Dixon stared intently at him. "What's got you so worried, Garrett? Is it rainin' inside your head, too?"

"I don't know. I've just been thinking about why things happen the way they do. Reverend Wright says God doesn't cause things like this to happen—that sometimes people just make bad decisions and then there are consequences." Walker frowned. "He's probably right, but I think I might rather God *was* doing it. I trust him more than I trust people."

"Doesn't matter what you think or want," Dixon replied bluntly. "It is what it is. Whenever you decide to do something, do you think it's *your* decision, or do you think you're just doing it 'cause God made you?"

"Of course not," Walker frowned. "It *feels* like I make my own choices."

"Then don't get yourself all confused about it. Every day, millions of people all over the world make their own choices, too—some good and some bad. Somehow, the world keeps on turnin'. Just take it a day at a time, and quit worrying 'bout things you can't control."

"Yeah, I guess so." Walker sighed and cocked his head to one side as he looked at Dixon. "How did you get to be so smart, anyway?

"Wasn't my choice," Dixon smirked. "God made me this way."

Walker nearly choked on a laugh, and reached out and knocked Dixon's hat off his head. Dixon returned the favor and mussed Walker's hair. They were swatting and poking at each other when Stover entered the car.

"Well, you two seem to be in good spirits," he said gruffly. "Nobody else is, for sure."

"How is the president doing?" asked Walker.

"Sleeping. He's had a close call, but his temperature is almost normal, and he seems to be resting peacefully. It seems that his infection was found in time. It could have been much worse."

"Much to be thankful for," Dixon nodded.

"When we get to Washington, we won't be going to the White House," Stover said in a businesslike tone. "The renovation work isn't finished yet, so the family will be staying at a house nearby, on Jackson Place. I understand that it's a lot smaller than the White House, so it should make our job easier."

Walker and Dixon exchanged a puzzled look. "How is that you know this, and we don't?" Walker asked.

Stover looked a little uncomfortable. "With Foster demoted and Craig dead, Mr. Wilkie decided to make me the new chief agent. Cortelyou shared the telegram with me in Indianapolis, and I'll be meeting with Wilkie as soon as we get back. I've been on the detail longer than anyone else, and I'm the oldest agent, so. . . ." He shrugged as his voice trailed off.

"Congratulations, Stover!" Dixon stood to shake his hand.

"They certainly picked the right man," Walker agreed, also standing and extending his hand. "You'll do a great job, I'm sure. Let us know if there's anything we can do to help out!"

"I appreciate that. I'm sure we'll all work together just fine—we have a good team." Pausing briefly, Stover continued. "The D.C. police will have men on the street, so we'll only have agents inside the front and back doors. It should be pretty boring work, but boring is good. We don't need any more excitement." After another round of handshakes and congratulations, he left to return to the president's Pullman.

"Well, how about that!" Walker commented, with raised eyebrows.

"For some reason, that makes me hungry," Dixon replied. "Let's go to the dining car and get some donuts and coffee."

"Right behind you." Walker took his notebook with him wrote a few more paragraphs for his book while they sat and talked until very late. His story now reached to the point when General Wheeler left the Philippines to return to the States. They reminisced over their experiences, and Walker jotted down a few notes for future reference. When he finally went to bed, he slept soundly until Stover shook him awake shortly before the train arrived in Washington.

As it turned out, the president's health crisis was not finished. Four days later, on a Sunday afternoon, Roosevelt was taken to the hospital for a second surgery. His temperature was rising sharply, and the incision on his left shin was red and swelling. Although he wouldn't admit it, he was clearly in a lot of pain. This time, the surgeons cut all the way to the bone and scraped it clean. Roosevelt spent the next two weeks in a wheelchair with his leg sticking straight out in front.

During those two weeks, Walker had a daily posting at the front door of the house, where he observed a steady stream of visitors, including government officials, foreign dignitaries, and various well-wishers bringing flowers and gifts of cakes, pies, and other sweets. He also knew from reading the newspaper that some of the visitors were owners of the largest coal mines in the United States, and others represented the coal miners' union. When Roosevelt led these two groups to a settlement of the months-long coal strike as winter approached, it made the headlines, and Roosevelt was celebrated as a hero.

"He's saving the country from a wheelchair," Walker marveled, pouring a cup of coffee in the kitchen while taking a few minutes break.

"Somebody needs to save *me* from this lemon cake," Dixon replied, cutting a generous slice.

"Like you saved somebody from that blueberry tart yesterday? You better wipe that icing off your face before somebody sees it."

"Mmmm," Dixon murmured, his mouth full. "The Good Book says, 'Don't muzzle the ox that treads the corn.' Reverend Wright said so, last Sunday."

"Speaking of the reverend, did you ask him to introduce you to that young lady you were wanting to meet?"

"Nope," said Dixon with a straight face, but then couldn't contain a wide grin. "*She* asked him to introduce *her* to *me*! I ain't touched the ground since."

"So *that's* where you were all Sunday afternoon!" Walker nodded approvingly as he blew gently on his steaming coffee. "What's her name?"

"Sally. She's a graduate of Booker T. Washington's school in Tuskegee, and teaches in the colored school here. She likes that I've met him and read his book, and that I help protect President Roosevelt. That dinner at the White House earned him a lot of credit with colored folks. I'm not as educated as her, but she seems to like me."

"'*Seems* to like you?'"

Dixon grinned again, almost embarrassed. "Yeah, she likes me. And I like her. A lot."

"I can tell! I knew something was going on. Glad to hear it! I hope this leads to something really good."

"So do I," Dixon said, very seriously. He swallowed a bite of the slice of lemon cake, and wiped yellow icing from his mouth. "Heard anything else from Dancy?"

"Just that she's coming to Richmond for her usual fall visit. Arriving sometime in late November and staying through the New Year." Walker held up a warning hand. "Don't say it again! I ain't throwing my hat in nobody's ring. I've got plenty of time for that, later."

"Well, I just hope Old Man Dancy don't starve to death while she's out of the kitchen, gallavantin' around Old Virginny." They both burst out laughing at the thought, and then it was quiet for a moment while Dixon finished his cake and Walker his coffee.

"Stover was right," said Walker. "This is the most boring work we've done since joining the agency. I'm not sure how much more of this I can take."

"Don't bother me none," Dixon replied nonchalantly. "I got plenty to think about." He adjusted his shoulder holster and straightened his tie. Bending forward and pointing at a plate of cookies, he growled menacingly, "I'll be back!" Then, with a grin, he strolled back to his post at the back door, doing a quick little dance step along the way.

Walker stared in disbelief and shook his head. *I've never seen him like this. Is that what it's like to be in love? I sure hope Sally feels the same way.* He put his empty cup in the sink with some other dishes and returned to the front door.

Despite Roosevelt's efforts, the Republican Party lost seats in Congress in the midterm elections, but fewer than was normal for the lead party in midterms, so the president was jubilant. His family had moved back into the renovated White House, and he was freed from the wheelchair and walking without a limp. The president was bursting with energy and ready for some action. A hunting trip was just what the doctor ordered, he decided.

"Garrett! Dixon!" called out Stover. "Get your bags ready to go. I'm assigning the two of you to go with the president. You're leaving tomorrow morning at sunup for Mississippi on a hunting trip, so pack accordingly."

"What are we hunting?" asked Walker.

"*He's* hunting black bear. You're *guarding*—not hunting."

"Any special threats we should know about?" asked Dixon.

"Nothing specific," replied Stover, frowning. "But there is some reason for concern. The president just appointed a black man to be the customs collector for the port of Charleston, and that has some southern whites pretty stirred up. There's been some careless talk, which we take seriously. The hunt will be on private land, and we're not announcing it in the press—so keep it quiet. There will be armed sentries patrolling around the property, but I want you two in there with the president just in case anything develops. We're not taking any chances."

"I didn't know there *were* any bears in Mississippi," Walker said, scratching his head. "Wouldn't it be better to hunt in the Smokies, or further north?"

"Why don't you suggest that to the president, Garrett," Stover snapped sarcastically. "And then come back and tell us what he says."

Walker blinked. "I reckon I won't," he conceded. "We'll go to Mississippi, if that's where he wants to hunt."

As it turned out, the hunt was a dismal failure. Roosevelt, who had a well-known reputation as a big game hunter, shot nothing in five days. The weather was unremittingly wet and rainy, and the woods thick with vines and briars, dripping and steaming. Despite the best efforts of the hounds and riders to drive game toward the president, nothing was stirring. Roosevelt's mood became increasingly irritable as each day passed.

Walker and Dixon, riding spirited horses provided by the plantation owner, shadowed the president at a discreet distance, trying to keep him in sight without being noticed. Each carried a repeating rifle in a saddle holster, along with their .38 revolvers concealed under their Mongolian camel-hair coats. Walker also wore a machete in a scabbard hanging from his belt—a sentimental reminder of his Cuban friend, José, who had fought alongside him against the Spanish.

On a mid-week morning, they crept slowly through the tangled growth, tracking the president's party more by sound than by sight. They snaked their way through a maze of gnarled tree trunks and rotting logs heavy with moss and mushrooms. Steam from the forest floor rose to meet the Spanish moss hanging from the weirdly twisted limbs. The oblique sunlight did not penetrate the heavy mist, creating a spooky, otherworldly scene. There were no bird calls, no squirrels chattering, and no wind.

Dixon motioned to stop, and they reined their horses to a halt. The only sound was that of dew dripping constantly onto the wet leaves and pine straw. "Can you hear them?" he asked quietly.

Walker strained his ears, but shook his head. "I don't hear nothin'. Where do you s'pose they went?"

Dixon shifted his weight and the saddle leather creaked faintly. "I'll head over this way, and you go that way. If you don't pick 'em up pretty soon, angle back towards me."

Walker prodded his mount forward, stopping frequently to listen. His horse snorted and shied as a rat scurried into the bushes. Walker could sense that the eerie gloom of the silent, damp forest was making the horse edgy, so he patted its neck and spoke softly to calm it. As they proceeded, he observed a particularly large mossy log blocking their path. With thorny thickets at each side, there was no good way to go around, so he urged the horse forward, intending to clear it, since the log was only about three feet in diameter. The horse took a couple of running strides and gathered itself for the jump, and just as it left the ground, the unexpected happened.

A large black bear, weighing probably four hundred pounds, suddenly rose from the other side of the log where he had been sleeping. Apparently awakened by the horse's approach, he stood up on his hind legs and turned to face them with a snarl. The horse was already airborne, and yet somehow managed to defy gravity and, with an indescribable neigh of terror, spun completely about in midair, lashing out and kicking the bear as he landed. Walker was catapulted from the saddle, spinning and flying head over heels to land face down, not a second too soon, as the terrified horse galloped over him, miraculously missing him with its hooves. Had the ground not been so soft and wet, he could have been knocked unconscious by the landing.

Rising to his knees, he saw the angry bear getting back on its feet, not happy about having been kicked by a horse. He also saw his revolver lying on the ground between himself and the bear, which bared its fangs and charged. There was no time to think. He had the machete only halfway out of its scabbard when the bear struck. The hours of training by "Big Bill" Craig came in handy, as he raised his left arm to ward off the bear's smashing blow and rolled to his right. The roll was not entirely a matter of choice, as the force of the bear's slap sent him several feet into the brush and ripped open his left sleeve from shoulder to elbow.

As he rose to a crouch, he pulled the machete free and gripped the handle with both hands. The enraged bear lunged, snarling with saliva dripping from its hideous jaws, reaching out with long black, curved claws. Instinctively screaming the "rebel yell," Walker drove the blade upward into the animal's chest with all his strength, and hot blood spurted into his face. The impact of four hundred pounds of fury bowled him over, and he felt the claws raking his back and heard the jaws snapping in his ears, and smelled the stench of the beast and its foul breath.

Lying in the wet leaves and vines with the bear atop him, he thought, *This is the end. I'm a dead man.* But the bear was still. Afraid to move, Walker lay there for a long moment in the quiet, his heart pounding, listening to the forest's dripping sounds all around him. Finally deciding that it was safe to get up, he began to try to wriggle out from under the bear. It proved to be a difficult task, and after several minutes of struggle, he stopped to rest.

"Garrett!" He heard Dixon's voice. It sounded close.

"Over here!" he croaked. After multiple calls back and forth, Dixon finally found him. Tethering his nervous horse to a small sapling, he stepped through the bushes and stood looking down at Walker.

"What the—?" he exclaimed. "Garrett, how'd you manage to get underneath the biggest bear in the state?"

"Just lucky, I guess. Get this monster off me."

Dixon grunted as he dragged the bear, rolling it over until Walker could clamber back to his feet. He pulled his machete from the carcass, wiped it on the bear, and returned it to the scabbard. Dixon watched, slack jawed, as Walker fetched his revolver and hat.

"You killed this bear with a *machete*?"

"He didn't give me no choice. It was me or him. I thought sure it was gonna be me, but thanks to José and the good Lord. . . ." His voice trailed off.

"Well, if that don't just beat all!" Dixon marveled, hands on hips and shaking his head. He then gave a Walker a critical look, frowning. "There's a creek a little ways up yonder. You need to wash that blood off b'fore the president sees you. You know Roosevelt wanted to bag the first kill."

"Considering the circumstances, I ain't gonna apologize. I don't reckon he has to know about this, anyway. Lucky for me, it's all the bear's blood, not mine."

"No, I don't think so," disagreed Dixon. "You got some gashes there, and there. And your coat is pretty tore up. Let's get you to the creek."

Walker stripped to the waist and washed himself and his clothes in the chill waters. The sharp stinging alerted him to cuts he hadn't known were there. His coat and shirt were shredded, and he had multiple lacerations on his back and a long gash in his left arm, as well as bloody scratches in his scalp. There were less serious cuts on his face and hands. Wringing as much water as possible out of his shirt, he put the ragged clothes back on, and pulled his hat over his wet hair.

"Maybe Roosevelt won't notice what a mess I am," he said hopefully.

"Just tell him your horse threw you and you fell in the creek. That coat looked pretty ragged already, anyway. Soon as we get back to camp, I'll put some ointment on those cuts and bandage your arm. Don't want to get an infection, y'know."

"Did you see my horse?"

"I b'lieve that's him coming, yonder." Sure enough, Walker's horse was watching warily from a short distance away. Dixon rode slowly to the animal. The presence of another horse seemed to reassure him, and he allowed Walker to approach and mount.

They heard the baying of the hounds in the distance. Knowing that the hunters would be following the dogs, they headed in that direction. It took the better part of an hour before they came upon a clearing where the hunting party was gathered. A young bear half the size of the one that fought Walker was tied to a tree with a rope around its neck, exhausted and bleeding. Roosevelt had been summoned to make the kill. The president arrived at the same time as Walker and Dixon. He did not even bother to dismount.

"Put that poor creature out of his misery," he snapped. "There's nothing sportsmanlike in killing an animal like that." Reining his horse about, he left the clearing in disgust.

"Wish he coulda run into *my* bear," whispered Walker, covering his mouth with his hand. "That woulda been real sportsmanlike."

"'Specially if he just had a machete," grinned Dixon. "Let's go," he added, slapping the reins against the horse's neck. "Don't want to lose him again."

The rest of the week went no better for the hunters, and it was a quiet train ride back to the capitol. The country's newspapers were divided between poking fun at the president for failing to make a kill, and praising him for refusing to kill a helpless animal just for the sake of killing it. On the whole, Roosevelt found his reputation enhanced by the incident.

Walker healed quickly, thankful that his injuries were not more serious. He was sentimentally attached to the camel hair coat, and got Daisy to stitch it back together. With Dixon spending most of his free time visiting Sally, he focused his mind on the writing of his book. It seemed that life was returning to a normal routine when, a few days before Thanksgiving, he was surprised to receive a letter from Abigail Dancy, in her usual pastel yellow envelope.

November 18

Dear Walker,

I arrived here in Richmond a few days ago. It is a relief to get away from Decatur! I plan to stay here longer than usual this time. I hope that you will come down for a visit. My uncle says to invite you to Thanksgiving dinner. I know it is short notice, but please do come! I would love to hear about your adventures in person. Give my greetings to Beulah and Daisy.

With kindest regards,

Abigail Dancy

On a second piece of paper, she had written her uncle's address and a telephone number. *So, the family has its own telephone. No surprise there,* he thought. He looked at the yellow stationery again, tracing the gracefully curving script with his eyes, without actually reading it.

Lying on his back in bed, staring at the ceiling, Walker argued with himself whether to accept the invitation or not. *You're just asking for trouble,* one voice said. *She's a rich man's daughter, and you're a farmer's son. It means nothing to her. Forget it and move on.*

But, another voice replied, *she wrote notes and sent you needlework while you were away, turned down a marriage proposal from a rich man, and now she's cooking in the kitchen at home. Maybe she's not what you think.* Then he remembered Dixon's words—"You don't know, 'til you know."

Impulsively, he made his decision. Moving to the chair at the small table by the window, he reached for a sheet of paper, and began writing a reply.

Dear Abigail,
Thank you for the invitation to Thanksgiving dinner with your uncle's family. I will be happy to accept. . . .

20

HAT IN THE RING

"Are you sure this is the place?" Walker asked, peering from the carriage.

"Yessuh," replied the cab driver over his shoulder. "This be Rosemont." Walker stepped down to the graveled surface of the long, circular driveway, lined with oaks and perfectly trimmed shrubs. He looked up at the four massive white columns, behind which was a second-floor balcony high above ten-foot tall, carved wooden doubledoors. Each window was flanked by red shutters, and rose bushes climbed trellises ringing the porch. He had assumed that Abigail's uncle would have a large, expensive house—after all, he had his own telephone—but this was beyond his wildest imagination. "Lordy mercy!" he exclaimed under his breath. He could feel his palms beginning to sweat.

The sound of the driver clearing his throat brought him back to reality. Fishing a fifty-cent piece out of his pocket, he tipped the cabby and watched him drive away. Standing alone in the drive, contemplating the imposing mansion, he felt very small and out of place. *Coming here was a mistake,* he thought. *But here I am, so might as well make the best of it.* He was glad that he had sought the advice of Reverend Wright and purchased a new gray three-piece suit, with a frock coat and matching wide-brimmed fedora, and patent leather shoes. Adjusting his new silk tie, he consoled himself with the knowledge that, even if he didn't belong here, at least he was well-dressed. "Act like you own the place," the reverend had said, "and nobody will know the difference."

Walker wiped his hands on his pants and, taking a deep breath, he ascended the steps to the front porch and approached the towering double-doors, where a carved wooden lion's head gripped a brass ring in its mouth. He rapped the door sharply with the ring, stepped back, and waited. Momentarily, the door was opened by a white-headed black butler in red livery. "Mistah Garrett, I presume?" he asked, in a slow, dignified voice. He ushered Walker into the foyer and relieved him of his hat. "I'll see that Miss Abigail knows you are heah, suh."

Walker stood on a thick, crimson rug, hands clasped behind him, taking in the sumptuous setting. The entrance hall extended some forty feet from the door, leading to a wide staircase whose steps were covered with the same crimson carpet. A crystal chandelier with electric lights hung on a brass chain in the middle of the space, and there were decorative vases displaying freshly-cut red and white roses. A massive grandfather clock made the only sound, its large pendulum swinging slowly as it tick-tocked in a rich, resonant voice. Family portraits looked down from the walls. Through rounded arches on each side of the foyer, he could see a parlor to the left, with sofas, padded armchairs, and an elaborate fireplace with a moose head mounted above it. To the right was the dining room, its twenty-foot-long table covered with a white cloth and red lace, decorated with candlesticks and roses, and set with white plates and red napkins. He caught the pleasing aroma of something cooking as it wafted from the kitchen through the dining room.

I can see why this place is called 'Rosemont.' I think I'll plant some rose bushes at the house when I get back. And put a moose head over the wood-burning stove. The last thought made him snort through his nose, and he pretended to cough to hide it.

"Mr. Garrett!" A heavy-set, middle-aged man emerged from the parlor, cigar in hand, and approached Walker. He had thin gray hair and a closely-trimmed mustache, and wore wire-rimmed spectacles and a brown suit, with a red rose in his lapel. "James Dancy," he said, as they shook hands. "You are Abigail's friend from Washington, I believe?"

"Yes sir, Mr. Dancy. Walker Garrett. Thank you for inviting me to dinner with your family, sir. It's an honor, sir." Walker thought that James Dancy did not resemble his brother Frank, in Decatur, very much.

"Glad you could make it! We've heard a lot about you from Abigail. It sounds like you've had some amazing adventures, and we're eager to hear all about them." He gestured for Walker to join him in the parlor. "We are expecting some other guests shortly—all family, mind you. Have a seat. Care for a cigar?"

"No cigar for me, thank you, sir." He was about to make a comment about the moose head when he saw a column of smoke rising from one of the chairs which had its back toward him. A man arose from the chair, took a draw on his cigar, and blew a cloud of smoke upward. He was a good bit younger than James Dancy, with a full head of curly brown hair, bushy eyebrows, a swooping mustache, and a receding chin. Observing his black coat, Walker initially thought he might be a clergyman, but the bright pink necktie and diamond stickpin suggested otherwise.

"Garrett, meet my nephew, Sidney Montague Callahan. Sid, this is Walker Garrett, a friend of Abigail's, from Washington—he's a Secret Service bodyguard for the president."

Callahan nodded civilly, but did not extend his hand, and sat back down. He fixed his eyes on Walker so intently that Walker felt he was being evaluated and measured, and he sensed Callahan's disapproval. Taking a seat on a sofa, he returned the nod. "Pleased to meet you, Mr. Callahan." Callahan took another pull on his cigar.

"Sidney is from Charleston. Came up yesterday," continued Dancy. "He's just become a partner in the top law firm in the state of South Carolina—maybe in the entire South!" He raised his cigar as if it were a champagne glass, toasting his nephew's success. Callahan returned the gesture with a modest nod.

"I'll pass your compliment on to daddy," Callahan smirked. "He'll appreciate that."

"And I meant it sincerely," returned Dancy emphatically. "He's the finest legal mind I know of, anywhere! I've always expected him to be appointed to the bench, maybe even become a federal judge, you never know."

"That won't happen until we get a Democrat back in the White House," scowled Callahan in disgust. "All these n----r loving Republicans care about is pleasing their damn Yankee voters by interfering with Southern ways of life. Roosevelt thinks he can put that coon in charge of our port down in Charleston, but—" He paused to take another pull at the cigar.

Before he could resume his tirade, there was a rapping at the front door, and the butler admitted more guests—two couples, each with small children in tow. The children ran into the parlor shouting "Grandy! Grandy!" and climbed onto Dancy's lap. Mrs. Dancy appeared, greeting her children and grandchildren, giving hugs all around. The next few minutes were rather hectic, as the newcomers —Dancy's son and daughter and their spouses—were introduced to Walker, and the children rushed off to play elsewhere.

Just as everyone was settling down in their seats, Abigail sailed into the room. Walker blinked twice and caught his breath. She was even more lovely than he had remembered. Her cream-colored, long-sleeved dress flattered her figure, the bodice and sleeves accented with red embroidery. Her dark hair was arranged in a soft bun at the nape of her neck, which was encircled by a delicate gold chain, bearing a single pearl. Her eyes sparkled as she came and took Walker's arm, and sat beside him on the sofa. His heart was beating much faster than usual, and he forced himself to take his eyes off her and breathe deeply and slowly. She warmly greeted the two couples, but did not acknowledge Callahan's presence. *Probably because he's been here since yesterday already,* Walker speculated. *No need to greet him again. I wonder why he's staring at her like that. Does he dislike Abigail?*

Dancy resumed the conversation. "Garrett, I hear that you're from Decatur, or around those parts. Is that right?"

"Yes sir, Courtland, actually. I attended the Decatur Academy, which is where I met Abigail."

"I grew up in Decatur, myself, and went to the Academy, too. Decatur's the original homeplace for the Dancy clan. I'd probably still be there, but there's not much work to be had for an architect, and I came east to seek my fortune." Danny gestured toward the richly ornamented room with both hands—proof that he had succeeded.

Callahan joined the discussion, with cigar smoke puffing from his mouth and nose with each syllable. "So, Garrett, how is it that you come to be in the Secret Service?"

"Mr. John Wilkie, the director of the Secret Service, offered to hire me when he learned of my experience in the Boxer Rebellion. He said he could use young men like us—that's me and another soldier, Dixon. We were together."

"The Boxer Rebellion! How did you come to be in *China*? I thought Abigail said you went to *Cuba*." He seemed almost irritated at this new information.

"I did. And after Cuba we were all sent to the Philippines, and when the Boxer Rebellion broke out, some of us were sent to China to rescue the diplomats, businessmen, and missionaries."

"Didn't you also go to Hawaii for the annexation?" interjected Abigail, squeezing his wrist. "I remember you wrote about that in a letter."

"Yes, and we annexed Guam, too. And we crossed Panama right where the president wants to build a canal. That's going to be a real job, I can tell you. Some of the worst jungle I've seen anywhere."

The butler appeared in the archway and announced that dinner was ready. Everyone rose and began moving toward the dining room. Walker looked down into Abigail's dark eyes. "You look beautiful, Abigail," he murmured.

"You're quite dashing, yourself!" she replied, white teeth flashing behind red lips. "I'm so glad you could come!"

Dancy's wife, children, and grandchildren sat nearest to his seat at the head of the table, with Walker, Abigail, and Callahan further down. Uniformed house servants served the food, Dancy said grace, and the meal began. Roast turkey, cornbread dressing and gravy, sweet potatoes, green beans, and many other dishes filled the table. There was little talking at first, as everyone was hungry and the food was delicious. The children chattered gaily, sometimes with mouths full. Walker gathered from the conversation that James' son and son-in-law were a history professor and a surgeon, respectively.

"What do soldiers eat for Thanksgiving dinner?" asked Dancy's daughter, Emily, with a friendly smile.

Walker laughed and shook his head. "The same thing as the day before and the day after—hardtack, oatmeal, sometimes rice and beans, and fruit if you can get it."

"That sounds horrible!" she exclaimed.

"There wasn't much variety," he admitted, "but there was always plenty of it. We didn't go hungry."

"Did you ever kill anybody?" asked her six-year-old son.

"Thomas! That is a rude question!" she reproved him. "You don't ask that to anyone—especially not at the dinner table!" Walker gave the boy an apologetic smile as he took another bite of turkey. Conversation turned to other things for the next few minutes, until it appeared that everyone had eaten their fill.

"Let's retire to the parlor while the table is cleared and dessert is served," said Mr. Dancy, standing up. Walker noticed that Dancy seemed to suggest that these things happened by themselves, and did not acknowledge the existence of the servants. "You children run along and play until it's ready." They immediately leaped from their chairs and charged noisily up the stairs. "Didn't have to tell *them* twice!" he chuckled. They all returned to their seats in the parlor, and each of the men—except for Walker—lit cigars.

"I'm curious, Walker," said Dancy's daughter-in-law, Rebecca. "Of all the places you went, which was your favorite?"

"You know," Walker mused, "I can't believe I'm saying this, but I think the Gobi Desert was my favorite. We spent three weeks riding camels in blazing heat during the day and freezing cold at night, eating boiled millet three times a day, going from water hole to water hole—it was miserable. But it was incredible how many stars you could see at night! So beautiful! The desolation, and the quiet remoteness of the place—it was like being on another planet. It was quite an experience. I wouldn't want to go back, but it was something special to me."

"Oh my!" she responded with wide eyes. "That is remarkable! How interesting!"

"As you know," intoned Dancy's son, Charles, the history professor, "we've had quite a debate here about the wisdom of annexing these foreign territories in Hawaii, Guam, and the Philippines. Did you form any opinions about that while you were there?"

Walker cleared his throat and hesitated before answering. "General Wheeler explained to me that soldiers follow orders and don't question their superiors." He cleared his throat again and rubbed his hands together nervously. "But I don't think the public grasps the real reasons why we wanted control of those places. President McKinley said it was 'to civilize and Christianize' the Filipinos, and to bring prosperity and democracy to Hawaii, but those people already had their own schools, hospitals, churches, newspapers—everything they needed. Hawaii already had a constitution and electric lights."

"So then, what do you think was the real reason?"

"I think Captain Mahan's book explains it. Have you read it—*The Influence of Sea Power Upon History*? He said we should take control of strategic locations around the world to have coaling stations for our navy. It's all about projecting power and defending national interests. It doesn't sound as nice as 'we're only trying to help them,' but it's more true, I think."

"Yes, I've read that book," Charles nodded. "It's one of the most influential books of the last century. So, do you agree with Mahan and the imperialists, or do you, like Bryan and most Democrats, oppose annexation?" All eyes focused expectantly on Walker.

"Well, since the annexations have already happened, my opinion on that doesn't matter much," he shrugged, "but there were certainly two sides to that debate. The Hawaiians and Filipinos didn't need us to give them a better life, but they were not strong enough to defend themselves alone. If we had done nothing, some country like Japan or Germany would probably have seized them. Maybe we could have done something short of outright annexation to help them. I'm sure they would have been happy to let us build naval bases there to help secure their independence, and we could have traded with them just as much. But I'm no expert, so that's just my opinion."

"A very insightful opinion, Walker," Charles smiled. "One of the most reasonable and balanced that I've heard. Maybe you should run for office!"

"Not me!" Walker shuddered. "General Wheeler says that politicians see things the way they want them to be, and soldiers see them the way they are. I guess we need both, but I'm definitely not a politician."

"You were familiar with General Wheeler?" asked James Dancy. "How's that?"

"I was practically a member of his family, growing up. It's because of him that I went to Cuba. He made me an aide to his son, Joseph—Captain Joe. We spent a lot of time talking."

Callahan shifted in his seat, leaning forward and fixing his eyes on Walker. "It's the Secret Service's job to protect the president, right?" His tone was aggressive and challenging.

"Well," Walker hesitated. "Yes and no. It's actually kind of complicated."

"Either it *is* their job, or it *isn't*," snapped Callahan. "Was the Secret Service not responsible for protecting McKinley in Buffalo last year?"

"Sidney!" protested James Dancy. "Mr. Garrett doesn't—"

Callahan raised his palm. "I'm just trying to establish who was responsible for the president getting killed while the Secret Service was protecting him, that's all."

"I'll be happy to explain," Walker said, agreeably. "But like I said, it's kind of complicated."

"I don't see how it could be complicated," Callahan growled. "But please enlighten us."

Walker could see that the others in the room were very uneasy, giving each other nervous looks. Accordingly, he chose his words carefully and spoke calmly at a casual pace. "We have protected the last three presidents to some extent, but all of them have objected to having guards around them. For example, the McKinleys liked to take carriage drives around Washington by themselves. Even after the assassination, Congress still hasn't budgeted any money to pay for presidential security—"

"What!" exclaimed James Dancy. "That can't be true!"

"It's true," Walker assured him. "Director Wilkie has to take money from the counterfeiting funds to pay us, which isn't actually legal, but he has no choice. And the Secret Service still has no authority to control security around the president. Local police have more authority than we do. There were a lot of policemen and a squad of artillery soldiers in the Temple of Music that day, and only three Secret Service guards—and we weren't allowed to be next to the president because other political leaders wanted to stand next to him."

He looked at Callahan and shrugged. "Besides that, it's hard to stop someone who's willing to die to carry out their plan. Czolgosz didn't care about escaping. He knew he would be caught and executed for it, but he didn't care. He said 'I done my duty.' When a man is that fanatical, he's dangerous. It may be time to make a choice about whether to keep presidents safe, or to let them mingle with the people. It's hard to do both."

"So true!" echoed Dancy, and the couples on the other sofa nodded agreement. Callahan grunted and sat back in his chair, chewing irritably on his cigar and exhaling another column of smoke into the air.

Charles spoke up again. "If I'm not mistaken, Walker, when you crossed the Gobi Desert you would have been in Mongolia. How did you get back to the U.S., with Boxers on the rampage all across China?"

Walker laughed. "That was a bit of a problem! We had to head north into Russia and take their Siberian Railway across to Moscow and St. Petersburg, and from there we passed through Berlin, Paris, London, and Glasgow before crossing the Atlantic on a liner. It was quite a trip!"

"You should write a book about it!" exclaimed Abigail, patting his hand.

"As a matter of fact, I'm working on that already," Walker grinned, blushing a bit. "I'm up to the point where we are crossing the Gobi. It's been like reliving the experience."

"Excellent! Let us know when you get it published," James said, waving his cigar in the air. "I want to read it!"

"Speaking of Russia," interjected Charles again, "according to the newspapers, it sounds like Russia and Japan are about to mix it up over there. I can't believe the Japanese would be so foolish as to go up against one of the greatest powers in Europe."

"They are definitely about to go to war," Walker agreed. "I saw the preparations underway. But I don't think it's going to turn out the way everyone seems to expect. Russia is going to get embarrassed badly, I think."

Callahan emitted a derisive cough, smoke exploding from his mouth and nostrils. Ignoring him, Charles protested, "You can't be serious! Why do you think so?"

"In the international rescue expedition, we saw the Russian and Japanese soldiers fighting against the Chinese army, and there was no comparison. The Japanese soldiers were cold, hard killers, and the Russians were brave but disorganized, poorly led, and generally incompetent. Besides, the war will surely be fought on the Pacific coast, practically in Japan's backyard. Russia will have to send its troops and equipment thousands of miles across the continent on a single-track rail system. They're at a big disadvantage."

Charles leaned forward intently as Walker continued. "Furthermore, remember that Mahan showed that naval power wins wars, and Russia has no naval power in the East. Japan will dominate at sea, and Russia doesn't stand a chance, in my opinion."

"Well, you certainly have given this some thought!" Charles stroked his chin. "I'm afraid I can't rebut anything you've said. I guess I'm just not ready to accept that an Asian country can defeat a European power. It's never happened."

Dixon's words from two years ago flashed back into Walker's mind, and he smiled as he repeated them: "After this war, I think you'll be calling *Russia* a 'country' and *Japan* a 'power.' I know that Tocqueville predicted that America and Russia would become the two greatest powers in the world, and I think he's right about America—but Russia's not even close yet. I don't know if it ever will be, but as of right now, I think they are pretty soft."

Charles clapped his hands and grinned in delight. "Fascinating! I enjoy talking to you, Walker! I wish that my university students could think and express themselves as clearly as you do!"

"I hate to interrupt this stimulating conversation," James said as he stood abruptly, "but Jefferson says that dessert is ready in the dining room! Let's all head that way!"

As everyone made their way toward the dining room, Walker felt a great sense of relief at having survived the battery of questions. It was intimidating to converse with such highly educated people, but he thought he had acquitted himself reasonably well. He felt a squeeze of his hand and looked down at Abigail. She was looking at him a bit oddly, he thought.

"Is something wrong?" he whispered.

"You amaze me, Walker," she whispered back, bumping her shoulder against his arm and squeezing his hand again. She then walked slightly ahead of him into the dining room, and Walker brought up the rear, admiring the knot of perfectly arranged hair against her neck.

An hour later, Walker bid farewell to the Dancy household and went out to await the cab to take him to the train station. Abigail joined him on the front porch, and for the first time, they were alone together. He thanked her again for the invitation, and they both agreed that it had been a very pleasant afternoon. A moment of silence followed, and he felt awkward, unsure what to say next. He held his hat in both hands, sliding his fingers around the brim. Abigail broke the silence.

"Do you know why Sidney was so rude to you?" she asked, somewhat shyly. "Why he tried to embarrass you in front of everyone?"

"I wasn't offended. I just assumed that's how he is—how he talks to people in general."

"That's true, to some extent, but he had a special reason for arguing with *you*." She paused as if unsure whether to continue. "He's my cousin from Charleston—the one who proposed marriage to me a few months ago, and I turned him down. He came here to ask me to reconsider, and I turned him down again."

"Oh!" was all Walker could say. He wasn't sure how this explained Callahan's hostility.

"I didn't know he was going to be here when I invited you to come today. Maybe Uncle James didn't know about the proposal, I don't know. I was horrified when I realized that you were both going to be here, and I feared it would be a disaster. But, Walker—" her eyes met his and sparkled as she smiled. "You were *magnificent*! I was so proud of you!" She reached out and touched his arm. "You must come back for Christmas! Promise me!"

"If your uncle is willing to have me, I'll be happy to come," Walker said. Something seemed to be in his throat making it difficult to swallow, and his voice sounded like someone else was speaking. He couldn't feel the floor under his feet.

Neither of them had heard the approach of the cab. Suddenly, it was there in the drive, waiting. Flustered, Walker took a step toward it, but then turned back to face Abigail. He reached out impulsively and took her hand. Bending, he gallantly kissed the back of her fingers, and she squeezed his hand. He raised his eyes to hers, and saw that they were wide.

"I'll see you Christmas," he said in a strained voice. He released her hand, but she did not release his. Stepping close and rising on tip-toe, she kissed his cheek.

"I'll be waiting."

21

TWISTS AND TURNS

"If you ever do that again, I'll have you *fired*!" shouted Roosevelt, his head jerking even more than usual as he furiously spat out the words. He added emphasis by striking Walker's shoulder sharply with the stout six-foot long pole in his hands.

"What did I do, sir?" Walker expostulated, wide-eyed.

"You had a *perfect* chance to give me a solid *whack*, and you didn't *do* it!" Roosevelt's bared teeth looked particularly fierce. "I won't have you going easy on me! Either fight like a man, or—" The president finished his sentence by swinging his cudgel at Walker's helmeted head. Walker ducked, and the blow whistled harmlessly overhead. He promptly took a swing of his own, smacking Roosevelt in the ribs. "That's more like it!" Roosevelt exulted, and proceeded to skip about, swinging right and left, pressing the attack. A few more minutes of combat and both men stopped to rest, leaning on their sticks, breathing hard. Sweat dripped from Walker's nose.

"That's enough for today," Roosevelt announced with satisfaction. "Good round, Garrett! You're holding your own! Come back on Thursday and we'll do it again!" He was out the door as the last words were spoken, before Walker could even respond. Walker stowed the two padded helmets and vests in the corner, and leaned the two sticks against the wall. *Nobody would believe this,* he thought. *I'm not even sure I believe it, myself. Me, stick-fighting with the President of the United States. On the other hand, when the president is Teddy Roosevelt, maybe they would believe it.*

"How did it go?" chuckled Dixon as they walked to Pennsylvania Avenue and turned toward home. It was already dark, and they turned up their coat collars against the blustery March wind. Snowflakes swirled in the light of the streetlamps.

"I survived," Walker grunted. "I don't know which is worse— boxing, jiu-jitsu, or stick fighting. Whichever one it is, he's gonna kick your butt."

"No," corrected Dixon. "He's gonna kick *your* butt. *I* ain't gettin' in a ring with that maniac."

"Why not? You'd be the only colored man who ever hit the president and lived to tell about it."

"Very funny, Garrett. Except I couldn't *tell* about it *and* live. It's one or t'other." Shivering violently, he added, "Got news to tell, but I'm too c-cold to talk. Let's just w-w-walk."

After the dishes were cleared from the supper table, Walker scooted his chair back and folded his arms across his chest. "That was mighty good, Beulah," he sighed. "I'm going to get fat, eatin' like that all the time."

"Daisy made the biscuits," said Beulah over her shoulder as she worked the pump with one hand and rinsed the dishes under the flowing water with the other.

"I couldn't tell! Daisy, your biscuits are just as good as your mama's! And hers are the best in the South!"

"Thank you, Walker," Daisy smiled. "I do my best."

She's turning into a fine young lady, Walker thought. *She's changed a lot in the past few months. Miss Hannah's school is really making a difference for her. It's a good thing Dixon brought her here.*

"So, what's that news you've got to tell?" Walker asked Dixon.

"Two things, actually," Dixon began, with a slight frown. "We had a meeting while you and the president was beating on each other. Stover says they got another speaking tour planned for April. This time it's all the way to California again. Twenty-five states, fourteen thousand miles, and more than two hundred speeches. Nine weeks travelin'. It'll make McKinley's tour look like a Sunday School picnic."

"Nine weeks!" Walker, Beulah, and Daisy gasped in astonishment.

"Yup," Dixon confirmed, tight-lipped. "Two whole months." There were several seconds of silence as this sank in. "Daisy will be out of school b'fore we get back."

"That means Sally will be out of school, too," observed Beulah, giving her son a penetrating look.

Dixon sighed. "I reckon it ain't no secret that me and Sally are getting pretty close. *Real* close. She's on my mind all the time, and being gone for two months is gonna be tough. *Real* tough." He sighed again, and grimaced.

"Which brings me to the second news. I'm thinkin' about leaving the Secret Service and joining the D.C. police. They're looking to add some colored men to the mounted force, and I'd be a shoo-in for a position, with me being ex-cavalry, Secret Service, and all."

Walker could only stare, speechless.

Beulah walked over and put a hand on Dixon's shoulder. "You been giving this a lot of thought, L.G.?"

"I have, but I ain't made a final decision yet. It's a big change, and I need to find out more about what the police job would be like."

"Will you be going with us on the tour?" asked Walker.

"Yeah—it's too late now to back out of that, and I don't want to leave y'all short-handed. Besides, as much as I don't want to be separated from Sally for two months, it might help me—it might help *us* —to see where things stand. I may be lookin' to settle down. I've about had my fill of traveling. All we've done since we got hired is travel all over the country. North, South, East, and West—there ain't no end to it."

Beulah and Daisy hugged him, patting his shoulders and giving him words of encouragement. Walker sat quietly, absorbing the news.

"What are you thinkin'?" asked Dixon, giving him a look that said 'Tell me the truth.'

Walker shrugged. "I don't know yet. It wouldn't be the same

without you, but if you are with the D.C. police, at least you'd still be around. But then, if you and Sally get married, you'll probably want your own house. It's a lot to think about."

"Yeah," Dixon nodded. "Lots of twists and turns in the road ahead. We'll just have to take 'em one at a time."

Later that night, lying in bed under two quilts and listening to the wind moaning at the window, Walker stared at the ceiling in the dark. He could hear Dixon's slow, regular breathing across the room, and tried to imagine what it would be like if that bed was empty. After all they had been through together, the thought of separation from Dixon was disturbing. He knew that change was inevitable—he just wasn't ready for it. *He has his family here, and now he has Sally,* he mused. *I'm happy for him, but. . . .* He realized that he was only feeling sorry for himself and resolved to stop those thoughts, but it wasn't easy.

His thoughts naturally turned to his own relationship with Abigail. His visit to Richmond at Christmas had gone well. James Dancy's children and grandchildren were there again, and the conversation was lively. They had wanted to hear more about his foreign adventures, and he had talked for more than two hours with Abigail sitting beside him, paying rapt attention to his stories. On leaving, he had kissed her hand again, and she had kissed his cheek —almost the corner of his mouth—and brushed his cheek with her eyelashes. "You must write me longer letters," she had murmured.

She had returned home to Alabama in early January, two months ago. Since then, they had exchanged two lengthy letters each—not exactly "love letters," but still personal and warm. Walker didn't know what to think or expect, but he knew he wanted to find out. She definitely seemed drawn to him, but he could not yet believe that a rich man's daughter could have real feelings for a farmer's son. *What can I offer her?* he wondered. *She gave me an expensive pocket watch for Christmas, and all I could afford to give her was a simple gold bracelet. If we are going to be together, I'll have to make something of myself. But what?*

He turned on his side with his face to the wall and pulled the quilts up to his chin. *It's like Dixon said,* he thought as he closed his eyes. *Lots of twists and turns in the road ahead—I'll just have to take them one at a time.*

The next three weeks were filled with meetings for the Secret Service agents as they studied the itinerary for the president's trip. Stover exchanged dozens of telegrams with the local police departments across the country to coordinate security for the president's arrival, lodging, and public events in their cities and towns. Seeing how stressed he was with so much responsibility, Walker offered to help, and Stover gratefully accepted. Dividing the list of presidential stops between them, each handled a part of the list, thus saving time. At Walker's suggestion they visited the D.C. police chief and asked for advice on how best to work with the police in the cities and towns. They also paid a visit to George Foster, who gave them the benefit of his experience. With no authority to make demands, they wired requests and security needs to each police chief, asking for their cooperation as diplomatically as possible. With only four agents accompanying the president, they would need all the help the local authorities could provide. As the time for the launch of the tour drew near, they felt that they were as prepared as they could be. But then, a day before the departure, the unforeseen happened.

Walker and Stover had stayed late at the White House in the communications office sending final telegrams to a few police chiefs. It was dark when they left, and the streetlights did little to help. Walker turned down the sidewalk toward home as Stover crossed the street, holding an umbrella against the wind and a drizzling rain. Apparently the umbrella obscured his vision, and perhaps he was preoccupied with thoughts about the impending two-month western tour, but he stepped off the curb directly into the path of a taxi pulled by a trotting horse.

Walker heard a shout and cry of pain, and turned to look. The cab stopped and the driver jumped to the pavement and bent over a body lying there. Walker slowly took a few steps back toward the scene, and then realizing that it was Stover, he broke into a run. Stover was in great pain, clutching his left leg, which was bent at an unnatural angle. Walker could see blood glistening in the dim streetlight, and Stover's face was contorted in agony.

"Henry!" exclaimed Walker, recognizing the cab driver. "What happened?"

"Mistah Garrett! I do declare he just walked right out in front o' me. I couldn't hardly see him in the dark. I hollered and tried to miss him, but he just kep' comin'!"

"Stover! It looks like your leg is broke. We got to get you to the hospital right away." Stover nodded, teeth bared and his head tossing back and forth with the pain. "Henry, can you help us get Agent Stover to the hospital?"

"I be happy to, Mister Garrett! Napoleon'll get us there 'fore you know it. I sho' am sorry 'bout this. I done my best to not hit 'im, but he just kep' comin'!"

"Wasn't your fault," Stover gasped, and groaned loudly. Walker and Henry lifted him into the cab and hurried to the Georgetown hospital, six blocks away. They watched as the attendants whisked Stover away on a wheeled stretcher.

"You needn't wait," said a young doctor. "Looks like the carriage wheel ran over his leg below the knee, and it's a pretty bad break. We'll be working on it for a while, and then he'll be sedated overnight. You can come back tomorrow and see how he's doing." The doctor then followed the stretcher through the swinging double-doors marked "Staff Only."

Henry gave Walker a ride home and refused to accept payment, though Walker did insist on giving him a dollar to buy some extra oats for Napoleon. They stopped by the White House on the way, and Walker told the man on duty in the communication office to send a messenger boy to Director Wilkie with the news. With the president scheduled to leave town within hours, there was no time to waste in making adjustments to the security detail.

The family had finished supper by the time Walker arrived. Beulah took a plate of food out of the oven where she had been keeping it warm, and put it on the table. Dixon came out of the bedroom and sat across from Walker as he ate. The look on Walker's face signaled that all was not well.

"How come you're so late? Anything wrong?"

Walker sighed. "You won't believe it," he said, shaking his head. "Stover got run over by Henry Brown's cab and broke his leg bad. He's in the hospital." He proceeded to tell the story in detail.

"Henry must feel awful," Beulah said sympathetically, wiping her hands on a dish towel. "That's just terrible!"

"Yes, he does, but it wasn't his fault. Stover just had too much on his mind and wasn't paying attention. Besides that, it was dark and rainy, and his umbrella blocked his view. Just an unfortunate situation all around."

"What are we going to do about the tour?" asked Dixon. "If Stover can't go, we don't have an agent-in-charge. The trip can't be postponed—we have to do something."

"*Wilkie* has to do something, you mean," returned Walker. "Maybe he'll go with us himself. Or maybe they'll bring Foster back to active duty, I don't know. I'm just glad it's not *my* responsibility. We'll probably find out tomorrow morning as we're leaving."

Sure enough, an emergency meeting of the Secret Service presidential detail was called the next morning. They gathered in the small office—all five of them, and Director John Wilkie. Wilkie closed the door, sat on the edge of desk with one foot on the floor, and gave them a long, intense look. Finally, he heaved a deep breath and spoke in a growling voice.

"By now, you've all heard what happened last night to Agent Stover. He's going to be fine in a couple of months, but it couldn't have come at a worse time. He'll be laid up in the hospital for at least a week, and the president leaves on his western tour in two hours. We have to make some adjustments, and do it fast. Here's what I've decided."

He stood up and walked around behind the desk, leaning forward slightly with his hands on the back of the chair. "We're a man short on the detail, so I'm assigning Peters to be our fourth man. Peters, you'll have to hurry home and pack a suitcase and meet us at the train station. Get going!" Without a word, Agent Peters exited the room, quietly closing the door behind him. Wilkie clasped his hands behind his back and paced back and forth in the confined space, obviously wrestling with what he was about to say next.

"You're all probably wondering who is going to replace Stover as the agent-in-charge for the trip. This has been a difficult decision due to the short time frame. Any one of you could probably handle it if you had time to prepare, but there is no time. Each of you knows the security protocols and knows your individual responsibilities, but the agent-in-charge has to interact with the local authorities and must know what they are doing and what our detail is doing. Coordination is the key, and it's political and diplomatic. We need someone who is already familiar with the local police departments that we'll be dealing with across the country, and that takes time. Fortunately, we have someone who can do that—someone who has spent the last few weeks alongside Stover, communicating with those police chiefs, and already knows the plans that are in place." He paused—or hesitated—before continuing.

"I refer, of course, to Agent Garrett. He has spent countless hours assisting Stover in laying the groundwork for this trip, and is well-prepared to assume the leadership role. You may feel that Garrett is too young for this, being the youngest member of the detail, but he toured with President McKinley in '01, and with President Roosevelt several times last year, so he knows what is involved. I am confident that he will do a fine job."

If the other agents had any objection, it was not apparent. Each turned toward Walker and gave him an approving nod. Walker, though, was stunned. He stared at Wilkie, speechless.

"Garrett," Wilkie added, sensing Walker's anxiety, "I apologize for not speaking to you privately about this first, but there was no time. You have my full confidence, and don't hesitate to contact me if you need anything." With that, Wilkie left the room.

The other agents quietly congratulated Walker as they filed out. "Glad it wasn't *me*," one grinned, slapping Walker's shoulder. Only Dixon was left in the room. He put his hands on his hips, cocked his head to one side, and gave Walker a studied look with a raised eyebrow.

"Well, if that don't beat all!" he said wryly. "Agent-in-charge!"

"I sure didn't see *that* coming," Walker said, rubbing his temples. "This can't be real."

"You deserve it. Like he said, you've been burning the midnight oil helping Stover get ready for this. Nobody knows the plan like you do. You'll be just fine."

"Thanks. I guess it's like you said a little while back—the road is full of twists and turns. We have to take them one at a time."

"Yup, and remember that's a 'we.' You ain't by yourself."

"Thanks. Well, I've got a lot to do before we leave. See you at the train station."

22

WESTWARD, HO!

The train made a brief stop in Pittsburgh at about 8:30 that evening. As usual, Walker and the other agents made their way to the rear deck of the president's car for his customary speech while the engine took on water. This time, however, Roosevelt was nowhere to be found. Walker's heart was in his throat as he panicked. *We can't have lost the president on the first day of the trip!* he thought frantically. Then he saw the president on the train platform, mingling with the crowd, vigorously shaking hands and booming "Dee-lighted!" He sprang to the platform and hurried to the president's side, while the other agents stared, confused.

When the train had left the station, steaming into the night, Walker knocked at the door of Roosevelt's private stateroom. "Mr. President—may I have just a moment of your time, sir?"

"What is it, Agent Garrett? Make it quick—I have guests to attend to."

"I'm concerned for your safety, sir, and you're making it very difficult for us to protect you. You left the train without notice twice today, and—"

"I'm perfectly capable of defending myself, Garrett," snapped Roosevelt. Reaching behind his back he produced a revolver and laid it on a polished mahogany table with a loud thud. "I don't need protecting!"

"Sir, with all due respect, I'm sure that Lincoln felt safe in his box at Ford's Theater, and Garfield thought he was safe at the Washington train station, and I know for a fact that President McKinley thought he was safe shaking hands in the receiving line at the Temple of Music. There are people who would not hesitate to do you harm, sir, and you must let us do our job."

"*With all due respect*, Agent Garrett, that is *your* concern—not mine! Do your job, but don't try to confine me with your bodyguards!"

"I was at San Juan Hill, too, Mr. President," Walker persisted. "I know that you do not lack bravery, but you sometimes expose yourself to danger. As a soldier, that is proper, but for a president who doesn't have a vice president—it is *not* proper. Who would lead the country if you were—"

"*Enough!*" Roosevelt was clearly angry, jabbing at Walker's chest with his finger, his eyes spitting fire. "That is *my* concern! Don't tell *me* what is proper, and don't bring this up again!"

"Yes sir," was all Walker could say, and closed the door softly behind him. He found the rest of the team waiting for him in the dining car.

"How did it go?" asked Peters. Walker repeated the conversation, describing the president's anger.

"He carries a *gun?*" exclaimed Kelly, the fourth agent. "You're lucky he didn't use it on *you!*"

"That did cross my mind," admitted Walker. "But you all see what we're up against. He's going to do whatever he pleases, without regard to his own safety. Like he said, that's *our* concern. So, we're going to have to be extra vigilant. Every time the train stops, two of us are going to have to get back there to the platform, and the other two will have to watch out the windows on either side to make sure he isn't getting away."

"Even on the side away from the station?"

"*Especially* on that side. I didn't tell you, but before dinner I saw him walking down the track coming from the front of the train. He'd been riding in the cab with the engineer ever since we left Altoona two hours back. Apparently, he got out and walked up there and no one noticed. If he keeps this up, we'll all have gray hair by the time we get back to D.C."

The agents exchanged wide-eyed looks as Walker's words sank in. "You know, Garrett," said Kelly, "when Wilkie made you the agent-in-charge, I really thought he was making a mistake. I thought you are too young for this. But *now*, I'm *glad* you're in charge. Anybody that can say what you said to Roosevelt has all the grit they need. Just tell us what you need us to do, and we'll do it." Peters agreed, and Dixon gave Walker a faint smile and nod.

"Thanks, men," Walker said appreciatively. Taking a creased piece of paper from his inside pocket, he gave it a glance, even though he had it memorized. "There aren't any more speaking stops tonight. We'll be in Chicago before nine in the morning, so let's hit the sack and get some shut-eye while we can."

The president spent only a day in Chicago, leaving at midnight, but it was a day packed with activity. He delivered three speeches, rode in two processions, laid the cornerstone for a new building, received an honorary degree, and attended a luncheon and a dinner banquet, inundated by cheering crowds throughout the day. In the processions he was escorted by a company of cavalry soldiers, and was blanketed by Chicago police officers at every venue. There wasn't much need for the agents, but Walker assigned Peters and Kelly to ride as coachmen on the president's carriage in the processions, and all four stood by the platforms while he gave the speeches.

During the luncheon at the Auditorium Hotel, Chicago police chief Francis O'Neill called Walker aside and asked him to come to the police headquarters nearby. Walker gestured for Dixon to accompany him, and they briskly walked three blocks in the chilly air to the station. Through gaps between buildings, they caught glimpses of Lake Michigan, barely a half-mile away. At the station, O'Neill led them through a large open space filled with desks at which a dozen young women noisily clattered away on typewriters. Walker stared curiously as he passed.

A cute blonde, wearing the dark blue police uniform with brass buttons and busily chewing on something, returned his stare icily. "What you lookin' at, mister?" she snapped.

Walker blinked and blushed. "Nothing—I just haven't seen anybody typewriting before. You're really fast at that."

"You ain't seen nobody *typin'* before? Where've you been—*Alabama*?"

Walker's eyes narrowed. "Do they let you eat while you're typewriting?"

"*Eat*? I ain't *eatin'*—I'm chewin' *gum!*" She displayed a wad of pale green resin between her teeth. "Don't tell me you ain't never seen Wrigley's mint chewin' gum before, neither?"

"Of *course* I've seen chewing gum," Walker lied. Glancing in the direction of Chief O'Neill's office, he turned to go.

"I can tell from your accent—you *are* from Alabama!" she hooted at his back.

"Enough of that!" said a stern male voice, and all of the typists immediately stopped giggling and returned to their work. Walker looked back and saw a black man in police uniform with sergeant's stripes on his sleeves. He gave the man a quick nod and hurried to rejoin O'Neill and Dixon.

O'Neill wore a dark blue uniform similar to the other police officers, except that his had a double row of brass buttons and four stripes around the sleeve cuffs. In his office, Walker was surprised to see a fiddle and a flute lying on a table to one side of the desk.

"Are you a musician, Chief?" he asked.

"Very much so, Agent Garrett," the chief smiled. "I'm Irish, and I love Irish dance tunes. I've collected quite a few of them." He picked up a polished wooden box and handed it to Walker. "This is a gift for President Roosevelt. I hope you'll give it to him for me."

"I'll be happy to, sir. May I ask what's in it?"

"A gun. Open it and see."

Walker opened the box and gasped at the sight of a gleaming, brass-plated automatic pistol. "That's beautiful, sir! Is it a real gun? I've never seen one made of brass!"

"Oh, it's real alright. We've just apprehended a gang of four murderers who killed several people in Chicago recently. The 'car barn murders'—you may have read about it in the papers. Anyway, this is one of their automatic pistols. When I learned that the president was coming to Chicago—I know he loves guns, so I had it brass-plated as a gift for him. It's real, but I wouldn't recommend firing it now."

A card in the lid of the box told the story of the case and explained the background of the weapon. Walker and Dixon marveled at the streamlined design. "The president will be thrilled! I'll give it to him as soon as we get back to the train later today, sir."

"By the way," Dixon said, somewhat hesitantly. "Do you have other black officers like that one out there?"

"Sergeant Childs? He's our first black sergeant—a fine man and a fine officer. I hope we have more like him in the future. Times are changing, Agent Dixon! There's light at the end of the tunnel—just you wait and see!"

"Yes sir. I hope you're right, sir."

They exited the office and passed through the typing room again. Walker glanced toward the cute blonde and saw her eyeing him. She wrinkled her nose and mouthed the word '*typewriting*,' and began giggling silently, though Walker was sure he heard her snort through her nose. On impulse, he reached out as he passed and bumped the chromed lever extending out to the side of the type-writer. He didn't know its purpose, but his action produced an instant reaction from the blonde, who sucked air noisily between her clenched teeth and smacked her fist on the table. With a quick look back he saw her pick up an eraser and begin furiously rubbing the paper. Scowling at him, she mouthed the word '*Alabama*.' The green gum fell out of her mouth when she did, but she caught it and popped it back in again.

Emerging onto the street, Walker exhaled through pursed lips. "Well, *that* was interesting!" he said, relieved to be out of the stuffy building and back in the cold breeze. Snow had begun falling while they were indoors, and the sidewalk was already covered in white.

"What was interesting? asked Dixon, shivering. "The typewriters, the girl, the chief, the gun, the sergeant, the fiddle—"

"All of it," Walker cut him off. "But especially that *girl*. They oughta let her interrogate prisoners. She'd get the truth out of 'em, or drive 'em crazy trying."

"A black police sergeant in Chicago," Dixon murmured, almost to himself. "I wonder how long it'll be before that happens in Alabama, or anywhere else in the South. I hope he's right."

"You hope who's right about what?"

"He said there's light at the end of the tunnel. I hope he's right, but I'm 'fraid it's gonna be a pretty long tunnel."

"Wait right here," Walker said suddenly, handing the wooden box to Dixon. He darted into a small shop, and returned in less than a minute with two small objects in his hand. He handed one to Dixon.

"What's this?"

"Wrigley's Spearmint Chewing Gum. We may be from Alabama, but we can chew gum, too."

They each unwrapped a stiff green stick and began chewing as they walked. The strong mint flavor and the wintry air made for a potent combination. After several seconds, Dixon grunted in surprise. Walker breathed loudly through his nose, his eyes wide.

"Feels like my head is 'bout to fly off," Walker wheezed.

"Feels like somebody's lit a match in my mouth," Dixon said through bared teeth, chewing rapidly.

"It ain't nothin' like a jalapeño pepper, but it's got kick," observed Walker. "I think I like it."

Dixon shook his head. "Jury's still out. This stuff'll take some gettin' used to." He then added, "I don't see how them women can chew this stuff and still work on typewriters like that. Seems like it would be real hard to concentrate."

"Maybe that's why that girl was so feisty," Walker speculated. "She's all lit up with mint chewing gum. Make sure you don't give any of this to Sally, unless you want trouble."

"That ain't gonna happen, no siree," declared Dixon, spitting his gum into the gutter drain. "Here—you can have the rest of this back. I'm done with chewing gum!"

The rest of the day's busy activities went smoothly, and the train left Chicago at midnight, arriving in Madison, Wisconsin early the next morning. After two speeches there, the president traveled across the state, making short speeches to large crowds at several stops until reaching Milwaukee in the early afternoon. There was hardly an idle minute, as Roosevelt rode in carriages in two processions with military escorts, reviewed veterans at the Soldiers' Home, gave four speeches, attended a lunch reception and a dinner banquet, and was entertained with a musical program. By the end of the day, he was exhausted. Walker had never seen him look so fatigued.

When Walker expressed his concern to the other agents, he was surprised at Dixon's response. "Good!" he declared. "The tireder he is, the less likely he is to be hoppin' off the train and gettin' away from us. Makes him easier to keep up with." The other agents grinned and nodded. Walker had to admit they were right.

The hectic pace continued across Minnesota. Thousands lined the streets cheering as the president rode in processions, often standing in the carriage and waving his silk top hat. Receptions, banquets, speeches too many to count—Walker wondered where he found the energy. He decided that it must be the enthusiasm of the people that drove him onward. When Roosevelt was addressing his audiences, there was no sign of weariness. Often speaking outdoors to thousands in forty-degree temperatures, he stomped briskly back and forth on the platforms, shaking his fist and splitting the air with his high-pitched, penetrating voice. Cheers interrupted him at virtually every sentence. Walker could feel the energy emanating from the crowds, and began to feel invigorated himself.

On Sunday morning, the party arrived in Sioux Falls, South Dakota. Roosevelt had requested that no events be planned for the day, and his request was observed, for the most part. There was a brief reception at the train station as he was greeted by the mayor and other dignitaries, followed by a carriage procession from the station to the hotel, with military escort through streets lined with people. After settling in at the hotel, the president attended a church service. Walker rode in the front seat of the president's carriage, and the other agents followed in the one behind. In the small German Lutheran church, Walker was surprised to see the women sitting on one side and the men on the other. The songs and the sermon were in German. Roosevelt enthusiastically joined in the singing, and listened attentively to the sermon. Walker was mystified—he remembered seeing a book written in French in Roosevelt's tent in Cuba. *How many languages does this man know?* he wondered.

At lunch back at the hotel, Roosevelt was joined by a number of congressmen, senators, cabinet secretaries, and local leaders. By four o'clock, the participants were leaving, and Roosevelt motioned to Walker.

"I've arranged to go for a ride with Seth Bullock, an old friend from my days in the Dakotas," he whispered, pointing to a tall, broad-shouldered man with a prodigious mustache. "We'll be slipping out the back of the hotel to avoid the crowd. No need for you to come."

"Yes sir," Walker whispered. "Did you know that Agent Dixon was a Buffalo Soldier, and spent four years in the Dakotas before the war? Perhaps he might ride along, if you don't mind, sir."

"Bully!" exclaimed Roosevelt, forgetting to whisper, and causing Walker to recoil from the unexpected blast. "By all means, have him saddle up. You might as well come too, Garrett." He motioned to Bullock with two fingers and loudly whispered the words, "Two more horses."

The president exchanged his top hat and frock coat for a black slouch hat and fleece-lined corduroy jacket, and the riding party managed to escape the notice of the waiting crowd and get to the stable where the horses were already saddled. They galloped out of town across the Big Sioux River, into the rolling hills of the prairie. The landscape was new to Walker, and he studied it with interest. There were few trees, except along the river and its tributary streams. Spring had not fully arrived yet, and the grass was still brown and the trees lacked foliage. Farmers' fields were not yet plowed. The scenery was quite bleak, but the sky was a deep, stunning blue, with only a couple of fluffy white clouds. The wind was not strong, but was steady and penetrating, and got progressively colder over the two hours of the ride. By its end, Walker's face was pink and numb.

As they reined in their horses at the Cataract Hotel, Roosevelt spoke to them for the first time. "Did that bring back any memories for you, Agent Dixon?"

"Yes sir, Mr. President. It reminded me a little of how cold I was for four years!"

"Indeed!" boomed Roosevelt, with a laugh. "There's nothing I love better than a good gallop in freezing weather! Brings the whole body and mind to life! I must do this more often!"

The ride was completed just in time for the president to attend an evening church service at the Dutch Reformed Church. The building was ringed about by both the police and a military guard. The church members were plain, simple people, and Roosevelt seemed to enjoy mingling with them. The four agents followed him closely, but there clearly were no threats to his safety. However, this made Walker even more uneasy, because he could not forget the scene in the Temple of Music and the harmless-looking young man with the handkerchief wrapped around his hand. The more innocent and peaceful it appeared to be, the more vigilant he became. He was resolutely determined that there would be no reenactment of that tragedy, especially not while he was in charge.

The next morning, Roosevelt gave a brief outdoor speech to a crowd of four thousand as flurries of snow fell, and then bid the town farewell. During the day he gave eleven speeches as the train rumbled toward North Dakota. Some were brief remarks from the rear platform of the train, and others were longer, delivered from specially erected stands to which he rode in carriage processions escorted by troops and brass bands. Crossing into North Dakota, he spoke twice more before reaching his destination of Fargo early the next morning.

The torrid pace continued. For example, in Fargo there was a reception by city officials at eight-thirty, followed by a three-mile parade, a speech at a high school, another speech at the opera house, and a final speech from the rear of the train prior to departing at ten o'clock. There were eight more stops throughout the day. Roosevelt was thrilled to be back in North Dakota, and the people were thrilled to see him. He had owned a cattle ranch there more than twenty years earlier, and considered it to be "home."

Walker found the towns depressing with their weathered buildings, muddy streets and snow drifts. He thought it ridiculous that so many of these isolated, rugged communities featured an opera house! However, he had to admit that the warmth and enthusiasm the residents displayed at the president's visit equaled or surpassed that seen in more presentable eastern cities, and he began to understand the president's affection for these hardy plainsmen.

The only cause for alarm to the Secret Service agents—especially for Dixon—was in Bismarck, when Roosevelt met with a delegation of chiefs from the Sioux nation. This occurred at the state capitol, in the governor's office. As always, there were police and soldiers about, but still the agents crowded close to make sure the warlike chiefs did not attempt any violence. Dixon, as a Buffalo Soldier with the U.S. cavalry, had sought to contain the Sioux on their assigned reservation lands, and distrusted their intentions. There was no reason for concern, however, as the chiefs presented Roosevelt with a carved peace pipe and a pouch of tobacco, professing their good will toward the "Great Father."

The last stop of the day was the small town of Medora, where Roosevelt had lived during his ranching days. He personally knew most of the people, and the brief hour spent there was a true homecoming celebration. It was dark when the train pulled out, heading further west. By morning the party would be in Montana, and Roosevelt was about to disappear into Yellowstone Park for a two-week escape.

23

EDEN

Walker shaded his eyes with his hat as he squinted up into the perfect blue sky. A majestic eagle soared motionlessly, circling slowly, thousands of feet above the valley floor. The only sound was that of the wind in his ears. There were no leaves to rustle, nor even any tall grass to whisper with the wind. Scattered patches of snow almost obliterated the trail they were following toward the summit, visible a mile or more ahead, covered in a blanket of white. His breath fogged in the air briefly and then disappeared. The silence was beginning to feel eerie, but shifting his weight produced a reassuring creaking sound from the saddle leather.

"Better keep movin'," came a muffled voice from behind him. "Them donkeys'll be here in a minute." Dixon had tied a red bandana around his face, covering his nose and mouth against the cold wind. A column of donkeys loaded with camping gear was bringing up the rear of the expedition, and an occasional braying could now be heard faintly. They prodded their mounts forward, topping a rise, and caught sight of the president and his entourage a few hundred yards ahead.

A herd of about two hundred pronghorn antelope suddenly descended from the steep slope to their right and crossed the trail, splitting around them as they bounded downward toward the valley. Individual bucks passed so close that Walker and Dixon could hear their breathing and see the movement of their brown eyes. The spiky black antlers looked dangerous, but the herd was gone in only a few seconds, and the startled horses calmed down.

"Not scared of nuthin', are they?" Walker's question was more of a statement. Dixon grunted in reply. "This place is kind of like the Garden of Eden," Walker continued. "I've never seen such natural beauty and wildlife!"

"Watch out for talkin' snakes," Dixon warned with mock serious-ness. "And don't eat no apples—'specially not if a nekkid woman gives it to you."

"I don't think there's any danger of *that* happening," Walker laughed.

The group spent the night on the mountain at Fort Yellowstone, and the next day descended a ten-mile trail to the valley floor and made camp on the banks of the Yellowstone River. Roosevelt shared a tent with the white-bearded nature writer, John Burroughs, and Major John Pitcher, park superintendent and commander of the small military unit which set up the tents, tended the animals, and cooked the meals. Walker and Dixon shared a tent with two of the half-dozen soldiers. Not wanting to be idle, they gathered armloads of firewood and piled them outside the cooking tent, and then warmed themselves by the fire while a large pot of beef stew simmered. Roosevelt, Burroughs, and Pitcher chatted casually a short distance away.

"You fellas don't look like Secret Service agents to me," commented one of the soldiers, giving them a critical look.

"Y'all look purty seedy," added another, with a strong southern accent.

Walker pulled open his ragged camel hair coat and showed the silver, five-point-star badge, and Dixon did the same. "We usually wear suits and ties," Walker explained, "but not out here in the wilderness."

"Where'd you get them awful lookin' coats, anyway?" grinned a soldier. "They home-made?" Several of them laughed as if they thought that very funny.

"Mongolia," Walker and Dixon replied in unison. The soldiers laughed again, but with a harsher tone, and some of them turned and walked away.

"Maybe we shoulda said 'Sears and Roebuck?'" suggested Dixon quietly. Walker chuckled and nodded.

"Are they really lettin' n----rs in the Secret Service now?" asked the southerner with a look of disgust.

"Are they really letting idiots in the army now?" responded Walker, fixing him with a hard glare.

"Who you callin' a idiot?" The lean private stepped threateningly around the fire to face Walker.

"You."

"Garrett, I can take care of myself," said Dixon.

"I know you can, but when he insults you, he insults me, too, and I don't intend to put up with it."

"Well, what're you gon *do* about it, Mr. Mongolia?" sneered the private.

Walker reached out quickly and lightly slapped the man's face twice. It had the desired effect—the soldier lunged forward, swinging a fist at Walker's head. "Big Bill" Craig's training proved valuable, as Walker deftly flipped the man onto his back and twisted his arm, putting him face down in the dirt, keeping him there with pressure on the backward-bent arm as the man yelped in pain.

"What's going on over there?" snapped Major Pitcher, walking in their direction, followed by Roosevelt and Burroughs.

"Just demonstrating some judo we learned in the Secret Service, sir," Walker said calmly, releasing his hold and letting the man scramble to his feet and dust himself off.

"Bully!" boomed Roosevelt, smacking his fist in his hand. "I love judo! Every soldier should be instructed in judo and jiu-jitsu. Supremely valuable skills! Glad to see you learned it well, Garrett!"

"Thank you, sir."

"By the way—Garrett and Dixon—I meant to tell you before now, but your Medals of Honor have finally come through! I don't know why it took so long, but I'll be proud to pin them on you both when we get back to Washington! Congratulations, men, for a job well done!" Roosevelt shook hands vigorously with both of them, flashing his trademark toothy grin and squinting through his pince nez spectacles. Pitcher and Burroughs added their congratulations, also shaking hands. The soldiers stared silently in amazement and then busied themselves with camp chores.

The stew was soon ready to eat. It was a simple meal—just beef stew and hardtack crackers, with coffee and water to drink. Everyone sat on the ground, rocks, or logs, or stood to eat. Roosevelt dominated the conversation, rambling about his experiences as a cowboy, Rough Rider, New York police commissioner, and president.

When Roosevelt paused to take a few bites of food, Major Pitcher interjected a question. "Mr. President, I'd like to hear what your two Secret Service agents did that led to their Medals of Honor. I didn't know Secret Service agents could get that."

"Oh, no, Major! It wasn't for their work as Secret Service agents, though they've done a fine job at that, too. No—this was for their service in the army during the war. These two men accomplished some amazing feats! For example, they jumped through a shell-hole in the roof of a blockhouse, and wiped out the last Spanish resistance at San Juan Hill. In the Philippines, they were with Funston when he captured Aguinaldo. They fought the Boxers in China, and Garrett climbed the Peking city wall and opened the gate from the inside. They escorted a caravan of missionaries across the Gobi Desert to Mongolia, and came back to America the other way around the globe! Someone should write a book about their adventures! Bravo, men! You should be receiving two or three medals!"

"Amazing indeed!" exclaimed Burroughs.

"Most remarkable!" echoed Pitcher.

The soldiers just stared.

Conversation around the campfire continued until well after dark. As the talking died down, the flames also died down to glowing embers, and a penetrating chill set in. Rising abruptly, Roosevelt headed for his tent, and the others did likewise. In the darkness of the tent, Walker lay on the ground, wrapped in coarse blankets. He sat up suddenly with a grunt. With crystal clarity, the lonely, haunting howl of a wolf sounded like it was almost overhead. It was followed by a chorus of other howls, apparently a pack inspired by the full moon. Walker felt a shiver run up his spine, and the hair on his neck stood up.

"Good Lord!" came Dixon's voice out of the darkness. "How are we s'posed to sleep with that goin' on?"

"Welcome to Yellowstone," growled one of the soldiers. "You get used to it, eventually."

Walker lay back down, but did not close his eyes. He felt his heart pounding, and he hardly breathed at all. He listened with fascination, fear, and an undefinable sense of sadness until the howling finally faded away and he lapsed into dreams of wolves racing through the heavens. He was the last of the party to awaken the next morning, emerging from the tent into daylight, rubbing the sleep from his eyes.

"Well, if it ain't Mister Mongolia!" sneered Walker's adversary from the night before. "So, you decided to join us ordinary folks for breakfast?"

Walker ignored him and poured a cup of coffee. Dixon handed him a pan of steaming oatmeal. "Thanks. That howling kept me awake for a long time," he muttered.

"We used to hear it all the time in the Dakotas," Dixon nodded. "It's been a few years ago. I'd forgot how it cuts into you." Pausing briefly, he added, "Hurry up. We're leaving with Roosevelt and Pitcher on a ride. I'll saddle your horse."

Walker, kneeling with his coffee cup on the ground, gulped down the oatmeal as rapidly as he could without burning his throat. The obnoxious cavalryman sauntered over to him and stood with his back to the others, and said in a low, menacing voice, "You caught me by surprise yesterday, Mongolia. Next time, I'll be ready for you."

"What's your name, soldier?" Walker asked coolly.

"None of your damn business, Mongolia."

"Then I'll just call you 'Johnny Reb,'" Walker said, putting his empty plate down and standing up. "I don't need surprise to take *you*. Anytime you're ready, I'll give you lesson number two, but you won't like it."

"We'll see about that!" Johnny Reb glowered, as Walker walked away.

They camped on the Yellowstone River for four days and nights, and each day Roosevelt and Pitcher, followed by Walker and Dixon, explored the river for miles along its course. They didn't expect any trouble, but were well-armed, just in case. Each man carried a repeating rifle in a saddle scabbard, and a revolver. Walker and Dixon's revolvers were in their usual shoulder holsters. Walker's machete swung from his belt on his left side, and the palm pistol was tucked in the pocket of his coat. *You never know when we might run into a wolf pack*, he thought, *or maybe a bear, or even some outlaws. Better safe than sorry.*

Each day provided a visual feast. Herds of antelope, deer, and elk grazed peacefully, oblivious to the riders' approach. Mountain goats negotiated invisible paths among the craggy cliffs above, and eagles floated weightlessly in the blue beyond. Trout jumped and splashed in the rushing waters of the river, and songbirds embroidered the air with their calls. Walker heard the squall of a mountain lion once, and the occasional yipping of coyotes. No wolves or bears were in evidence, however, and no other human presence was detected. *Truly, this is the Garden of Eden,* he thought. *Nothing could be more beautiful than this!*

Each night, however, his sleep was disturbed by the incessant howling of the wolves. He lay awake for hours, envisioning the pack high up in the snowy reaches of the mountain, with noses pointed skyward, serenading the moon with their awful song. The mournful sound was carried on the night wind, and seemed to permeate his very soul. *Dixon was right—it really does cut into you. I don't think I'll ever get used to this.*

Each evening around the campfire the group was entertained by Roosevelt's storytelling. Burroughs and Pitcher contributed stories of their own, but the president dominated the conversation, as usual.

Walker and Dixon were coaxed into describing some of their experiences in Cuba, the Philippines, and China. Dixon insisted that Walker tell about his nighttime fight to the death with a huge python in the jungle, and he had to remove his shirt and show the scars left by the snake's powerful jaws to prove that it really happened. Even Roosevelt was impressed.

Johnny Reb tried repeatedly to get under Walker's skin with his sarcastic insults and taunts, but Walker ignored him. Emboldened by Walker's passivity, he followed him into the trees when he collected firewood and continued his verbal attacks. On one occasion, Walker, in exasperation, dropped the wood and challenged the noxious private. "Put up or shut up," he snapped. "Talk is cheap. Nobody's watching—show me what you've got."

"You'll see what I got soon enough," his tormentor jeered. "That *judo* won't help you none then."

"Coward!" Walker hissed. "If you were a real man, you'd stand up and fight like one. People like you are why the South lost the war—all mouth, no guts."

Johnny Reb's face twisted with hate. "You'll regret them words, Mongolia," he growled. "I'll make you sorry you messed with me." He wheeled about and stomped back to camp, fists clenched by his sides.

Walker shook his head in disgust, watching him go. *I may need some eyes in the back of my head,* he frowned. *Cowards are the most dangerous people—they don't fight from in front of you.*

On the third night in the camp, Walker gave up trying to sleep through the wolfpack's din, and quietly slipped out of the tent to take a walk. The moonlight was brilliantly reflected in the river as he trudged along the bank, hugging his camel-hair coat around him. He stopped frequently to listen to the forest, and distinguished the sounds of several night birds, including owls. A Great Gray Owl with a five-foot wingspan swooped within a few feet of Walker's head to pounce on a careless chipmunk. A beaver slapped the water with his tail, almost giving Walker a heart attack. Coyotes barked shrilly in the distance. After an hour, noticing that the howling had ceased, he headed back to camp.

244 | WALKER GARRETT, SECRET SERVICE

A low, dry cough from the underbrush startled him—it didn't sound like a human cough. *Cougar? Bear?* He walked faster, and heard a second cough, and saw movement in the brush. Alarmed, he reached inside his coat, only to discover that he had forgotten to bring his revolver. *A palm pistol won't do much good against a wild animal,* he thought. The hike back to camp seemed to take forever— he hadn't realized how far he had gone. He continued to hear and see movement along the bank, and walked faster and faster, stumbling over rocks and driftwood.

Finally reaching the tents, he looked back, and to his amazement saw a solitary wolf standing on the riverbank, hardly fifty yards away. He was a big one, with thick gray fur and a powerful neck and shoulders. It looked at him balefully, its breath fogging in quick pants, and then, like a gray ghost, melted silently into the forest. Walker suddenly felt weak, and bent over with hands on knees. His heart raced and his breath was shallow and fast. Had he really been stalked by a wolf? Had it intended to attack him? If so, why didn't it? He couldn't help feeling that he had escaped certain death, and whispered "Thank you, God!" repeatedly.

Trembling, he crawled back to his blankets. Just as he was finally able to relax and close his eyes, the howling resumed, much closer and louder than before. He sat up with a jerk and groped for his six-gun, grasping it in his shaking hands. *If this is Eden, that must be the Devil,* he shuddered. *Daylight can't come too soon.*

The final day in the Yellowstone River camp was a Sunday, and Roosevelt insisted on taking a hike by himself, to commune with nature. Major Pitcher reluctantly agreed, and Walker, concerned about the wolves, could only persuade him to take his rifle along. The president set out on foot at a brisk pace, and Walker and Dixon soon departed in the opposite direction for a horseback outing of their own. They spent the entire day following the river upstream, past two waterfalls, and climbed to a rocky promontory from which they could view a broad vista. The spectacular scenery and abundant wildlife that surrounded them elicited their enthusiastic exclamations and alternately left them speechless with awe.

They arrived back in camp just minutes before Roosevelt returned, glowing from his exertion and refreshed by his hours of solitude. After another supper of beef stew and hardtack, he talked excitedly for an hour about the unusual birds and rodents he had seen, and then everyone turned in early, anticipating a tiring day of travel tomorrow as they would move the camp to a new location. Walker lay down and fell instantly asleep, only to be awakened with a start around midnight by the soul-piercing song of the wolves. He groaned in despair, putting his hands to his head. *I can't take another night of this! I have to get out of here!* He crept softly out of the tent, remembering to take his revolver this time.

The sky was lightly overcast, veiling the moon except for occasional breaks. The howling, like the night before, was very close, sending chills up Walker's spine. He chose his steps carefully as he walked along the bank, making sure not to trip over rocks or step on sticks that might make noise. He reached a high outcropping of rock which loomed over the river, and paused to listen. All was suddenly silent, and this agitated him even more than the howling.

The clouds parted momentarily, and the scene was flooded with soft moonlight. Looking up, Walker was terrified to see the silhouette of a large wolf on the rocks above. He caught his breath as he recognized his tormentor from the night before. The beast turned its face toward the moon and unleashed a long, unnerving howl that froze Walker in place, unable to breathe or move. A cloud then shrouded the moon again, and just like that, the wolf was gone. It took Walker a moment to regain his equilibrium, but as soon as his pounding heart quieted down and he was breathing normally, he realized that he was in danger. The wolf might very well be stalking him again! *I better get back to camp, fast,* he thought.

Before he could take a single step, however, a fist-sized rock smashed into the back of his head, knocking him to the ground. Stunned, he struggled to rise to his feet but got only as far as his knees when a boot in the back shoved him back down again. Turning over, he peered up to see Johnny Reb leering at him.

"Not so tough *now*, are you, Mister Mongolia?" He jabbed

Walker in the chest with a sharpened pole, pressing it in and twisting it. "That judo stuff ain't helpin' you *now*, is it, Mister Mongolia?"

"Have you lost your mind? What are you doing?" Walker felt the back of his head and saw blood on his hand.

"I'm teachin' you a lesson you won't soon fergit," he replied venomously, pushing the sharpened point again, making Walker gasp. "If'n there's one thing I hate worse'n n----rs, it's n----r lovin' white bastards like you. You're gonna be beggin' for mercy 'fore I'm done with you."

With lightning quickness, Walker grabbed the pole with both hands, straining to push it away. Johnny Reb leaned in hard, trying to drive it into Walker's chest. Walker suddenly kicked the other man in the knee, knocking him off balance and allowing Walker to roll to his right and come to his feet. He realized in dismay that his revolver lay on the ground between them, and Johnny Reb quickly picked it up and pointed it at Walker, who raised his hands.

"Big mistake, Mongolia," he said, with an evil grin. "Why don't you try some judo?"

"You're going to shoot me?" asked Walker in as calm a voice as he could muster. "How will you explain that to the rest of them?"

"No problem. I'll just put the gun in your hand, and it'll look like you committed suicide. I'll say a prayer over your grave here by the river. Maybe even cry a little bit." He laughed harshly and his thumb cocked the hammer. "Say your last words, Mongolia."

The brush behind Johnny Reb suddenly exploded as a huge wolf sprang snarling onto his back. Walker fell to his all fours, not by choice but out of sheer terror and shock. It was over in a matter of a few seconds, as the man's scream was cut short, his throat ripped open in a gush of crimson that Walker didn't need moonlight to see. He crawled backward until he was half in the river, trembling with fear. The snarling beast stood over the body, blood dripping from its muzzle, a deep growl rumbling from its chest. The amber eyes, narrowed to slits, fixed on Walker as if the wolf was considering taking a second victim. But then, just as quickly as it had come, it turned and vanished into the trees. Walker immediately threw up in the water.

Walker reclaimed his gun and stumbled as quickly as possible back to the camp. Twice he heard the dry cough in the darkness, and did not slow down until he reached the tents. He decided not to wake up the others—there was nothing that could be done for Johnny Reb, and he didn't want to have to explain what had transpired between them. Returning to his blankets, he did not stop shaking for a long time. The chorus of howling resumed, making sleep impossible and filling his mind with bloody images of what must be happening on the river bank. When Dixon shook him awake the next morning, he was astonished to realize that he had actually slept.

"Get up, Garrett! We're 'bout to take the tent down. You gonna sleep all day?"

Walker collected his things and staggered unsteadily into the daylight. The camp was buzzing with activity as the soldiers dismantled the tents and loaded the donkeys. There was no oatmeal for breakfast—just canned sardines and hardtack. Walker turned away, nauseated at the thought.

"What's that on your shirt?" asked Dixon, pointing to a palm-sized red stain. "That looks like blood—and there's a *hole*. What happened?"

"Later," Walker mumbled, with a quick shake of his head. Dixon gave him a puzzled look, and let it pass. Walker washed himself in the icy waters of the river while the tents were taken down.

"Anybody seen Thompson?" called one of the soldiers. "He wasn't here when we got up, and his bed don't look slept in." When Thompson couldn't be found, Major Pitcher sent the men to search for him. They were shocked to find his shredded uniform and what little was left of his body on the river bank a half-mile downstream. It was quickly determined that wolves were the cause of his death. A shallow grave was dug, and rocks were piled to cover him. Using a hatchet, a cross was fashioned from two small tree limbs and pushed into the soft soil at its head.

"I reckon he was defending himself with this," observed Pitcher, holding up the pole with the sharpened tip. "There's blood on the point," he added, "so he must have gotten one of the devils. He went down fighting, like a good soldier." Dixon blinked and looked at Walker, his eyes narrowing suspiciously. Walker remained silent and expressionless. Pitcher concluded, "Let this be a reminder to everyone not to go out by yourself, especially at night!"

"And always take a rifle or pistol with you," added Roosevelt. "Sharp sticks aren't worth anything against a wolfpack."

Dixon came alongside Walker as they walked back to the campsite. "One of those rocks had blood on it," he said in a low voice. "Can you think of a reason why?"

"Maybe he hit a wolf with it."

"Of course!" Dixon muttered, in mock amazement, snapping his fingers. "Why didn't I think of that?" A few steps later, he spoke again. "I can't figure why he went out with a rock and a pole, but didn't take a gun. Does that make sense to you?"

"Nope. Maybe he wasn't planning to use a gun. Not his own gun, anyway." Seeing Dixon's look of confusion, he added, "I'll tell you more later."

The company traveled down the river valley for the next four days, making camp anew each day. The scenery continued as beautiful as before, and the wildlife as abundant, but what pleased Walker the most was that there was no howling to be heard, and he was able to enjoy a good night's sleep for the first time in days. His impression that Yellowstone Park was an Eden had been badly tarnished, but he now began to think that he had been right after all. After another week of riding and hiking the trails, witnessing the fantastic geysers and towering waterfalls, and marveling at the snowy mountain vistas, he was sure of it.

24

EYES AND EARS

The first day after resuming the presidential tour provided some excitement for the Secret Service agents, and especially for Dixon. By the time the party returned to the train and Roosevelt spoke at a cornerstone-laying ceremony for an archway at the entrance to Yellowstone Park, it was getting late. The train travelled through the night and was in Wyoming by daylight. During the night, however, an alarming incident occurred on the train.

Agent Peters discovered a stowaway. A husky, unshaven, strong-looking man clad in rough workman's clothes, he was trying to conceal himself in the vestibule between the baggage and club cars. Peters summoned the other agents and they collectively tried to take him into custody, but he put up a determined fight. The vestibule was very crowded with five men wrestling and punching at each other—it was almost impossible for more than one man at a time to engage with the intruder. They eventually managed to handcuff him and force him to sit on the floor, but not before Peters suffered a black eye and Kelly a bloody nose. Walker and Dixon each took a few bruises, and Walker finally subdued him with a chokehold learned from "Big Bill" Craig.

An identification card in his pocket revealed that he was a

member of a union in San Francisco. He said that he was trying to get to St. Paul, Minnesota, to visit his mother. The agents concluded that he was not an assassination threat to the president, and decided not to press charges against him. Walker telegraphed ahead and they stopped briefly in Billings, Montana, to hand him over to police, and immediately continued on their journey.

There were three stops in Wyoming, and then two in South Dakota, and by afternoon the train had crossed into Nebraska. The first stop was in the town of Crawford, where Dixon and Walker enjoyed a special treat as the president addressed a large crowd from the rear platform of the train. Forming a line alongside the track, mounted in full dress uniforms and holding sabers aloft, was the Tenth Cavalry regiment—Dixon's old "Buffalo Soldiers" unit, with whom he had patrolled the western range prior to their deployment to Cuba! Roosevelt acknowledged their presence and praised the men for their contribution to the fighting in Santiago. He did not mention their key role in capturing San Juan Hill.

Dixon was so excited to see some of his former comrades that he jumped from the train and ran to shake hands with several of the troops, barely making it back on board as the train began moving again. When Walker leaned from a window to wave, "Shorty" Anderson stood in his stirrups, waved his saber overhead, and shouted, "Snake Man!" – a reference to Walker's battle with the python in the Philippines. Walker laughed out loud and gave him a "thumbs up" gesture. The unexpected pleasure of seeing their old friends again rejuvenated Walker and Dixon, and led to an afternoon of reminiscing about old times.

"I reckon this is how Roosevelt feels every time he sees some of his Rough Riders," Walker reflected.

"Prob'ly so," agreed Dixon. "And it seems like there's a bunch of Rough Riders in most every town we go through. I didn't know there *were* so many Rough Riders. I don't believe you could swing a dead cat without hittin' one." There was a note of sarcasm in Dixon's voice, and Walker laughed. He had forgotten how much the Tenth Cavalry troops had resented the attention lavished on the Rough Riders. They got the distinct impression that Roosevelt thought he and the Rough Riders had won the war all by themselves. It was five years since San Juan Hill, and the bravery and initiative displayed by the Tenth had been almost forgotten, while the Rough Riders had achieved mythical status as heroes.

Roosevelt's progress across the West was a continuous celebration. He crossed ten states in eleven days, giving innumerable speeches, shaking thousands of hands. There were eighteen speaking stops in one day across Kansas, alone. The emotional intensity of the crowds was still amazing to Walker, though he was somewhat used to it by now. The deafening cheers, waving flags, screaming steam whistles, blaring brass bands—each town seemed to try to outdo the others in its enthusiasm. Every town was decorated to the hilt, even if the president was only going to be there for a few minutes and spoke only from the train. Having seen this kind of reaction to two presidents now, Walker decided that it must be normal, and secretly wondered why he didn't feel the same way.

Arizona's Grand Canyon was perhaps the most spectacular site they visited on the entire tour. That, at least, was Roosevelt's emphatic opinion. He led the entourage on horseback to the rim of the canyon and stood surveying the panoramic scene, for once speechless. Upon reaching the rim, Walker's jaw dropped. He had heard that the Grand Canyon was big, but he'd had no idea it was *this* big. It wasn't just a canyon—it was an entire landscape of colorful rock layers and formations. Looking down into the depths of the abyss made Walker's stomach queasy, and he took a couple of steps back, bumping into Dixon, who turned away and muttered, "I ain't lookin' down there."

"They say that little river way down there in the bottom carved all this out of rock," Walker mused, "but I don't think so. If a river can do that *here*, then why is this the *only* grand canyon? Why's the Mississippi, the Ohio, and the Potomac all still on the surface, instead of hundreds of feet down in a canyon? Why ain't *every* river in a canyon? No sir, it just don't make sense to me."

"That's 'cause you got common sense, 'stead of a library full of books," Dixon said, turning up his nose. "You only get ideas like that from books. Did they ever think to ask if maybe the canyon made the *river*, 'stead of the river making the *canyon*?"

"That's really good, Dixon," admired Walker. "I think I'll write that in my book."

"Go right ahead. That's D-I-X-O-N. Be sure to spell it right."

"Got it!" Walker laughed, and edged carefully back up to the rim for another look. It was truly a fabulous scene, like something on another planet. He found it hard to tear his eyes away.

Roosevelt spent almost the entire day at the canyon, besides the usual luncheon, speech, and handshaking. As the sun began to set in the late afternoon, the train left for California, where the president would spend the next two weeks.

The tour of California brought back poignant memories for Walker and Dixon, reminding them of their travels with President McKinley just two years earlier. The train stopped in most of the same towns and cities as before, and the president was greeted with the same enthusiasm. As much as Walker tried to accept this, it still seemed fickle that the crowds reacted the same way to both presidents. He expressed these feelings to Dixon privately, shaking his head and frowning.

"Would you feel the same way if McKinley hadn't been *assassinated*?" Dixon asked. "If he had finished his term and Roosevelt was elected to follow him, would it still bother you that people cheer for him like this?"

"No, I guess not," Walker admitted. "I guess I just want people to show a little sorrow for McKinley getting killed. It seems cold to just cheer for the next one like nothing happened."

"True," Dixon agreed, "but it's been almost two years since Buffalo. People have to get on with their lives. You don't wear black for the rest of your life."

Walker sighed. "You're right. I need to get on with my life, too. Don't pay me no mind."

"Say, did you notice who got on board this morning at Riverside?" Dixon changed the subject.

"No—who?"

"General Otis. Remember him? The newspaper boss in Los Angeles?"

"You mean he hasn't been blown up yet?" The both laughed, remembering the two bungling men with the dynamite. Walker then added, more seriously, "I don't know if it's safe for the president to be around him. We better keep our eyes peeled when we get to Los Angeles."

Walker's words were prophetic. When the train pulled into the LaGrande station, thousands of people jammed the street outside, blocking traffic. Others packed the train platform, and still others swarmed onto the track around the rear of the train, pressing closely to the president's car. There were police and troops ready to part the crowds for the president to get to his carriage, but the size of the crowd was almost overwhelming. The cheering of the people and the shouts by the police for them to move back made for a very noisy scene.

When Roosevelt stepped out onto the speaking platform of his car, the crowd erupted into boisterous cheers and applause. He was followed by Otis and two cabinet secretaries, to be greeted by the governor. All four of the Secret Service agents positioned themselves on the deck also, watching the crowd with eagle eyes. Walker stood next to Otis. Scanning the multitude before him, he looked specifically for a weapon, thinking perhaps a pistol would most likely be an assassin's choice, and also watching for any suspicious movement, such as pointing toward the group on the deck.

When Roosevelt shouted that he was 'dee-lighted' to be in Los Angeles, the crowd burst out in another frenzy of cheering. At that instant, Walker's eye picked up a sudden movement about forty feet from the train—a man raised his arm in the direction of the car, and it appeared to Walker that there was something in the man's hand. He immediately stiff-armed Otis, knocking him aside and to his knees, falling against Roosevelt, who leaned over the railing to shake a hand and didn't even notice. The pistol shot was almost lost in the noise of the crowd, but Walker saw the flash of the muzzle. Vaulting over the ornate brass railing and knocking a couple of spectators sprawling, he charged into the crowd, shoving people out of the way, making a bee line for the shooter.

The man turned to run, but the crowd was so thick that he constantly collided with others and hardly made any progress at all. Walker tackled the man before he had gone twenty feet, forcing him to the ground, his head slamming against the steel rail. With a knee in the man's back, he twisted his arm and removed the pistol from his grip as the man yelped in pain, and then hauled him to his feet, blood trickling down the side of the man's face. Most of the crowd was unaware that anything was happening, but some soldiers on the station platform noticed and came over. Showing his badge, Walker handed them the pistol and asked them to escort the man to the police. They gripped his arms between them and led him roughly away.

By the time Walker returned to the train car, the president's entourage was being escorted through the station to the street where carriages awaited. He caught up just as they were boarding, and jumped into the front seat of the president's carriage. With a quick backward look to check on the other agents, he saw that Peters—who had been standing directly behind Otis—was holding a white hand-kerchief to the side of his neck, apparently having been grazed by a bullet.

At the hotel, he gathered the agents in the lobby to make sure they were all aware of what had happened. His arm was suddenly grabbed roughly from behind and an angry voice demanded, "What do you mean, shoving me like that—you damned pathetic excuse for a—"

"I saved your life, General," Walker interrupted Otis. "Do you see the blood on that man's neck?" He pointed to Peters, who held up the handkerchief with its bright red stains. "He was standing behind you on the platform. That bullet was meant for you, sir."

"Bullet? What bullet? I didn't hear any gunshot! You're making this up!" Otis's white goatee shook as he snapped his words, and his eyes flashed with fury.

"Why would I do that, sir? If you don't believe me, check with the police. They have the shooter in custody. You came very close to being killed just now, General."

"That's a lie! Why would anyone want to kill me?" Otis jabbed a finger angrily at Walker's nose. "If I have anything to say about it, you won't have a job by tomorrow! Who is in charge here?"

"I am the agent-in-charge, sir."

"*You? Impossible!*" The stocky old general sputtered and fumed, and then spun about and marched away, fists clenched.

Unruffled, Walker turned back to the group and said calmly, "Otis won't be with us at the parade, but just the same, keep your eyes peeled."

"Eyes and ears!" Dixon smirked, tapping the side of his head.

"Garrett—" spoke Kelly, "How did you know the shooter was aiming for Otis, and not for Roosevelt?"

Walker and Dixon exchanged a cautious look. "Let's just say that when we were here with McKinley two years ago, we saw firsthand how Otis's workers hated him. *And,*" Walker added, "when I saw the man raise the gun, it looked like it was pointing at the center of the platform, where Otis was standing, and not to the side where the president was standing. Fair enough?" Kelley and Peters both nodded assent, and Walker left the group to find the police officer in charge and review the security plan.

The city of Los Angeles had timed its annual *Los Fiesta de las Flores* celebration to occur while the president was in town. The four-hour parade took up the entire afternoon, as Roosevelt reviewed hundreds of flower-laden floats, marching bands, thousands of flower-scattering children, and marching military units—including, of course, former Rough Riders. Walker and Dixon agreed that the spectacle was even more breathtaking than the one they had attended with President McKinley. Before leaving the hotel, Walker had spoken with the police officer in charge and made arrangements for the president's return to the train after the parade. The gunshot at the station made security even more of a priority than before, and plans had to be changed.

As soon as the last float passed, a closed carriage was brought to the review stand and the president was rushed into it. Mounted police and troops encircled the carriage and, with other police clearing the way ahead, carried out a high-speed dash to the depot. Astonishingly, the mounted escort rode their horses directly into the station, forming two lines from the front door to the platform exit. Roosevelt, surrounded by the Secret Service agents flanked by foot soldiers and police, breezed through without a hitch. Upon boarding the train, Roosevelt went directly to bed, thoroughly exhausted from the long day's activities. The president never spoke to Walker about the incident with Otis, and Walker concluded that he was completely unaware of it.

The presidential route up the Pacific coast was almost identical to that taken by McKinley. After several days in San Francisco, Roosevelt left his Secret Service agents behind while he spent four days alone with naturalist John Muir in Yosemite Park, and then proceeded northward through Oregon to Washington. Along the way, besides speeches, processions, receptions, luncheons, dinners, and various ceremonies, the president also laid several cornerstones for buildings and monuments—including one in honor of President McKinley—planted trees, received honorary degrees, and of course, shook countless thousands of hands. When the presidential train finally turned eastward, even though it was in the farthest corner of the country from the national capitol, Walker and the other agents felt a deep sense of relief. There were still nine days of travel ahead of them, but just knowing that they were homeward bound gave each man a boost of energy and put a smile on their tired faces.

They crossed Montana on a Wednesday, Idaho on Thursday, and Utah on Friday. Upon arriving in Salt Lake City, the president was welcomed with a sixty-carriage parade, escorted by mounted troops, including an honor guard of fifty Rough Riders. Dixon leaned over to Walker and growled, "If I never see another Rough Rider, it'll be too soon for me!"

The president spoke at the Mormon Tabernacle to a packed house, and then had lunch at the home of Senator Tom Kearns. The guests at the lunch were quite a mixed group. Besides President

Roosevelt, it included the Secretary of the Navy, both Utah senators, a congressman, the governor, Mormon church president Joseph F. Smith, a Catholic bishop, an Episcopal bishop, and a few other men and women, including one of Smith's plural wives and Seth Bullock, the famed frontier lawman who had traveled extensively with Roosevelt on the tour. Walker and the other agents ate sandwiches and fruit in a small room beside the kitchen.

"The Book of Mormon," Walker read aloud the title of a thick book lying on a side table. "I wonder what this is about," he said as he idly opened it and turned a few pages. "Looks a lot like the Bible to me."

"You've never heard of *The Book of Mormon*?" asked Peters. Walker shook his head, chewing on a sandwich. "It's the Mormon Bible. Some of my relatives back in Missouri joined the Mormons for a while, but they didn't stay with it," Peters continued. "They couldn't go along with some of their beliefs, like polygamy, Jews turning into Indians, and such."

"You're pulling my leg, ain't you Peters?" hooted Dixon. "You can't be serious!"

"I'm not kidding," insisted Peters. "They believe that centuries before Christ a bunch of Israelites came to America, and that some of them were cursed and were turned into Indians."

Just then, a young woman entered the room carrying a pitcher of fresh water and a basket of strawberries. "Are you men getting enough to eat?" she asked pleasantly.

"Yes ma'am," said Walker courteously. "Can you tell me something about your religion? Do Mormons believe that Indians are Jews who were cursed?"

"That's what *The Book of Mormon* says," she replied. "Anyone who rejects the Gospel of Jesus Christ will be cursed, also."

"But a white man who rejects the gospel today won't be turned into an Indian, right?" asked Kelly.

"That's true!" she laughed. "If it worked that way, there would be a lot more Indians around!"

"And what about polygamy?" asked Dixon. "Is that something Mormons do?"

"Not anymore," she smiled. "We quit that a few years ago, though some plural marriages still exist. Apostle Smith has five wives, and one of them is in there at the table now. But we don't do that anymore."

"*Apostle*? I thought apostles were only in the Bible!" Walker was confused.

"We have twelve apostles, and one of them is the president of the church. Gentiles don't understand the Latter-Day Saints religion, but it's not really that complicated."

"*Gentiles*? Who are Gentiles?" Walker rubbed his temples. He was reaching his limit for new information.

The girl smiled patiently. "Anyone who isn't a Mormon is a Gentile," she explained. "You're a Gentile, but you can be converted and be saved."

"Sarah!" a woman's voice called from the kitchen. "I need you in here now!"

"Coming!" she called back. "Sorry," she said apologetically, "but I have to get back to work! I hope you have a pleasant stay here in Utah!" She hurried away, as the agents looked at each other in silence for a moment.

Peters grinned. "See? I told you. That's why my relatives didn't stay in their church. There's more besides that, too. But they've got really good strawberries," he grinned again as he bit into a large, juicy one.

"I'd like to hear the conversation around that table in there," Walker exclaimed. "There's a Mormon apostle, a Catholic bishop, an Episcopal bishop, and the president's Dutch Reformed. Not to mention Seth Bullock and his forty-four!"

"The Gentiles are outnumbered at least two to one," observed Dixon. "But my money's on Roosevelt and Bullock!"

"I'd like to watch somebody call Bullock a 'Gentile!'" chuckled Kelly. "They wouldn't do *that* but once!"

"Alright, men," said Walker, interrupting the banter. "We've got to get back to work, too. Dixon—you're with me out front. You two take the back door."

"Eyes and ears!" reminded Dixon again, grabbing a handful of strawberries.

"Eyes and ears," they echoed, filing out to the back porch.

On Saturday, the train steamed into Wyoming for the second time on the trip. Here Roosevelt enjoyed what was for him the highlight of the return trip—a sixty-five-mile horseback ride from Laramie to Cheyenne. The riding group consisted of fifteen men, including Walker and Dixon, besides Bullock, Roosevelt's personal secretary Loeb, and an assortment of state and federal political figures. Five changes of horses along the way allowed them to make exceptionally fast time, despite reaching an elevation of over eight thousand feet while traversing Sherman's Summit, with views of fourteen-thousand-foot peaks around them.

It was a grueling ride, ending at the city square in the heart of Cheyenne. Walker noticed that several of the men appeared a little unsteady as they dismounted. He and Dixon walked rather stiffly, also, but the president was ebullient as ever. He sprang to the ground, loudly praising the day as a "dee-lightful" outing and a "bully" time. Handing the reins to a waiting officer, he climbed the steps to a speaking platform, and proceeded to deliver an energetic forty-five-minute address to a crowd of several thousand while still in his boots and spurs.

Fortunately, the next day was Sunday, and according to Roosevelt's rule, it was a day of rest, with no scheduled activities. The president's party attended services at the First Methodist Church in the morning, and had only a luncheon and a dinner for the rest of the day. Walker took advantage of the opportunity to write a letter to Abigail—his third of the trip. He was proud of his effort until he learned that Dixon had written Sally every week for the past eight weeks, besides writing his mother and Daisy twice.

"You got some fences to mend, Brother Garrett," he observed critically. "She's gonna think she don't mean much to you."

"I'm doing the best I can," Walker sighed, with a downcast look.

"When you ain't gettin' any letters back, it's hard to keep it up all by yourself. Maybe I should have spent more time writing her and less time writing my book."

"You'll prob'ly have a letter waitin' on you when you get home," Dixon said, encouragingly. "And you'll have more time to write letters once this trip is over. I'm ready to be done with it, myself. Nine weeks is too much, and I bet you he's planning to spend the summer on Long Island again. No rest for the weary." He frowned and closed the envelope on his letter. Walker had a sense of foreboding that Dixon was thinking of leaving the Service, but let it pass. There would be time to discuss it later.

Upon leaving Cheyenne, the rest of the trip eastward was a blur for Walker. At this point, towns and cities had become indistinguishable from one another, and he heard not a word of any speech given by the president. The only distinct memory he retained was the ceremony at the Lincoln tomb in Springfield, Illinois. A company of black soldiers served as an honor guard for the occasion, and in his remarks Roosevelt noted that this was only fitting. With its one hundred-seventeen-foot-high obelisk, the tomb was impressive without being ornate.

He was studying the monument when someone bumped against his shoulder. Dixon heaved a deep sigh. "If we'd been there, he wouldn't got assassinated," he murmured. "I'd a'put that Booth fella six feet under."

Walker nodded. "That's where he belonged," he agreed. "Remember the Surratt House? We stood in the same room where he slept, almost forty years ago. Made my skin crawl."

"It was too easy for him," Dixon scowled. "Garfield was too easy, and McKinley was too easy. This country's gonna have to get more serious about protecting its presidents. We can't let it be so easy. We can't let this keep happening every twenty years or so."

Walker stood beside Dixon in silence for a long minute. Finally, he turned and said softly, "Eyes and ears, Agent Dixon. Eyes and ears." They walked slowly together down the granite steps toward the carriages and waited for Roosevelt.

The train roared through the night, passing through Indiana, Ohio, and Pennsylvania in hours. With only a few stops, the president speaking mostly from the rear platform, the trip concluded with a rush. It was after seven o'clock in the evening on Friday, June 5 when the locomotive finally hissed to a halt in Washington, D.C. A crowd greeted the president at the station, and thousands lined the streets cheering during the procession to the White House, where he gave a brief speech to another crowd before retiring.

Daylight lasted well into the evening, as summer was at hand. The sky in the west was pink with the glow of sunset, and the air was warm and muggy. Walker thought longingly back to the cool, dry air he had come to enjoy during the last two months. As he and Dixon walked down the street toward home, they heard their names being called. Turning, they saw a cab approaching at a quick trot. It was Henry Brown and Napoleon, and inside were Sally and Daisy! Walker shook hands warmly with Henry, while Dixon was embraced by the two. He then sat in the cab between them, while Walker climbed onto the front seat beside Henry.

During the ride home, Walker felt a sense of bone-deep tiredness come over him. All he wanted to do was lie down in a bed that wasn't moving and sleep for a long time. For a moment he doubted that he would be able to stay awake until he reached the bed, but when he did, it was sweet surrender. "No more 'eyes and ears,'" he mumbled to no one, and was gone before his head touched the pillow.

25

COUNTING CHICKENS

Director Wilkie leaned forward, his hands on the back of the desk chair, and the ends of his mustache lifting as he smiled. "Well done, men!" he beamed. "Nine weeks on the road, and no incidents! The president wanted me to tell you all how pleased he was with your service. Considering the last-minute adjustments we had to make to the squad, I think it is a great testament to your flexibility and hard work that everything went so smoothly." He paused to scan the room, looking directly at each agent, giving each an approving nod. "You've got almost a month before the First Family heads to Sagamore Hill for July and August," he continued, "so get some rest and spend some time with your families." With another approving nod, he abruptly turned and exited the room, closing the door behind him.

Stover rose from his chair with some difficulty and, using a walking stick, limped to the front of the room. He grimaced as he saw everyone's eyes fixed on him with concern written on their faces. "It was a bad break," he shrugged. "I'll be fine in another month or two. Until then, it is what it is." Taking several envelopes from his inside coat pocket, he handed them to Peters, sitting closest to him. "Pass those out, Peters. Everybody gets a bonus for all the extra work you did while on the tour—an extra twenty dollars for each month. Don't spend it all in one place!"

"Forty dollars bonus!" exclaimed Kelly. "I can sure use *this!*"

"Thanks, Stover!" said Dixon, tucking his envelope into his pocket.

"Don't thank *me*," demurred Stover. "Your agent-in-charge—Mr. Garrett—asked the president to approve it, and Director Wilkie requested the funds. You earned it." The agents turned to Walker in surprise and enthusiastically slapped him on the back. "Keep the noise down, men," Stover said sternly, but with a one-sided smile. "Now, get out of here and go to your stations."

Walker waited until the others had left the room, and held up his envelope, giving Stover a questioning look. "I think somebody made a mistake on my check, Stover."

"There's no mistake, Garrett. The agent-in-charge gets paid more than the other agents. Your check is two month's salary, plus the traveling bonus, plus the agent-in-charge stipend. It's a nice payday, wouldn't you say?"

Walker gave a soft whistle. "Almost four hundred dollars—that's more money than I've ever had in my life!"

"Like I said, you earned it. By the way, depending on how my leg heals over the next month, you may be the agent-in-charge at Sagamore Hill, also. I'll keep you updated so there's no last-minute surprise, this time."

Walker was floating on air as he left the office. The unexpectedly large paycheck gave him a boost of energy almost as powerful as the lengthy letter from Abigail that had been waiting for him upon his return home. Beulah had waited to give it to him until he woke up the next day. Since it was Saturday, he and Dixon had slept late. Walker had sat down at the table, groggy and cradling a cup of steaming black coffee while Beulah scrambled some eggs for his breakfast. When he noticed the familiar handwriting on the envelope on the table he had almost choked on the coffee. Four pages of *real paper*—not that little, yellow stationery she used to send. He had read it obsessively for two days, mulling over every sentence. There was no misinterpreting her feelings. She said that she missed him, and wanted to know if it was possible for her to come to Washington for the Fourth of July. He had mailed a reply already this morning on the way to the White House, explaining that he would be on Long Island with the president for the months of July and August, but promised to come to Decatur to visit as soon as that was done. His heart and mind had been in a whirl for two days now.

Dixon was no better off. He and Sally had spent every waking moment together. Strolling the streets, eating ice cream, going to church—every time Walker saw them, they were holding hands and looking into each other's eyes. *He's got it bad,* Walker mused. *Something's gonna happen soon. They can't go on like this much longer.*

That afternoon, as Walker was manning the guard post in front of the White House, Dixon stopped by while patrolling the grounds. He stood beside Walker for a couple of minutes without saying anything, and Walker began to get the sense that something was wrong. "Everything alright?" he asked casually.

Dixon sighed. "During lunch break, I went to talk to the police chief about maybe joining the force." He sighed again, this time impatiently. "He said they want me, but they don't plan to hire any colored officers until the first of the year—which I don't mind, I can wait a few months. I asked him what they planned to pay, and when he told me, I almost choked on my own spit." He turned toward Walker with an incredulous expression. "Garrett, they ain't gonna pay *half* what we make now! How do they expect anybody to live on that? I garn'tee you that's not what they pay the *white* officers." He lifted his hat and ran his hand over his hair. "I reckon with Sally teaching school, we would make enough together to get by, but—" he shook his head and frowned.

Walker blinked. "Are you saying that you and Sally are getting *married*?"

Dixon looked quickly at Walker with wide eyes, and then closed them as if in pain. "I let the cat out of the bag, didn't I? Don't tell Mama and Daisy yet—we need to work some things out first."

"Of course!" Walker gasped, reaching out and grabbing Dixon's hand to shake it. "Absolutely! I'm really happy for you—for both of you!"

"Yeah," Dixon grinned sheepishly. "After I was gone for two months, we both knew we have to be together. That was torture. I ain't got a ring yet, so it's not official, but it will be soon. With that extra forty dollars we got today, I can buy her a nice gold ring. I'm nervous, but I'm happy too." Looking Walker in the eye, he added emphatically, "I *want* this, Garrett. I *really* want it."

"I want it for you, too," Walker smiled, clapping Dixon's shoulder. "I'm really happy for you!" Suddenly, Walker froze and exclaimed, "Oh no!" He pulled the gold watch Abigail had given him for Christmas from his vest pocket and opened it. "I'm going to be late for my stick fight with the president! He won't like that!" And he dashed toward the White House, leaving Dixon to take the post.

After a vigorous half-hour of combat, both men were sweaty and panting. Roosevelt tossed his stick to Walker and dropped his helmet and padded vest to the floor. "Good session, Garrett! You got in some good licks this time! Keep it up!"

"Yes sir—thank you, sir! Could I ask you a quick question, Mr. President?"

"What's on your mind, Garrett?"

"Sir, I've written a book about my adventures traveling around the world. It starts in Cuba and tells about what happened in all the places we went, all the way back to America. I'd like to get it published, and I was wondering if you could—" Walker was about to ask the president to recommend a publisher that he might approach with his manuscript. He did not expect the response he received.

"Bully!" interrupted Roosevelt, practically shouting as he smacked his fist into his hand, teeth flashing. "That is *outstanding*! I'll be absolutely dee-*lighted* to write you a letter of introduction and recommendation to my publisher in New York. That should open a door for you! My secretary will have it ready for you later this afternoon!" Roosevelt smacked his fist into his palm again, and with another flash of his famous teeth, was gone.

Walker stood with his mouth open, staring at the doorway. It was several seconds before he recovered his senses enough to put away the equipment. True to his word, the president's letter was waiting for him in the outer office that afternoon as he was leaving to go home. It was typed on official White House letterhead stationery, graced by the president's signature flourish. He stared at it, still disbelieving that it was real. That evening, he showed it to Dixon, Beulah, and Daisy. They were so excited—their eyes were wide and mouths open. They celebrated by going to the local black-owned ice cream parlor and sat at an inside table to enjoy dishes of Neapolitan.

When he went to bed that night, Walker had a hard time going to sleep. Thoughts raced constantly through his mind—would he really get his book published? Would people actually buy it? What would Abigail think? He decided not to tell her about Roosevelt's letter— better to wait until the book was actually accepted by the publisher. *Don't want to count my chickens before they're hatched,* he thought.

The most important thing to occur during the rest of June was that Dixon proposed to Sally, and she accepted. She was so proud of the gold ring, and they were obviously so much in love that Walker could feel only joy at their happiness. He had thought that he would be sad at Dixon's taking this step. He had feared that losing his best friend and brother would leave his own life empty and lonely, but those feelings did not come. His smiles were not just on his face, but in his heart. He wondered if he and Abigail would ever reach this point, but he decided not to think about that, for now. There would be time for that later, he thought.

July arrived, and the First Family departed for the Roosevelt estate on Long Island. An enlarged team of eight agents accompanied them, lodging in the famous, eight-sided Octagon Hotel in Oyster Bay, three miles from Sagamore Hill. Stover, still hobbling with a cane, set up an office at the hotel with a direct telephone line to the estate. To protect the president from unwanted hordes of visitors, Stover stationed one agent on the drive during the day, out of sight of the house, and two at night. This was later increased to two during the day and three at night. The reason for the increase was an incident that occurred late one evening.

At about ten o'clock on a Monday night, a buggy came up the road from Cove Neck, driven by a man sporting a mustache, and wearing a dark suit and an old-fashioned derby hat. "What is your name, and why are you coming to Sagamore Hill?" asked Walker, holding the horse's bridle.

"I'm Henry Brenner, and I have an appointment to see President Roosevelt."

"At this hour of the night? That's not true. Who are you, and why are you here?"

"Yes, it *is* true. I'm Henry Brenner, and I have a farm a few miles away. I spoke with the president earlier this evening by wireless, and he agreed to meet with me."

"That is preposterous! The president doesn't speak with anyone by wireless, much less a local farmer. Turn your buggy around, Mr. Brenner, and leave immediately. That's an order!"

"But—" the man began to protest.

"No buts!" Walker interrupted. "Turn it around right now! You're not going to see the president, and that's final."

Grumbling, he turned the buggy around and left. Half an hour later, however, he returned. "I insist on seeing the president," he demanded. "He invited me to come and discuss a personal matter with him, and I refuse to be turned away."

"What is the nature of this 'personal matter?'"

"It concerns his daughter, Alice. She and I are to be married."

Walker laughed so loudly the horse snorted and tossed its head. "You are either joking or insane!" he snapped, beginning to get irritated. "Turn this buggy around, Mr. Brenner, and I mean it. Don't come back again or I will arrest you. Now get going!"

Brenner objected and became agitated, but did comply with the order. At about eleven o'clock, however, the buggy returned for the third time. "You have no right to prevent me from seeing the president," he argued angrily. "I don't care what you say, I'm going to the house and talk to him about Alice. We are in love and want to get married."

"Get out of the buggy, Mr. Brenner." Walker let go of the bridle and walked slowly toward the buggy along its right-hand side.

"No! I'm going to see the president!" Brenner raised the buggy whip and was about to strike the horse. Walker sprang forward and seized him by the arm, and flung Brenner out of the buggy to sprawl full length on the ground. He marched him to the stable, where he was guarded by Dixon while Walker notified Stover by telephone. While waiting for the police, Walker searched the buggy and found a loaded pistol under the seat, which he handed to the police when they arrived.

The incident, though bloodless and mostly non-violent, was disturbing to the security team, and led Stover to increase the number of agents on duty. The incident was reported in the press for several days, with varying degrees of accuracy. Most reported it as an assassination attempt, and depicted it as a narrow escape for the president. Walker testified at a hearing for Brenner, but most of the reporters preferred their highly sensationalized versions of the event to the relatively dull account provided by Walker.

Walker made an appointment to meet with an editor at Parson and Sons, Roosevelt's publisher in New York City. On his day off, he took the train into the city, and then a cab to the publishing house. He wore his usual gray suit and fedora, and carried a worn leather satchel containing his five-hundred-page handwritten manuscript, wrapped in brown paper and tied with string. Until now he had only seen the city from train windows, except for the time almost three years ago when he had arrived in the port, relieved to be back on American soil. On that occasion, however, he and Dixon had been arrested, charged with desertion, and taken to Washington for court-martial. He hadn't really noticed the city then, having had more serious matters on his mind.

This time, however, he absorbed the hustle and bustle of the city's crowded streets, listening to its many noises, and smelling its scents. He had been in large cities from coast to coast, but New York was different. The buildings were taller, the countless people more diverse, the streets noisier and livelier. There were skyscrapers that stood twenty or even thirty stories high, and there were more auto-mobiles than he had seen anywhere else. The pulsating energy of the city was mesmerizing. He was so distracted by the stimulation of it all that he was surprised when the cab stopped in front of an ornate fifteen-story tower— Parson and Sons, Publishers.

He gave his name to the receptionist at the front desk, and waited while she perused a large register. "Mr. Walker Garrett? Ah, yes—*here* you are. Your ten o'clock with Mr. Cross will be in his office on the seventh floor. The elevators are right around the corner there."

Upon reaching the seventh floor, Walker found another reception desk waiting for him when he got off the elevator. The woman behind the desk was reading a book and chewing gum. Walker waited, but she paid him no attention. He cleared his throat to no effect, and then cleared it again, more loudly. She looked up with irri-tation. "Yes?" she asked impatiently.

"I'm Walker Garrett, and I have a ten o'clock with Mr. Cross in his office."

She consulted a large appointment calendar on her desk. "I'll let him know you're here," she said curtly, and went back to reading. Walker didn't move. Several seconds passed. Without looking up, she growled, "You can sit down over there," and pointed to some chairs by the wall. Walker still didn't move. Finally, she looked up and snapped, "What do you want?"

"I want you to let Mr. Cross know that I'm here for my ten o'clock." Walker nodded toward the wall clock, which showed two minutes until ten.

"I *said* I would, didn't I?"

"Yes ma'am, but you haven't done it, and it's almost ten o'clock."

Just then, a door opened across the landing and a short, thin man stepped out. He was coatless, there were sweat patches under his arms, and his shirt sleeves were rolled up over the wrists. He wore thick glasses, brown suspenders and a gray bow tie, and his thin hair was combed over the top of his head to cover its baldness. "Mr. Cross—this is Walker Garrett. He's here for your ten o'clock." She gave Walker a 'so there' look, and went back to reading. Cross gestured for Walker to come, and went back into his office without saying a word.

Walker sat facing Cross's desk with his satchel in his lap. "Good morning, Mr. Cross," he began, but Cross remained expressionless. "I've written a book, and I'd like to show you my manuscript. I'd like to see if I can get it published."

"Don't you have an agent?" Cross spoke for the first time. His tone was not friendly.

"I *am* an agent," Walker replied with a tight smile. He pulled back the lapel of his coat to show his badge. "I'm a Secret Service agent."

Cross glared at him over the top of his glasses. "Don't joke with me, young man! What do you take me for? You need a *literary* agent to get your manuscript in the door, if you want to have any chance of getting it published. You can't represent your own book!"

Walker reached into his coat and produced an envelope, which he extended to Cross. "You might say that I have an agent, in a way. This is a letter of introduction and recommendation from President Roosevelt. I'm here because of him."

"*President Roosevelt!*" sputtered Cross furiously. "He's not a literary agent! And if you expect me to believe that you have a letter from *him*, you're out of your mind!"

Walker produced another envelope. "These are letters of recommendation by Generals Funston, Wheeler, and MacArthur—"

Cross smacked the top of his desk with his palms. "I have never heard such nonsense! That badge is obviously fake, and you're some kind of shyster, young man! *Out!* Get out of here, before I call the police!" He stomped around the desk and opened the door, pointing out.

Walker, red-faced with anger, exited quickly and was soon back on the street. He didn't stop grinding his teeth until he reached the Octagon Hotel in Oyster Bay. As he walked briskly through the lobby, heading for the stairs to his room, a well-dressed middle-aged man with graying hair and a trimmed mustache waved at him. "Young man! Are you a Secret Service agent? Could I have a word with you? I won't take but a minute of your time!"

Walker, still in a foul mood, was about to snap that this was his day off and continue to his room, but his sense of good manners prevailed. "Yes sir," he said civilly. "I am an agent in the president's detail. What can I do for you?"

"I really need to see the president about—"

"Everybody wants to see the president," interrupted Walker, raising his palm. "If you want an appointment, you should contact Mr. Cortelyou or Mr. Loeb. They can—"

"I've tried that," protested the man, spreading his hands. "They won't talk to me, and there's no one who can help me get my foot in the door."

Frowning, Walker was about to tell the man to leave when it struck him that he had been in the same frustrating situation just a couple of hours earlier. *The man needs an agent,* he thought. *I can't take him to the president, but maybe I can speak to Loeb.* "What is it that you want with the president?" he asked in a more considerate tone of voice.

A look of relief came over his face, and the man began to explain, speaking quickly. "My name is George Page. I'm a book publisher— Page Turner Books. My family has been in the publishing business for three generations, but now we're struggling to survive. I need to publish something that will sell—something that the public will want to read. If President Roosevelt would let me publish something of his—even just an essay or short article—it might do the trick— might get us noticed—might bring more business my way. If I could just talk to the president, I think I could persuade him to give me something. Can you help?" His look of desperation made Walker want to help, but he didn't see how he could. He motioned toward a pair of upholstered chairs and a coffee table in the corner of the lobby, and they sat down.

"Most of the president's books have been published by Parson and Sons, you know," Walker countered. "Why would he let you cut in on their business?"

"Parson is one of the biggest names in the publishing industry," admitted Page. "It's hard for small companies like mine to compete with them. They get all the top authors, and the bestsellers. My company tries to work with the less well-known writers, especially those who are trying to get started. Unfortunately, there's not as much money in that—which is why I want to publish something by Roosevelt. We need the revenue and the attention it would bring."

Walker studied the man's face in silence for a moment, and then leaned forward and spoke in a confidential tone. "Mr. Page, you and I may be able to help each other."

"What can I do to help *you*?" Page seemed ready to agree to anything.

Walker opened the satchel and took out the brown paper parcel tied with string, and set it on the coffee table with a solid thump. "I've written a book and I want to get it published. I just came from Parson and Sons, but they threw me out because I don't have an agent. They didn't even look at the manuscript. Would you be willing to take a look at it and give me your opinion, if I can get Loeb to make an appointment for you to talk to the president?"

Page instantly grasped Walker's hand and shook it vigorously. "Absolutely! I'll take this to my room and begin reading right now. I can't tell you how much I appreciate whatever you can do for me! I'm in room 210—just knock on my door any time!"

"But I haven't done anything yet, Mr. Page."

"I have confidence in you, young man—what is your name, by the way?"

"Garrett, sir. Agent Walker Garrett."

"Garrett? Aren't you the one who saved Roosevelt's life last week when the assassin tried to get to him at Sagamore Hill? I read all about it. You're a *hero*!"

"It wasn't as exciting as the newspapers made it sound, believe me. I was just doing my—" He was about to say "duty" when his mind flashed back to Buffalo and he remembered Czolgosz's words. "Uh," he floundered, "I was just doing my *job*."

"Maybe so," Page enthused, "but you did a mighty fine job *of* it! We need more young men like you in this country. I'm looking forward to reading this. By the way, what's it about?"

"It's the story of how I came to travel all the way around the world. I joined the army and fought in Cuba with Wheeler, Roosevelt, the Rough Riders, and the Tenth Cavalry. I was sent to the Philippines, stopping on the way to annex Hawaii and Guam, and was with Funston when he captured Aguinaldo. Then I was sent to China when the Boxer Rebellion broke out, and we rescued Tientsin and Peking—"

"You can't be serious, Garrett! You fought in all those places?"

"And in the Gobi Desert and Mongolia. Nobody believes it, sir, but it's true, and I've got letters from Wheeler, Funston, MacArthur, Pershing, and Roosevelt to prove it—besides a couple more. I have several medals, including the Medal of Honor. All the stories in the book are true."

Page stared at the parcel in his hands. "I *really* can't wait to read it, now!" he exclaimed in a tone of awe. "This could be something *special.*" He walked toward the stairs, saying over his shoulder, "I'll be in my room if you need me."

Watching Page ascend the stairs carrying his manuscript, Walker's hands began to shake. He returned to the upholstered chair until his breathing and shaking were under control. *Is this really happening?* he wondered. *Don't count your chickens before they're hatched,* he warned himself, but he couldn't help feeling excited. Wiping his sweaty hands on his pants, he stepped to the front desk and asked to use the telephone. He lifted the receiver to his ear and tapped the key twice.

"Your party, sir?" inquired the female operator's voice.

"Sagamore Hill, please."

"One moment, please."

There was some static, followed by a loud popping sound that made Walker flinch. The voice on the other end was familiar.

"William Loeb speaking. Please state your business."

"Hi William, this is Walker Garrett. Listen—I've got a big favor to ask. . . ."

26

DECATUR

Walker touched the napkin to his lips as he rose from his breakfast table in the dining car to stretch his legs while the train took on water, coal, and passengers in Chattanooga, Tennessee. He checked his pocket watch—it was three hours yet to Decatur. He strolled into the station for a quick look around, and bought a copy of *The Chattanooga Press* for a nickel, tucking it under his arm. The Terminal Station had a large main waiting room with a soaring domed ceiling, complete with a skylight and large brass chandeliers. *Fancy!* he murmured to himself. *But not nearly as fancy as some others I've seen,* he added smugly.

He caught a glimpse of himself in a full-length mirror outside a barber shop, and stopped for a closer look. Gray pinstriped suit, vest, silk tie, and fedora—*I look like a businessman,* he thought, hooking his thumbs in his belt. *Nobody will take me for a farmer's son now!* he smiled confidently. *Frank Dancy will definitely give me a second look!*

Returning to his seat, he browsed the ten pages of the newspaper. It was mostly full of advertisements for everything imaginable, with a few news items. There was a lengthy article describing the fortieth anniversary commemorations of the Civil War battles of Chicka-mauga and Chattanooga. Another extolled the dominance of "King

Cotton," which will "never be successfully challenged." *That's true,* he nodded. There was an analysis of the threat of war between Turkey, Bulgaria, and other Balkan states.

By the time he finished reading these, the train had left the station and Chattanooga behind, and was rumbling through the Tennessee River Valley. The scenic beauty of the river and the rolling hills was pleasant to behold, and he relaxed comfortably as he gazed out the window. September was harvest time for the corn and cotton crops, and the fields were bursting with vitality as field hands loaded wagons with bales and sacks of produce.

The scenes reminded him of bygone days at Pond Spring when he had shadowed his father as he supervised General Wheeler's sprawling plantation. Thousands of acres of crops, along with horses, cattle, mules, hogs, and chickens, besides the barns, stables, and granaries—how did one man manage it all? In addition to all that, there were the field workers, herdsmen, and craftsmen to oversee. *Lemuel Garrett, you were a real man,* he mused. *No detail was too small for you to notice, no problem too complex for you to solve. No wonder the General left his affairs in your hands—and you didn't let him down.*

He suddenly felt a pang of guilt—hadn't he just been congratulating himself on his gentlemanly appearance—not looking like a farmer's son? Was he ashamed of his father?—a voice in his head demanded. *Of course not,* he argued indignantly. *That's ridiculous! I'm proud of my father, and I'm proud to be his son!* But the nagging, guilty feeling didn't go away, and the rest of the way to Decatur he tried to distract himself.

He read again the letter he had just received from George Page, thanking him for his help. Roosevelt had given him the manuscripts of three of his speeches from the recent tour to publish, and Page was thrilled. The letter concluded with the exciting announcement that he had decided to publish Walker's book! A contract would be arriving in the mail soon, and the wheels would then start to turn. It could be in bookstores by Christmas! Walker couldn't help but grin as he put the letter away. *I'm going to be a published author!* he exulted. Frank Dancy would have to be impressed by that! He wasn't sure yet why that was so important, except that he had begun to think about his future possibilities with Abigail, and her father's opinion of him mattered. She had invited him—no, practically begged him—to come visit her in Decatur. She would be back in Richmond in December, but that was months away. It had already been too long since they had been together. The trip was costing him half a month's pay, but he didn't mind. The money didn't matter. She was on his mind constantly, and he needed to find answers to his questions.

In her letters, Abigail frequently said how proud she was of the work he did, protecting the president. While this made Walker feel good, it also gave him concern. He had just spent four of the last five months away from home doing this work, and that much separation would definitely put a strain on a relationship. With next year being a presidential election year, he was sure that more touring was in store for the Secret Service agents. He thought about Dixon and Sally— Dixon had negotiated a better salary with the D.C. police, and was committed to making the change at the end of the year for this very reason. Dixon wanted to be home with his wife as much as possible, not spending half his time traveling the country. Walker thought it ironic that his work with the Secret Service, which seemed to inspire Abigail with so much admiration and attraction for him, was also a potential barrier to their being together—and he had no idea what to do about it. He hoped that taking a week off to come to Alabama would bring some clarity to the situation.

When he stepped out of the car at the Decatur depot, he couldn't help but contrast the scene with the last time he had passed through, on McKinley's tour more than two years ago. This time there were no banners, flags, or brass bands, no waving crowds. No one noticed him as he carried his suitcase through the waiting room and out to Railroad Street. The red-brick chimneys of the two-story Dancy house peeked through the topmost branches of the towering magnolias that surrounded it—a thin column of gray smoke rose from one, plainly visible against the cloudless blue sky. Taking a deep breath, he began walking slowly down the street, hoping that the right words would come to him when he got there.

Frank Dancy, an attorney in Decatur, was wealthy, but not nearly as prosperous as his brother, James, in Richmond. His front porch was a dozen feet wide, graced by four slender columns which supported a roofed balcony, which also featured four columns. At eighty-years old, it was the oldest residence in the city, and was attractive, but nothing like the newer, elaborate Victorian beauties—known as the "Painted Ladies"—across town. The close proximity of the railroad track, the depot, two hotels and a saloon lent a somewhat seedy atmosphere to the area.

A colored hired man tended to the yard and carriage house, but there was no liveried butler to answer the door. The hired man's wife did the housework and laundry. Since Beulah left for Washington, Dancy had employed three cooks in succession, but each had eventually quit for better paying work elsewhere, with the result that Abigail had assumed the kitchen duties, and was becoming a competent cook, though with a limited repertoire.

When Walker knocked, the door was opened by Dancy himself. He had come home for lunch, and was still dressed in his business suit. Tall and well-groomed, with a neat gray beard and gold-rimmed glasses, he was a more impressive figure than his wealthier brother. He stood silently for several seconds, staring at Walker. "Garrett?" He sounded confused.

"Yes sir," said Walker, politely lifting his hat. "I hope I'm not interrupting anything."

"Not at all," Dancy recovered quickly, a little embarrassed. "We were—ah—we were expecting you—" He stepped back with a sweeping gesture. "Please come in!" As Walker put his suitcase down in the foyer, Dancy turned to the black housekeeper coming down the stairs with a basket of rumpled bed linens—"Mandy! Fetch Abigail from the kitchen! Her guest has arrived."

"Yes suh, Mistah Dancy."

Walker hung his hat beside others on the coat tree, and followed Dancy into the parlor. Across the way, he could see into the dining room—where he had never eaten during his two years living in the house—and could see that the table was set for five. Upon entering the parlor, he found a middle-aged couple there, apparently the reason for the other two places set at the table. The woman was expensively attired, with a flowered hat, pearl necklace, and navy-blue silk dress. The man, plump, bald and mustached, wore a plain brown suit, and rose from his seat to be introduced.

"Garrett, this is Stafford Moseley. He owns the Dixie Hotel just up the street, across from the train station. Stafford, this is Walter Garrett —a friend of Abigail's, come down from Washington for a visit."

"It's 'Walker,'" Walker corrected, as they shook hands. Dancy's eyebrows came together in a frown. Walker turned to the woman. "And how are *you*, ma'am?"

"I'm 'Dixie,'" she said bluntly, remaining seated but extending her gloved left hand. "It's *my* hotel." Moseley reddened and coughed into his fist.

"Yes ma'am," Walker nodded. "It looks very nice."

Just then, Mandy stuck her red-kerchiefed head into the doorway. "Miss Abigail say she cain't come right now. She stirrin' gravy." She disappeared with the basket of laundry, and a few seconds later they heard the back door slam. Walker couldn't tell if Dancy was embarrassed or irritated, or whether the cause was that his daughter was working in the kitchen or that his directive had not been obeyed.

"So, Walker," said Moseley, making conversation, "what do you do in Washington?"

"I'm a Secret Service agent—a bodyguard for the president."

"Oh my!" exclaimed Moseley, blinking in surprise. "That sounds dangerous!"

Dixie sat up straight, glaring. "How can you protect a Re*pub*lican who's trying to put n----rs back in charge ovah white people?" she snapped. "He put one ovah the port in Charleston, anothah one in the post office in Miss'sippi, and ate dinnah in the *White* House with that nasty Bookah T. Ah you a *Yankee*, Mistah Garrett?"

Walker looked her in the eyes for a couple of seconds, and then said, very calmly and quietly, "I'll go see if Abigail needs any help in the kitchen." Not a word was spoken as he left the room. When he entered the kitchen through its swinging door, Abigail's eyes went wide and she nearly dropped the skillet of gravy she was holding with both hands.

"Walker!" she exclaimed excitedly. And then, with equal fervor, "Walker—help me pour this gravy into that bowl! I'm about to drop it!" He quickly reached around her with one arm and added his grip to the long handle of the skillet, while steadying the large porcelain bowl with his other hand. Together they poured the thick white gravy into the bowl, and set the skillet back on the stove. Taking advantage of the opportunity, he kissed her temple and gave her a quick one-armed hug. "I'm so glad you're here!" she whispered, leaning against him. And then, pulling away abruptly, "Let's get this food on the table while it's hot!"

She backed through the swinging door with a plate of cornbread in one hand and a bowl of black-eyed peas in the other. "Everybody to the table!" she called out. "Let's eat while it's hot!" Walker followed with the bowl of gravy and another of fried okra. Abigail returned to take a pan of pork chops from the oven. A glass pitcher of water and a dish of sliced lemons completed the menu. She had baked a bread pudding with raisins for dessert. Walker was astonished—he'd had no idea Abigail was capable of preparing a meal like this. As they sat down at the table, he looked at her more closely, and saw that her forehead was shiny with perspiration, and strands of dark hair had fallen across her face. She brushed them back, flashing him a smile and modestly lowering her eyes. To Walker, it seemed that he was seeing her—*really* seeing her—for the first time. And he liked what he saw.

Dixie reached across the table to touch Walker's hand, her gloves now removed, and said earnestly, "Mistah Garrett, I am so *sorry* for being rude just now. I don't know why I accused you of being a Yankee! I didn't know that you ah from right heah in Alabama! I hope that you will be so kind as to foh*give* me."

Walker shrugged. "No need to apologize, Mrs. Moseley. I know a good many Northerners, and they're fine people. In fact, people from other countries call *all* Americans 'Yankees.' We're all Yankees to them."

"How *dare* they!" she seethed in fury, her face turning pale. "Why, if some foh'ner evah called *me* a 'Yankee', I would—I would—" She gripped her table knife with white knuckles.

"Now, angel," remonstrated her husband, patting her arm. "There ain't no for'ners 'round here, so let's not worry about *that*. Abigail, this all looks wonderful! And *smells* wonderful, too!"

"Thank you, Mister Moseley!" Abigail smiled, and then turned to her father, sitting next to her at the head of the table. "Papa?" That was his signal to say grace, and all bowed their heads for a short prayer of thanks. Then, tucking napkins, they began passing dishes around the table, serving their plates and filling glasses. It was quiet for several minutes then, as everyone eagerly devoured the food.

"Abigail, that was delicious!" admired Walker, putting his napkin on the table. "I've never eaten a better meal."

"Don't be silly!" she laughed, blushing. "But thank you, just the same!"

"Garrett was in Cuba with General Wheeler," Dancy interjected. "And in the Philippines."

"We *do* love the Gen'ral, don't we?" gushed Dixie. "It's a *shame* we didn't win the waw."

"He meant the Spanish-American War, angel," explained Moseley. "Not the Civil War."

"Of course—that's what I *meant*," she frowned. "But it's a shame we didn't win *both* of them."

"Walker's writing a book about his adventures!" Abigail beamed, putting her hand on Walker's arm. "I can't wait to read it!"

"Actually, I've finished it," Walker said, proud to be making the announcement. "I just got a letter from the publisher, and it should be in bookstores by Christmas!"

"*No!*" she exclaimed breathlessly. She gripped his arm with both hands, eyes wide and shining. "Walker, that is *wonderful*! I am so happy for you!"

"Congratulations, Garrett!" Dancy said approvingly, looking a bit surprised. The look in his eyes suggested that he was reevaluating Walker in a new light.

The Moseleys also congratulated Walker, and expressed curiosity about his experiences. He obligingly described briefly how he came to travel around the world, being sure to mention General Wheeler frequently, and added a couple of stories from his time in the Secret Service.

"Well, you've certainly experienced a lot for such a young man!" observed Moseley. "What plans do you have for the future?"

"I don't rightly know," admitted Walker. "I may stay in the Secret Service, or I might look into some other possibilities. I just don't know right now."

"*I* want to know what Miss *Abigail's* going to do," Dixie said sternly, giving Abigail an arch look. "Yuah twenty-two yeahs old, and *no* prospects. You can't live at home and do kitchen work *fo-evah*, you know."

"Thank you for your concern, Miss Dixie," Abigail replied politely, her cheeks turning pink. "I'll take that under consideration."

"If *I* was you, *I'd* take a look at that Robert *Murphy*," Dixie continued. "He's a *fine* young man, and he's got *money*. His family—"

"*Thank* you, Miss Dixie," Abigail interrupted firmly. "Let me clear these plates, and we'll have some dessert." Rising, she began collecting everyone's plate and used utensils.

"I'll take those," Walker said, also rising. He carried the plates into the kitchen and placed them in the sink. Abigail handed him a stack of smaller dessert plates and, carrying the pan of bread pudding, led the way back into the dining room without looking at Walker or saying a word. He had never seen Abigail angry before, but he could tell she was incensed.

Conversation during dessert was a bit strained at first, focusing on the weather and the upcoming church social, but then shifting to the temperance campaign to ban alcohol in the state. Regarding the latter, Dixie was against it, saying it would be bad for business, and Dancy opined that it would prove unenforceable. Moseley thought it would make for more crime, and Walker thought it should reduce crime. Then, Abigail suggested that reducing drunkenness would be good for marriages and families, and everyone agreed that she was right. Afterward, the Moseleys took their leave, and Dancy announced that he was returning to his law office for the afternoon. Walker helped Abigail wash the dishes while they chatted casually. "Abigail, you're a really good cook—I mean it," he said. "That was a great dinner."

"Thank you," she replied. "The pork chops were a little dry, though."

"I didn't think so, but that's what gravy is for." She gave him a quick, sharp look, and he grinned impishly. She flicked some soapy water at him, and giggled. They continued washing the dishes, talking, and bumping elbows frequently.

At Walker's suggestion, they took a walk when the kitchen chores were done. Crossing the railroad track over an arched pedestrian bridge, they strolled to the center of town and shared a dish of Neapolitan at an ice cream parlor. Abigail put her spoon down and studied Walker's face. "If you don't mind my asking," she said shyly, "what future plans *are* you considering? You said you might not stay with the Secret Service. Is there anything specific you are thinking?"

Walker cleared his throat and hesitated for a few seconds before replying. "I really like being a Secret Service agent. I travel a lot, and meet a lot of important people. I'm at the White House all the time, and spend time with the president." He paused again. "The problem is that we travel *so much*—since Roosevelt became president, we've made at least six trips, ranging from a few days to nine weeks. Every summer, we're at his family home on Long Island for two months—it just takes over your life."

"If you enjoy traveling, why is that a problem?" she asked innocently. "You're not married, and don't have a family."

Walker felt his heart beating faster. This was moving more quickly than he had expected. He knew it was time to have the conversation that he both feared and desired. There was something about the way he was looking at her that made her blink, and suddenly pick up her spoon and take a big bite of the chocolate ice cream, breathing rapidly through flared nostrils. Walker wasn't sure what that meant, so he continued talking.

"Dixon met a really nice young woman at church in Washington —Sally is her name. They're getting married this December. He's crazy about her. Because of all the time agents are away on trips with the president, he decided to leave the Secret Service and work for the D.C. police, on their mounted police force. He starts the first of the New Year." He paused again, and Abigail took another big bite, this time of strawberry ice cream. Her eyes seemed to be focused on his necktie, he thought.

"Anyway," he continued awkwardly, "I've just been thinking that I —I don't know—that I need to—I want to find out—I have to *know* if —" He finally stopped and put his spoon down. "Abigail, I came here to find out what you think about me. I've never felt like I was—like I was—*worthy* of you, but I couldn't help thinking that maybe—" He stopped again, helplessly staring at the almost empty dish of ice cream.

The sharp sound of Abigail's spoon being slammed down on the table startled him. He looked up to see her glaring fiercely at him, with a smudge of chocolate at the corner of her mouth. "Walker Garrett! I don't know how I can make it any clearer than I already have! I've done everything I know to show you that I think you are the bravest, smartest, finest man I know. Nobody holds a candle to you— and yet you think *you're* not worthy of *me*? What else can I do to get through to you? Open your eyes, Walker! I can't wait forever!" Their eyes locked for a tense moment, and then she scooped the last of the vanilla into her mouth, dabbed with the napkin, and rose to her feet.

Walker, searching vainly for words, also stood up. He donned his fedora, while she put on her wide-brimmed sun hat with a blue ribbon around the crown, hanging off the side and fluttering behind her. Parasol in hand, she walked out to the street and waited for him. *She is perfect,* Walker thought, pausing in the parlor doorway to admire, before catching up with her. Coming across the street toward her was a man with unruly red hair, smoking a cigarette and wearing a suit with an open-necked shirt and no tie. Walker recognized Robert "Red" Murphy. They both reached Abigail at the same time.

"Abigail!" Murphy boomed. "I haven't seen you in two weeks!

Have you reconsidered my invitation to the social? It's right around the corner, you know!" He reached out to put his hand on her shoulder, but she quickly popped the parasol open and put it over that shoulder.

"Hello, Robert," she said politely, ignoring his question. "I believe you know Walker Garrett? He's visiting from Washington D.C."

Murphy gave Walker a startled look. "Garrett? Is that you? I didn't recognize you in that suit."

"Hello, 'Red.' Yes, I've moved up the world since we last met."

"Well, good for you," Murphy replied icily. "The social, Abigail? I can pick you up in my new car, and—"

"Thank you, Robert, but I'll be going with Walker. He's come a long way, and won't be here but a few days."

"I see," Murphy frowned, his eyes narrowing as he blew cigarette smoke toward Walker's face. "I didn't think she was your preferred complexion, Garrett." With a sneer on his lips, Murphy walked away, but his harsh, mocking laugh could still be heard.

Walker briefly imagined driving his fist into Murphy's freckled face, but instead smiled at Abigail. "So, when is this social, exactly?"

"Walker!" she exclaimed in exasperation. "We were talking about it at dinner! Didn't you listen?"

"No, I was looking at you."

"Oh, you men!" She playfully swatted him with the back of her hand, and gave him a mock reproving look, but he could see her smile as she turned to cross the street. When they reached the other side, she slowed to a snail's pace, twirling the parasol over her shoulder. "What did he mean—that I'm 'not your preferred complexion?'"

Walker laughed contemptuously, and then sighed and shook his head. "He was trying to insult me. When I came home three years ago, Dixon and I were walking along Railroad Street and 'Red' came out of the saloon with two of his friends. They were all drunk, and called Dixon some ugly words. I stood up for him, and they threatened to beat us with pool cues. Fortunately, his friends thought better of it, and went back inside, so he did, too. He was pretty angry, and I guess he hasn't forgotten it."

Abigail was quiet for a moment. "You and L. G. are pretty close, aren't you?"

"We traveled all the way around the world together, fighting battles and facing death a dozen times. We're both in the Secret Service, and rent a house together in Washington. Beulah and Daisy joined us a year ago. They're my family now. I wasn't going to stand by while he got beat up by three drunks with pool sticks—though he probably could have handled them by himself. It wouldn't do for a colored man to beat up a white man."

"I see." She walked slowly, deep in thought. The parasol was not twirling now.

After a moment, Walker said in a low voice, "What you said to me in the ice cream parlor—that was what I needed to hear. I needed to know for sure. Thank you for saying that." Abigail only nodded.

It was a quiet walk back to the house, and by the time they reached it, Walker was feeling anxious. He stopped and turned to face her. "Is anything wrong? Does it bother you that Dixon's family and I are close?"

"No, of course not. They are wonderful people, and after all that you and he went through together, you *should* be friends."

"You're being very quiet," he observed, with concern. "What's the matter?"

Abigail looked at Walker pensively. "Walker, you've changed. You've outgrown Decatur. You'll never be at home here again. That's a good thing for *you*, but it's something I have to think about."

"I see." He paused. "How long do you think you need?"

"That depends on you," she said tartly, with a raised eyebrow. "Maybe I need to hear some things from you, too." She quickly ascended the steep steps to the front porch, and then turned back. "Father said you could have your old room again. I put fresh sheets on the bed. Supper is at six." And then she went inside, leaving him standing at the foot of the steps.

27

CLARITY

The next day was Sunday, and Walker joined the Dancys at church in the morning. Afterward, their friends, the Jones family, invited them to their "Gingerbread" house—one of the fancy, Victorian "Painted Ladies.' Reverend Dryson, a middle-aged bachelor, was also a guest. It was a short, four-block walk from the First Methodist church building, and Walker, who had not spent much time in this part of Decatur, enjoyed seeing the lovely homes along the way.

The Jones's daughter, Lily, was Abigail's best friend, and they kept up a constant chatter as they walked. Lily had also been a student at the Decatur Academy, and remembered Walker. "Walker—do you remember me from the Academy? It's so good to see you again—Abigail has told me all about your exploits! That is so exciting!"

"That's right," nodded Abigail. "I told her everything, so, you have no secrets."

"Don't be too sure," Walker laughed. "There might be a few things in my book that you haven't heard yet."

"Tell us something, then," Abigail entreated, squeezing Walker's arm with both hands. "What have you not told me?"

"It will have to be short," said Lily. "We're almost to the house."

Walker thought for several seconds, and then said slowly, "I don't know—it's all pretty dark and violent. I don't think you'd want to hear it. Maybe you shouldn't read the book, either."

"Don't be silly," coaxed Abigail. "Just one short story you haven't told me yet. Please!"

"Well, alright. Here's one. When we were crossing the Atlantic on a cruise liner—the *City of Rome*—we struck a small iceberg, called a 'growler.'" Walker went on to describe the terror and pandemonium that resulted on the ship, and how he was saved from falling overboard by a Jewish rabbi, but was never able to find the rabbi again to thank him. He added that the rabbi was probably staying concealed below decks to avoid persecution and harassment, due to antisemitic prejudices. "He was a good man," Walker concluded. "Unfortunately, there are a lot of good people in the world who are mistreated because of their religion, color, or poverty. But they're still good people, and one of them saved my life that night."

"Oh *my*!" Lily breathed, eyes wide.

"Thank you, Walker," Abigail said softly. "I'm glad you told me that." She squeezed his arm again, and bumped against him as they walked up to the front steps. "Now I want to read your book more than ever!" she added, brightly. "It must be *full* of such wonderful stories!" Walker smiled uneasily, but he didn't argue with her. *Wait until she reads about the reconcentrado camp in Cuba, or the sack of Tientsin,* he thought grimly. *Those aren't such wonderful stories, but people need to know about them.*

Once inside the house, the men hung their hats and coats on the coat tree in the foyer, the women removed their sun hats, and everyone went directly to the dining table. The Jones's black cook had prepared a meal of fried chicken "and all the fixin's," as Beulah would have said. Reverend Dryson said grace—much too long, in Walker's opinion—and the meal began. Pleasant and lively conversation filled the room as everyone enjoyed the tasty food. Walker answered questions about his travels in the army and Secret Service, and related some of his experiences with both presidents. At one point, Dryson asked Walker if he was a member of the Methodist church.

"No," said Walker. "My family always attended the Baptist church in Courtland. Since I've been living in Washington D.C., I've been going to a Baptist church whenever I'm in town. When we travel with the president, we go to whatever church he goes to."

"So, Mister Garrett, are you required, as a presidential bodyguard, to attend worship services at churches to which you do not belong, and whose doctrines you do not believe?"

"Well, Reverend," Walker shrugged, "they're all Christian churches, and I haven't noticed all that much difference in the sermons I've heard preached in them. They sing the same songs and read the same scriptures. I don't have any complaints."

Dryson cleared his throat and gave Walker a penetrating stare. "But all churches are *not* the same, Mister Garrett! The Baptists and the Campbellites reject infant baptism, for example. What if your child died, unbaptized? It makes a great *deal* of difference!"

Walker chewed a few times and swallowed, and took a sip of water. "Last spring, I was with President Roosevelt on a nine-week tour across the Western states. In Salt Lake City, he attended a luncheon at a senator's house. At the table with him were a Catholic bishop, an Episcopal bishop, a Mormon apostle with one of his plural wives, and a mix of other Protestant faiths. The president himself is Dutch Reformed. They got along just fine, without arguing or debating their differences. I think we should do the same."

Dryson inhaled sharply, and sat up very straight in his chair, his face reddening. "Young man," he snapped gruffly, "what if you married a Methodist, and she wanted to have her babies baptized? Would you debate that with *her*? Would you say it makes no difference *then*?"

There was an uncomfortable silence around the table, and Walker could feel Abigail's eyes on him. "Reverend," he answered calmly, "if my wife wanted to baptize our babies, I would be happy to let her. And when they became old enough to decide for themselves, I would let them be baptized for their *own* sins—not for those of Adam and Eve thousands of years ago."

Dryson almost choked on his mashed potatoes, and managed to sputter, "But that's not—"

Mrs. Jones quickly spoke up in a panicky voice. "We have apple pie for dessert! Would anyone like a cup of coffee to go with it?"

"That would be wonderful, Mrs. Jones!" Abigail joined in quickly. "Walker—" she put her hand on his arm. "Why don't you tell the story about the man who saved your life on the ship? That was so interesting! I would like to hear it again."

Walker obliged, and everyone but the reverend seemed to enjoy the story. The ladies diplomatically steered the conversation away from religion and into other topics for the rest of the meal, doing most of the talking themselves—which pleased Walker. Dryson bade farewell, explaining that he had to finish his sermon for the evening service, and went on his way. When the door closed behind him, there was a noticeable lessening of tension in the room.

"Let's finish our coffee in the gazebo, shall we?" suggested Mrs. Jones brightly.

"Splendid idea!" seconded Mr. Jones, and they all filed out to the gazebo, which was attached at the front corner of the house.

"I apologize for provoking the preacher," Walker said, taking a seat on the circular bench at the railing. "I didn't mean any harm."

"Don't worry about it," Mr. Jones smiled with a wave of his hand. "I was raised Baptist, myself. I don't see that much difference in them, but y'all don't tell Dryson I said that. He'd never let me hear the end of it."

"But what if you *did* marry a Methodist?" asked Lily, fighting to conceal a grin. "Wouldn't that just be a *disaster*? I mean, how would you *ever* get along?" Abigail shot her a look that could kill, and Lily covered her mouth with her hand, shoulders shaking.

"I wouldn't marry someone I couldn't get along with," Walker shrugged. "It takes two to argue, and it takes two to get along. If both of us want to make the other happy, then it shouldn't be a problem."

"That's a wise answer!" praised Mrs. Jones. "Too many men are tyrants in the house, and treat their wives as servants. If you *want* to make each other happy, then you *will*!"

"I agree," Dancy said quietly and seriously. All eyes turned his way, and he hesitated, appearing to regret having spoken. "I just mean that, if you realize that you are happier together than you are apart, then you do whatever it takes to be together. You make it work." Those words struck Walker with their simplicity, and he suddenly felt that a light had broken through the fog. He made a decision at that moment. Walker also had the impression that Dancy was expressing something deeply personal, and was curious to know what it was. He kept his thoughts to himself, waiting for the right time.

Later that afternoon as they were walking back home, Mr. Dancy excused himself, saying that he was going to visit a friend, and headed up a side street, leaving them to walk the rest of the way by themselves. "You might as well know, Father is visiting a lady friend," Abigail confided, matter-of-factly. "Her husband died around the same time that Mother passed away. They met at a concert on the square."

"I, uh—I'm happy for him—for them," Walker said, taken by surprise. "Is that what he was thinking when he said that in the gazebo—when he said you do whatever it takes to make it work?"

"I'm sure it was. They're both lonely. She is a very nice person, and I have no objection if they want to get married." After a short pause, Abigail added, "She's Baptist." Startled, Walker looked at her quickly to see if she was joking, and then they both laughed. "I don't think Reverend Dryson knows anything about it yet," she giggled.

"He's gonna pop a cork," Walker grinned. Turning serious, he continued, "What your pa said today clarified some things for me— helped me understand my own feelings. Abigail, I believe that we are happier together than we are apart, and I'm willing to do whatever it takes to make it work."

She looked at him with an angelic smile. "So am I," she said, and then added, "There are a lot of decisions to be made before that can happen."

Walker mulled that over in his mind until they reached the Dancy house. Putting that thought aside for the moment, he ventured a question. "I'm going to Pond Spring tomorrow. The Wheelers will all be there, except for the General. Would you come with me? I'd love for you to meet them—they were like family to me while I was growing up."

"That sounds delightful! Yes, I would be happy to meet the Wheeler family."

"Bully! – that's what President Roosevelt always says when he likes something," Walker explained with a grin. "We'll take the morning train to Courtland, and Captain Joe will meet us with a carriage. We'll be back in time for supper."

The next morning, they stood on the platform waiting for their train, enjoying the cool late-September breeze. A small locomotive puffed up to the station, pulling four cars. Its high smokestack and prominent cow-catcher marked it as an antique. "Oh! What a quaint little engine!" Abigail laughed. "It's so cute!"

"It's the *Southern Belle*," Walker said, pointing to the faded, old-fashioned lettering on the side of the cab. "I've ridden this little train a hundred times or more. The last time was five years ago, when I left home to go to the war. I'm surprised it's still running."

There was no conductor on the *Southern Belle,* so the station master came out to collect their tickets before they boarded. When Walker drew them from his pocket, a small object came out with them. He held up a small, crocheted yellow diamond with a green circle in the middle, and a blue ribbon tied to the top corner. "Remember this?" He handed it to Abigail. It was her work, and she had given it to him when he returned home, almost three years ago.

"Walker! You still have it!" She beamed, her eyes sparkling with pleasure.

"Of course I still have it! You said the colors represent the Earth, ocean, and sun, and it symbolizes my journey around the world. I'll always keep it."

With a blast of its steam whistle, the *Southern Belle* chugged out of the station and headed west. Walker draped his arm across the back of the bench seat so that Abigail could sit closer to him. She held her wide-brimmed sun hat in her lap, and he leaned his head close to hers so they could hear to talk. It was fifteen miles to Courtland, and with a couple of brief stops in tiny hamlets along the way, they were there in less than an hour. He pointed out the white buildings of Pond Spring as they passed, three miles from Courtland.

When they stepped out onto the platform of the little station, Walker was surprised to see not only Captain Joe, but also Annie Wheeler waiting for them. Joe was wearing his army uniform, and Walker could see that he was no longer a captain, but a major. A speckled hound lay on the platform, ignoring the world. They walked around the dog to greet and embrace each other.

"My goodness, Walker!" exclaimed Annie. "You look so grown up now! You're not a boy anymore!"

"I completely agree!" nodded Wheeler. "You've come a long way from Tampa, five years ago!"

"Thank you—I appreciate that. I understand the General is not here? He's in New York?"

"Yes," said Annie. "He's not in good health, and since Joe is teaching at West Point, they are close by and get to see each other frequently." Turning to Abigail, she smiled, "And you must be Abigail!" and extended her hand. "It's so good you could come!"

"Let's go to the carriage," interjected Wheeler. "We can talk on the way." Walker rode on the front seat beside the major, while Annie and Abigail sat together and chatted through the half-hour ride. Joe engaged Walker with questions about his experiences after the Wheelers left the Philippines to return to the States. He was especially interested in Walker's account of the capture of Aguinaldo. The time passed quickly, and Walker was surprised when they arrived at the Pond Spring plantation.

"Does anything look familiar?" Wheeler asked, with a grin.

"I'll say it does!" Walker exclaimed. "It looks just like it did when I left."

All the Wheeler siblings were present, except for young Thomas, who had drowned at the end of the war. Lucy, the oldest at thirty-seven, along with Julia and Carrie, met them at the door. They sat in the parlor, drinking lemonade and munching on cinnamon crackers while they reminisced over old times, sharing stories about General

Wheeler. After a while, the major gallantly begged forgiveness of the ladies, and took Walker on a horseback tour of the property. They rode a couple of miles through fields of cotton and corn, pastures of livestock, and orchards of pecan and fruit trees. Black workers were everywhere, singing and carrying out their tasks.

They reined in the horses on a ridge with an expansive view of the estate. It was even more impressive than he had remembered, Walker thought. "I remember that you used to ride along with your pa while he managed all of this," Wheeler commented. "Seventeen thousand acres! It is amazing to me that one man could keep track of all that was going on, and keep it running smoothly. We couldn't have done it without him."

"Even as a child, I knew it was a big job. I was in awe of him," Walker nodded.

"Since his passing, we have struggled to find someone to fill his shoes. We've hired and fired two men, and the one we have now isn't working out too well, either. We're looking for someone who is smart and hard-working enough to do this job properly." He paused for a long minute, and then went on. "Nobody knows this place better than you, Walker. You know what needs to be done, and how to do it. I think you'd be perfect. We'd pay a thousand dollars a year, with bonuses for good harvests. You wouldn't have a lot of living expenses —you could stay in the Sherrod House here on the property. If you marry Abigail, she would have my sisters for company, and it's not far to Decatur."

He paused again to let it sink in. "I know this is rather sudden, so take your time and think about it. Discuss it with Abigail. Let me know what you decide."

Walker could hardly speak, but he managed a hoarse 'thank you' and then fell silent. His mind and emotions were in a whirl. This was the last thing he had expected, and he was stunned. From somewhere inside him the words came—"Can I see the graves?"

Joe blinked and then nodded. "Of course! Forgive me for not thinking of that, myself."

Walker's parents were not actually buried in the family cemetery, but under the shade of a large oak nearby. Wheeler waited a short distance away, giving Walker some privacy. He dismounted, removed his hat, and bowed his head. After a moment, he spoke softly, "Hello Ma, Pa. It's been a long time. I miss you." He sighed heavily, and was quiet again. "Y'all have a pretty place here. Nice and shady. Right at home." Another pause. "Pa—I'm proud to be your son. I don't know if I can take the job they're offering me, though. This is home, but in some ways, it's not home anymore. I'm not better than you—I'm just different. It's something I'll have to think and pray about." He paused once more, and then, putting his hat back on, "I love you both. God bless you, and good-bye." He mounted his horse and rode to the major without looking back.

Walker was quiet during the meal, and also in the buggy on the way back to Courtland. They said their good-byes to the major and Annie at the station and waved as they drove away. Before they could even go inside, they were accosted by a well-dressed, heavy man with graying hair. "Excuse me, but aren't you Walker Garrett? I thought I overheard the major call you 'Walker.'"

"Yes sir, that's me. Have we met?"

"I'm Norman Richards—president of the Bank of Courtland." He shook Walker's hand. "Do you have a few minutes to come by the bank and discuss your father's account? It's been more than three years since he passed, and we really need to get some things settled. It shouldn't take long."

"I didn't even know he *had* a bank account," Walker said, surprised. Glancing at Abigail, who gave him an imperceptible nod, he agreed. "Alright—we'll go right now."

When they reached the bank, Abigail said, "You go ahead, Walker. There's a sewing goods store across the street, and I need some more thread. I'll see you in a few minutes."

Inside the banker's office, Walker, hat in hand, perched on the edge of a chair facing the desk while Richards pulled a folder out of a filing cabinet and plopped down in the cushioned rolling chair. Slightly out of breath from the short walk, he wiped perspiration from his face with a handkerchief and opened the folder. "There is a balance on your father's account," he began. "I'd be happy to keep it here, of course, but I understand you're living in Washington now, and you'd probably like to liquidate the account and take it with you." Walker gave a wordless nod, and Richards continued.

"Your parents didn't have a lot of living expenses out at Pond Spring, so they were able to put aside three or four hundred dollars a year for nearly thirty years."

"*Excuse me?*" Walker exclaimed in shock, almost falling out of the chair. Calculating quickly in his head, he asked, "Are you telling me that my pa has ten thousand dollars in his account?"

"Oh no!" laughed the banker. "Nothing like that!"

"I didn't think so," Walker breathed, settling back in the chair.

"No, he has right at fifty thousand dollars in his account."

Walker sprang from the chair and, putting his hands on the banker's desk, leaned over it, almost into the man's face. "*What!*" he practically shouted. "That's impossible! How could a farm manager save that much money? You can't be serious!"

Leaning back in his chair, Richards put up both palms. "Easy now, Mr. Garrett. I can explain. First, he did deposit almost ten thousand dollars over the years. Second, there's the effect of compounding interest, which nearly doubled that amount. Third, he wisely invested in railroad stocks during the Great Panic back in the early 'nineties, when they fell to only a few cents per share. It was a gamble, but when the Southern shares recovered, he sold for several times what he paid. Altogether, it comes to a little over fifty thousand dollars. I can't offer you the full amount in cash, but I can write you a check."

Walker collapsed back in the chair, speechless. He stared at the banker with his mouth open. A tingling feeling in his feet and hands warned that he was about to faint. Suddenly, a gunshot rang out in the front of the bank, and a scream came from where the single cashier window was located. A man's harsh voice shouted, "Give me all the money in the till! Put it in this bag, and get the bank manager out here right now, before I start shooting people!" An elderly lady screamed weakly and collapsed to the floor.

"Mister Richards!" cried the cashier in a panic. "Come out here—quick!"

Richards peeked out his office door and found himself looking down the barrel of a revolver in the hand of a man wearing a Klan-style white hood. "Open the safe! Right now—or I'll shoot you dead!" Another man, similarly disguised, was pointing a gun through the speaking hole in the glass at the cashier, who was frantically fumbling with the cash box, sobbing hysterically.

Richards appeared to be on the verge of a heart attack as he inched past the gunman. "The—the—the safe—the safe is—is over—there!" he gasped, trying to point while holding his hands up overhead.

Walker stepped casually from the office, hands in pockets. "What's going on here, fellows?" he asked calmly.

The gunman swiveled to point his weapon at Walker. "Get your hands up! Before I—" He never got to finish his threat. There was a loud bang, quickly followed by a second, and he fell backward to the floor with a bloody circle spreading on his chest.

"*What*?" exclaimed the other gunman, in shock. And then he blurted out, "*Garrett!*" and fired a shot in Walker's direction. As Walker leaped over the prone body on the floor, he felt the bullet strike his chest and knew he was wounded. A second shot passed over his head as he stooped to grab the revolver from the dead man's limp hand. Crouching, he fired two shots through the cashier's window, shattering the glass and sending the hooded man spinning to the floor. Rushing past the counter, he found the man lying face down with blood running from him, legs twitching. Twisting the revolver from his grasp, Walker turned him over and snatched the white hood away to reveal a shock of red hair.

"'Red' Murphy!"

"Damn you, Garrett!" mumbled Murphy, and then his body relaxed and his eyes fixed in space. Walker dropped the hood back over his face and turned away.

Suddenly smelling something burning, he looked down and saw his coat pocket smoking from a blackened circle the size of a large egg. Hurriedly patting out the scorched area with his handkerchief, he shook his head. *That's the second coat I've ruined like this,* he scowled.

Then, remembering that he had been hit by a bullet, he pulled his coat open and looked at his left chest. There was a gaping hole in the coat over his heart, another in his shirt, and a groove across his chest and left bicep. Blood was running down his arm and side. He stared, wondering. His chest was hurting, so the bullet clearly had an impact, but why didn't it penetrate? He opened his shirt to examine his chest and saw the imprint of a five-pointed star, and could even read most of the letters of "Secret Service." He fished his badge from his breast pocket and saw that it was badly dented and flattened. The bullet had apparently struck at an angle and ricocheted off the badge, driving it into his flesh. He kissed the badge. *You saved my life!*

He was helping the elderly lady to her feet and Richards was comforting the cashier when the sheriff arrived, gun in hand. "What's all the shootin' about?" he demanded.

"Two masked men tried to rob the bank, sheriff," Walker answered, holding up his battered badge. "They're both on the floor. Nobody else got hurt."

"Looks like *you* got hurt," he disagreed. "Lemme see that badge."

At that point, Abigail burst into the bank. "Walker!" she cried. "Are you alright? What happened?" She ran to him and grabbed his arm, only to discover that his arm was bloody. She recoiled in horror with blood on her hands. "You're *bleeding*! Walker! You've been *shot*!"

"It's alright," he said calmly. "I've been shot worse than this plenty of times. It's nothing."

"This man saved us!" declared Richards, pointing at Walker. "Those thieves were pointing guns in our faces, threatening to shoot us, and that one there fired two shots at Mister Garrett. He's a *hero*, sheriff!"

"That 'pears to be the case," agreed the sheriff, as he bent to pick up the white hood.

Abigail screamed. "*Robert Murphy*!" With both hands to her face, leaving bloody prints on her cheeks, she stared at his frozen expression. "Robert Murphy is a *bank robber*?"

"Was a bank robber," Walker corrected her. "I was shocked, too. When he saw me, he said my name. Then he took two shots at me, and hit me with one. If it hadn't been for my Secret Service badge, he might have killed me."

"Walker Garrett, Secret Service agent," the sheriff said thoughtfully. "Say, ain't you the feller that saved the president's life last month up in New York?"

"That's what the papers said," Walker shrugged.

"And his pa was Lemuel Garrett, from Pond Spring," added Richards.

"I remember Garrett!" exclaimed the sheriff. "He was a good man. Fought in the war with General Wheeler. If you're his son, then you're alright! Let's get you to the doctor's office and get you patched up." To Richards, he said, "I'll send somebody to get these bodies out of here as quick as we can. You might want to get a mop bucket ready."

Walker stopped at the door and called to the banker, "I'll come back and finish our business as soon as I'm done at the doctor's office. Then we've got to hurry to make our train."

At the doctor's office, Walker stood shirtless in front of Abigail while the doctor cleaned the blood away and put a bandage on Walker's chest and arm. Walker joked about being able to read "Secret Service" on his chest, but no one laughed. Abigail stared wide-eyed at the many scars on Walker's back, chest, and arms and shoulders. Then, when he had donned his blood-stained shirt and coat again, they returned to the bank.

"I'll take that check, Mister Richards," he said. "But I'd like you to make two checks, please. Divide the amount in half and make one check to me, and the other to L. G. Dixon." Abigail gave Walker a confused look. "I'll explain later," he whispered.

He put the checks in the pocket on the clean side of his coat, and they hurried to the train station. He had feared that the last train to Decatur would have already left, and was surprised to find that it was waiting for them. The sheriff grinned at them on the platform. "I told 'em to wait for you," he said. "It's the least we can do for the man that saved our bank!"

They walked around the speckled hound again and boarded the *Southern Belle*. Walker put his head out the open window and pointed to the dog. "Does that hound ever move?" he asked.

"Twice a day," nodded the sheriff. "Like clockwork." Walker grinned and waved as the train blasted its whistle and crept jerkily from the station.

Settling back in his seat, Walker reached for Abigail's hand. "This has been quite a day," he said in her ear. "We have a lot to talk about."

"Yes, we do," she agreed, and squeezed his hand.

It was a quiet ride back to Decatur.

28

NEW BEGINNINGS

"You can't *possibly* be serious!" Abigail was aghast, leaning forward on the sofa with mouth open. Frank Dancy stared and slowly put down his newspaper. "Your father did *not* have fifty thousand dollars in his bank account!"

Supper was finished, the dishes washed and the kitchen cleaned up. Abigail had fried eggs and bacon, and served grits and buttered toast. "My biscuits are a disaster," she had sighed apologetically. "But I'm working on them." They had then relaxed in the parlor to talk, and Walker had just shared the news about his shocking discovery at the Courtland bank.

"It's true," Walker insisted. "See for yourselves—" and he showed the two checks, each for a little over twenty-five thousand dollars.

"That's just incredible!" marveled Dancy. "But why are you giving half of it to Beulah's son? That's a lot of money!"

Walker took a deep breath, hesitated, and then told them. "Do you remember when Beulah came to work for you? She had been at Pond Spring, cooking for the Wheelers, and the General recommended her to you." Dancy was nodding thoughtfully, rubbing his chin. "Her son was born a few months later, so she was already pregnant when she came here." He paused—this would be painful, but it had to be told. "My father, Lemuel Garrett, was the father of Beulah's son. That's why she named him L. G. The letters stand for his father's name. The General told me all this right out in front of your house three years ago when I came home." Walker paused again to give them time to process this information. Abigail's mouth and eyes were still wide open, and neither she nor her father were saying a word.

"My pa never acknowledged Dixon as his son, and never had any contact with Beulah after that. When I found out that Pa had that money, I knew that I had to share it with Dixon. After all, it's his father, too. He's entitled to it."

"But, Walker—" began Dancy in a remonstrating tone.

"I am so proud of you for doing that, Walker," Abigail cut him off. "You are the most honest, good-hearted man I've ever met. You are absolutely doing the right thing."

Dancy spread his hands. "If Abigail is for it, and you are for it, who am I to object? You two seem to be a perfect match, as far as I can see."

"There's another thing that happened today," Walker continued. "When Capt—I mean, *Major* Wheeler—took me riding around the plantation, he offered me the position of overseer—the same position my pa had for all those years. He said I was the right person for the job, and we could live there with minimal expenses. With a salary of a thousand dollars a year, we could save a lot of money, just like Pa did."

Abigail stared in shock. "Did you tell him you would take it?" she asked quietly.

"No. He said to talk it over and let him know. What do you think? Would you like to live at Pond Spring?" Their eyes met for several seconds. "You have to be honest with me," Walker added.

"If I'm being honest, no, I don't want to live there," she shook her head slowly. "I know it's your childhood home, and your parents are buried there, but it's not the life for me. The Wheelers are wonderful people, but I could not be happy there."

"Where *do* you want to live?" he asked. "Here in Decatur?"

"No!" she replied quickly, and then glanced at her father with an embarrassed look. "I'm sorry, father, but I have to get away from here. I want to go to Washington with Walker."

"Why?" asked Dancy, taken aback. "Is it because of Mrs. Thomas? I thought you liked her."

"No no—it has nothing to do with her. I am happy that you have found each other, and I want you to be happy together. It's—this is something that goes back a long time—I can't—" She stopped and took several deep breaths with closed eyes. Walker went over to the sofa and sat beside her, taking her hand and squeezing it.

Abigail's face was pale, and her hands trembled as she began to explain. "It was nine years ago—I remember it like it was yesterday—I saw—" she swallowed hard. "I saw Beulah's husband get lynched in the grove. It was awful. You told me not to leave the house that night, but I could hear the crowd yelling and whooping—it sounded like a big party, so I slipped out and went over there. I couldn't believe my eyes—" and she closed her eyes tightly for a few seconds and gave her head a quick shake as if trying to clear her thoughts of something unpleasant. "To see the people you know at church and in town acting like savages, celebrating the murder of a man like he was some monster—like he was a rabid dog—I can't even explain how it made me feel. I've had nightmares about it ever since."

"But they say he raped a white woman," began Dancy.

"Whatever he did, this was worse!" cried Abigail. "I saw how it devastated Beulah and Daisy. Daisy told me that her daddy was at home the night he was supposed to have done it—he was innocent! Beulah sent L. G. off to join the army, just to get him out of town. When I saw how sad they both were—I'm ashamed to admit it, but for the first time I realized that colored people are just like us! They have the same feelings—they love each other, and grieve just like we do. I began to see how wrong it is for white people to treat colored people the way they do. I started helping Daisy with her schoolwork, and she taught me to crochet—she's so smart and sweet! When they left to go be with L. G. in Washington last year, I felt like I was losing a friend."

Tears were streaming down Abigail's cheeks, and she stopped to wipe them with her hand. "When Walker stayed here for two years while attending the Academy, he had to sleep in the attic and eat in the kitchen with the help. Most white boys would have refused, but Walker didn't seem to mind. He got along just fine with them—I could hear them laughing together, and wished I could be in there too. That's when I started to understand that you were different, Walker! I wished that you would notice me—and then you wrote me that letter when you left to go to Cuba! I was so excited—and afraid! I didn't dare go to the train station to see you, so I sent Daisy. I still have every letter you have written me—and I'll keep them forever."

Walker felt as though the past five years were a book that was suddenly being opened to him for the first time. He saw more clearly than ever what kind of person Abigail was, and understood why she cared for him. He put his arm around her shoulders and kissed the side of her head. "Abigail," he said earnestly, "I love you! We are definitely a perfect match. I'll tell Major Wheeler that I won't be taking their offer. We'll go to Washington together."

She leaned against him, putting her head on his shoulder. "Can we go tomorrow?" she asked. "It won't take me long to pack!" Walker and Dancy both stared at her, trying to decide if she was serious, and she laughed, wiping her cheeks again. "I'm kidding," she smiled, with shining eyes. "I can wait until the end of the week." Looking up lovingly at Walker, she said firmly, "You're not leaving Decatur without me!"

"I wouldn't think of it," replied a rather dazed Walker.

"You'll need to be married first," insisted Dancy. "It would be a scandal...."

"Not Reverend Dryson!" Abigail shook her head adamantly. "Ask Mrs. Thomas if her preacher will do it."

"Wait just a minute, there!" expostulated Walker, feeling that the situation was getting out of control. "Are you—do you—" He stopped, at a loss for words.

"My answer is 'yes, I will marry you,'" Abigail smiled, taking his hand. "I was hoping you would ask." She snuggled up to his side, and then remembering his fresh wounds, asked in a concerned voice, "Am

I hurting you? Is your arm better yet?" Turning to her father, she explained, "Walker got shot today."

Dancy threw his newspaper to the floor and leaned forward. "You got *shot* today? Where? Who shot you? What happened?"

"It was just a minor thing," Walker shrugged, with a dismissive wave of his hand. "While I was talking to the banker in Courtland, two hooded men came in with guns to rob the bank. They were threatening to shoot everyone, and a bullet nicked me. That's all."

"That's *not* all!" Abigail demurred. "Walker shot both of them and killed them, saving the lives of everyone in the bank. And father, you won't believe this, but one of the bank robbers was Robert Murphy! He's the one who shot Walker, and it was Walker's Secret Service badge that saved his life! Walker is a hero—again!"

Dancy sank back in his chair. "I don't know how much more I can take in one evening! Everything is upside down." He rubbed his temples with his fingertips. "Let's talk about this some more tomorrow. I need to go to bed." He stopped at the door and turned to Walker. "I'm glad you weren't hurt more seriously. Let me know if you need a doctor—or a lawyer." He went up the stairs, and Walker and Abigail stayed on the sofa talking until midnight.

Walker was awakened the next morning by pain in his chest and arm. He checked the bandages for blood, and peeled back the one on his chest to see if the letters were still legible. They were. He grimaced as he pulled on his shirt and pants, and then headed downstairs from his attic room, emerging into the kitchen washroom. Abigail was stirring a pot of oatmeal on the stove, and turned to give Walker a welcoming smile. "Good morning, hero!"

Walker grunted in reply, and helped himself to a cup of black coffee. As his brain gradually focused more clearly, he began to remember the previous night's conversation. Something about getting married—*this week*. Surely he was mistaken, he thought.

"How are your bullet wounds this morning? Are you alright?"

"Yeah, I'm alright. I should probably change the dressings, though."

"I'll help you with that after breakfast. Have a seat—Father has already gone to his office." She put two steaming bowls of oatmeal on the table, and they sat down across from each other. Walker raised a spoon to his mouth and blew gently to cool it. "How do you feel about our plans?" she asked quietly, watching him closely.

He swallowed the oatmeal and took a sip of coffee. "When I arrived here last Saturday morning, I had no idea that I'd be getting married on Thursday. I have to admit I'm kind of shocked. Can we even *do* it—I mean, it will take a lot of work to get ready for a wedding, won't it?"

"I didn't expect to be getting married this fast, either, so I understand completely what you're feeling," she agreed. "But we both know that we want to be together, and when you leave here you'll be going back to Washington, several hundred miles away. We won't be able to see each other for three or four months, and even then I'll be in Richmond. Waiting for a better time doesn't seem to be a good idea to me." Walker listened, nodding thoughtfully.

"And as for the wedding, we don't need a fancy church wedding. We can wear clothes we already have, and just invite our closest friends. It can be small and simple. We can buy rings, or I can use my mother's ring—that would suit me just fine."

"Where would we live when we get to Washington?" Walker wondered aloud. "The house there isn't big enough for all of us. We'd have to find our own place right away."

"You've got a check for twenty-five thousand dollars," she reminded him with a smile. "That shouldn't be a problem." She reached across the table and put her hand on his. "I promise you won't regret it, Walker. We'll be happy together!"

"I know we will. I just have to get my mind around this. It's a real head-spinner."

"We'll make it work!" she smiled. "Now, let's change those bandages!"

Walker removed his shirt and watched her face as she scrubbed away some dried blood from the gash on his chest and arm. She blushed faintly as she touched his skin. "I could never be a nurse!"

she murmured. Pointing to the double-row of marks around his left bicep, she asked, "What caused those scars there?"

"The teeth of a really huge python in the Philippines," he answered casually. He'd forgotten that he hadn't told her about that before, and her reaction was electric. Stepping back, she gave him a look of sheer horror. It took her a few seconds to decide that he was not fibbing. She turned and put the wet cloth back into the bowl of soapy water and refused to look at him again until his shirt was back on.

"I don't want to know any more about that right now," she gasped. "I don't need any more nightmares. You can tell me about it someday —a long time from now."

The next two days were busy. Walker visited a tailor shop to buy a new suit, since his old one now had several bullet holes, including a blackened pocket. This required taking measurements and making several adjustments, which consumed a half-day. He paid extra for the suit to be ready by Thursday morning. They went to a jeweler and found rings that they liked. Last of all, they went to a bakery and ordered a cake with strawberry icing. Frank Dancy arranged for his lady friend's Baptist minister to perform the ceremony in the flower garden of her Victorian house. A photographer was hired to take wedding photos. The Moseleys and Joneses were invited to attend. In addition to these preparations, Abigail was busily packing a trunk and two suitcases for the trip to Washington—they planned to leave on Thursday's afternoon train, arriving in Washington before noon Friday. Walker bought the train tickets in advance. By Wednesday evening, it seemed that everything was finally in place.

As the three rested after supper Wednesday, Dancy cleared his throat as if about to make an announcement. "I hope you won't mind," he said apologetically, "but I have made some plans for tomorrow, too. If you object, I can change them, but I hope you will be pleased." He paused, and had their full attention. "Watching you two jump into this on such short notice put an idea into my head. I talked to Ruth, and we'd like to make it a double wedding tomorrow. I don't want to—"

He was interrupted by Abigail's squeal of delight. She sprang across the room and threw herself into his arms. "Oh Father! I am so happy for you! I was so worried that when I left, you would be all alone, and I couldn't stand it. This is the most *wonderful* news! I know you will be so happy together!" She wrapped her arms around his neck and they hugged each other for a long minute. They talked excitedly until it was time to go to bed.

Walker had a hard time getting to sleep. Lying in the tiny room where he had stayed during two years of school, his mind roamed back over the years that had passed since. *What a path my life has taken!* he mused. *And it's about to take another unexpected turn. What was it Dixon said? Lots of twists and turns in the road ahead—just take them one at a time? That's what I'll have to do. I wish he could be here tomorrow. I can't wait to give him that check!* His thoughts continued rambling until finally, in the wee hours of the morning, he dozed off and slept fitfully for a few hours.

The big day arrived, and the weather was crisp and cool, with a clear blue sky. The wedding party gathered at the home of Ruth Thomas, whose flower garden was a riot of color, with a large trellis over which a beautiful rose bush had climbed, forming an arch. The minister stood under the arch, and the two couples posed with him for photographs. Major Joe Wheeler and Annie came on the morning train, and with the Moseleys and Joneses, and Ruth's three married children, formed a semi-circle. The ceremony was about to begin when a man's voice spoke from the back porch—"Am I too late? I got here as fast as I could."

Walker's jaw dropped. "*Dixon!*" he yelled, and literally ran to embrace him. "How on earth did you know—"

"Abigail telegraphed me. I wouldn't miss it for the world." Dixon joined the circle after shaking hands with Wheeler, and stood between the Moseleys and Joneses. Walker introduced Dixon to the rest as his best friend and fellow Secret Service agent. Ruth stepped over to him and introduced herself with a smile, and made him welcome. Dixie Moseley, however, was suddenly taken ill and asked to be excused.

The wedding sermon delivered by the minister was short. The vows were repeated and the rings exchanged, and then Walker kissed Abigail's lips for the first time. They were now married. They ate a slice of cake and drank punch, posed for photographs, and chatted with the others. Then it was time to go to the train station. A carriage waited at the curb as Abigail said a tearful good-bye to her father.

Walker and Dixon stood together to one side. "Are you going back to Washington today?" asked Walker.

"No—I thought I would spend the night with some of my old friends that I haven't seen in years. I'll catch the train tomorrow."

"Thanks for coming! This really means a lot." They shook hands and clapped each other on the shoulder. "Before we go," Walker added, "there's something I want to give you." He took a couple of steps away, turning his back to the group in a secretive manner. Dixon followed, giving him a curious look. Walker pulled an envelope from his coat and extended it to Dixon. "I closed Pa's bank account in Courtland this week," he said quietly. "He was your father, too, and you deserve half of what was in it." Dixon did not reach for the envelope, but only looked at it blankly. "I insist," Walker said firmly. "This is yours." When Dixon still did not take the envelope, Walker reached over and stuffed it into Dixon's inside coat pocket. "Take good care of it," he said in a low voice. "And don't let anyone else see it."

He and Abigail arrived at the train station in time to see that their things were loaded into the baggage car, and then took their seats in the coach compartment. Looking out the window, Abigail whispered, "I hope it's a long time before I come back."

The train's whistle screamed two long blasts and the five-foot-tall driving wheels began to turn. Glancing back at the platform one last time, Walker was surprised to see Dixon waving his hand. Walker waved back, and Dixon saw the movement and pointed to him, patted his coat where Walker had put the envelope and lifted his hat. "What does he mean by that?" asked Abigail.

"He opened the envelope and saw the check," Walker grinned. "I'm surprised he's still got both feet on the ground!" They both waved until Dixon was lost to view.

Abigail settled back into her seat and leaned against Walker, resting her head on his shoulder. "I can't believe we're actually *married!*" she sighed. "It's like we're going on an adventure together—but nothing like the ones *you've* had for the past five years!"

"Not true," Walker murmured, kissing the top of her head. "This is much better than any adventure I've ever had. I'm the luckiest man alive."

"We'll be so happy together," she whispered, squeezing his hand. "Even when you have to travel with the president, I won't complain, as long as you come back to me."

Walker reached into his pocket and drew out his dented, mangled Secret Service badge. For a quiet moment they gazed on the silver, five-pointed star that had saved his life only a few days earlier, and Abigail ran a finger across its letters. "I want you to always have this to protect you," she said. "Wear it always!"

Walker put his arm around her. "Yes ma'am," he smiled. "I'll do that—for *you!*" She looked up, and they kissed for the second time.

The train steamed eastward through the Tennessee River valley, under clear blue skies. The gently rolling autumn landscape was lovely, with occasional glimpses of the broad river. Walker and Abigail, however, were oblivious to all of it.

THE END

HISTORICAL NOTES

1 "Just Like Old Times"

- The train on which McKinley traveled left Washington, D.C., on April 29, 1901 traveling south through Virginia, and passed through Decatur, Alabama, on its way to Memphis, where it arrived in the afternoon of April 30.
- Four agents had been assigned to the White House during the Spanish-American War for presidential security, and four were assigned on Roosevelt's early tours, so it seems reasonable to assume that four would have traveled on this tour.
- The White House was called The Executive Mansion until late in 1901, when President Theodore Roosevelt changed its name.
- George Foster's comments to Dixon about being "useful" are entirely fictional and may not accurately represent the historical Foster's attitudes or beliefs. There actually were no black agents assigned to the presidential security detail until the early 1960s. Agent Stover is fictional.

Descriptions of the training received by the new agents are not based on any historical sources.

- Shoulder holsters began to be used in the late 19th century.
- The president's visit in Memphis is accurately presented, but the assassination attempt is fiction. "JJ" Williams was the mayor in 1901. The cool reception given to the president by Memphis is reported in the May 8 issue of the *Weekly Corinthian*, of Corinth, Mississippi. Readers who are familiar with modern Memphis should note that the current locations of the Peabody Hotel and the Nineteenth Century Club are not the same as in 1901.
- Civil War rifled muskets typically fired a .58 caliber projectile called a 'minie ball,' which caused a great deal of damage to its victims.

2 "Lost Cause"

- The St. Charles Hotel was where President McKinley and his entourage stayed in New Orleans. Recently rebuilt after a fire in 1894, it was one of America's premier hotels.
- The description of Homer Plessy as "light-skinned" is accurate, and he was indeed 7/8 white, but there are no known photographs of him. The internet image widely labeled with his name is not of him. The comments attributed to him here are consistent with his life, but are based on no historical sources. He was a shoemaker, and would have been 38 years old at the time of this fictional incident. He was famous for the 1896 Supreme Court case, *Plessy v. Ferguson,* which gave us the phrase "separate but equal."
- McKinley's tour of the waterfront was on the steamboat, *St. Louis.* The famous 1870 steamboat race of the *Natchez* vs. the *Robert E. Lee* was historical, and the explanation offered by the dock attendant reflects common folklore about the event.

- McKinley is regarded as one of our most religious presidents. Baptized by immersion in a stream near Poland, Ohio, at a camp meeting revival at the age of ten, he was faithful to the Methodist Church for the rest of his life, and read the Bible daily.

3 "Remember the Alamo!"

- The warm reception given to the president in the cities of Texas is described accurately, and Mrs. McKinley did visit the Alamo. All details of that visit presented here are fictional.

4 Cinco de Mayo

- The president arrived in El Paso on May 5. The McKinleys had a quiet day after attending church services, and Ciudad Juarez was celebrating Cinco de Mayo. Otherwise, the description of the events of that day are fictional.
- The palm pistol was invented in 1882. A man carrying one was prevented from attempting to assassinate President Taft and/or Mexican President Diaz in El Paso in 1909. The threatened use of a palm pistol here in 1901 is fictional.
- When Mrs. McKinley attended the breakfast (or brunch) hosted by banker Juan Ochoa in Juarez on Monday morning, May 6, she was the first First Lady to leave American soil.

5 Silver Bugs, Gold Bugs, and Red Bugs

- Walker's comment about "going to hell in a handbasket" was actually made by a reporter who participated in the deep-mine tour.
- Descriptions of the town of Congress and the mine are

generally accurate, based on historical sources and online images.

- Stover accurately explains the "Free Silver" vs gold standard debate, which was the focus of the 1896 election.
- The Phoenix Indian School was real, and the description of the day's event is based on historical sources. The discussion of the school's assimilation methods is also based on historical sources.
- Dixon had been promoted to lieutenant in the army. See *The Odyssey of Walker Garrett*.

6 Grim Ends

- The *Los Fiesta de las Flores* festival began in Los Angeles in 1894 but was canceled during the Spanish-American War. It was resumed in 1901, the year of McKinley's visit. The description of it is taken from historical sources.
- Gasoline-powered automobiles began appearing on the streets of Los Angeles as early as 1896. By 1901 there were several hundred, and by 1905 several thousand.
- Sources differ on how Ida McKinley's finger became infected (some sources say it was her left thumb—I was unable to determine definitely which finger). Her comments here reflect a popular view. Her poor health was widely known, though epilepsy was not well-understood at the time. When she had seizures in public, her husband would drape a napkin or handkerchief over her face until it passed.
- Descriptions of Harrison Gray Otis and his home, "the Bivouac," are based on historical sources. An explosive was found in the bushes at his home in 1910, the same year that a bomb destroyed his *L.A. Times* building. and a ticking package of dynamite was mailed to his house in 1913. Otis's anti-unionism was the apparent reason. No

attempts at blowing up Otis's home were made during McKinley's visit—this is fiction.

- Dixon reminded Walker of an incident which is described in *The Odyssey of Walker Garrett,* in which they released some Filipino insurgent prisoners rather than deliver them to the Manila stockade.
- Called 'Westlake' at the time, it was renamed MacArthur Park Lake after World War Two.

7 Trouble in Paradise

- Stover's comments about the political issues of the day, and his description of McKinley's earlier visit to Georgia and Alabama, are historically accurate.
- The scenery described by Walker and Dixon depict their experiences presented in *The Odyssey of Walker Garrett.*
- From the veranda of the Hotel del Monte, Walker would not actually have been able to see Monterey Bay, since the front veranda was on the southern side of the hotel, and the bay was to the north. However, in the interest of historical accuracy, there really was a half-moon on that date.
- The descriptions of Mrs. McKinley's health crisis in San Francisco and all historical aspects of that part of the trip are accurate.
- Walker's comment about "praying up a thunderstorm" refers to a scene in *The Odyssey of Walker Garrett.*
- Donaldina Cameron and her missionary work rescuing Chinese girls from sex slavery were real. She did not always enter brothels alone to liberate girls, but was sometimes accompanied by Chinatown police. Known to the *tongs* as the "white devil" and "the Jesus woman," she reportedly rescued as many as three thousand girls.

8 Unleashed

- Captain Thomas is fictional, but his description of the *USS Ohio* is factually correct.
- Father Yorke was a historical figure, and his comments about violence are based closely on his actual words.
- Andrew Foruseth was a historical figure, a union leader. The words attributed to him are mostly based on his actual statements. His response to Dixon's warning about jail is a verbatim quote. By the way, the San Francisco waterfront general strike began in the summer of 1901 and lasted through the end of September, and involved significant violence. The outcome was considered to be a victory for the unions.
- The description of the launch of the *Ohio* is based on contemporary newspaper accounts.
- Major Walter Schuyler was the commander of the 46th Volunteer Regiment in the Philippines. The swimming of the river was an actual event, as noted in *The Odyssey of Walker Garrett.*

9 "A Close Thing Indeed"

- The Baltimore & Potomac Railroad Station was located on the Mall, just a short distance from the Capitol. Within a decade it had been replaced by the Union Station.
- I have found some evidence that a unit called the White House Police played a role in presidential security, but other sources say that unit was created in the 1920s, and also, the White House was called the Executive Mansion until Theodore Roosevelt changed it, so there would have been no "White House Police" during the McKinley presidency.
- Reverend Wright is fictional, but AME churches did often operate schools for black children. Wright's AME church is not based on any historical congregation.

- Mary Surratt's house continued to operate as a boarding house under its later owners into the 1920s. Its role in the Lincoln assassination made it a well-known landmark, less than a mile from the White House.
- I found an obscure source stating that the Secret Service uncovered an assassination plot against President McKinley, but no details were provided as to when, where, how, or who the plotters were. That is the inspiration for the incident in this chapter. Otherwise, it is entirely fictional.
- It is true that the McKinleys went on carriage drives in Washington D.C. without security. Like many other presidents, he objected to having guards around him.
- In 1901, the National Mall did not offer a grand, open vista as it does today. It was fairly crowded with trees, according to pictures taken from the top of the Washington Monument at the time.
- As the reader of *The Odyssey of Walker Garrett* may recall, Walker had acquired a modest Spanish vocabulary while in Cuba and the Philippines.
- It would be the city's job to prosecute the case because, until the late-1960s, it was not a federal crime to assassinate the president. It was treated as a murder, and was dealt with by local or state law enforcement.

10 Revolutionary Wheels

- "Dancin' Dancy" was Dixon's sarcastic nickname for Abigail Dancy, due to her privileged lifestyle.
- Canton, Ohio was the McKinleys' hometown. They shared a large (over 8000 sq. ft.) mansion (the Saxton-McKinley House) there with Ida's sister and her family of 7 children (one of whom died in 1900 and one had moved out by 1901). The McKinleys did not actually live in the house where he conducted his famous "front porch campaign."

Historical sources disagree as to whether they stayed in
the Saxton-McKinley House in the summer of 1901, or in
the "Campaign House." Since President McKinley publicly
referred to the Saxton house as his home, and since it *was*
their home for much of their marriage, I chose to use it for
the story. Details about the house are presented accurately,
though my sources did not agree about whether there was
a lift at that time. Considering Mrs. McKinley's health
issues, I assumed that a small lift would have been present.

- There was a Farmer's Hotel across the street from the
  Saxton-McKinley House at that time, but I have been
  unable to find any detailed information about it. However,
  I found hotels by that name in other cities which were
  described as plain, but clean.

- The personnel and accommodations described for
  McKinley's staff are consistent with his usual practice
  when away from Washington. Cortelyou, the president's
  personal secretary, was the equivalent of today's chief of
  staff.

- Katherine (Kate) Barber was a real person, but my
  presentation of her is based on no historical sources. Her
  Aunt Ida would almost certainly have approved of the
  Kate I've described. She would have been 17 in the
  summer of 1901.

- The description of Meyers Lake amusement park is based
  on historical sources. Kate's comment about the bicycle's
  liberating effect on women is based on numerous such
  statements by women of that era.

- McKinley was the first president to ride in an automobile.
  Depending on your source of information, it was either in
  1896, 1899, 1900, or 1901, and took place in either
  Washington D.C., Canton, Ohio, or Paterson, New Jersey.
  The vehicle was either a Stanley Steamer or an electric
  car, and was driven either by F. O. Stanley, Zeb Davis, or

"Junior" Hobart. McKinley's comment that automobiles would not replace horses is supposedly a verbatim quote —but as you can see, sources are hardly unanimous about any aspect of this event.

11 Goodbye and Hello

- Ida McKinley actually did crochet at least three thousand pairs of slippers for charity fund-raising. Her comment about the wave of European assassinations by anarchists is historically accurate.
- Ida McKinley had not wanted her husband to serve a second term, and she feared for his life.
- It is true that, after spending two months in Canton, the McKinleys went from there to Buffalo, and that they were guests in the home of John Milburn.

12 The Unthinkable

- Sources disagree as to whether Mrs. McKinley accompanied the president to Niagara Falls.
- The description of the scene of the shooting is generally consistent with historical facts.
- "Big Ben" James Parker knocked Czolgosz down. He was of African and Spanish descent. Secret Service lead agent George Foster, and multiple policemen and others assisted in the apprehension of the shooter. Secret Service agents Samuel Ireland and Albert Gallagher were involved. However, sources disagree on who played what role, with some denying that Parker was involved at all. One source claims that the local policemen initially grabbed Foster, thinking he had fired the shots.

13 The Face of a Killer

- Leon Czolgosz, an anarchist, fired two shots from a .32 Iver Johnson revolver. Czolgosz refused to talk to his appointed lawyers, but spoke freely with his prison guards. Most of the words attributed to him about his beliefs and actions are actual quotes or are slightly modified from his statements and writings. His name was pronounced "sol-gosh," approximately.
- The description of the surgery at the Exposition infirmary is historically accurate, considering that sources differ in some details.
- The description of the arrangements for McKinley's care at the Milburn House is historically accurate.

14 Life in the Balance

- Walker and Dixon's experiences at the Paris International Exposition the previous year are described in detail in the preceding novel, *The Odyssey of Walker Garrett.*
- There were two cycloramas at the Exposition. The other one depicted a Hawaiian volcano.
- "The Old Plantation" was a feature of the Exposition Midway. The description was originally printed in the *Buffalo Evening News.* I found the quote in an online (buffaloah.com) excerpt taken from *High Hopes: The Rise and Decline of Buffalo, New York.* Pub. by State University of New York at Buffalo, 1983 by Mark Goldman. To be fair, the Exhibit of the American Negro which Walker and Dixon remembered from the Paris International Exposition, was also present at Buffalo, but was set up in an out-of-the way location and was seen by relatively few visitors.
- My sources differ as to who and how many assailants fell upon Czolgosz. Different accounts refer to multiple Secret Service agents, policemen, U.S. Marines, and artillerymen, besides Parker.

- Some sources say that "Big Ben" James Parker worked at the Exposition for the Bailey Catering Company, others that he was unemployed at the time of the shooting, having been laid off from his job waiting tables. However, a contemporary news account in the *Cleveland Gazette* stated that he was a waiter at the Boston Inn, which is the version I chose to use.
- Parker's comment "I tried to do my duty. That's all any man can do," is taken from an article in the *Buffalo Times*, found online. His statement "I'm glad I was able to be of service. . . ." was found online, sourced to the *Buffalo Commercial.*
- Parker's comments about lynchings are based loosely on Booker T. Washington's article printed in the *Atlanta Constitution* in September, 1901.

15 The Changing of the Guard

- The medical treatment and subsequent death of McKinley are accurately described. Some experts disagree about what actually caused his death, but gangrene was the standard explanation for most of the next century.
- The court-martial hearing referred to by Walker is described in *The Odyssey of Walker Garrett,* as is the battle at San Juan Hill and the recounting of their round-the-world travels, recalled by Roosevelt.
- The account of the swearing-in ceremony is based on Edmund Morris's *Theodore Rex,* with very minor modifications, mainly involving the roles of the fictional characters.

16 "Booker T"

- As previously noted, the White House was officially

known as the Executive Mansion until Roosevelt changed it in 1901.

- Details presented concerning the dinner are accurate, except that BTW was not driven to the train station afterward by Secret Service agents, as far as I know. His autobiography, *Up From Slavery,* had been published earlier in 1901.
- BTW led the Tuskegee Normal and Industrial Institute. The school's name was changed to simply "Tuskegee Institute" in 1937, and became a university in 1985.
- The outcry against TR which followed the White House dinner has been well-documented, and was worse than indicated here.
- I am aware of no historical evidence that agents were assigned to protect Booker T. Washington, either at Yale, or elsewhere. This is fictional.
- The interaction between BTW and the man on the train platform is based on an actual alleged incident, though I cannot confidently vouch for its authenticity. The incident, if it actually occurred, did not take place in New Haven. The second incident, in which BTW's life was threatened, is entirely fictional.
- The remarks by Yale's President Hadley, in his presentation to TR, have been condensed for brevity. The remark by SCOTUS Justice Brewer that Yale recognizes "a true Washington," etc., exists with various wording in different sources, but is essentially the same.

17 Home

- George Foster was demoted to a clerical position in the aftermath of the assassination.
- Some sources say the electric chair in which Czolgosz died used 1800 volts instead of 1700. In later years, 2000 or even

2500 volts were used. An angry mob tried to lynch the assassin, but police were able to fight them off.

- General Joseph Wheeler resigned his seat in Congress shortly after winning reelection in 1900, and retired to New York.

18 Guarding Roosevelt

- Such outings were typical of Roosevelt's hikes and horse rides. He was a devotee of "the strenuous life," having been a competitive boxer in college, a cowboy out West, and a hero of the Cuban campaign.
- William "Big Bill" Craig was a real person, and is accurately described here. He is one of two Secret Service agents to have been killed in the line of duty. The training session presented here is not based on historical sources.
- Roosevelt did indeed work out in the boxing ring while in the White House, and he loved judo and jiu-jitsu. An injury during one of these boxing matches led to blindness in his left eye.
- Craig was close with the Roosevelt children, and read comics with Quentin. Other comments about his playing with the children are imagined.
- The Sagamore Hill house originally had 22 rooms, but TR added the famous "North Room" to display his hunting trophies in 1905, making it 23 rooms. The house was built in 1884-85 for the modern equivalent of about $600,000 (2023).
- Franklin Roosevelt idolized TR and was a frequent visitor to Sagamore Hill in his youth, but I have no evidence that either he or Eleanor were there during the summer of 1902.
- Roosevelt became the first president to ride in an automobile in a public event. Photographs show the police on bicycles and horses.

- The description of the barnstorming tour is accurate. For those who want more detail, I recommend "When Teddy Roosevelt Barnstormed New England," on the website of The New England Historical Society. TR actually was once observed throwing up after a long series of speeches.
- Craig's death is accurately described. The trolley driver was found guilty of manslaughter, sentenced to six months and made to pay a stiff fine. Sources disagree as to whether Roosevelt was thrown from the carriage or not.

19 Surprises

- It was navy medic Captain George Lung who assisted Roosevelt in walking to the carriage in Logansport. I have relied heavily on Edmund Morris's *Theodore Rex* for details of the campaign tour.
- The White House underwent a major renovation during the summer of 1902 while the Roosevelts were away. Upon returning to D.C., they stayed in a row house at 22 Jackson Place, overlooking Lafayette Square, until they moved back into the White House in October.
- Roosevelt appointed Dr. William D. Crum, a black man, to be customs collector in Charleston. This led to fear of possible assassination attempts against the president.
- Roosevelt's refusal to kill the young, undersized bear quickly became an international news story, reinforcing his reputation for character and sportsmanship. He reportedly said, "Put it out of its misery." Toy-makers quickly marketed small, stuffed "Teddy Bears" in commemoration of the incident.

20 Hat in the Ring

- The Rosemont mansion and James Dancy's family are fictional.

- Walker's comments about presidential security issues are historically accurate. Until 1906, the Secret Service budget provided funds only for its anti-counterfeiting work, and the director had to shift funds to pay for presidential security forces.
- Walker's travels are described in *The Odyssey of Walker Garrett.* In it, he has the opportunity to read famous books by Mahan and Tocqueville, as mentioned here. He recalls a comment by Dixon regarding the prospect of war between Russia and Japan.

21 Twists and Turns

- One of Roosevelt's exercise routines was what he called "singlesticks." The two men wore padded helmets and vests and wielded "heavy ash rods" with which they beat each other. I am not kidding (see *Theodore Rex*, by Morris, p.185). His favorite singlesticks partner was former Rough Rider comrade General Leonard Wood. Therefore, the description here is partly historical and partly fiction.
- Four agents are all that had been typically assigned to presidential security in the previous decade—except for times when only two were assigned—and I have found a source confirming that number (4) for the western tour of 1903. Beginning in 1906, eight agents accompanied presidents when away from Washington. By the end of Roosevelt's presidency, there were a total of ten agents available for presidential security.

22 Westward, Ho!

- Walker's statement that TR had no vice president was correct. At that time, vacancies in the vice presidency were not filled until the next election, and the line of succession beyond the vice president was not spelled out in the

Constitution. This changed with the 25th Amendment in 1967. Under the tradition then in place, the next in line for the Oval Office would have been the elderly Secretary of State, John Hay.

- Roosevelt did indeed evade Secret Service guards twice on the first day of the tour. He also carried a concealed pistol when away from the White House.

- The description of Roosevelt's activities in Chicago is accurate. O'Neill was the police chief at that time, and he was an Irish music and dance expert. He appointed William Childs the first black police sergeant in Chicago, though that occurred in 1905, not 1903. O'Neill did not give a gift to Roosevelt. The "car barn murders" were a major event in Chicago in 1903, but the case was not actually closed until August. The pistol was described in 1903 as an "automatic," but would be called a "semi-automatic" today.

- Typewriters were widely in use in offices by then, but the federal government was among the last to adopt them, so it is believable that Walker had not seen one in use before this.

- The high temperature in Chicago on April 3, 1903 was 39, with 2.6 inches of snow.

- Roosevelt did make that horseback ride in South Dakota. The description of the visit to Sioux Falls is historically accurate.

- Roosevelt met with chiefs of the Sioux, Mandan, Arickaree, and Gros Venter tribes.

23 Eden

- In fact, the Secret Service agents were left with the train at Cinnabar, Montana, along with the reporters, political aides, and others, and did not accompany Roosevelt into the park. However, I'm sure that Roosevelt would have wanted Walker and Dixon along, due to their history with him. My account of the 16-day camping trip is necessarily greatly condensed.

- Roosevelt commented on the tameness of the animals he encountered in Yellowstone Park. Herds of antelope, deer, and elk were common. Roosevelt did not report having heard wolves howling, but it could have happened. They were aggressively hunted, but not exterminated from Yellowstone until the 1920s. Wolves were reintroduced in 1995. In case you're wondering—yes, there really was a full moon during their time camping on the Yellowstone River.

24 Eyes and Ears

- There was indeed a stowaway on board the train. The facts stated about him are accurate. For this and many other details about the 1903 western tour, I am indebted to James Blase's *Keep it for Your Children*, 2019.
- The Tenth Cavalry was on duty in Crawford, as described here. The regimental band welcomed Roosevelt with "Hail to the Chief!" See my previous book, *The Odyssey of Walker Garrett*, for background on Walker and Dixon's connection to the unit.
- General Harrison Gray Otis accompanied the president from Riverside, at Roosevelt's invitation. No attempt was made on Otis's life at that time. Nevertheless, the high security precautions taken for Roosevelt's return to the train after the parade are historically accurate.
- Although the Mormon church discontinued polygamy in 1890, existing plural marriages were allowed to continue. The guest list at the luncheon and the presence of a plural wife of President Joseph F. Smith are found in James Blase, *Keep it for Your Children*, p.323. Smith had five wives at the

time. You can confirm the Mormon teachings mentioned here on LDS official websites.

- The 65-mile ride actually happened. Observers said that Roosevelt was the freshest-looking one of the group when they reached Cheyenne.

25 Counting Chickens

- Based on historical data about the earnings of a cross-section of workers in many fields, I have estimated the salary of Secret Service agents in 1903 to be about $100/month.
- Neapolitan was the most popular ice cream of the early 1900s. A white-owned restaurant would not have allowed blacks to sit inside, even in Washington D.C.
- The so-called "assassination attempt" by Henry Weilbrenner actually happened. (I chose to shorten his name to Brenner.) Contemporary newspaper reports generally sensationalized and exaggerated the danger. According to Edmund Morris's *Theodore Rex*, Weilbrenner (a local farmer) announced that he had come to kill Roosevelt because he had not done enough for labor unions. However, in his endnotes, Morris adds that Weilbrenner believed he was going to marry Alice Roosevelt. Weilbrenner, twenty-seven years old, was judged to be insane and was committed to the State Asylum at Kings Park for the rest of his life. Roosevelt dismissed the matter as unimportant, and Alice, who was not present at Sagamore Hill at that time, never spoke of it. Roosevelt joked that his wanting to marry Alice proved he was insane.
- Most of Roosevelt's early books (pre-1900) were actually published by G. P. Putnam's Sons, in New York. Parson and Sons is fictitious, as is Page Turner Books (except for the imprint of *this* book!).

- The court martial mentioned here is described in *The Odyssey of Walker Garrett,* along with the letters of recommendation by Generals Funston, Wheeler, and MacArthur.
- The tallest building in NYC in 1903 was 31 stories tall.
- William Loeb was Roosevelt's personal secretary. He had accompanied TR on the just-completed western tour, and would have been well-acquainted with Walker.

26 Decatur

- *The Chattanooga Press* was a weekly Republican newspaper, which cost five cents. The news items mentioned appeared in the September 18 and 25 issues. The Terminal Station described actually did not open until 1909, so its appearance here is a bit premature. It was one of the most imposing buildings in Chattanooga, and is currently the home of the "Chattanooga Choo-Choo."
- Walker had slept in an attic room at the Dancy house for two years while attending the Decatur Academy. He had eaten meals in the kitchen with the hired help, and had minimal contact with the family. See *The Odyssey of Walker Garrett.*
- The description of the Dancy house and its surrounding area is mostly accurate for that time, though subjective— "seedy" might be disputed by some. There are many lovely Victorian-era homes in Decatur, known as "Painted Ladies."
- Stafford Moseley is fictitious, though the Moseley family was prominent in the history of Decatur. The Dixie Hotel is also fictitious. FYI, Alabama prohibited alcohol in 1907, after years of campaigning by temperance groups and churches.
- The earlier confrontation between Walker and "Red" Murphy is found in *The Odyssey of Walker Garrett.* The first

automobile registered in Decatur was in 1906, so "Red" is a little ahead of his time in owning a car.

27 Clarity

- The Jones family and Reverend Dryson are fictitious. There was, however, a Victorian-style house in Decatur known as "the Gingerbread House," owned by a Jones family.
- The story about the iceberg incident, and the others recalled by Walker, are found in *The Odyssey of Walker Garrett.*
- The Bank of Courtland, Norman Richards, and Robert Murphy are all fictitious. The two bank robbers were not actual Klansmen, of course, but were only using hoods to shield their identities. The KKK was dormant from the late 1870s to about 1915.
- When the banker refers to "the Great Panic" of the early 1890s, he means the Panic of 1893, the worst depression the country had yet seen.

28 New Beginnings
No historical notes for this chapter.

ACKNOWLEDGMENTS

I would like to express my appreciation to all those who have assisted me in the writing and publishing of this book. Without their support and input, it would have been extremely difficult to complete the process. Many thanks to each and every one! In alphabetical order, I thank David Anguish, Scott White, and Tim Weekley. Special thanks to Wayne Joyner for the cover art.

ABOUT THE AUTHOR

Michael Glenn is a native of Mont-
gomery, Alabama. He is a graduate of
Harding University, and earned his
master degree in history at the
University of Mississippi. He
currently lives in the metro-Atlanta
area with his family and a neurotic
Sheltie. He is the author of The
Odyssey of Walker Garrett and The
Resurrection of Jesus: Fact or
Fiction?

Made in the USA
Columbia, SC
23 December 2024

50503923R00207